When We
Lost Our
Heads

ALSO BY HEATHER O'NEILL

The Lonely Hearts Hotel

Daydreams of Angels

The Girl Who Was Saturday Night

Lullabies for Little Criminals

When We

Lost Our

Heads

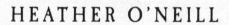

HEATHER O'NEILL

HarperCollins*Publishers*Ltd

F
O'NE

When ~~we lost our heads~~

Published by HarperCollins Publishers Ltd

First published in Canada by HarperCollins Publishers Ltd in this hardcover edition, 2022.
Published simultaneously in the United States by Riverhead Books,
an imprint of Penguin Random House LLC.

HarperCollins books may be purchased for educational, business,
or sales promotional use through our Special Markets Department.

HarperCollins Publishers Ltd
Bay Adelaide Centre, East Tower
22 Adelaide Street West, 41st Floor
Toronto, Ontario, Canada
M5H 4E3

www.harpercollins.ca

Library and Archives Canada Cataloguing in Publication

Title: When we lost our heads / Heather O'Neill.
Names: O'Neill, Heather, author.
Identifiers: Canadiana (print) 20210333308 | Canadiana (ebook) 20210333316 |
ISBN 9781443451574 (hardcover) | ISBN 9781443451598 (ebook)
Classification: LCC PS8579.N387 W43 2022 | DDC C813/.54—dc23

Printed and bound in the United States of America
LSC/H 9 8 7 6 5 4 3 2 1

When We

Lost Our

Heads

PART ONE

CHAPTER 1

The Duel

In a labyrinth constructed out of a rosebush in the Golden Mile neighborhood of Montreal, two little girls were standing back-to-back with pistols pointed up toward their chins. They began to count out loud together, taking fifteen paces each.

Marie Antoine and Sadie Arnett had met in the park on Mont Royal behind their homes when they were little girls of twelve years old. It was 1873. The two of them seemed to have been born with the same amount of thick hair on their heads. Except that Sadie had dark-brown hair and Marie's was blond. Sadie had large dark eyes that were almost black, cheekbones that were already high, and lips so dark red they looked as though they had makeup on them. Marie had blue eyes and a complexion that looked porcelain and a mouth that was the lightest pink. It was almost as though they were two dolls that were being marketed to girls, one fair, one dark.

That day, Marie had on a white tailored jacket with blue embroidery down the sides. It fell just below her knees, revealing her white stockings and pretty blue leather shoes. Sadie had on a burgundy hat with a black ruffle. It was about the size of a cupcake. It was propped on her head uselessly. But at least it didn't take away from the impression her black velvet coat with burgundy buttons made. She had small black shoes with black bows on the toes.

The pistols had roses engraved on the handles.

A maid looked down from the second-story window. She was buttoning up her chemise and whistling. From her perspective, she could see into the labyrinth and its clearing in the middle. At first, she doubted what she was actually seeing. It did not seem possible at all. There is always something surreal about children embarking on something dangerous. They are oblivious to the danger. They act as though they are about to defy all the laws of physics.

For a moment the adult is suspended in the realm of childhood disbelief. The maid broke the spell. She ran down the stairs with only her drawers on and her chemise half-undone. Her red hair flew behind her, as though she were carrying a torch.

She ran out through the labyrinth screaming. Finally, she arrived there. She stood in the middle and opened her mouth to tell to the girls to stop at the precise moment they both spun around and fired their guns at each other. As the two bullets hit the maid and she fell to the ground, the words alerting the girls to their idiocy were forever silenced.

CHAPTER 2

Introducing the

Lovely Marie Antoine

The amount of wealth in Montreal in the late nineteenth century was increasing exponentially, although the number of rich people was not. The personal wealth of the English-speaking elite was growing out of all proportion. The mansions being built and expanded to house this muchness were glorious. They were grand artworks. They were truly majestic. They were placed on the side of the hill as though on a pedestal. The dome of the Anglican cathedral looked like a scoop of mint ice cream in the middle of them. The streets of the Golden Mile, as it was known, snaked up the hill. You had to go up the winding roads patiently in your carriage. But it was well worth taking the ride slowly because there was so much to see. The gardens were as beautiful as the homes.

All the parks were modeled by British gardeners. They were to have a disciplined feel. They weren't supposed to exhibit the brash, tangled almost jungle-like quality of North American nature. Some of the trees didn't behave—they ripped up the streets and stretched the sidewalks in precarious ways. And the trees that didn't follow the rules found themselves covered in children who perched on all their branches wearing bloomers and tiny black boots and bows in their hair. The children whispered to one another, pretending they were on pirate ships and that there were vicious sharks below. And they clung to the branches of the trees as if for safety, as though the trees were their mothers. And the trees could not help but be domesticated, and found themselves longing for children in their arms.

The most glorious house of all in the Golden Mile was inhabited by the widower Mr. Antoine and his only child, Marie.

AS FAMILY LEGEND HAD IT, Marie's first steps were ballet moves across the floor. Whereas most children take a few awkward and stumbling steps, she did a petit pas de chat. She walked around with her tiny ballet slippers, looking very much like a duck, with the ribbons trailing behind her like marks in the water. She performed for people. As she grew, she spent more time on the name of the dance than the choreography itself.

"And now I present to you a deer who has been separated from its family." She put both hands with her fingers spread out to resemble antlers. And she walked around on tiptoe, looking about herself desperately for her other deer family.

Her nursery was constantly being repainted with new murals. Her father told the painters to consult with Marie, as it was her room and she was the one who had to be pleased with it. There was a life-size image of a goat sitting on a chair, sipping a glass of milk. In general, guests were never taken up to the nursery. But Louis felt inclined once in a while to bring people up to see it. Everyone was so delighted by the whimsy displayed.

It was a very new idea to regard childhood as a period of life that was to be revered and worthy of consideration on its own. People used to consider children to be inefficient adults. But now they were regarded as being in an Edenic state where they had access to an imaginative faculty superior to reason. Everything they said contained a wisdom that had been lost to adults. Childhood needed to be encouraged. People had to spend all their time focused on making this the most magical of all periods in life.

Louis often thought of himself as the originator of this kind of thinking. He thought Marie was the baby who had started the Victorian craze for babies. Ever since her mother had died, when Marie was in infancy, it had always been just the two of them. He was the owner of the largest sugar factory in the country. So there was no expense too great to develop Marie's childhood. When she was six, he had Marie's silhouette printed on every bag of sugar.

Because they were the most influential family in Montreal, nothing they did could really be interpreted as gauche. The minute they engaged in an activity, it went from being considered uncouth to being something others did not have the money to pull off.

It was not considered polite to bring a child to any gathering of adults. But Louis made it clear that he and his daughter were inseparable. And thus like a child who comes to the throne early, Marie found herself surrounded by adults. Given Louis's wealth, everyone was quick to comply with his eccentric demands. Everyone knew there was very little way to capture Louis's heart; he was immune to their sycophancy, in a manner only someone who once mastered the art themselves could be. Everyone knew the only way to please Louis was to do it through his daughter.

Guests found themselves frequently asking Marie what she was going to do when she grew up. Of course, none of them actually believed she was going to do anything when she grew up other than get married. That gave an even more comic ring to Marie's charming prophecies.

"I would very much like to travel in a circus and be a lion tamer," she told the mayor and his wife. "I would be very gentle with the lion. I would brush his mane. And I would give him caramels. He would let me put my head in his mouth. And he would never dream of clamping down his jaws. We would walk down the street. And I wouldn't need to put a leash on him."

"I think I shall be an opera singer," she announced to a group of society women. "But I don't really like singing loudly. So I shall sing into a speaking trumpet. What I mostly like about the idea of being an opera singer is that I will get to eat whatever I want and become fat. I think it would be nice to be so fat!"

"I would like to become an arctic explorer," she told a group of dour investors. "I like wearing many coats. And I should like to murder my own walrus one day. I love all animals, but I don't like walruses. They are too frightening."

She would blink charmingly. And adopt a look of naïveté, knowing that what she was saying was at once precocious and endearingly idiotic. Marie had a natural gift for being charming. She could be coy and naïve and silly. But she did it in such a creative way, anyone might say she had a genius for it.

She enjoyed uttering the most nonsensical things she could ponder: "I worry that when it rains, the rocks in the yard will turn into frogs and hop away." Nonsense literature was in vogue, so her idiotic remarks were interpreted as ingenious.

Adults understood the subtext to her sense of humor. They understood when she was being absurd and coy and fanciful. Other children did not. She was frankly more amused by her own conversation than that of people around her. She was quite aware that she had a mastery over social interaction, that she, despite her young age, was more amusing and sophisticated than the people around her. She rarely paid much attention to what others said, using it merely as a springboard for her witticisms.

WHETHER OR NOT SHE was actually intelligent was something debated by her tutors. She fell asleep whenever anyone began reading to her. As soon as one or two sentences were read, her head would nod with alacrity. She decided anything she could learn was too difficult to learn. She was satisfied by having access to whatever came to her intuitively and without effort. But the truth was that she knew very little, so nothing could undermine her arrogance and confidence. If she pressed herself to learn, she would be aware of her own limitations and that frustrated her.

She put up quite a fit when it came to her piano lessons.

"If only those tunes weren't so long," she complained. "I can only learn a ten-second song, or else my brain and hands begin to ache."

"Well, then let's work on a ten-second song."

"I simply can't today. I'm exhausted. Perhaps tomorrow."

They sent for a doctor to see why it was that Marie became so tired in her lessons. Her tutor said she had never seen anything like it. In fact, she thought it might be dangerous. Marie fell asleep so abruptly and deeply when she was reading aloud from *Le Morte D'Arthur*, the tutor was afraid for a moment she had killed the child.

The doctor suggested Marie eat fewer sweets. The amount of cakes and treats she ate over the course of a day might be what was causing her to sink into mini comas. Marie's sweet tooth was a phenomenal thing.

What were the sweets she had eaten that day? A rum ball that had been set on fire in front of her, so when she ate it, it was warm, as though she were biting into the heart of a beast. A chocolate mousse that melted in her mouth and filled her whole body with sweetness. There were chocolates filled with brandy that she had sucked the alcohol out of. She felt how a bird would feel after drinking nectar and then flying about high in the sky. And there was a princess cake. It was a round dome covered in a hard pink shell you had to strike with your spoon. When the hard icing cracked, it was like witnessing an earthquake. It made her shiver with delight. There was a tiny rose on the cake. Sometimes the rose was made out of icing and sometimes it was a real flower. She couldn't help but bite into it to find out.

MARIE HAD A WAY of consuming culture too. She was fascinated by any sort of theatrical performance. No matter where she was sitting in an audience, she always acted as though the play was being put on just for her. When they came home from a puppet show, she'd explain to the maids the tragic entanglements the puppets had gotten themselves into. She explained it as though the puppets were very dear friends of hers and their happiness was her own. One of the maids instinctively threw her arms around Marie, in sympathy for the hardship she had suffered on account of the puppets.

Marie began screaming during a play when a villain plunged a knife through the heart of a heroine. Her father had to take her out into the foyer. She was inconsolable. Afterward, her father brought her backstage to see how the actors were all alive and well.

She was upset by a doll that had a dour expression. She tried over and over to make the doll happy, but nothing seemed to work. She had so many different dolls, and yet she became focused on that one. Her father brought it to the doll hospital to have it repaired. The doll maker painted a different smile on the doll's face. This pleased Marie to no end. How it made the doll feel, on the other hand, was harder to say.

But once the doll was repaired, Marie immediately transferred her affection to a sad bear with a blue velvet coat. It had black fur in tufts on its head that made it look as though it had fallen in the water. It had a look on its face that made it seem as though it had gotten into trouble all on its own and couldn't blame anyone but itself.

"I love you so much," Marie said to the bear at her play tea party. "But of course I love you so much. How could I not? You are so lovable. Any girl would fall in love with you. I want to be the only one who knows how to love you. I want you to think that if you didn't have me to love, then you will be all alone in the world. I want you to be as afraid of losing me as I am of losing you. Is that cruel? I'm so mean, I know. Can I make it up to you in kisses? I could never get tired of kissing you. Do you fancy some cookies?"

She took a spoon and scooped out some buttons and dropped them on the plate.

"Oh, it's always important to eat. Or you will become too skinny. And do you know what happens to bears when they get too skinny? Well, their eyes fall out of their heads, of course. You'll be on your hands and knees looking all over the floor for them. But you'll never find them, since you'll be blind."

Marie stared at the bear, who refused to respond. Every time she spoke to her dolls, it was as though she were speaking to the same person. All the dolls were the same. They were all disastrously bored. They took their chagrin out on her. The bear was much the same.

"Do you think about other bears? Ones in the zoo? Do you imagine you would be happier with them than you are with me? You wouldn't be. But I don't tell you that you are very different than they are. You aren't wild. You belong in the house here with me. You wouldn't be happy at

11

the zoo. They don't have teatime. They don't have a warm, cozy bed for you. Oh, I've had it. I'm so tired of begging you to love me all day long."

She stood up and stormed off but then found herself turning and heading right back hurriedly.

"You have to forgive me. You can't believe a word I said."

Marie seemed not at all concerned by the amount of love she had to give. Her reach was enormous. She had the ability to make large groups of people feel loved by her. Her affection was like sunlight, and it could fill an entire room.

THE GOVERNESS TOLD LOUIS that Marie needed to play with other children. The governess came to this conclusion when she encountered Marie in the midst of a heated argument with a pig. She was pushing around a toy perambulator. It was a lovely pink contraption with gold trimmings. It was indeed fancier than any the governess had witnessed any child riding in. She imagined Marie was pushing around one of the dolls she was so fond of. But the blanket began to stir. For a moment she was terribly apprehensive, wondering who had given Marie a baby to play with.

But then a head emerged from the blankets. She thought she was looking at an unruly pig. But then she thought she must be wrong. So she looked closer, only to realize she had been right. There was a pig in the carriage. Marie had a look of exasperation on her face. An expression ordinarily reserved for new mothers of very young children.

"You are being very difficult. What do you want? If I give you a cupcake, you are going to want another one. You have gone mad since I gave you that cupcake. Don't you wish you had never even tasted it? You wouldn't know what you are missing out on all the time. I worry I've driven you mad. Please don't tell the other pigs about how good it tasted. They will never leave us in peace. They will sneak into the house in the middle of the night. They will eat all the food. But they won't stop there. They will eat all the pillows and the blankets. They will eat the couch cushions. They will eat the carpets. They will eat the heads of all my dolls."

The mansion was overrun by animals. Whereas most homes had a menagerie of taxidermized creatures on display, the Antoines had ones that were insistently alive.

Marie had begged and begged for a piglet for her birthday. She fed it with a bottle of milk. She had her tailor make small collars and bonnets perfectly shaped and suited for his head. It wasn't an uncommon sight to witness Marie walking down the boulevard with a pig wearing a bow tie. Or she might be lying in her yard reading a book with her head propped on a sow for a pillow.

Louis thought animals were attracted to Marie's maternal sweetness. But it was more likely they were attracted to her wildness. The animals believed she was one of them.

AS SHE GOT A LITTLE OLDER, Marie befriended the girls in the neighborhood, who were much easier to impress than her stuffed animals and pets were. Her adorable personality and her wealth made her very attractive to other little girls. She was good at getting girls to fall in love with her. She couldn't really love them back though. Like her dolls, they were all interchangeable. And loving everyone is the same thing as loving nobody at all.

She accepted that she was the leader. She would present to them her latest mechanical trinket, such as a silver bird that sat on her finger and chirped. She loved technology and having a young audience to impress with her scientific acquisitions and knowledge. Gradually the adulation of others began to replace and satisfy her need for other feelings. She became addicted to praise. She became especially addicted to being looked at, because she had no other emotional sustenance. It was as though she were eating cupcakes expecting to be filled up. And they made her hungrier for more food instead of making her feel full.

Marie was becoming a more darling and extravagant version of herself. She was never alone. She never had time for introspection. She never had time for loneliness and self-loathing.

ONE CHILLY AFTERNOON, Marie saw a small procession of children walking across her lawn and headed into the woods of the mountain behind it. She had been about to hurry inside when the snow had started rushing at her face, but she paused to look at the group. Their assuredness struck her as peculiar. They all seemed very sad. They were wearing their black Easter Sunday coats. A little girl and boy at the front of the line were helping each other carry a rectangular box. They were both weeping. The other children also looked so sad it made them appear anxious. It was as if they'd snuck out of a nightmare and they were trying to find their way back to it.

Except for a little girl with a thick mane of black hair that appeared to have been mussed up by the wind. This strange girl looked absolutely calm. Her back was straight. When the children began to falter, she moved to the front of the procession. She was different.

CHAPTER 3

Introducing the
Devilish Sadie Arnett

The Arnetts had come to the Golden Mile when Sadie's father inherited the mansion from his great-uncle. It was a beautiful house made of polished, square gray stones that seemed indifferent to harsh winters. Mr. and Mrs. Arnett moved in on their third wedding anniversary. Their son, Philip, was a baby, and their daughter, Sadie, had not yet been born.

The house in the Golden Mile was their ticket to security and prosperity. Mr. and Mrs. Arnett were both determined to use their address to climb to the top of the social ladder. Mr. Arnett was a politician known for his zealous advocacy of moral decency. He repeatedly requested that prostitutes and houses of ill repute be closed down. The minute he criticized a play, it extended its run, knowing full well the publicity would bring people out in droves.

His address loaned him an air of respectability. The illusion of wealth was what had kept his career afloat. The Arnetts often thought of selling it because they needed the money. But they knew if they did sell it, they would no longer have the status of living in the Golden Mile.

They kept the house freezing cold in the winter to save money. The third floor was entirely cordoned off so they didn't have to clean or heat it. They had only one maid, who was Mrs. Arnett's seventeen-year-old cousin. She was more or less posing as a maid instead of actually being one. Mrs. Arnett did the lion's share of the housework. She got down on her hands and knees and scrubbed the floor viciously with a brush. She had to make it look as though she had three maids working all the time. They never encouraged visitors. It was such a great expense to them to entertain.

They could have led a normal life if they were humble. If they lived in a house suitable to a politician and sent Philip to a less expensive school. But they needed to ally themselves with real money. They had to truly be accepted into the Golden Mile if Mr. Arnett were going to rise in the political ranks.

WHEN SADIE WAS A YOUNG GIRL, she did not scream and cry and fuss unnecessarily the way some babies do. She never spoke until she spoke in full sentences. She was so clear about what she wanted.

Sadie was very self-sufficient as a child. Perhaps she had to be, since she had only one maid who didn't clean up. She didn't like when anyone dressed her. She despised certain outfits. She put on the same navy-blue dress with black stripes on the collar every day and tied on her black boots.

She opened books before she could read them. She refused to ever play with her brother.

She sat next to Philip while he was being taught to read and write. She was absolutely still. She learned the lessons quicker than he did.

She seemed to know this would be the only time she was exposed to teaching in the same way. So she sat as quietly as a mouse and took it all in.

She was always shocking members of the household. They would enter a room and not know she was in it. Then they'd turn and leap almost out of their socks. It seemed truly as though she had appeared out of thin air. But she had been standing right there the whole time.

WHEN SADIE WAS SEVEN YEARS OLD, her mother went to the extra expense of hiring a governess, in hopes it would make her ladylike. The governess had to be let go after she had allowed Sadie to fall off a cliff. But she swore Sadie had thrown herself deliberately over it. No one could accept this. But the governess had seen what she had seen. And no one could convince her she had been in any way mistaken in her interpretation.

She had taken her eyes off Sadie for a brief moment. When she looked again the girl was smiling at her, with her back to the cliff. Although Sadie was about twenty feet away from the edge of the cliff, the governess still considered it too close for comfort. She summoned Sadie to come back to her on the picnic blanket.

Sadie smiled wider and began to walk backward. Growing more alarmed, the governess rose to her feet and yelled at Sadie to stop walking at once.

"Sadie, darling. Be careful, please. Turn around! The cliff is right behind you, darling, you'll fall. You'll fall."

When Sadie refused to stop her backward motion, the governess began to run toward her, arms outstretched. She was sick to her stomach and terrified. She began to plead with Sadie, "Please, please stop." It was as though she were pleading for her own life. She was pleading to be spared from this experience.

Sadie got to the very edge of the cliff. She stopped for a moment. Instinctually, the maid felt herself stop too. It was as though her propulsive movement might remind Sadie of her own seemingly unstoppable trajectory. Then, and most unsettlingly and most unbelievably, Sadie held up her hand to wave good-bye. And took one step back off the cliff.

Sadie recovered but had a broken arm and a concussion. She seemed very proud of her broken arm. It was one of Sadie's first memories. She remembered thinking if she could throw herself off a cliff, she would be able to throw anyone off a cliff.

Deliberately. "Deliberately" was a word the governess heard herself repeating over and over in the following days. She repeated it so often, unable to have anyone take it seriously, that she began to wonder whether she truly had any understanding of the word.

The governess sat on the trolley with all her bags on the way to her mother's home. For the rest of her life she would forever after be uncertain about the concept of deliberation and free will.

AFTER THIS, SADIE WAS SENT to school. She was the smartest in her class. She dominated in every subject. Her drive was not just for knowledge, in which case she might have found herself lazily daydreaming through her subjects. She wanted to be better than the other girls. She was as good as she needed to be to master and humiliate them.

She came back from school with her scarf wrapped almost up to her eyes and her hair a mess. This always alarmed her mother. She couldn't understand what had happened. How had her daughter become so ruffled and rumpled? Sadie looked at her mother without a hint of expression on her face, the way she looked at most people. Sadie's mother could be so infuriated by her daughter's rudeness.

SADIE HATED THE SOUND of the piano and refused to learn it. She looked stubbornly at the snow falling out the window.

"I don't like it. It's too twinkly. It's too pretty."

"You can dance to it," the tutor pleaded.

"No. I think music should be terrible. It should make people weep. Would you teach me a funeral dirge?"

"For what kind of funeral?"

"That of a young mother who drowned herself when she was rejected by her husband."

SADIE ARNETT HAD NO FRIENDS before she met Marie. Sadie had learned to read when she was very young. The larger the novel she read, the more she was able to disappear from the world, and all the people in it. Each novel was like a voyage she embarked on. She specifically looked for enormous books. Then she would be gone for a longer period of time. She might disappear for an entire winter.

She often wondered why she was allowed to read novels. The subtext in them always ran counter to the ideas taught at school. There were murderers and degenerates all over the pages. And they were often the heroes!

When she was called for dinner, she sat at the table, not really present, her mind still absorbed by what was happening in the book she'd been reading. She rarely made conversation with anyone, as she was clearly not interested. She deemed whatever they said to be pointless.

Sadie had the distinct impression her parents loved her brother more than they could ever love her. Her mother even eyed her suspiciously.

Sadie did not know why her parents were so disappointed that she was a girl. They didn't have any hope for her the way they did for Philip. She didn't understand how they could not see how much better she was than him. She was always ahead of him in all aspects of life, despite being younger. She had caught up to him by the time she was three years old. Everyone in her family regarded her precocious behavior as a direct insult on her brother.

SADIE BEGAN KEEPING A DIARY when she was eleven years old. It made Mrs. Arnett nervous how Sadie was always recording things. She watched the ink dance out of the tip of her daughter's pen like the tail at the end of a kite. She didn't know what made Sadie believe she was the arbiter of what was worthy of being recorded. When Philip choked on his milk at the dinner table, Sadie took out her book and jotted it down. Once her father was complaining, rather ungenerously, about a political opponent. Sadie took out her notebook to jot that down too. Her mother snuck into Sadie's room one afternoon to get a look at the diary. Sadie was scolded for having a list of all the idiotic things Philip had done that day. It was wicked that Sadie had been judging her brother in that way.

Her mother at first decided to take Sadie's journals away altogether. Sadie had such an intense reaction though. She seemed so pathetic. She begged her mother not to do it. She couldn't live without the notebook. Sadie got on her knees and clasped her hands together and looked up to her mother in a supplicating manner. Her mother, knowing how much pride Sadie had, and so how begging went against everything in her personality, was rattled by Sadie's level of passion.

She was ashamed she had witnessed this in her daughter. She would have been ashamed after witnessing it in anyone, to be honest. But it was particularly difficult to see an emotion so base in someone so close to her.

Later, when she contemplated whether Sadie had any feelings whatsoever, she would remember that moment. She didn't consider it evidence of her daughter having feelings, however. Rather that Sadie would pretend to have feelings to get what she wanted. That was how manipulative Sadie was.

At the time, Mrs. Arnett relented but told Sadie she was only to write poetry or fiction. There was no good that could come from an eleven-year-old memoirist or political satirist, or whatever it was she thought she was. And to be honest, there would be no need for a female one of any age.

MRS. ARNETT WAS PLEASED WHEN she saw her daughter had taken up poetry. She liked poetry herself. Poetry was very popular in that day and age. She thought poetry was inherently beautiful. By its syntax, it forced everything you put in it to be beautiful.

She asked Sadie to read her a poem. The young girl stood in front of her family in the dining room. She held her notebook in her hand. Sadie looked around. She knew this was a bad idea, but that made her want to read out loud even more.

The small crow is naked at night.
Black is its eye. Black is the sky.
There is no more difference between light and fright.
The small crow is naked at night.
Round in its belly is the rat's eye
How many did you have to eat to give you sight?

Sadie had a look on her face. She knew her poetry was good. And she was proud of it. Even though she knew her mother was going to criticize it. She knew it was not the kind of poem little girls were supposed to write. She also knew the poetry little girls wrote wasn't very good. She had no intention of emulating it. She was going to get in trouble for her poetry because she had made it good and different.

Sadie's mother decided not to say anything about her daughter's poetry. Instead, she nodded. And she gestured for Sadie to run along. From then on it was implicitly understood that Sadie should keep her writing to herself.

Every mother engages in an act of parenting they know isn't a great idea. They allow something to slide. And this is the thing that causes the child to develop a personality and also all their worst inclinations and predispositions and habits. The mother's neglect seals the child's doom. Thus we can safely blame all crimes on mothers.

THE WALL OF SADIE'S ROOM was covered in her collection of butterflies. She had gathered them over the years. Whenever Sadie did anything, she did it with a great passion. Her favorite part was killing the butterfly. She poisoned it, and its wings began to slow as though they were a pair of sleepy eyelids trying their very best to stay awake but growing heavier and heavier.

It is customary to be worried about an older child hurting a younger one. But Mrs. Arnett was always worried Sadie had designs on the life of Philip. Watching her daughter's infatuation with killing butterflies made her worry for Philip's safety. She needed to ask someone for advice on her children. But she was too ashamed to ask. How could she go about asking whether it was normal if your children tried to murder each other?

Sadie never played with dolls. She did not seem to care whether they lived or died. When they were clearly in a state of distress, such as lying upside down on the ground with their legs in odd directions and their shoes off, she did nothing to alleviate their distress.

Mrs. Arnett found a doll hanging by its neck from a noose in the toy cupboard. Her mother thought she had outgrown her youthful sympathies for dolls. But Mrs. Arnett felt horrified for this doll.

Sadie's mother sent her to play with other girls, hoping she would pick up some of their graces. She stole things from the houses of girls she went to visit. She stole food and desserts from the table. She didn't eat them but let them rot in her pocket. The only time she seemed to have much to do with other children was when they invited her over to offer up a few words for a dead cat or a monkey. The animal would be curled up in the shoebox, like a slipper that would never find its mate.

Sadie arrived at the funeral of a cat wearing her black coat over her navy-blue dress. It was cold outside. The ground was frozen. So the children had had trouble digging the grave. Their knuckles were all red from the effort. She brought a small Bible with her. It was useless, since animals don't go to heaven. But the children appreciated any nod to ceremony.

After the cat was buried, Sadie took out the eulogy she had tucked into her breast pocket and read it to the assembled children. "Although this cat was not much bigger than a sock, he was loved enormously. Although he was named Gaston, he will be remembered as the Black Cat with Four White Paws by people in the neighborhood forever. He had a very funny meow. It sounded like a baby crying. It sounded like it was unhappy. Then we would check on it and it would be happy. And that made us happier. He had such a funny way of making us happy. As long as we remember, we will remember him. Because we always remember friends." Sadie then folded the paper and put it solemnly back in her pocket, not believing a word she had just read. The snowflakes landed like tiny stars in her black hair.

Whenever she walked down the street and a child whose pet's funeral she had officiated passed her, the child would often stop, thinking they were friends, and greet Sadie amicably. But Sadie would look at them coolly, as though she had no idea why they might believe themselves to be on the same level as her, and she might nod but would then move on.

BY THE TIME SADIE MET MARIE, her mother had entirely given up on her. She still hoped something about Sadie's personality would improve so she would not hinder her brother's marriage prospects. He had enough going against him without alienating an eligible woman with a disagreeable sister-in-law.

She allowed Sadie to retreat out of her line of vision. She decided not to observe her. As though she were a stain on the wallpaper your eyes eventually train themselves not to see. Sadie was safe in this space. She existed outside of her mother's gaze. And she was content there.

And then Sadie befriended Marie. Her mother believed everything could begin all over again.

CHAPTER 4

The Friendship

Sadie Arnett arrived at the park one windy summer afternoon when she was twelve. She looked for a bench on which to sit in peace and read the book she had brought with her. Sadie's mother had insisted she go for a walk. Taking a constitutional was important, according to the family's physician. There was always a male doctor who was determining what were appropriate activities for young women. Who knew how they decided these things?

Sadie thumped down on the bench, her hair bouncing freely about her head, and settled into her book. Sadie's attention was dragged from the story only when Marie Antoine stopped in front of her. She had an enormous book balanced on her head. It was as though she were indicating to Sadie that this was the appropriate way for a young girl to use a book. Marie spread both arms to the side and balanced on one foot. She bent her right elbow and touched the tip of her nose with her finger and did the same with the left. She then smiled, relaxed her limbs, and moved on.

Sadie did not know what to make of Marie. She was behaving in such a painfully idiotic manner, she had to be aware it was foolish. She was instantly enchanted by Marie. She couldn't concentrate on her book afterward. There was something about this girl that made Sadie want to know her, that made her think she might be fascinating. She was probably wrong. Whenever she had been introduced to girls before, she felt they were painfully inferior and she was miserable afterward. They made her feel as though the world could only be considered a disappointing place filled with boring people. She didn't know how she would make it through her whole life.

The next time she saw Marie in the park, she had a girl on either side of her, their arms interlocked. The girls were rapt with whatever Marie had to say, while Marie looked as though she were basking in the light of their attention. Suddenly, Marie ran off from the other girls to the side of the pond, where she began blowing kisses at the swans. Marie then confessed her love to a swan who was paddling away from her.

"You can't leave me. I've done nothing but love you. I'll do anything! You've ruined me socially. No one will have me after you've rejected me. Please, you can't do this to me. I shall drown myself for you. You are so handsome. Swans mate for life. I won't be able to bear it."

Sadie found it very peculiar. It was as though Marie were a character in a novel. She had snuck off the pages of one the books Sadie was reading. Sadie wondered what it would be like to speak to a character in a novel. They always spoke about things that mattered, or that revealed their character. Even their small talk was heartbreaking.

Marie's friends were blushing. They would never be so bold to speak these words aloud. They glanced around nervously to make sure no one was listening. Sadie was immediately angry with the girls. She knew they were not worthy of Marie's friendship. She wished Marie would turn around and tell them she was not really their friend. She needed a friend who wasn't ashamed of her brilliance.

The next time Sadie saw Marie at the park she was standing in a circle of stones as the sun was going down. A ring of girls surrounded the stones, while Marie stood in the middle of it with her arms spread and daisies in her hair.

"Fairies! You must come for me," Marie cried out. "I am willing to come to your world. I will be immortal and I will be your queen. I will lead your armies into battle against trolls. I will risk my life again and again. I am called from the higher forces to be your leader. I will renounce my family and my name. I will no longer be Marie Antoine. I will be Titania Fae, Queen of the Fairies!"

She raised her hands in the air. The groups of girls looked at one another, having no idea what they should do at this point. They were unable to do anything unless Marie told them. They were too timid to lose themselves in an imaginary world.

"Go, go!" exclaimed Marie.

The girls all took the lids of the jars of fireflies they were holding, and suddenly Marie was surrounded by a galaxy of twinkling stars. Sadie thought it was breathtaking.

Marie had also noticed Sadie. She was curious why they weren't already friends, especially since she was adored by every girl in the neighborhood. It never occurred to her that someone might dislike her. She felt so peculiar around Sadie. She felt herself wondering whether Sadie liked her. She was more curious about Sadie than any other girl. But she did not know how to approach her. What she was feeling was intimidation, but she did not know this because she had never experienced it before.

Even though she was very young, Marie felt she had a grasp on the world around her. But Sadie was an enigma. Every time she spotted Sadie, she went home with a troubled feeling. It was as if she were totally ignorant about the world. And that she might be a fool.

Marie had a nightmare she was in the woods. She was walking along when she encountered a deer. The deer stopped in its tracks and stared at her. She had always thought deer were among the most beautiful animals. They were like horses in a ballet. She held out an apple for the deer. The deer approached her, opened its mouth, and let out the cry of a young troubled girl.

Marie sat up in her bed. She began to cry loudly. The dream had made her feel so alone. It was as though the voice inside the deer had come from her own throat. She had never felt alone in life. There were always so many people around to amuse her and tell her she was wonderful. But now she sat up in her bed and cried as though she were totally abandoned, as though there were no one to hear her for miles. Two maids and her father rushed through the door that joined their bedrooms in order to come to her aid. One of the maids was naked except for her bloomers, while the other had on nothing but a bonnet and her father's robe. "Now, now," her father said.

Marie had been reading *Goblin Market* for the last few weeks. She was memorizing it for the annual Girls' Elocution Contest. She brought the small book of Rossetti poems in her hand to the park. She intuitively knew that people who read books a lot always wanted to talk about them. It was a communal language. This was a book she thought she knew well. She would be able to use it as an excuse to speak to the inscrutable and reclusive Sadie.

Sadie and Marie had figured out that the other was often in the park around four thirty. They had arranged to be in each other's presence even though they hadn't yet spoken. Marie looked around for Sadie. She spotted her from a distance, seated on her favorite bench.

Sadie took a notebook out of her basket and scribbled a thought down with a fountain pen. Marie was overcome by a desire to know what Sadie had written. What was it like to have a thought so interesting it belonged in a notebook? She didn't know whether she had thoughts like that. She felt that she didn't leave a thought in her head long enough for it to be organized, thoughtful, and worth recording. For a moment she considered turning back. But instead she approached the dark-haired girl.

Another girl skipped up to Marie to say hello. Marie was curt with her and sent her away. She had never been rude like that to another girl, but she didn't want Sadie to know they were friends. She would be humiliated by the association. She had seen Sadie standing and looking at a group of girls the day before with a dour expression, as though she was judging them. She wondered what was wrong with the girls. What was it that Marie wasn't seeing? Marie decided this girl was trivial and silly, and she wanted nothing to do with her.

"Hello," Marie said.

"Hello," Sadie answered, looking up.

They stared at each other. And that was it. They were already shackled together.

"What are you reading?" Sadie asked.

"*Goblin Market*."

"Ah! I like that poem."

"You can't possibly know it. It's brand-new. That's why I've chosen it."

"It is the story of two sisters who go for a walk in the woods and come across a goblin market. One of the sisters eats the fruit and becomes poisoned and mad. So the other sister must return the next day for an antidote to save her."

"Oh," said Marie, chastised.

"I have been reading *The Lady of Shalott*. It's truly ridiculous what women do for men. She has to kill herself to look at a handsome man? She doesn't even know him. That's totally ridiculous. I don't find men good-looking at all. In fact, I find them all ugly. I would gladly never have to look at any of them ever again."

"But my father is beautiful. All the maids tell me they find him handsome."

"Perhaps. But men always tell you what to do, don't they? I want to live a passionate and tragic life. Because then I will have things to write about. The way things are now, I have no subject matter. Everyone here is positively boring. Everyone acts the same. They don't care at all about ideas."

Marie didn't know you could be critical of the Golden Mile in this way. She had accepted the world around her with great delight. She was beyond satisfied with it. It had never occurred to her that she might be living in a false, inadequate world that was robbing people of their true experiences. She was startled.

Marie was immediately smitten by the manner in which Sadie complained about things. Sadie analyzed everything. She found everything wanting. Her distaste for the world around her caused her to visualize and desire more. Marie had never realized how intelligent being negative made you.

She went home confused. What else was she not seeing? She would have to spend more time with Sadie. She had something to learn from Sadie. She wanted to know everything Sadie did.

SADIE WAS SURPRISED WHEN SHE received a written invitation from Marie to come over to her house the next Saturday for tea. But if she was surprised, her parents were shocked. Her mother had no idea why Marie Antoine would want to spend time with her dour, inhospitable child. But although she could not fathom the motives, she immediately saw the opportunity for what it was.

That evening Sadie's parents made her aware of how important her relationship with Marie was. Sadie needed to understand the scope of the Antoines' fortune. Louis Antoine had so much money, he could fund a political campaign to victory. He could easily buy anyone a seat in Parliament. And that was what Sadie Arnett's father wanted more than anything.

Her mother got on her knees in front of her and fixed her large bow around her neck.

"Sadie, my love," her mother said. "Be sweet with Marie. Daddy needs this very much. We are very proud of you."

Her mother kissed both her cheeks and her father patted her on the head. It didn't really make Sadie feel loved. In fact, quite the opposite.

MARIE MET SADIE AT THE GATE of her mansion and walked her around the estate. Marie paused to give Sadie a few minutes to look at the roses, as guests generally liked to do. The mansion was surrounded by a thick bed of beautifully kept pink roses. They were like ballerinas taking a break and sitting down in their tutus. It was so incredibly lovely. Each rose seemed to be a vision of health. It was as though each were in such a good mood.

Sadie stared at the rosebush dutifully. The roses gave her a strange feeling of foreboding. She thought it would be impossible for a girl to sneak out a window of this house. If she was to lower her legs into the bushes, the thorns would tear her legs and stockings apart. It was as though there were a moat surrounding the house. But it was meant to keep people in rather than keep them out.

Marie waited for the compliment she usually received about her garden. But when it didn't come, they walked on. Marie brought Sadie to a promenade that looked over the city. Marie pointed to the edge of the city by the water. "Do you see the smoke coming up from that building? It's from the sugar factory. And do you want me to tell you something about it that you are going to have trouble believing but is true nonetheless? It belongs to me."

Sadie was very impressed by Marie's power. She felt powerless as a young girl. Her parents were always talking about Philip's future. But they never mentioned hers.

"You are the boss?"

"Not now, of course. I'm too young. But I will be when I'm older. I think about what I am going to do all the time. Whenever there is a baby born to one of my workers, I am going to send over a trousseau of beautiful clothes. And we are going to have an annual parade and the most beautiful girl in the factory can be the sugar queen and ride on a carriage. And there will be a huge, huge cake everyone can take a piece of. We will set it up in a park there. It will be called Sugar Day. It will be the opposite of Lent. The archbishop will come and bless the sugar."

"That sounds wonderful."

"Working at a sugar factory is quite wonderful. We have the world's most splendid machines. And what's more, you inhale and sugar gets in your lungs and stays there. And when you cough, you cough sugar. You go around life smelling like a cookie."

"Now that you mention it, you do smell like sugar. After I saw you the last time, when I went home, I kept feeling as though something sweet was baking."

"It's my magical power. Would you like a sugary kiss?"

"I would."

They kissed. And Sadie found her lips tasted like sugar. She was afraid to lick her lips in case the taste would go away.

"I like to write in a notebook every day."

"I've seen you. What do you write about?"

She reached into her pocket and pulled out her notebook. She flipped through the pages, settled on one, and began to read.

"'The Swan, a poem. A swan has white feathers, but it does not want to be clean. It only wants others to look at it. Then hates them when they do. The swan hates anyone except its life partner. They spend all their time gossiping about everybody else. And they cannot have anything but contempt for other swans. Or any other creature. But why should they? Nothing. No creature can ever get between two swans. And you cannot tear them apart. Once they fall in love, they become horrible in exactly the same way.'"

"I love that so much!" said Marie. "You have made me think about swans differently. It is true they are so difficult. But that's what makes them beautiful. They don't want to be only what we make of them. They want the right to be ugly too. I think you are my favorite writer, Sadie. One day you will write books and everyone in the whole world will read them. Everyone will know of your ideas."

Sadie felt her cheeks flush red when Marie complimented her poetry. After the visit, Sadie went home to her room and began to write. She now had a reader. And Marie was open to her idea that there was power and beauty in being original. It made her devotion to her burgeoning craft even more feverish.

She spent all her free time apart from Marie writing. If ever she paused, she thought of Marie enjoying the poem she was working on, and her pen immediately went back to the page. The tip of her pen made the flight pattern of neurotic birds mating. The looping words on the page were like knots in a girl's hair that have formed after she's been standing in the wind. They were like the tendrils of a plant if spring happened all in one moment. The page sucked the words out of her pen. It wanted to be marked.

⁓

ONE AFTERNOON, MARIE ASKED SADIE to show her how to be darker.

"You make everything into a sad story," Marie said. "And I mean that as a compliment. You always make me want to cry. That's the most beautiful thing: to cry for no reason at all, only because you are feeling someone else's sadness."

"I don't know how to make you feel it," Sadie replied. "It is always just there for me. This sadness. It's just like using the color black. I think sometimes I am too sad, and it taints everything I do. When I read, I always imagine myself as the main character, and then every book becomes a sad book."

Then Sadie had an idea. They sat at the veranda table in front of two bowls of chocolate pudding. They both tied blindfolds around their eyes. They spoke to each other with their blindfolds on. Sadie thought up a bleak idea and then they took a bite of the pudding. The dark idea would forever be associated with something delicious.

"Imagine you wake up and your house is very quiet. You tiptoe through the rooms and notice your family and all your maids have been murdered," Sadie said.

"Even Papa?"

"Even Papa."

There was a pause as they both ate a spoonful of pudding.

"Imagine you are standing on trial in front of a crowd. Everybody begins to yell that you are guilty."

The girls sucked on their spoons.

"Imagine you are being brought to the guillotine. Your head has been placed on the guillotine and you hear the slice."

"Yes, yes," Marie whispered. They heard the sound of each other's spoons striking the bottom of their bowls.

"Imagine your head is on a stake," Sadie said. "It's still conscious and you don't have a body."

"You two need to stop this instant!" a voice said in the darkness. The two girls pulled the blindfolds from their eyes to take a look. A maid named Agatha was standing there, having overheard everything they said and looking appalled. Both girls reflected on what their conversation must have sounded like to an impartial listener who had not descended by degrees into their madness. And they began to laugh. In truth they were delighted by their indecency.

SADIE HAD A STRANGE SIDE. The best way to describe it was as a perversity. She liked grotesque things. She saw a frog and she stepped on it with the heel of her boot. She wanted to see the maid's broken ankle. She squealed with delight, put her hands up to her mouth, and declared with admiration that it was absolutely disgusting. Marie was always startled by this but decided never to bring it up.

AFTER PLAYING ONE AFTERNOON, Sadie felt overcome by a wave of affection for her friend. The two girls were sitting in the large garden behind Marie's house. Their parasols were open and lying on either side of them. It was as though they had both hatched out of an egg, like the twins Helen of Troy and Clytemnestra.

"I didn't think I could have a friend," Sadie said. "I thought spending time with other children was a waste of time and it kept me away from reading. But I like your company very much. It makes me think in a more creative way."

"I have no interest in any of my other friends," Marie declared in response. "I was playing with Melody the other day. We had been such close friends since we were very little. But when we were together, I became so bored that I fell asleep. She was, of course, terribly offended, but what could I do? She didn't say one thing that was funny or strange."

"I really like going home and writing about our experiences together. I always find the way we spend our days as interesting as something in a book."

Marie flung her arms around Sadie. She believed Sadie to be so wise that this type of affection was entirely beneath her. She was a cerebral little girl who lived in her head and not her heart. And yet this unobtainable girl had confessed that not only was her heart something that could be charmed but it was Marie who had charmed it.

Sadie knew she had stolen Marie's heart completely and none of the other girls could compete. The other girls felt a shadow cross the whole neighborhood as Marie's affection was withdrawn from them. Marie no longer invited them over for tea and cookies. She preferred to be alone with Sadie.

The girls were playing in the labyrinth in Marie's garden one afternoon when they declared their love for each other. Every declaration of love is a magic incantation. It casts a spell on your future. They knelt in front of each other in the middle of the labyrinth. Marie had a wreath of white flowers on her head. Sadie had a wreath of red ones on hers.

"I declare my love for you for the rest of my life. Nothing will ever tear us apart. I will never love anyone as much as I love you."

"My heart is hereby bequeathed to you. I will give you my heart."

"We will exchange hearts. Your heart will be beating in my chest. And my heart will be beating in yours."

"I am as much you as I am myself. When you are away from me, I will never feel whole. There will be an empty space in my chest. And I will be heartless."

Sadie found her family's obsequious behavior toward Marie's family to be distasteful. She found it made them repugnant. When she came home from Marie's house, they would ask her for a very detailed account of the time she had spent over there. There was no detail that was too mundane for them to hear. They didn't want her to leave anything out. It was as though they did not trust her to know which were the important details. So they had her recount everything.

"We sat by the fountain today. We had some tea and cake brought out."

"You were nice to her?"

"Of course."

"Did you see her father?"

"Yes."

"Did he speak to you?"

"No, he did not."

Her parents showed more interest in these stories than in anything she did. She watched the desperate attention in their faces. They reminded her of animals. Dogs. It was as though she were holding treats in front of them.

Sadie didn't want to share any information with her parents. She would feel complicit with their need to commodify her friendship. She did not want to feel that the moments she spent with Marie were part of a grand scheme for her parents' advancement. They belonged to her alone. But naturally, Marie wanted to come to Sadie's home one day.

There was a knock at the door. Sadie had been watching for Marie from her window ledge. She ran down to the door to invite her friend in.

They sat at the tea table the maid set for them. She told the maid to bring out her own tea set. She had inherited it from a great-uncle. It was an extremely questionable heirloom. All the handles had been broken off at some point and then glued back on. You could see the cracks in the porcelain. They were like the black veins on the arms of dead people. But Sadie liked the tea set because it was one of the few items in the world that was genuinely hers. She had an affection for its ugliness and brokenness. That's the reason the tea set remained hers. Nobody else wanted it. She knew Marie would love it.

Mrs. Arnett came into the room. Sadie was confused. She was sure she had indicated quite clearly to her family she wanted to be alone with Marie. If she hadn't said it explicitly, they should have certainly assumed it, since Sadie wanted to be alone without the presence of her family no matter what she did.

"Hello, Marie. Allow me to introduce myself. I am Mrs. Arnett. I'm Sadie's mother. I can't tell you how thrilled the whole family is that you have taken an interest in Sadie. Her personality has simply bloomed. We see her smiling, and usually she's such a dour little thing. I only hope she can learn to be more like you. I saw you at the elocution contest last year. Your bearing was so lovely. And your delivery was splendid. Are you competing again this year?"

"Yes, Mrs. Arnett. I look forward to the event every year. I very much enjoy seeing the entire neighborhood come out. And also listening to the poems other children have chosen too. I think theirs are just as good as mine. I'm always surprised when I win."

"Your modesty is part of your charm, dear. Your father must be delighted to have such a perfect child. I can't imagine how he must feel. He has raised you in an extraordinary manner. You inherited his looks and manners, but there is part of your charm that is yours and yours alone."

Marie smiled magnificently, in the way she always did toward sycophants. Sadie clicked her tongue, making the sound of croquet balls striking against each other.

Why couldn't her mother ever say such things about her? Why couldn't she compliment one of Sadie's poems in this manner? She must truly think she was awful. Sadie assumed her mother would treat any female child with contempt. But it was clear she would love to have Marie as a daughter.

It was a strange feeling, jealousy. When she saw the way her parents treated Marie, she was jealous. Once this feeling had been awoken in her, it was impossible to make it dormant again. She now became acutely aware that Marie drew everyone's attention. When Marie walked down the street, people looked at her and couldn't stop. They acted as though looking at her were a rare phenomenon they had to stop everything they were doing to observe.

Sadie had perfected the act of being invisible. But this was absurd.

Sadie looked at the silhouette of Marie on the bag of sugar. She was well aware that other girls all over the city gazed at this image with unreciprocated adoration. But she was the one who had stolen Marie's heart. It filled her with a pride that was unfortunately tinged with a desire to squash her. She was aware of the status she had acquired in the eyes of other little girls by association. She thought she should have that status on her own.

SADIE WAS NOT THE ONLY one to experience this stirring of new emotion. The two little girls had profound superiority complexes. Sadie performed a puppet show she had written for Marie. She held the puppet of a crow in one hand, and that of a wolf in the other. The two puppets argued for fifteen minutes about who was the more wicked.

"When did you write that?" Marie asked.

"On that rainy day when it was impossible to go out."

Marie felt so taken aback. How could her friend simply sit at a desk and write a play that was both cynical and brilliant? She was clearly a genius. It immediately made Marie feel she was not.

Before she had met Sadie, she had always been the best girl her age at whatever she did. But now there was someone else their age who was very good at things. While this was fascinating and attractive, she found it stirred odd and ugly emotions in herself. It planted the seed of jealousy in her. And that seed began to grow and it bore thoughts that were like tendrils. Every decent friendship comes with a drop of hatred. But that hatred is like honey in the tea. It makes it addictive.

WHILE PRACTICING ARCHERY IN MARIE'S backyard, the girls discovered the other had particularly good aim. Because they both hit the mark so easily and so often, they could not impress each other. They were both used to thrilling at least somebody with their skill.

They stood facing each other. They both had a sack of arrows slung over their backs and bows in their left hands. They were at the back of Marie's property, which was demarcated by a tall black fence with stakes that were twisted like licorice.

"Since we have perfected our aim," Sadie said, "we must now perfect our courage."

"In what way?" Marie inquired.

"There's no point in shooting again and again at a stationary object, is there? We need to be pursuing foxes and living things. It's not that the target is moving that makes it hard to kill. It's the act of taking life away from something else, for sport. It's the morality of it, Marie!" Sadie had a look of absolute glee in her eyes. "I would love to kill a fawn. Its darling head would look adorable on my wall. My mother thinks hunting is a morbid sport for a lady. She won't let me go with my father and brother."

"That's a pity," Marie said, although she was unconvinced.

"It's for the best. If I went with my brother, I would be possessed by an urge to put an arrow into him. I would like to have him stuffed and used as a coatrack."

"You don't like your brother?"

"He's awful. And he hates girls. He hates me because I'm a girl. He can't even look at me because he hates me so much."

There was a black cat climbing on the fence. They say that black cats are unlucky, and this one certainly was. Especially as it had decided to leap up onto a fence the very moment after Sadie had delivered her sadistic speech.

Later, Marie thought she would have tried to stop Sadie if she had thought her friend was serious. If she believed Sadie was actually going to murder the cat. But she didn't. She didn't think it was possible. It was so out of the realm of what an ordinary girl might choose to do on a Thursday afternoon.

Sadie pulled out an arrow from her sheath and set it in the bow. She then let it go. It struck the cat. The cat let out a sharp cry and fell off the fence. He made a small thud when he landed. He rolled onto his back with the arrow in his chest.

It was almost comic. As though the cat were a puppet in a play and were performing its own death. They huddled next to the dying creature. The cat looked up at the sky. He had expected many possible endings to the day, but this had not been one of them.

"I liked that cat," Marie declared. "He had a very merry way about him."

Sadie had no interest in cats or any understanding of why anyone might care about them. She quite enjoyed drowning kittens in the bucket in the kitchen. Sadie personally believed there was a proliferation of cats in the neighborhood because they weren't being used as target practice.

"I think that was excessively cruel of you," Marie said.

"If you think I'm cruel, we don't have to be friends. You have so many anyways. I'm taking you away from them."

"No, no, no. I didn't mean that. I meant it as a compliment."

Both girls shrugged the death off. And Marie walked Sadie home.

"I'm competing at the elocution contest at Lady Brickenton Hall," Marie said. "You should read a poem too."

"You won't mind?"

"Of course not. But I've won this competition for three years in a row. So don't be disappointed if you lose."

They pressed their pretty lips against each other's and kissed.

THAT SATURDAY, MUCH of the Golden Mile filed into Lady Brickenton Hall, a grand building made of red bricks. There were squirrels and rabbits and foxes carved into the masonry around the large front door, looking like a spell had been placed on them by settlers, turning them into stone. Marie went up on the stage. She was wearing a pink dress and had pink roses in her hair. She announced she would be reciting Christina Rossetti's *Goblin Market*.

Marie stood on her tiptoes and waved her arms about as she recited the words in her pure and melodic voice. The audience was bewitched by Marie's performance. They did not take their eyes off her. There was a look of delight on the spectators' faces as they followed Marie into the land of fairy tales. They were in a forest where they could meet goblins and eat a strawberry that would steal their souls.

Marie was open with her gestures, she allowed the audience members, each and every one of them, to enter her body. She behaved in a manner that would normally be considered unbecoming to a young girl or lady of the time. Ladies were supposed to moderate their physical behavior. They were supposed to speak in an articulate and reserved fashion. They were not supposed to act as though they were transported by their emotions. Because look what power the female imagination had. People lost their grasp on reality when Marie spoke to them. Marie could lead people straight into the ocean. She could make them accept the most sordid behavior. She could start an orgy of some sort. And she was so young. She was only at the very beginning of her power.

SADIE WENT UP IMMEDIATELY after Marie. To everyone's surprise, she announced that she, too, would be reciting *Goblin Market*. Marie was the most startled that Sadie had chosen the same poem as her. It worked to her disadvantage. The audience would have just heard it. They would be bored of it. The story itself would hold no suspense for them. Their attention would wane.

Sadie did not move her body around the way Marie did. She glared at the audience as she recited the words, curtly and viciously. Her dark seriousness pervaded every word. The audience followed Sadie even if they didn't want to. They were now in a menacing fairy tale with perverted goblins pulling at their hair and sticking poisonous berries in their stomachs.

Marie began to think of the poem in a different way. It had hidden meanings. Sadie was offering a completely opposite reading of *Goblin Market*. The audience was silent and troubled, but they were also rapt. They were quiet at the end, pondering the darkness Sadie had revealed to them.

In any case, the two readers had both broken many rules about what it meant to be a young woman and had gotten away with it.

THE JUDGES TOOK A LONGER time deciding on a winner than they usually did. And when the judges came back, they made an announcement that would have far-reaching consequences and wreak havoc on many lives. They decided that there had been a tie that year. There would be two winners. The judges had decided the girls were both so eloquent, they couldn't decide who to give the ribbon to. Sadie and Marie were both given first-place ribbons.

If the judges had decided then, once and for all, which of the girls was superior, it would have saved an awful lot of trouble. The girls might have accepted their ranking. One would have been slightly superior and proud of it. And the other might have reconciled themselves to a secondary role. But to posit they were equals put each of them in an impossible situation vis-à-vis the other.

This was absurd to both Sadie and Marie. How could first place be given to two children? They both knew it was a lie.

AFTER THE GIRLS WERE AWARDED their ribbons, Marie was surrounded by a swarm of girls and their parents, all of whom wanted to congratulate and compliment her. Sadie stood off to the side, all by herself. Nobody could even look her in the eye.

Sadie didn't feel as though she had won. She didn't even feel as though she had tied for first place. She felt she had been robbed of the award. Her interpretation was better; she was sure of it. But the judges refused to let an unlikeable girl like her win the competition.

She felt bitter that night in her bed. She closed her eyes. She imagined inviting Marie to come cycling with her along the river. She imagined the wind blowing Marie over into the water. It would be very hard to swim in the type of fancy dresses Marie wore. She would probably drown.

The only manner in which she could get over her feeling of rejection was to fantasize about Marie dying in strange ways. In these fantasies she always went to great lengths to save Marie but would never succeed.

She had a fantasy wherein Marie fell through a hole while skating on a thin patch of ice on the river. She imagined lying on top of the ice, banging on it. And Marie banged from the other side of it. It was very macabre, but it was wonderful. Marie would be lifeless underneath the ice and Sadie would be staring at her, alive, alive, alive.

MARIE FELT LIKE SUCH A phony after obtaining the ribbon. Everything she took pride in was a lie. People had complimented her because she was rich and for no other reason.

She wasn't especially pretty. She was fat and blond and silly-looking. She still looked like a harmless baby. On the other hand, it was impossible to keep one's eyes off Sadie. She was going to get prettier and prettier the older she got. Whereas Marie would become fatter and more ridiculous and people would recall how adorable she had been as a child.

Sadie would become more and more brilliant. Marie would always be an idiot.

She had been told she was better than other girls her whole life. It wasn't true at all. Other girls had been holding themselves back so she could win. She was held up as a standard of success, and because the bar was so low, all the other girls were idiotic.

Marie put her head against her pillow and wept, wishing she had never met Sadie. She wanted to go back to feeling the way she did about the world before meeting her blackhearted friend.

NONETHELESS, THE TWO GIRLS FOUND themselves in Marie's garden talking about poetry less than a week later. It was a beautiful day. The clouds were like the tutus of ballet dancers dropped all over the floor. The dandelions had sprung up like a group of eggs had hatched the night before. The girls were discussing the duel scene in a play they had seen.

"Why would anyone agree to a duel?" Marie asked. "You're risking your life to make a point to someone you don't like."

"Sometimes two people can't be alive at the same time. Because they both want the same thing. They hate each other so much that if they both stay alive, it will negate both their existences. So it's a simple solution if you think about it."

"But I think they should be able to work it out," Marie said, her face scrunched up in thought. "I don't know what killing each other will do. Even if one person is dead, do you really stop hating them? You might go crazy because you will never be able to make peace with that person."

"No, no, no. Some people can never be friends no matter how much they try. They try again and again and it just makes things worse. There is nothing they can do about it. That's the thing about mortal enemies, they can never stop trying to destroy each other."

"Shall we play at being in a duel?" Marie suggested.

"Absolutely," Sadie said.

"I don't mind dying."

"You always get to die," Sadie complained.

"Let's both die."

"Perfect!"

"And shall we murder each other with our fingers?" Marie asked.

"I'll borrow my father's guns. They are so beautiful."

AFTER A BRIEF TRIP to her house, Sadie returned out of breath, holding a box with her father's guns inside. She opened the lid for Marie to admire how beautiful they were. Sadie took the box of bullets out of the side and put them on the bench, so no accidents would happen. They went deep into the labyrinth in the backyard together.

CHAPTER 5

Louis Antoine and His Conquests

The maid Agatha was getting dressed very slowly by the window. Louis's favorite thing was to watch maids get dressed and undressed. He appreciated when they did it slowly. Agatha, however, wasn't doing it to please Louis but because she didn't want to go back to work. She considered making love to be part of the job. She considered getting dressed to be her own time. She was lazy about it. She watched a dove tossing about in the sky, looking like a young boy pulling his white shirt over his head.

Louis's reputation with maids was notorious, even though he tried to keep it within the walls of his large home. Louis Antoine hated the opinions of outsiders. Gossip had plagued him his whole life, even when he was a child and innocent of wrongdoing. Louis Antoine's father was a moron and lost all the family's money in bad investments. He did what people normally did when they had a reversal of fortune like that—he blew his head off in his office. His mother had a cup of tea and arsenic and followed suit.

Louis Antoine had wanted to marry someone very pretty. He was very pretty, so he thought he really deserved to marry someone pretty.

He believed he had exquisite taste in girls. He could rank who was the most beautiful. He didn't consider himself shallow because he also took into account women's personalities. He believed that a woman's happiness enhanced her looks. He believed a woman looked her most beautiful right after she laughed. Her cheeks were flushed pink and her mouth was partly open. Equally, he admired the way they looked after they had been dancing. They were sweaty, their curls stuck to their forehead, and they looked desperate to take their clothes off.

But the most beautiful and eligible girls were always encouraged to marry rich men, because they could. They courted men who were less charming and beautiful than him because those men had large fortunes. The only woman he could get to marry him was Marie's mother, Hortense. Her parents had also died when she was young, but they had left her with an enormous fortune and an entire sugar factory. She was so rich that she could afford to marry a handsome, penniless aristocrat. But she was plain and melancholic.

He met Hortense at the Ice Ball when he was nineteen. What had the theme been that year? It had been Cyrano de Bergerac. All the men were wearing large prosthetic noses attached to their faces with elastics. And they had swords on their sides. There was something unexpectedly perverse about the costumes.

Hortense sat on a bench by the wall all evening. She was too self-conscious to skate. She was always about to burst into tears. Every time he saw her, he thought she was crying, even if she didn't actually have tears in her eyes. She couldn't bear to embarrass herself. How boring someone that self-conscious would be in bed. No one else wanted to marry her. However, none of the other young men were for sale in the same way that he was. She could afford to buy his love. And so he was purchased.

She understood. And she knew it was her money in large part that he was after. Yet he was kind to her. He plied his seduction with her. She was, of course, insulted when her aunt and uncle insisted he only wanted her money. Because how else could she interpret it other than them implying that she was unlovable. And so that was how it came to be that two very unlovable people came to be wed. One got what he wanted, and the other was deeply depressed and killed herself before her daughter's first birthday.

There's no one more brutal than a rich man without money.

After his wife's death, Louis insisted all the girls working in the house be jolly. He said he didn't care if they were incompetent as long as they were happy. He had had enough of women's sadness. He viewed his wife's sadness as something he had endured. Something he'd had to live through. He acted as though he'd had to cope with his wife's suicide. It was a selfish act she had perpetrated against him and also against Marie.

The maids in their household changed all the time. They lost their joie de vivre abruptly once Louis seduced them. They inevitably went mad. There was a maid who spoke only French who tried to run off with Marie when she was a baby. She left the father a note that said, *You took my heart, now I will take yours.* But she had written it in French and Louis had no idea what she meant. She took the train with Marie all the way to a small town outside of Trois-Rivières. They slept together in a bed at an inn. They were too tired to even take the blanket off the bed. They lay on top of it and fell asleep in each other's arms, and that was how they were found by the detectives.

But of all the strange fates the maids who were Louis's lovers had in store for them, it was Agatha's fate that made the most impression.

Marie was always affectionate with the maids. She accepted the runoff of emotions they had for her father and relished it. But she was always wary when Agatha was solicitous of her. She found it alarming, although she couldn't put her finger on why. And she knew she was being unfair to Agatha. Nonetheless, she couldn't help but put her defenses up around this maid. It felt as though Agatha was always asking Marie for some sort of reciprocal attachment she had no right to demand.

That day, while getting dressed, Agatha looked out into the magnificent rose garden below. For a moment she considered it to be her own. And then her heart fell into her stomach, her face went pale, and she screamed, "Oh no!" and flew out of the room half-dressed.

She had spotted the two girls engaging in a duel. It was to be the end of her.

CHAPTER 6

Eulogy for a Pair of Pistols

The girls had been practically knocked off their feet by the force of the guns' blows. They were stunned that there were bullets in the gun. They stood there with tiny clouds of gunpowder over their heads, wondering if they were ghosts, whether they were going to be made aware that bullets had entered them and had stopped their hearts. They knew there were consequences to what they had just done, but they couldn't ascertain what they were.

The maid lay on the ground with two bullets in her chest. The front of her chemise was soaked in blood. It kept spreading outward. There was no saving her. She didn't move a muscle. She looked wide-eyed up at the sky. Although neither girl had encountered a dead body in their lives, it was clear they were now looking at one.

Marie seemed to react first. She threw the gun onto the ground, as though it were a live thing, an accomplice that would cause her to murder someone else.

She had a look of such panic on her face that Sadie knew she would have to save her friend. Of course Marie was going to react more strongly. She had seen this woman alive so many times. So naturally the fact of having to look at her dead was overwhelming. But Sadie did not know the maid. She seemed as though she had run out of the house with the express wish to become a corpse.

Their eyes met, and Marie's whole being begged for Sadie to help her. Ordinarily, Sadie's face would have the same look of aghast comprehension that Marie's had. But Marie had beat her to it. They could not both be petrified. Sadie would bestow the privilege of being alarmed and hysterical to Marie. She would take care of this mess and then Marie would know just how much she loved her and would make her sure to always, always keep Sadie at her side.

Sadie stepped around the dead maid. She knew immediately the best course of action would be to deny the whole event. She had read about such things in detective novels. She picked up the guns and hurried off with them in her arms to the woods behind Marie's house. She stepped carefully over the roots so as not to trip. As she walked, her heart was beating so loudly, it felt as though she were marching in a procession that was signaling to everyone around that war had begun. Sadie buried the guns in the pet cemetery.

She realized it wasn't the best plan to try to hide the *guns* in order to conceal the crime. But she had never murdered anyone before. And in the detective novels she had read, there always seemed to be an effort to throw the murder weapon in the river. She wished she could dispose of the body.

She sat between two giant tree roots that held her in their arms as though she were a baby. Her hands were completely covered in mud. She needed to let her little heart stop beating so quickly. The mushrooms at the base of the trees were shaped like ears, as though the forest were listening and waiting for her to explain.

There was a space the noise of the gun had cleared out in her head.

All other outside noises were muted. She could not hear the sound of the stream passing by the tips of her boots. She couldn't hear the branches rustling against one another above her. She looked up in the sky, and there were birds overhead but she couldn't hear them. She could only hear what was going on inside herself. She sighed, and the sound of her sigh echoed through the whole forest.

She went back down to Marie's yard, now empty of people, including Agatha's body, and waited for her friend. She was waiting to find out if they were in trouble. Feeling faint, she reached into her pocket and pulled out an apple. She often carried a piece of fruit around on the off chance she felt hungry. She took a bite from it. Then seeing that she was all alone and not knowing what to do, she headed home.

Marie will take care of this, she thought. She and her father can fix everything. Marie is going to be the owner of a sugar empire. It will be nothing for her to find an answer to this problem. She had no idea how Marie would pull it off, but Marie thought in different, more worldly ways than she did. It was as though the day were a page in a huge book and they would rip it out if they chose. It wasn't their fault the maid had hurled her body between them. No, this event need never have happened.

She walked home and found it was already dinnertime. She didn't say a word to anyone at the table, but nobody noticed. They didn't notice she was deaf and mute. They didn't notice her thoughts were about a million miles away from them.

She lifted up her fork to take a bite, but it trembled in her hand. She put it down abruptly and looked around. It was as though the fork were asking how dare she hold it after what she got up to today. It was as if the fork were trying to notify everyone at the table what she had done. The fork was not inclined to feed her any dessert. The raspberry remained untouched in the center of the flan. Red juice began to seep out of it, like a bullet wound in the chest of a white chemise.

She asked to be excused, then went to the bathroom to puke.

THE MAID HAD BEEN CARRIED quickly inside by three other maids. Marie ran after them. Agatha's undergarments were completely red and soaked in blood. They lay the maid on the carpet and unfastened her chemise. The other maids yelled her name and begged her to answer. "Agatha, Agatha, Agatha," they cried. Marie kept hoping beyond hope that the maid would be resurrected, that she wasn't actually dead. But she hadn't shown any signs of movement. Marie realized how obstinate the dead were. They simply refused to take the world seriously.

Marie hadn't even known people died instantly. She thought they were always given a bit of time. They would get to say famous last words if they were notable. And they could pass on messages to their favorite people if they were simple nobodies. She wished the maid had stayed alive long enough to forgive her.

Realizing how hopeless the situation was, Marie went back outside to find Sadie. She saw her at a distance. Her friend was sitting on a small white bench outside of the labyrinth, staring straight ahead. Marie thought she must be in an incredibly sad mood at the moment. Perhaps she had been unkind by abandoning her friend to run after a corpse. Sadie was clearly in a moral quandary.

Marie watched Sadie rummage through her skirt pocket clearly in search of something. She imagined it was a handkerchief, even though Sadie didn't appear to be crying. She pulled an apple out of her pocket and shined it with her sleeve. And then she bit into it as though nothing in the world had happened. For a brief instant, Marie doubted reality.

MARIE'S FATHER TOOK HER by the hand. He led her abruptly away from the scene. She had never had to hasten her pace for her father. He preferred to stroll than to walk. He pulled her quickly down the corridor. They passed all the paintings of landscapes that seemed to stand still despite all their hectic motions, like those in train windows. He brought her to her room. He opened the door and pushed her inside. He stood outside the door as though the threshold were a line she had crossed but he had not.

"Stay in this room," he said. "Do not come out until I tell you to. Do not let anyone come in other than me. Do you understand?"

Marie nodded. She couldn't speak. She was holding her words in her throat as though it were a dam and the second she spoke one word, a cry would be dislodged and she would weep forever. Her whole body felt like a Champagne bottle that had been shaken and was waiting to explode.

Louis closed the door, and Marie felt shut off from everything around her. She turned and looked at the green wallpaper adorned with tree branches and birds and felt like Eve when she had been kicked out of the Garden of Eden. But she didn't even have Adam to hold hands with.

Marie was shaking. She had been so concerned with the fate of the maid, she hadn't had a chance to really think about what the implications of these events were for her. She could not lose her father's love. Her father thought she was a perfect child. Could you be a perfect child if you were also a murderer? It seemed highly improbable. She could not bear the idea that she might be brought down in her father's estimation to any degree. He couldn't tolerate anyone on earth except for her.

She had no idea what they did to rich girls who murdered their servants. It could not be prison! Her factory! That would be what they would take away from her. She would never be able to execute all her plans. She had been looking forward to it. They would take her face off the side of the sugar bags. Who would she be if she wasn't on the side of the sugar bags? She didn't want to be ordinary.

Sadie did not have this problem. She was already living in a loveless home. She didn't have a factory. It wasn't fair! She had so much more to lose than Sadie.

If Sadie had stayed and thought about things with her, she probably would have come up with some different solutions. But Sadie had left her all alone. She had left her to face the music. She had left her to take all the blame for these actions herself. If Sadie was going to look out for herself, Marie decided, then she should look out for herself too.

So when her father came in and sat on her gold divan, she fell to the floor, onto her knees. "Sadie" was what she said.

She said Sadie had tried to shoot her. She said Sadie was jealous because she had won the poetry recital and she felt the results had been unfair. She said she had already been wary of Sadie, as she had murdered a cat in the backyard for no reason. And she hadn't cared at all. And she had buried it in a pet cemetery in the woods that had stone markers above where all manner of animals had been buried.

This almost seemed too farfetched to be true. Louis had the inspectors go to the burial ground Marie had described. Naturally, Sadie seemed like a calculating murderer from a novel. They found the guns buried in a fresh grave, which could only be the actions of a murderer who had engaged in predetermination. This act was deliberate. She was culpable.

There were inconsistencies in the story. The main inconsistency was that although at first glance there appeared to be one hole in the maid's chest, the examination of the body revealed there were two bullets.

Who could say whether it was one bullet or the other that had killed the maid? Louis was certain Marie was complicit. It did not make him turn against Marie the way she thought it would. All Louis knew was that he would protect his daughter at all costs.

Marie could not believe she had denounced her best friend. She felt as though it changed everything in her body. She would be a different person after this. She knew what she was capable of. That was perhaps a definition of innocence: not knowing what one was capable of.

CHAPTER 7

A Visit to the Lowly

Home of Agatha

When Louis went to visit Agatha's family, he found the maid lying on the living-room table for a wake. How monstrous and grotesque, Louis could not help thinking. But the other visitors did not feel this way at all. They all remarked on how young and pretty and lifelike she looked. No one could afford the services of a mortician. There was a woman who lived on Dandelion Alley who would come and fix up a body for a nominal fee. She wore a black kerchief with red cherries on it, wrapped tightly around her head. She came with a small beaten-up doctor's bag and asked to be left alone with the body. All she had in her bag were scraps of old cotton and a bit of costume makeup she had found behind a theater. She opened up the girl's mouth and tucked bits of cotton into it, then she put makeup on her face. She put a thick smudge on her lips and she applied pink to the cheeks. Since it was considered improper to wear makeup, no one was aware of its magical properties. Agatha had so much color in her!

Agatha also had a crown of daisies around her head. Louis thought about how daisies were so much like young girls. They hung around where you didn't expect them. They seemed perfectly unaware of their environment. You might see one of them in a garden standing prettily with its face turned toward the sun. You might equally see one leaning against a wall in the city, all by itself.

Everyone but Louis found the halo of daisies to be a wonderful tribute. They thought it made her look like an angel. They believed they had never seen her look so beautiful. And many of the older women made the sign of the cross and thanked God she had not been shot through the head. For her mother's sake, at least.

Louis did not want to look at Agatha's face. He had always found her very pretty. But he could not find her pretty anymore. It wasn't because she was dead either. It had to do with the house he was standing in now. It was dark and cramped. The ceilings were low and the wallpaper had water damage. This was the type of house she had grown up in. This was the type of house she had taken her first steps in. This was the house she had lived in up until she showed up at his door. He chose to believe the girls showed up fully formed as though by magic on his doorstep. It made him shudder to think they all came from this.

When all the guests left, Louis sat down with Agatha's parents. Monsieur Robespierre had a French accent, whereas madame had an Irish one. He was surprised Agatha had managed to have neither. Despite their different accents, Louis had trouble following who was saying what.

"She had such beautiful red hair," the father said.

"It was a shock! We never knew where she got it from," the mother said.

"She's got blond hair and I have dark. So we were expecting one or the other."

"He thought she wasn't his."

"I thought she wasn't mine!"

"She had his eyes though."

"I never understood how I could have a daughter that pretty."

Louis loathed how married couples ended up speaking as though they were the same person. He thought it rendered the couple asexual, and that seemed horrifying to him.

"She was very tidy," the mother said. "She always tidied up."

"She couldn't stand to see a crumb on the floor."

"I was in service myself," the mother added confidentially. "And I found it hard. So I wanted something different for her. But she never seemed to mind it."

Louis looked around the room. He couldn't imagine how anyone could tell whether this house was dirty or clean.

"I was never afraid of getting old," the mother said, "because I knew she was going to take care of me."

"I almost wish she worried less about us," the father said. "But she couldn't help it. She was always taking care of us."

They both cast their eyes downward but then looked up at Louis slightly, in order to see if they had led him to offer more money than he'd originally imagined.

"We also need a new breadwinner in the family," the mother said. "You were so good to give Agatha a job in your household. Would you consider taking on our granddaughter Mary? She has no once since her mother died. We don't have anyone either now that her mother is dead."

"Should you like us to call her in?" the father asked.

"No, no," Louis answered. "I don't need to see her."

Louis looked up and saw a girl standing in the doorway staring at him. His heart leaped up to his throat and his face went red. For a brief second he thought it was his own daughter standing at the door. She bore a remarkable resemblance to Marie. It was as though something horrible had befallen Marie. Someone had kidnapped her and kept her in a cabin in the woods, and she had been underfed and forced to wear wretched, threadbare clothes. She was thinner than Marie, but not in a svelte and lithe manner. She looked malnourished. Her limbs and face seemed more angular than they should be. There were dark circles under her eyes. She had the same mountain of blond hair, the exact same color as Marie's, but it was greasy and dirty. She had brushed it and put it up all by herself, and no one had ever fussed over it.

Louis always dressed Marie in the most expensive dresses. Her colorful clothes would have lit up the dark doorway. It would be like pulling curtains off a window and having the sunlight pour in. Marie always had the same effect that a large bouquet of flowers on a table would have. This girl was wearing the drabbest black coat. It didn't even have the energy to be black. It was gray like a chalkboard that had a poem recently wiped off it with a brush. She had on a pair of black boots. One was tied with a piece of brown twine, the other with a skinny ribbon frayed at the edges.

The thing about the girl that was the most different from Marie, however, was the expression on her face. Marie always had a curious and sweet look. She regarded everyone with such softness, as though she were forgiving you for the most terrible crime. But the girl in the doorway had a nasty look. It shocked him. She undermined his confidence. Her eyes animated all his repressed feelings of self-hatred. This was why girls had to have so much training and education about their expressions.

For a moment he felt ashamed that he had mistaken this impoverished child for his own Marie. She had shown up in the doorway like the ghost of his daughter. He would honestly rather Agatha sat straight up, pulled the flowers out of her hair and the cotton out of her mouth and say, *How do you do?* than see this girl.

There was no chance he would ever let her step across his threshold.

He handed the parents a large envelope of cash, promised a job for Mary in his factory, and swore the girl who had killed their daughter would be punished. In return, they were to keep quiet about the whole event.

CHAPTER 8

Sadie Is Exiled

L ouis really hadn't given Sadie very much thought before this terrible incident. He didn't see any of Marie's friends as being particularly different from the maids. He considered Marie to be so far above everyone. All her friends were interchangeable. Marie often took a fancy to a girl for a short period of time. The nature of Marie's strong passions caused each girl to believe herself singular in Marie's affections. Then she would grow very bored of them and choose not to see them again. The girl would always be replaced by another.

He wasn't fussy about who she spent time with. He didn't care if it was a maid or if it was a girl from a well-to-do family. He did, however, notice that Marie had a particular affection for the dark-haired girl who was an Arnett. They seemed to be together all the time.

He was surprised the Arnetts were willing to sacrifice their daughter so quickly and easily after the shooting. He understood for a moment the effect his wealth had on other people. It made them bend to his will before he asked them to. And before he even thought about it. It was peculiar to have your needs met before the desire manifested. The Arnetts had figured out what he needed them to do.

He hadn't dared to think about it. If any questions were asked about the dead woman, the shadow of a doubt had to be cast on someone. The Arnetts would let it fall on Sadie.

Louis had immediately paid money to the coroner to say there was one bullet. And with that, a child was framed.

OF COURSE, THE EVENT WAS hushed up. What in the world was anyone supposed to do with two murderesses, especially when they had murdered a servant? They couldn't actually put them in prison. They were much too well dressed. And to hold them responsible for such a grandiose crime might give women ideas of their own importance.

But Sadie had to be sent away. It was decided she would attend a boarding school for difficult girls in the English countryside outside of London. By separating Marie and Sadie, they would never be able to speak of this crime again. If you cannot discuss a crime with someone, then you cannot be sure it exists. It disappears into memory. It was also the excuse Sadie's mother had been waiting for to send her away. Sadie's father was struggling with his career in politics, getting very close to being very important, and she knew deep down that her daughter would destroy it one day.

WHEN SADIE LEARNED SHE WAS being sent to a boarding school filled with difficult girls in England, she was frightened. She knew the girls in the Golden Mile were no match for her condescension, but these ones might put her in her place. Sadie began to pack reluctantly, putting some books in her traveling bag. Her mother said it was not a wise idea to pack books, because they were so heavy. She wasn't sure why her mother was making her pack so light. It was as though she wanted her to know that she no longer had a right to anything in this world. She did not have a right to the clothes in her closet. She did not have a right to all the elaborate toys in the nursery she had outgrown. She felt as though the child who had grown up in the nursery wasn't her at all. It was a different identity she had no right to anymore.

She was a little girl without a family. And although she'd had an innate intolerance for her family, she could not help but be terrified. In the carriage on the way to the dock, seated between her mother and a maid, Sadie began to shake uncontrollably. She did not want to get on the ship. She could not even picture anything that was on the other side of the ocean. The idea of the ocean was too overwhelming. She found she could only equate it with death. Wasn't that what death was? The great unknown?

She followed her mother as she walked toward the ship. Just as they reached the ramp, Sadie felt her stomach sink violently. This was the time for revenge against her mother for abandoning her. The only way to achieve it was to perform indifference. She didn't believe it would be difficult to do, because she believed her indifference to be genuine. And she had counted on it. And yet it was at this moment that she debased herself. Like most moments of debasement, it came on without any warning. She found herself sitting on her trunk stubbornly, wailing and begging.

"Please don't send me away. I don't want to go. I'm afraid. I love you. I want to stay home. Mama. Mama. Mama. Say you forgive me. I don't know why I did it. I promise I'll change. I'm sorry if I was rude. If I wasn't nice enough to Philip."

Sadie was shocked by her own actions. They didn't even seem to be in keeping with her personality. She was appalled by her own behavior.

She was reacting the way another child would react. She was reacting the way an ordinary child would react. She was reacting the way an ordinary child who was being abandoned by their mother would react.

Perhaps no child thinks they are a child. They secretly think of themselves as adults. And when they act in the manner a child would, they are surprised. Perhaps every child is shocked by their own tears when they gush like blood from an injury.

Sadie's mother did not respond in kind. Her mother was distant and cold with Sadie, the way Sadie had expected to be distant and cold with her. The emotional tables had suddenly turned.

The maid pulled Sadie by her armpits, causing her to rise. Then Sadie hurled herself at her mother's breast. This alarmed her mother most of all. Mrs. Arnett aggressively pushed Sadie off, telling her not to make a scene. Sadie observed her mother turning around to see what the other passengers were making of this behavior.

"Why don't you love me? You can keep me in my room for months. I don't care. I will go to finishing school in Montreal."

"Sadie. You have been disagreeable. We asked you for your help in one simple way. Instead you have sabotaged your father and brother. I was always tolerant of your dourness. But since I can't teach you anything, perhaps this school will."

Sadie's vulnerability made her mother colder. She was having enough emotions for the two of them. At that moment, Sadie realized her supplications were fruitless, and she became silent. Sadie would never forgive her mother after this. Her mother had forced her to be weak.

Sadie let the maid lead her toward the gangplank. She felt terrified and as though she were dying. And in some respects, she was. How could she ever expect to be the same after climbing onto the ship? Her face was wretched. It was contorted into extreme expressions.

Sadie's mother knew her daughter could have been beautiful if she'd

70

had a different personality. Her thoughts were always written on her face. It was not easy to walk into the parlor and see your daughter looking at you with such disdain.

She had never bonded with Sadie as a child. But since she had so much love for her son, she was able to ignore Sadie. He was so obedient and affectionate even if he wasn't as clever as Sadie. And she wasn't even sure if Sadie was intelligent. She sometimes thought wickedness seemed to masquerade as intelligence. Certainly cruelty and criticism had a similar edge to intelligence.

When Sadie became friends with Marie, she suddenly had a power in her hands. She, of all people in the house, had held a key to the family fortunes. Her mother hated that. She had to be obsequious to her own daughter. Her mother was frustrated that Sadie was aware of her power but did nothing with it.

She could have finally become part of the household. It was great fun to have a common mission and to work toward a goal together. She could have helped strengthen the family name. She would have benefited enormously. It would have increased her marriage prospects. But whenever she brought up marriage or anything of that nature with her daughter, Sadie looked at her as if she were suggesting she hurry up and look at a unicorn in the backyard.

She watched Sadie moving about on the deck of the ship. She should have known not to take a hope and put it in Sadie's hand. Sadie could very easily have killed Marie. They would have been finished then. The only thing Louis Antoine had any affection for in this world was his daughter. He would never have allowed Sadie's family to survive.

Whereas Sadie had seemed surprised by her outpouring of emotion, her mother was surprised she herself didn't feel anything. She was relieved her daughter was going. It meant nothing to her when Sadie slumped onto her knees. The only satisfaction she had was that she knew she had been right about her daughter this whole time. She had been justified in being suspicious of her.

Sadie's mother stopped to look at the ship pulling slowly away from the port. She made out Sadie standing on the deck. Sadie was scanning the crowd for her mother in turn, but she did not see her. There were many people on the dock. They held out their handkerchiefs to the people on the ship and waved them. The people on the boat held out their handkerchiefs and waved them back. It was a beautiful thing to see all the handkerchiefs. They were like a group of seabirds congregating around a cresting whale.

Mrs. Arnett didn't wait for the ship to pull out from the shore before turning around and walking away.

CHAPTER 9

Sadie Sails Across the Sea

adie was seasick for the first two days. She was so angry that Marie hadn't been punished the way she had. She knelt with her arms around a bucket. She stared at the hole that was at the bottom of the bucket. She whispered, "This is Marie's fault." And then she vomited into it. If Marie had come with her, then she would not be alone in this predicament. They could hold each other's hair while they puked and tell each other to be brave.

She walked along the deck, muttering, "This is Marie's fault." Children got used to her walking along the deck and talking to herself. They came to accept that she was no fun to play with. And that there was something not quite right with her head. If she had been wearing black, they would have assumed she was in mourning, as she acted like a child who had lost her mother quite recently.

There was a group of girls on the boat who thought it quite the pity that Sadie was too odd to speak to. She was so pretty. And girls were always so attracted to one another. Sadie had such beautiful black hair, they all stared at it enviously. They hoped they would be able to get a lock of it before they landed on shore. But they would never get a lock of her hair.

Sadie's chant was so repetitive, it seemed somewhat like a skipping-rope chant: *An accident. An accident. You can't punish someone for an accident.*

Sadie's hands were always cold. She held them to her face and blew on them. She exhaled and little puffs of smoke came out of her mouth even though it wasn't winter yet. It was winter out on the sea apparently. Perhaps the winter didn't have anything to do with temperatures. Perhaps it had to do with distance and loneliness.

What bothered Sadie most was that she was certain Marie wasn't feeling tormented at all. She imagined Marie almost as though she were a pastoral painting. She imagined her lying on a large bed, completely naked with a black ribbon around her neck, eating grapes. She imagined her walking in the park. She imagined her sleeping on a canoe with a book on her chest as she moved gently down the river.

Sadie stood at the back of the ship one evening. There were animals underneath the ship. Entire cities of them. There were whales who opened their mouths and swallowed great gulps of the sea. Sadie considered jumping into the water and being swallowed whole by a whale. She imagined sitting in the belly of the whale with all the other suicidal children who had jumped into the sea. She imagined one could sit in the stomach of the whale only for so long before they began to be digested. She imagined trying to pick up a fish's rib cage to comb her hair, only to discover three of her fingers were gone. She would have to hold things in a delicate, awkward manner. She would sleep on a jellyfish but then wake to discover her legs had disintegrated. Perhaps it was better to go that way. Piece by piece. First you said good-bye to your toes. Then your ankles. Then your heart.

This sort of morbid reflection was very comforting to her.

Sadie was aware of the growing distance the ocean was creating. She didn't miss anything about the Golden Mile. She refused to experience homesickness. The only thing that would cause her to miss the Golden Mile was Marie. She decided to put Marie out of her mind.

She and Marie had been separated. There was no chance they would see each other again. She accepted this. Sadie headed back into the ship, turning her back on North America.

AFTER EIGHT DAYS AT SEA, the ship docked in England. The noise of the city was brutal and greeted them before they even landed. Sadie took in everything. When she stepped off the ship in London, she couldn't help but compare the world she saw before her to paintings of hell.

But Sadie wasn't frightened. Perhaps a pleasant surprise of this entire venture was that she found the chaotic, crowded scene before her curious. Her little heart was beating in her little chest quite rapidly—but it was not out of fear, she realized quickly. It was out of excitement. If she was not afraid of this scene, she would not be afraid of anything.

There was a woman from the boarding school who was there to meet her. Sadie curtsied.

CHAPTER 10

Marie Awakes from a Nap

Marie felt shaken up about the murder. Everything she touched seemed to be vibrating. First the doorknob was vibrating. Then the pen she was holding was vibrating. Until she realized it was actually her who was vibrating. She imagined Sadie would be punished for a time, as her friend was not able to manipulate her parents as well as she was. They would not be able to see each other for perhaps a week or so. Then Sadie would refuse to speak to her for a brief time before forgiving her.

Marie's father put her in a carriage and brought her out to their country estate. That was where he had brought her mother when she was feeling depressed. He had been told by a doctor that the best cure for nervous anxiety in women was to take them out to the fresh air. They could sit in the sunshine and wiggle their toes and not worry about fashion. Louis also felt there was something more natural about women. He thought they somehow belonged in nature: in fields of flowers, milking goats and holding sheep in their arms.

Her father had filled the bench of the carriage with pillows and the softest blankets. So her trip would be lovely and bouncy, and she could feel like she hadn't even left her bed. Louis knew that Marie was sensitive. And he had learned from his wife that maladies of the mind could be as devastating as those of the body. He squashed his large body in with hers. He let her rest her beautiful head on his lap.

They left the clamor of the city with all its new buildings that had been recently erected for a growing population. There was scaffolding everywhere, with men pulling up buckets of cement and bricks and yelling. There was never a moment of peace and quiet in the city. It was always in the middle of building itself. You couldn't even tell what the city looked like. A street would build itself up and then would catch on fire from a single cigarette butt and burn to the ground. It looked for trouble. Sometimes a building climbed up taller and taller and then collapsed in the middle of the street.

When they arrived at the country home, Marie was given lemon and honey tea. It was so strong her nose scrunched up when she drank it. The maid had been instructed to put drops of opium in her tea and to make sure she drank it all day. She placed the drug into Marie's teacups with a thin dropper, like a hummingbird pollinating a flower.

After she drank the tea, Marie felt so extraordinary. She stared at the sunbeams in the room that were filled with motes. She was sure if she were to put the motes under a microscope they would be tiny, fidgety fairies, lifting up their dresses and scratching their twats, picking their noses and pulling cobwebs off their wings. There had been quite a lot of documentation of fairies lately. Marie yawned, inhaling a hundred fairies up her nose.

Marie was stoned for two weeks. She was eating strawberries dipped in chocolate with her eyes closed. She missed her mouth on several occasions, causing there to be a chocolate mustache above her lip.

The fall came more quickly in the countryside outside Montreal. Marie sat in a lounge chair on the porch, wrapped in a fur blanket, and watched the trees begin to turn colors. The yellow leaves shone like they were made from the gold leaf in illuminated manuscripts. The red made the hills look like a battlefield after a holy war.

She was so impressed by the movements of a leaf, she felt the need to spread her arms and attempt to imitate it. She danced on tiptoe along the edge of an icy pond, pretending to be a leaf.

She had the maid bring in a baby rabbit for her to stroke. She could not get over how incredibly soft it was. She squished it so hard. She fell asleep with the rabbit in her arms, accidentally suffocating it. But she never knew because the maid replaced it with another one.

THEN ONE DAY, MARIE WOKE up from a deep nap and realized she had lost all sense of time. Her first thought was that she might have lost an entire week. But her sense of loss was too great for that. She believed she had lost a year.

She was terrified of how much time might have passed. She looked at her body for a moment. Almost as if to check if it was old and that her entire youth had passed her by. Everything about her body was the same. Her toes were the same. Her nose was the same. Her knees were the same. Her peach-colored pubic hair was the same. Her fingers were the same. Her thumb was the same. Her palms were the same.

But she had such an enormous sense of loss, as though something important had slipped through her fingers.

Then it hit her. It wasn't time she had lost. It was Sadie. Somehow Sadie was gone. The opium had made her oblivious to the effects of the murder. She was being treated for her possible reactions and guilt and horror and anxiety, but she'd also been cured of thinking about Sadie. She suddenly realized something had happened to Sadie. Sadie had disappeared from her reach. She had left Montreal imagining Sadie was confined to her room reading a book, which was something she loved to do. But she knew with a terrible, alarming sense of calamity this was not so.

She would feel that bullet hit her again and again throughout her life. It struck her. The bullet that was meant for her. It continued through space. It entered her heart. She put her hands to her chest. The hole was so palpable. It was the empty spot where Sadie belonged.

She went to see her father in his room. There was a maid in the bedroom who was wearing only a pair of white stockings while dashing about looking for the pieces of her maid's uniform. Marie was used to maids in her father's bedroom. She looked at the maid impatiently, waiting for her to hurry up. The maid gathered her clothes and slipped out.

Louis was sitting up in his bed reading the newspaper. Although this seemed like an intelligent activity, in truth he enjoyed looking at comic strips and illustrations of attractive starlets. He also relished reading about the scandals. As long as they concerned other people and not himself, he found it cathartic.

"Where is Sadie?" Marie exclaimed.

Louis looked up. He thought they had established an implicit agreement not to talk about it.

"Darling, Sadie has been sent to England to attend a boarding school there."

"I didn't want that to happen! Oh, Papa, Papa. I beg of you. Make her come back. This isn't fair. I'm as much to blame as she is."

"Something had to be done."

"Then send me away too. Send me to her. I want to be with her. I want to share the punishment. I can't live without Sadie. She is my best friend. Everything will be boring without her. I don't want to be in Montreal without her."

"You would choose her over me, Marie? That disappoints me in a way I can't begin to express. You are my whole life."

"Then why are you making me choose?"

"Marie!" he yelled. He stood up. He threw a vase against the wall. She stopped. She rarely saw her father get angry that way. He was always so indulgent with her. When you were that rich, you didn't have to be angry with your child. You hired a governess to do it.

She knew her father had been aware all along that she was lying and had betrayed her friend. Having betrayed Sadie was morally much worse than shooting the maid. The maid's death had been an accident. She could have stood on a chair in any room and yelled, "Accident!" at the top of her lungs, and felt good about herself. Whether people accepted this or not, she would feel justified yelling it. She would be an idiot, but she would also have the moral high ground.

She felt thoroughly chastised and ashamed for having pinned the murder on her friend. She had done this herself. That was always the hardest pill to swallow. If only we could have the luxury of blaming other people for the situations we find ourselves in. She had to swallow her pride. And she experienced the effect of digesting it. Her shame was absorbed in every part of her body. She felt it in her toes. The female body was particularly absorbent when it came to shame. If you wrung out any woman's body, you would discover it was soaked in shame.

She could not bear to have her father bring it up again. She would have to act as though it had not happened. Then her father would forget about it.

Louis observed Marie as she fell deflated on the couch. He was happy to see she was dropping the subject. He had no interest in being angry with Marie. Louis was able to be callous to everyone else because he had Marie. He had no fear of being alone. Because Marie would always, always be there for him. She was the only person who loved him unconditionally.

She had been sitting on his lap one day when she was five years old. Her hair was a bundle of gorgeous curls, with a bow stuck on top of them like a butterfly on a plant. He had looked at her and said, "Do you think Papa is a bad man?" And she had looked at him shocked and hurt. Her eyes welled up with tears and she'd exclaimed, "No, Papa! I will never leave you! I will never marry!" And he had believed her. And he would always hold her to it.

The maid hurriedly got dressed in the kitchen and went back to making soup. She wiped a tear from her cheek. But neither of the Antoines remembered she existed.

CHAPTER 11

A School for Girls
Who Refuse to Smile

The girls gathered around to see the new student. Sadie stood before them in her one dress, with her heavy, stained cloak around her shoulders. She could feel them assessing her appearance. She straightened her back and raised up her chin. She could not let them see she was frightened by them.

She felt self-conscious about her status. She knew she wasn't only comparatively less wealthy than they were. She was poor now. She was poor because of her lack of money and also a lack of love. She knew from the way they were looking at her they knew she had been accused of murder.

Walking down the large hallway behind the headmistress, she couldn't remember ever feeling so tiny. The heels of her boots made an echo on the floors. She wanted them to be quiet and not draw attention to her. But they were curious and nervous and so would not.

The headmistress's heels, on the other hand, made the sound of a gavel striking the block with every step she made. *Guilty, guilty, guilty,* they kept saying.

The headmistress showed her the classrooms briefly on the first floor and then the cafeteria with its large tables. She then led her up to the second floor, where all the bedrooms were. Each room had three beds in it. There was a small table next to each of the beds on which each girl had displayed her collection of most impressive items. There were vases with flowers painted on them, small bottles of perfume, bell jars with stuffed birds in them, rows of combs lined up neatly like utensils, dolls wearing dresses that looked fancier than anything Sadie had ever worn herself, jewelry boxes with ballerinas stretching their arms up to the sky. Sadie didn't have any of these pretty things in her suitcase.

The two girls she was sharing a room with stared at Sadie when she walked in. Sadie decided it was best not to say anything and began to unpack. She reached into her bag and took out her notebook and put it into the drawer. She took out her few books and placed them on the desk, hoping they'd take up more space than they did.

"So you are a murderer, are you?" one of the girls asked.

"I'm not."

"I didn't think you were. I think a murderer would be taller and prettier."

"She would have knives in her bags," the other girl added, their voices bouncing back and forth, so it was impossible for Sadie to follow which girl was saying what.

"Do murderers read books?"

"They read scientific books because they have to know how to kill a man with anatomical precision."

"It's harder to kill a man than you think. My mother tried to murder my father a few times. But she never succeeded."

"She's quiet like a murderer."

"What makes you think murderers are quiet?"

"They have to be stealthy. So they can sneak up on you."

"No, I think a murderer would have to be charming. He has to talk you into coming into a dark corner so he can murder you without getting caught."

Sadie refused to engage with them. The best way to get a girl to expose herself was to make her angry. It was like putting a kettle on an element, waiting for the water to scream. The dinner bell rang. The girls stopped mid-sentence and mid-gesture, and hurried off to the cafeteria.

Sadie felt like weeping. She was a solitary creature. That's how she thought of herself. But she had wanted at least one of them to take her hand and lead her to the dining hall. This desire caused her to feel profoundly humiliated. She had been someone's best friend. Now that she had felt the intimacy of having a friend like Marie, loneliness took on an entirely new dimension. It seemed like an emotion she could not get to the bottom of. She sat by herself in the dining hall, the other girls having already all lost interest in her.

OVER THE COURSE OF THE FOLLOWING WEEK, Sadie was introduced to her routine. Every minute of her day was accounted for. The school did not believe girls should be allowed idle hours. They were not at all encouraged to roam freely in their minds. It was as though their minds were dense forests. They were bound to get lost in them, panic, and lose their sanity.

There was a pervasive idea that girls were all on the brink of madness. It took much less than anyone had previously believed to push a girl over the edge. A single novel could do it. A complicated idea could do it. Having ambition and wanting to have an occupation could definitely do it. It was too taxing on the female brain. They had to be monitored carefully to make sure they stuck to exclusively feminine subjects. It was disturbing and unnatural for women to engage in male endeavors. Imagine, if you will, a cat barking, or a songbird opening its mouth to meow. How could anything be more unsettling? Each creature must stick to its natural life path. Otherwise all around us will be images of the grotesque.

The day began at six thirty a.m. when they were awoken by a bell. At this point they had to get out of bed immediately. They were not allowed to have those few moments in the morning when you lie in bed feeling everything is miserable and pointless. They were not permitted the luxury of being suicidal.

They then were to bathe themselves and dress before seven, when they were expected in the dining hall for breakfast. They were all given the same bland breakfast. Except the girls who were overweight and were put on a diet. They then had callisthenic exercises, to make sure their bodies were hale and firm enough to endure the rigors of happiness and childbirth.

They then had elocution lessons in the fine art of small talk. They were given reading and writing courses so they would be able to keep up with their correspondences and run a household. They had history lessons, wherein they were meant to learn the basics of history so they could follow men's conversation. They were not, however, to form an opinion on anything. It was up to men to do that. Women would simply marvel at their ideas.

They had art classes. The girls all donned white smocks and drew botanical still lives with frighteningly accurate skill. They had music lessons. They were all quite good at the piano. There seemed to be no point during the day when you could not hear someone playing the piano. At the school were girls from the ages of ten to nineteen. So they all played at different levels. There were times where the notes came out so slowly. They sounded like a woman taking off her jewelry and dropping each piece into a porcelain cup. Other times there was a veritable whiz at the piano. It was like a wind chime being blown about furiously in a storm.

Sadie loathed the piano. It never expressed any emotion she had inside her. The notes were too optimistic. She resented it for that. She seemed to never be able to escape it. It was like a young man you disliked who kept asking you to come join him on the dance floor.

How stupid this all is, Sadie thought one night as she looked out the window of her bedroom.

She suddenly thought of what it would have been like if she and Marie had both been denounced as murderers as would only have been right. She imagined the two of them standing next to each other on the gallows in gray prison dresses and nooses around their necks. They would be asked if they had anything to say before the floor was dropped from beneath their pretty naked feet. And that was when they would have spoken their most eloquent recital. They would have said the most emotional and beautiful words two girls could think of. And in that moment, they would have been so alive. They would have been alive in a way no one else in the whole world could ever be.

Sadie sighed and left the bodies of the two imaginary girls hanging in the yard. She climbed into bed and went to sleep. The toes of the hanging girls twitched and shook, and then they were still too.

THE HEADMISTRESS DECLARED ONE MORNING that all the girls had to work on their smiles. She explained that she had never seen such lousy expressions on a group of girls in her life. And that it was a great unkindness to make the teachers have to look on their miserable sardonic smirks and grimaces. They didn't seem to be aware that when girls didn't have a pleasant expression on their faces, they were in actuality quite unattractive. Being attractive wasn't something that came naturally to girls. It took great effort to be pleasant. A smile wasn't something that should be considered a spontaneous reaction. Instead, it was more like an arrangement of flowers or a memorized poem. Something that had to be labored at.

The headmistress made everybody line up and smile. When she was satisfied with a girl's smile, she pointed at them and told them to be seated. She critiqued them viciously, as though she had finally had enough and couldn't stand any more.

"You look foolish. And you look disgusted. For the love of Mary, you look as though you are constipated and on the toilet. Don't look like someone is behind you with a gun pointed at your head, forcing you to smile. You look thoroughly ridiculous. Don't smile with your teeth, they are not at all your strongest feature."

She had another teacher bring out a mirror for the girl to look at her smile because she couldn't find the words to describe how unattractive it was. "Look for yourself," she said, holding up the mirror.

Tears began to form in the girl's eyes and her chin began to wobble. It seemed impossible that she could form a pretty smile after this. But she produced a delicate, sympathetic, and kind smile. It was possibly the most tender and pretty smile of the day. The headmistress then held the mirror up to her face so she could see it. There was a drop of women's bitterness in anything of beauty. The headmistress nodded. The girl had realized that a smile is something forced. It is not for women to enjoy. A woman ought to be pleasing to others, even when she was at her most miserable.

The other girls learned the difference between their normal resting face and a smile. They learned to be conscious of their faces at all time. And to make sure it wore a pleasing smile even when they were distracted.

Sadie was another story. The headmistress said she would stand in front of Sadie all night until she presented a normal smile. Sadie's smile was perfect. But she made it and dropped it so quickly. It was as if to show she was perfectly capable of making a smile, but she chose not to. Smiling abruptly implied sarcasm, which was about the worst attitude a girl could convey.

Also, she was not smiling with her eyes. It was quite a feat to do this over and over again. To smile with your mouth but not your eyes was almost always an indication of sociopathy. It displayed a cleverness and control that was quite unattractive in a girl.

There was a look of such hatred and malaise and coldness in Sadie's eyes when she smiled, the headmistress was shocked by it. She contemplated at that moment that Sadie wasn't learning a thing while she was at boarding school. She was going through the motions of propriety without internalizing any of it. The headmistress saw exactly why her mother had sent her all the way across the ocean to be rid of her. She also suspected the duel had not been an accident, but something Sadie had planned.

The headmistress struck her staff on the desk. She yelled that all the girls would stand there until Sadie learned to smile.

The girls were not actually dismayed by this punishment. There was nowhere they would rather be. They wanted to see if Sadie might manage to hold out. They hadn't been able to themselves. They wanted to see whether holding out was even an option. Was it possible? And if Sadie could hold out, what would she gain from it?

Finally when dinnertime came and Sadie had still not produced an appropriate smile, the headmistress sent all the girls off to eat. And then she let Sadie go too. At which point Sadie smiled the most lovely and heartfelt smile and turned and hurried off to dinner.

CHAPTER 12

Another Mary, Quite Contrary

Louis decided he would take Marie to visit the factory one afternoon. Louis wanted Marie to understand her position in the world. He had not been born to this, and the enormity of it never ceased to please him. He wanted Marie to know she was living a life no one else had.

The carriage descended the hill and rode for a time on Sherbrooke Street. This was the area where the residents of the Golden Mile came to do their shopping. Women and men stepped out of their carriages in the latest fashions. Women especially, who wore dresses that were works of art. When the doormen helped them step out of the carriages, they were concerned not only for the safety of the lady but also of her dress.

As the carriage entered the poorer neighborhood known as the Squalid Mile, Marie noticed an immediate change. The carriage stopped for a moment as a man passed in front of it. He wore a shabby coat the color of mossy water. He smiled at the carriage and tipped his hat as though he were a handsome fellow. His yellow, pointy teeth reminded her of those that rats had. A woman wearing gray fingerless gloves approached the carriage and banged on the window. The edges of her fingernails were completely black.

There was a child walking barefoot down the street in a wool coat. Marie could not imagine walking down the street and having everyone looking at your toes. You might as well be naked. Marie had only seen wretchedly poor people in plays. But they were so much more alarming in real life. She had seen dragons in plays as well, and it had in no way prepared her for seeing one walking down the sidewalk exhaling flames.

The street was filled with carriage traffic. The driver began to shout at someone in French and there was a responding chorus of cursing carriage drivers. "*Merde! Va te faire foutre! Ta gueule!*" She had forgotten how many people spoke French in Montreal, since the Golden Mile was almost entirely English. She had learned a very polished French in school, of course, but she had never expected to actually use it. The French they were speaking sounded nothing like what she learned at school. Marie had not realized how sheltered she was from a whole world that was only a short carriage ride away.

Inside the factory, Marie was surprised to see so many children. There was a small girl working frantically at a table sewing the tops of the sugar bags together. The girl had pins sticking out of her mouth. It made her look like a voodoo doll. She was so thin that Marie could see her bones sticking out of her flesh. Little girls were supposed to be bouncy and rosy. So what sort of creature was this? She had a longing to reach out and touch the girl, to make sure she was actually there.

The girl was not the type of person she would have imagined working at a sugar factory. She had pictured the women being very fat and jolly, the way anybody who eats sweets all day would be. She imagined that since they worked around sugar their lives would be characterized by the sweet substance. They would be allowed to take home bags of sugar from the factory every day. They would always have friends over for tea. Because what in the world could be more wonderful than sugar in tea?

Everyone was dressed in dingy colors. Marie felt strange in her brightly colored dress. Instead of making her feel better about herself, it made her feel ashamed. She did not know why. All the workers stopped speaking when they saw her. She was just a little girl, but they were intimidated by her. Her father took her into the foreman's office. The foreman was smoking a cigar while a woman with pencils sticking in all directions from her tight hair bun seemed to be doing all the work. The secretary looked up for a brief moment from her stack of papers and smiled at Marie, then dove back to work. The foreman explained what was needed of them that day.

The tops of the flour bags needed to be stitched together. It was generally young girls like the one Marie had seen who were given this task. When they finished, they used a mechanical blade to cut the cord as close to the bag as possible. Sometimes a girl would hold her cord up to the blade while it was already coming down. And off would come two or three of her fingers, or only one if they were lucky. The girl would be standing there with fingers one moment and the next they were gone, as though by magic. She would start looking around her for her fingers as though she had dropped something.

Sometimes others noticed the girls' fingers were missing before they did themselves.

There was a young girl who had recently lost three fingers to a machine. The broadsides and newspapers were giving Louis a difficult time about accidents and mutilations in his factory. The readers of the Squalid Mile loved these types of stories. They loved that their daily, unspeakable horrors were making the news.

Whenever a young girl fell victim to a machine, it caused a much greater uproar in the newspapers. What fate lay in store for a mutilated girl? Would anyone marry her? There had been much ado about this latest young girl who had lost her fingers. The girl was beautiful, inasmuch as factory girls could be considered beautiful. Did the missing fingers condemn her to spinsterhood? How could you marry without a wedding finger?

Louis had arranged to meet her in the center of the factory floor. All the machines were closed down. All the workers gathered on the platforms and floors. They leaned over the railings to see Louis and the girl, as though they were spectators at a play, which, in a way, they were.

The girl was hardly recognizable to the other workers when she stepped out. She was wearing a dark-blue velvet coat and a pretty matching hat of the same material. These had obviously been purchased for the occasion. There was no way in the world any factory girl could afford these things.

The other little girls clenched their hands into fists when they saw her. They stuck them in their armpits or pockets. They did this after one of their own lost a finger. They felt their own fingers were somehow more precarious and would fall off. They might reach down to pick up an object and their fingers would stick to it like magnets.

Louis Antoine shook the girl's mutilated hand and pinned a medal on her coat. He handed her an envelope filled with cash. When she took it in her hand, her heels rocked back and forth slightly. She was excited by having an envelope of money even without counting how much was in there, and knowing full well her parents would snatch it the split second they had the opportunity.

"This will make sure you have a much-needed rest. And all your family will have a most enjoyable Christmas. There's enough in that envelope to heat your whole house and provide toys for all the children in your family. I bet there's something special you've always wanted. And now it shall be yours. And we are very much looking forward to your return."

Louis bent down and kissed her on the cheek. The girl was happy with her gift. Everyone at the factory was content with the scene. There was nothing in the world they could do about that girl's fingers.

But then Louis raised up his arms. "We've got one more surprise," he exclaimed. Suddenly it was his daughter, Marie, who walked to the center of the factory floor. She was leading an enormous turkey on a long black satin leash. The girl laughed and clapped her hands, as did everyone in the factory. How delightful it always was when an animal came onstage. There was general chatter of approval throughout the factory. The turkey had the effect of making everyone come alive and become more themselves and more animated.

The foreman, realizing the factory was getting out of control, and that everyone was behaving as though it were Saturday night, announced it was time to get back to work and pressed the buzzer that indicated machines would begin running in five minutes. Everyone went back to their stations, and the injured girl was left in the center of the floor, still minus three fingers but in possession of a turkey. For a moment she stood there, confused about where to go. Then she turned and walked off with the turkey following her.

MARY ROBESPIERRE WAS WATCHING this whole scene from the factory floor. As soon as she saw Marie, she knew why Louis had had such trouble looking at her when he came to visit. She and Louis's daughter looked shockingly alike. The woman standing next to her leaned over and said, *"Elle te ressemble, non?"*

"I don't see it," Mary answered.

Then the bell rang and they all had to go back to work, the turkey having disappeared like a dream. They were no longer able to even think about that turkey.

MARY ROBESPIERRE DIDN'T FEEL LIKE herself when she worked at the factory. She felt dehumanized. She felt like an automaton. The machines were more effective and productive than she was. The machines never missed a beat. They were steady. They were strong. They were never tired. They never daydreamed.

Anyone who had worked as a child at a factory had the same sort of experience. They were trained to keep moving their whole lives. They had to be faster, faster, faster. They did not have a second that was not bought. Were they to stop for a second and contemplate what existed before the universe began, or whether the pigeon they always saw outside their window had a personal vendetta against them, or whether their cat actually loved them, the whole assembly line would fall apart, and the machines would punish them in the most brutal way.

The Industrial Revolution had turned people into cogs. Their function was to keep the machines up and running. She was conceived and she was a tiny cog in her mother's belly. All the pregnant women in the city were manufacturing indispensable parts to the machine. The machines were living, breathing things. You could hear them coughing and sputtering through the day. They breathed heavily. As you passed by one of them you could feel their heart beating under your feet.

Mary had to take all the thoughts she had come to the factory with, remove them from her head, and put them in the small locker at the front where she put her coat and boots. As soon as she was done with work, she would run to her locker, wrap her scarf around her neck, and tuck her thoughts back in her head in order to think them.

MARY'S HEART HAD DROPPED when she saw Marie. At that moment, she had the answers to a whole bevy of questions she had never asked before. What she would look like in expensive clothes: wonderful. How she would feel if she had been spoiled growing up: happy. How she would act were she given a platform from which to speak to the masses: confident. How people would look at her if she were in Marie's position: with respect.

THE FACTORIES CLOSED DOWN COLLECTIVELY at seven. All the workers began to head home. Mary walked out of the sugar factory at the front of the group of workers, as though she were in a hurry. Once an idea was planted in Mary's head, there was nothing she could do to get it out. She felt the roots of it begin to spread. They wrapped around all the other ideas and countering opinions and strangled them.

The sunset was so beautiful that evening, it was as though men in scaffolding had painted it. Only Louis Antoine could have afforded to commission a sunset like that. The factory machines blocked out all other city sounds. Now that they had shut down, the horses began to make clopping noises again. The girls' voices took on sweet, confidential tones. The bottles began to clink together lightly. The city began to play its evening sonata, which was much more melodious and pretty than its daytime one. Mary skipped to the rhythms of the city as she headed to the drugstore of Jeanne-Pauline Marat.

Whenever Mary Robespierre was truly anxious, she would go see Jeanne-Pauline. Jeanne-Pauline was older than her and could truly offer her advice. The store was so tiny, you could barely notice it. The words

"Marat Pharmacy" were written on the window in gold paint. Mary stood outside the shop a moment contemplating Jeanne-Pauline, whom she saw through the window. Jeanne-Pauline was a tall, middle-aged woman. Her hair was white and she wore it in a bun on top of her head. The white of her hair had the effect of making her eyes sparkling blue.

JEANNE-PAULINE'S HUSBAND HAD DROPPED DEAD of a heart attack one morning. The doctor was surprised, since the man had previously been in such good health. But he had seen stranger cases in his time. Especially with men who were prone to rage. He knew that flying into a rage could do great damage to men's hearts. And he had seen similar fates arrive for men who were chronically upset with their wives. He noticed a bruise under Pauline's eye and determined this to be the case here. Bad marriages caused cardiac arrest and sudden death in men.

Jeanne-Pauline had every sort of poison at her disposal, and it became a widespread rumor throughout the neighborhood that she had murdered her husband. This conclusion was exacerbated by the general improvement in morale and lifestyle that Jeanne-Pauline exhibited after her husband's death. Despite trying to tone it down and project an illusion of grief, her joie de vivre was evident to all those who met her.

It wasn't only that killing a man had set her free, it had changed her completely. She became a woman no one could mess with. Murder has a strange effect on women. Her hair became more voluminous. She seemed to grow two inches in height. Her clothes began to fit her better. It was as though her long black coat was proud to be worn by her. Her scarf flipped itself in the wind in an arrogant way.

Colors changed whenever she came into the room. Reds became redder and began to glow. The bells on the doors always rang louder. These were all known ways nature had of informing you that a murderer was in the room. Stray dogs would often fall in love with her. There was always at least one dog trying to follow her down the street.

She made people's blood run cold. She made everyone feel insecure. Everyone felt awkward and self-conscious in her presence and couldn't bring themselves to tell jokes. It was hard to believe she had once been abused.

After wearing black in mourning, she realized how much she liked the color. She added a string of fake pearls to her hair that resembled dewdrops, as though she had been out all night killing people.

Now Jeanne-Pauline was the person to see if you wanted a man to die in his sleep.

A YOUNG GIRL WAS at the register when Mary arrived that day. She and Jeanne-Pauline were speaking in French. The girl said she needed pills to fall asleep. Her nose was crooked, as though it might have been broken a couple of times. She also had a broken tooth and her hand was in a bandage. She was still beautiful. She refused to stop being beautiful. No matter what men did to her, no matter how many times she was knocked down the stairs. The same reason she was still beautiful was the same reason she was here. She was resilient. She refused to be ugly.

"How much of these should I take to fall asleep?"

"One to begin with. You can slowly try more."

"I have to be careful, though, don't I? Because these could kill me if I take too many, right?"

"Yes."

"How many should I be careful not to take?"

Jeanne-Pauline stared at her for a long moment. The girl did not blink. "Never take more than four. Never grind them up and boil them. Always make sure you've disposed of any of the leftover tea. You don't want it to get inadvertently lapped up by a cat. Here, these are particularly potent."

The girl nodded, slid a bill across the table, and hurried out. Jeanne-Pauline promptly turned her attention to Mary. "Hello, Mary Robespierre. I suspect you're here for your grandparents. Will it be the usual salves?"

"I haven't come in for my usual medications. I just came to talk. I find myself feeling very unhappy."

"How do we deal with women's suffering?" Jeanne-Pauline asked. "We say there must be a point to it, but isn't the point of being human to push back against suffering? If we don't push back, then we aren't human beings really. There are other ways to testify to injustice than silence and pain."

"I feel too miserable to do anything at all."

"Don't think of melancholia as passive. Melancholia is a state of deep thought one's body enters into when it is looking for a way to act."

"What is permissible? How am I allowed to act?"

"Everything is permissible."

Mary paused thoughtfully. "I am angry all the time. I feel that I need justice. I feel as though my brain is a monster that I let out of a cage."

"The reason women aren't free is because they haven't shed the blood that allows them to be free. No matter how vehement and radical our words are, no one seems to listen. We need blood. Every revolution needs blood. Words don't mean anything unless they are followed by actions. A woman's freedom is the most important thing in the world. It is the end that justifies all means. One day you will figure out how to be free."

Mary did not know what to say to all this. She was too young to launch into whatever action Jeanne-Pauline was advocating.

When Mary Robespierre got home that night, she took off her boots and rubbed her feet. All the girls in all the houses in the city took off their boots and began massaging their feet and toes. There was a slight tremor from the sound of all the boots falling off the feet of girls and hitting the ground at the same time. They made the sound of an army being called to attention.

CHAPTER 13

Sadie Arnett Discovers
Her Life Passion

Since Sadie showed no interest in the piano, the headmistress thought another instrument might appeal to her. The headmistress told Sadie she should go to the attic to retrieve a violin that was up there. Sadie climbed up the narrow flight of stairs to the attic, whose ceiling grazed the top of her head. She found the violin, took it out of the case, and tried playing a note on it. It sounded like a black cat who was on the gallows confessing to all the bad luck it had caused. Sadie decided she might like the violin. She closed the lid and tucked it under her arm like a gun. While she was headed back to the stairs, she noticed a small trapdoor in the floor. She opened it up and saw a single book lying at the bottom of the shallow hole.

The book had paper wrapping on it, as though to further hide it from the world. Sadie picked up the book, undressed it, and then opened it up. She knew immediately the contents would be provocative. But she was not quite prepared for how they made her feel, given it was her first encounter with pornography.

She read the book as quickly as she could. She wanted to get through it and retain all the information, knowing it might be confiscated at any moment. Its existence was a miracle in itself. The minute it was discovered it would necessarily be burned. She read cross-legged in front of the trapdoor, ready to toss the book down it if anyone came up.

The pages of the dirty book seemed to glow when she looked at them. She was so turned on by the pages, she wanted to rip them out and eat them. Her whole body felt electrified. She was experiencing sensations she didn't know she had. Her desire was too intense. She felt as though she were made entirely out of water. She wasn't able to stop herself from masturbating. It would be painful to try to keep in all that desire. She needed to release it by having an orgasm. It was like a stick of dynamite that had been lit. It was going to explode. She reached under all her skirts, through the opening in her bloomers, and began to touch herself. The second she came, her whole body crashed to the floor. The book collapsed on her chest like a spent lover who had come at the same time as her.

THERE WAS NO WAY SADIE could take the book downstairs with her. It was too risky. Perhaps it was meant to stay here anyway, for another girl to find. She wrapped the book up again and placed it back into the floor, like she was placing a heart in a chest.

It was a revelation. She was normal. All her life she had looked for someone else to acknowledge how good the feelings between her legs were. There was perversion everywhere.

Later, she lay on her back on the large rug in the center of the tearoom. The flowers on the carpet made her feel as though she were lying in a garden filled with roses growing all around her. She imagined she was lying next to Marie. And she imagined the tips of their fingers touching. She closed her eyes. The rosebush grew denser and denser all around her. The matron walked by the room. The rosebush had grown too dense and thick for her to see Sadie lying there sleeping.

Her deep snoring made the sound of water disappearing into a gutter.

Sadie decided to write her own book of pornography. She began to write down her fantasies in her drawing book. She hid the drawing book under all her things in the chest at the bottom of the bed. She knew what a risk it was to have such a book. If it was found, it would be more than enough to send her to the insane asylum. It was a giant atlas of the land of sexual perversion.

It was the moment of her breakthrough. She had discovered the themes she would write about for the rest of her life: the violent delight of female desire.

AND THEN, TO FURTHER CEMENT her themes, Sadie was punished severely for laughing one afternoon. The girls were being instructed in how to converse with young men. They were to express no opinions of their own. They were to nod and say, "Is that so? How fascinating!" All the girls said it at once. The absurdity of this struck Sadie, and she began to laugh uproariously.

Sadie was brought to the front of the classroom for a caning. She climbed up the two steps and she knelt beside the pulpit. She leaned her head forward. She felt as though she knew precisely what it felt like to be decapitated before a crowd. She also knew this to be the most exhilarating of experiences.

She was turned on by what was about to happen to her. That the other girls were standing around made her more excited. What a spectacle this was! She looked around, taking note of her riveted audience.

Their eyes were wide with horror and fascination. Their cheeks were flushed with what she interpreted as a sexual desire to witness Sadie's bodily abnegation. Would she ever be able to procure this level of engagement with an audience again? Once she had a taste of it, would she ever be able to live without it? She would not.

The stick went down on her shoulders. The smack emptied all the thoughts from her head. She felt as though she were a pure being. The next one came down. She felt an erotic charge in her body. The sexual pleasure to the pain liberated her from any fear of it, and she found her body welcoming it. She felt as though she were on the brink of an orgasm. She had to press her thighs together to both enhance that sensation and to stop from peeing herself. She felt so naked. She wished she could take off all her clothes. She wanted to cry out. But she held her tongue. Not out of shame but out of fear her cries would be ecstatic ones.

Now that her body had been so debased in front of the other girls, she did not feel a need to keep any more secrets. Allowing others to witness your darkest, most ignoble self was a powerful thing. The act of being an artist of any kind was an act of self-confession and debasement. And now that the teachers had acted toward her in the most disreputable manner, did she really have to follow any of their rules?

She decided to read to the other students out loud from her book of pornography. In the evening, the girls gathered around to listen to her stories in her room. They weren't sure what to expect. Ordinarily they might have turned down the invitation, but the beating had left them susceptible to Sadie's charms and deeply curious about her mind. Sadie sat on a chair with the book open on her lap, while the girls crowded onto the three beds together. She began.

In one story, she was walking down a country road when she passed by a hole in the wall. She would have passed right by it without considering it at all unusual, but suddenly a prick poked out of it. Her first instinct was to run away. But she thought there would be no harm done if she got down on her knees and sucked it.

She met a society of physicians in another tale. They wanted to study the female orgasm. She lay on a table in the middle of an operating theater. The head doctor lifted up her dress and began to diddle her. The medical students all gathered around to see what the doctor was doing to her that evoked such pleasure.

She had a tale about a plague that killed virgins. The virgins all crowded into a carriage and had to hurry to the nearest town. They burst into an inn and begged men to make love to them quickly.

The stories made the girls feel so immensely. They made them feel disgusted and triumphant. They made them feel as though they no longer belonged to their families. They were somehow members of the criminal class now that they had listened to and digested Sadie's stories. None of them wanted to reject the experience, whatever it was. They requested new stories from Sadie every evening. Her awaiting audience caused Sadie to write more and more. She became addicted to transcribing her most absurd fantasies. She knew what she was doing was not only transgressive but revolutionary. Sadie began to see herself as a writer.

CHAPTER 14

The Travels of Marie Antoine

Much of Marie's adolescence, from fourteen to sixteen in fact, was spent on trains with her father traveling the East Coast of North America. Louis and Marie were both eager to explore the new technologies of the continent. During their train travels, as they went from city to city, when Marie felt lonely, she would go to third class to pick out a child to bring back to her cabin. She found the children from third class were better listeners. In fact, they sat there stupefied. One spring afternoon, Marie was wearing a green dress with a green bow at the end of her blond braid. Her dress was tiered and she looked rather like a layered cake. She found a young girl her age with tight black curls seated squashed next to a window and invited her to come and converse with her.

The girl was so surprised to see Marie had her own train car. There was a bed on one side of the car, in the corner. And a table by the window with chairs on either side of it.

"I am traveling the world. I own a factory. It makes sugar. Isn't that wonderful! It is filled with the most extraordinary machines. One day I will be in charge of it myself. That's why it's important for me to see everything that's happening. If you were to go into the kitchen and look at any sugar bag in Montreal, you would see my face on all of them. The name written on the bags is Marie, and do you want to guess what my name is?"

"I have no idea."

Marie changed the subject. "Look what we got when we were in Portland, Maine. You have to see them. They are only going to be sold once a year at Easter."

Marie pulled out a black wooden box that had flowers and a particularly alert-looking rabbit decorating it. The girl looked at the box with incredulity. She clearly had no idea whatsoever what could come out of that box.

Marie held the box in front of her like a proper magician. She lifted the lid. There were six eggs inside it. She held one up and bit into the shell. The girl looked horrified, as though she had just realized she was seated with an ogre. Marie laughed. She showed the egg to the girl. It was filled with chocolate.

"I know! When I saw it for the first time, I thought they had come from a magic sort of chicken."

"These are for Jesus?"

"No. They are absolutely not for Jesus. Everything is already for Jesus. He doesn't need any more. The holiday is already so sad. We needed to have some part of the day devoted to pleasure. Don't you think?"

The girl delicately accepted an egg and took a bite of it.

"When I run my own factory I will give a box of these eggs to all the girls working at my factory at Easter. And they will run home with them and share them with all the members of their family. I want to travel around the city and meet everyone who works for me and shake their hands and tell them I could not do this without them."

Marie reached into the pocket of her dress. She pulled out a large spider. She pressed a button on its belly. It began to dance a small jig across the table all around the teacups. It raised and lowered its legs.

"I'm going to take it apart to see how it works when I get home," she said. "There's so much to see in this world."

She stepped onto the table. She opened the window and stuck her head out, and her hair blew so wildly, it seemed almost certain the wind would blow her head right off her neck.

The girl had very little to say. She stared at the strange spider hurrying around the table, looking for a way to get free. It didn't occur to her until later that Marie hadn't asked her a single question about herself.

WHEN THE THIRD-CLASS GIRL LEFT, Marie's loneliness returned. She felt a nagging longing for a companion who truly complemented her like Sadie had. The absence of Sadie left a hole in her wherever she went. Since she was followed by this feeling through America, she realized it was not a feeling she could escape geographically. She began to think about the future. If she couldn't be happy now, then surely she would be another time. Like all unhappy children, she saw the future as a utopia. Children romanticized the lives of adults, believing they didn't have any of the problems children did. Adults didn't sit on their front steps and weep into their hands. Adults didn't hurl themselves on the ground in a fit of anger, tearing at the grass as though they were angry at the Earth itself. And since adults visibly did not have the problems children had, they therefore had no problems at all.

Marie imagined herself as a grown woman. Her father had told her since she was very little that the factory and all the people in it belonged to her. She visualized running the factory, and it gave her great satisfaction. She imagined tasting different spoonfuls of sugar and then pointing to the one she thought was best.

She had always assumed theirs was the greatest, largest factory in the world. She was surprised when her father referenced a larger one in Pittsburgh. Marie had insisted they go visit it.

IN THE YEAR BEFORE THEIR TRIP, Louis and Marie had become isolated in their kingdom of two. Louis's fear of Marie being taken away had led him to be more wary of society. Louis no longer found any joy in seducing the maids, as he would wake up from his affairs feeling gutted and lonely.

Automatons, extravagant creatures made of metal and wires and plaster that moved around mechanically, were very popular. But thirteen-year-old Marie was always disappointed by automatons. She had seen so many and they never seemed real enough to her. So her father had a mechanical deer sailed over from a watchmaker in Switzerland. It was said the watchmaker's machines were so life-like, he had been jailed for sorcery.

The automaton arrived in a huge wooden crate that was brought in by seven men. The deer stood in the ballroom looking delicate and poised. The household gathered around, waiting for it to move. It seemed frozen, as though it had heard the sound of a predator in the forest. Then a tinkling musical sound began to play. The deer moved its head in an almost imperceptible way. Even its little ears tingled as though it heard a sound, and its chin turned in a manner that caused it to look very sophisticated and intelligent. It bent its nose down on the carpet. It moved in a slow way that made each motion seem surreal and elegant. It began to walk a few feet.

Marie and the maids were all delighted. She ran up to it on her tiptoes and with trepidation. And put her hand out under its nose. The deer's head lowered and its nose grazed her palm.

The whole neighborhood came to see the fantastic deer. And at one point, Marie had it walk across the lawn for the children to see. Then, despite its cost and splendor, the Antoines grew bored of the deer. It was to be found grazing in remote corners of the house. And one day it had a pair of bloomers on its antlers.

THERE WAS TALK ALL OVER the world of the possibility of creating the first incandescent lightbulb. That autumn, as the skies were turning gray and the days were getting shorter, Louis had an experimental model brought in from Toronto. It was placed on the dining room table. The whole household gathered around to watch.

Louis ordered all the lamps in the room turned down, so they were all in darkness. There was a nervous energy in the room, as though they were at a séance and waiting for an apparition to step out of the afterlife and greet them. Lightbulbs were known to burst into plumes of fire and set young ladies on fire.

Then it suddenly lit up. The room was filled with such light as they had never seen. It was greater than the sun. Louis turned the lightbulb on and off to admire what had been harnessed, until it made an exploding noise and was extinguished for good. But for a few moments, they had beheld the future of light. Louis realized when he was turning on the lightbulb that no one needed to believe in God anymore. He let out a sigh of relief.

Louis hated the past, and anything to do with it. He liked inventions. He wanted to live in a world that looked and operated in a manner radically different from his childhood one. What was he looking for? He was looking for the object that would bestow him perpetual delight. It was as though his soul were a dark and lonely apartment. He kept trying to illuminate all the rooms. He went from room to room looking for the one that wasn't dark and not finding it. This missing room was causing the rest of his body to be cold. He couldn't find it.

Soon he began to dream of looking for inventions all over the world. This was a time of great travel and adventure. Rich people from the West were traveling all over the world, to the farthest reaches of the Congo and Peru. In Louis's study, there were books on all the shelves and maps all over the walls. It made him look as though he were a man of science and letters. It was in vogue for a man to appear cultured. When Marie walked into his study to see him, his vest and shirt were open as he leaned back over his desk. The doctor had a stethoscope up to his heart as though he were a thief trying to find the combinations to a safe.

"There is no way you can travel to the jungle," the doctor said. "Your heart would never survive that type of exertion."

"I am still a young man!" Louis protested. "I am in my prime. I am at the age men make their most significant discoveries."

The doctor sighed as he took out a small percussion hammer and began tapping it on Louis's chest while having him inhale deeply.

"How much do you drink?" the doctor asked.

"How much do I drink every night?"

"Do you drink every night?"

"Well, obviously. How can you get through that uneasy transition between day and night if not for alcohol?"

"You don't make an effort to exercise."

"If I need exercise, a trip to Peru would be the perfect prescription, I should think."

"I would be signing your death warrant. There isn't a chance you could survive. You are too fair. You would have sunstroke immediately."

Louis buttoned up his shirt. He picked up a saucer with a teacup on it. He took a sip. He then absentmindedly picked up a pastry and dunked it into his tea. It didn't seem like the type of pastry that could be eaten in one bite, but he opened his mouth, and when it was closed, the pastry had disappeared. All that was left was a sprinkle of icing sugar on his lips. It was closer to being a magic trick than it was to eating.

Marie also wanted to leave Montreal. She had started to find everything in the city wanting. She was impatient with other girls her age. She had tired of the parks and the museums. She was experiencing the lack Louis felt all the time. She wanted to get out into the world and fill this void with as much strangeness and excitement as he did.

"I don't know if I have an inclination to travel through a swamp just to find a butterfly no one's seen before and name it after myself," Marie said, finding a bright side. "I would like to see America. I'm more interested in inventions."

"Let's ride the train. I want to see all of America too."

When he told the doctor he was thinking of traveling along the East Coast in the spring, and going to the novelty museums and seaside resorts, his doctor thought it was a marvelous idea. He prescribed Louis a small container of cocaine. He was to snort a little should he ever experience lethargy or his heart slowing down. Louis opened the bottle and tapped a little out onto the back of his hand. He snorted it. He threw his head back and his arms up in the air. "We're going to America!" he yelled. "Show us your technological wonders, America!"

ON ONE OF THEIR STOPS, they had gone to a seaside resort on Long Island. The clouds were puffy and large like the foam at the top of a glass of beer. Marie had never seen the sea before. She stretched her arms out toward it. There was a large brass band playing as she ran about collecting seashells. A musician held a French horn to his head that looked like the ear of an elephant pricking up to hear a sound.

Marie stood in the sea. She ran after the waves in her bare feet. The sea changed its mind about retreating. It turned around and came after her. The sand on the beach tried to hold on to the impression of her footprints for as long as possible after she left. She screamed when the water hit her ankles. It was colder than the snow in Canada. It had the feel of bottles striking up against her ankles. She kept looking down to see if there were bottle messages from Sadie. But there was nothing there but the pain the ocean caused. Then seaweed grabbed at her ankles as though mermaids were casting their nets to catch her.

In that seaside town, Louis purchased a pair of roller skates that moved on their own. You could stand perfectly still and they would whip you down the street, to the surprise of all your neighbors. He bought a glass booth with a fortune-teller inside that told you your weight and your future. He acquired a machine that made bubbles come out of it for seventeen hours straight.

Whenever he made an enormous purchase, he justified it by thinking he would be satisfied by this acquisition. He would never want anything again. Signing a check for an enormous sum sent a shot of adrenaline and excitement through his veins that made him feel intoxicated. He was overcome with a feeling of well-being. If someone were to stab him with a knife, he would not feel a thing. His body was anesthetized.

PITTSBURGH PROVED TO BE NOTHING like the seaside town they had previously visited. The area the factory was built in was filthy. The sky was filled with black clouds. Marie kept feeling the urge to take out her umbrella to protect herself from an impending rainstorm. She felt her eyes burning. Everyone had been colored by the soot. She saw a white cat dart out from behind a building. She was certain by the time the cat returned, it would be black and unlucky.

There was a seven-year-old girl outside the factory wearing boots that were too big for her. She was coughing at the side of the building. She had a rag she was holding up to her mouth. The rag was filthy from all the dust in her lungs she had coughed up.

Louis was displeased by the state of the industrial district. He never liked being at a factory for longer than he had to. It distressed and depressed him. He held his hands over his ears to block out the pounding.

But Marie loved being near the factory. She liked the enormity of it. She felt her heart catching up or slowing down to the rhythm of the machines. She couldn't hear anything for the rest of the day because of the thrumming it had caused in her ears. But she didn't mind. She liked that she existed in a temporary realm of silence. She could then concentrate on all the marvels she had seen.

MARIE ASKED TO MEET THE CHILDREN who worked at the factory in Pittsburgh. The little girls were lined up. One little girl was still very pretty despite having worked at the factory for three years. She couldn't stop scratching her body, as she had contracted a bad case of scabies. Marie insisted at once a doctor be summoned to the factory to deal with all the children's afflictions.

She wasn't sure why the poor girls were too frightened to speak to her. Especially once she gave them license to do so. They still wouldn't give her their secrets. She walked up to a girl whose blond hair was tied up in a messy bun on the side of her head. She was wearing fingerless gloves and smoking a cigarette. She had her shoulder blades against the wall, her hips jutting outward. This was a pose Marie had seen being struck by many working-class women. The most extraordinary thing about this girl was an enormous black eye. Because she was so pretty, Marie had a great yearning to kiss her face.

"Excuse me."

"Yes."

"May I ask you a question?"

"All right."

"What happened to your eye?"

"I have no idea."

"You must know."

"I do. But I don't see how it's any of your business."

"I will give you a coin if you tell me."

The girl put out her gloved hand. There was a hole in the center of the glove into which the coin fit perfectly.

"I was having a spat with my brother. He was trying to take advantage of me."

"Did he learn his lesson?"

"What do you think? Boys never learn anything, do they? They are always going to be stronger than us. That's the nature of being a girl, isn't it? You're always at the mercy of the whole world."

"I'm not."

The girl shrugged. "You are though." She tossed her cigarette on the ground and went inside.

MARIE REQUESTED THAT LOUIS BUY her a box of a hundred pink ribbons. She handed one to each of the girls who worked at the factory. Louis watched Marie. She was interested in the workings of the factory in a way he himself could never be. He found the machines at the factory very crude. They weren't meant to evoke wonder, but to quickly manufacture tawdry goods he himself would neither use nor consume. Did a factory bestow delight on anybody? It found a way to manipulate human beings. There was a brutality he wanted to keep himself away from.

And the plight of the worker always made him feel so uncomfortable. It made him feel as though he might so easily be in their predicament. Marie's mind never went to these places. She never conceived of herself as sharing the fates or feelings of the factory workers. He knew, watching her with the ribbons, her ability to chat with and smile at the workers (although it was a demonstration of sympathy) showed a total lack of empathy.

MARIE REALIZED THERE WAS ONLY so much she could learn about the factory from the other children who worked there. So she turned to the owner of the factory for her inquiries. Marie knew there was a talent to asking questions. If you asked questions people didn't enjoy answering, they would quickly tire of you. You had to ask questions that were prompts for a person to tell a story about themselves. They had to talk about things they loved. She was exceptionally good at this. She was a wonderful conversationalist.

She followed the factory owner through the plant. "Why do you have so many children working here?" she asked him. "Isn't it a bad idea to hire children? I thought they were foolish."

"They are my best workers. They cost half the price. They never think of striking on their own."

"Does it matter to you whether the women you hire are ugly or pretty?"

"Either way, they both become pregnant and that slows them down."

"Do you ever give them days off of work?"

"I let them go to funerals. They get so sad otherwise. They get distracted and end up getting themselves crushed in one of the machines."

"Are you close to your workers?"

"Some of them spend their whole lives working here. That makes us a family of some sort."

"Is this the only factory you own?"

"It isn't impressive enough for you? You wanted bigger?"

"No, it's incredible. But I heard you owned several factories."

"I bought the sugar factories in the three neighboring cities. I don't have competition that forces me to reduce the price of sugar. It's an unfortunate business. But if you don't keep buying and expanding, you will be consumed."

Marie nodded, taking it all in. The factory owner looked her up and down, as though acknowledging to himself what a young woman she was.

"You will inherit your father's factory. They will all come for you because you are a young woman. You will have to be more cutthroat than any man. Take them all down or they will take what is yours."

LOUIS LOOKED OUT THE WINDOW, having a cigarette during the conversation, antsy to leave. He didn't appreciate spending time with other factory owners. They reminded him of the way he used to feel in society before he had married Hortense. Some of them had inherited their factories and enterprises. But none had come to their factories through marriage. He remembered why he avoided men mostly. He felt judged by them. They made him feel effeminate, as he had once been, standing at parties, being desperately social in an attempt to be purchased.

He felt Marie was his ambassador. He didn't have to worry about making an impression himself because Marie made such a good one. The factory owner was left with the impression he had spent time with the Antoines, even though he was essentially speaking to Marie. And he came away from the meeting with a good, warm feeling.

❧

Louis grew bored and irritated visiting factories and was very much looking forward to returning to Montreal. He was the richest man in the city. Everyone knew who he was and he didn't have to prove anything. He knew people in Montreal would be expectant of his return. He would not disappoint them. He would bring them wonders. It would be as though he had a time machine and had traveled to the far, far future to bring them back delights. People would tell him he was wonderful and marvelous and very rich. He wanted people to tell him these things over and over again, so he could believe them. That chorus of approval would drown out the small voice in his head that liked to remind him he was a nothing and a nobody.

The thought of returning to Montreal made Marie remember Sadie, and the fear of the absence she would feel returning home struck her. One afternoon in Florida, Marie sat down at a natural history display to fill in the back of a postcard that had a photograph of an automaton of a man with little screws for dimples on its cheeks. She had got it in New York. She thought the automaton looked handsome, like someone she could talk to. She had been carrying the postcard around in her coat pocket since then. Suddenly, she wanted to send the handsome automaton to Sadie, as a sort of valentine. A pride of taxidermied lions was mounted all around her, as though they were waiting for her to fill in the back of her postcard before they could descend and eat her.

She inscribed a note to Sadie. She had once snuck through her father's papers and had found a receipt for Sadie's tuition at a boarding school. She had written down the address and now copied it on the card. She held it up and looked at it. The cursive letters were like a wrought-iron fence dividing the two of them now.

CHAPTER 15

Sadie Lives on the Other
Side of the World

During the years she was at the boarding school, Sadie became the leader of all the girls. She was the most adventurous. Sadie flirted with the man who came with a cart to collect all the sheets. She put anonymous love letters in the basket so that when he returned, he didn't know which girl it was. They all leaned out the window and flirted coquettishly at him. His face went mordantly red.

She made a fishing rod out of a stick and some string. At the end of it she attached a pair of bloomers. When the grocer arrived with his crates of vegetables, she let the bloomers descend in front of him. He moved to the right, and so did the bloomers. He then tried scurrying to the left and the bloomers were still in front of him, the ghost of a shameless pretty girl who wanted to dance.

Sadie organized betting tournaments. She snuck a chicken out to the yard and the girls gambled on who could catch it. They were so delighted with the game, when it started raining they didn't want to stop playing. They ended up slipping around in the mud. They were all horribly dirty when they came in. The chicken, meanwhile, had run off and was on its way down the road. It would not stop running until it was crushed under the wheels of a cart.

Some of the girls would visit Sadie in bed. A girl named Alice arrived one night. Sadie lifted up the girl's chemise. She began to draw on Alice's belly with the tip of her finger. The illustrations became more and more ornate. She was drawing a rosebush with flowers blooming all over it. Then she would put her fingers between Alice's legs. Alice sounded as though she had stopped breathing.

"Imagine that my name is Frank."

"Oh, Frank," Alice whispered. "Frank. Frank."

It was all about pleasure. It was as though she were panning for gold and had finally come across it. A nugget. When they were done, Sadie and Alice both climbed out the window and sat on the ledge. Their bare legs swinging. As though the night sky were a pond of water. They smoked a cigarette together. It was the first cigarette the girl had ever smoked. And she went on to be a lifelong smoker afterward.

One afternoon, Sadie received a postcard from Marie. There was a strange-looking automaton gentleman on it. At boarding school, Sadie was in many ways sheltered from the wild changes and ambitions of the times. This was a deliberate act by the school. There was no need for girls to be kept abreast of the technological changes in the world. Being ladylike was an idealized existence that should not be affected by external considerations. External considerations were for men. When they returned home, what they wanted was a timeless bubble. A lady should be able to have a pretty tea party regardless of whether there were saber-toothed tigers or bombs dropping outside.

Sadie held the postcard and noted with a slight resentment how Marie was out in the world, traveling, seeing new and wonderful things, while she was being confined in the strictest way. Her friend had always been interested in technology. She contemplated the meaning of the card. Marie believed that technology was better than human nature. If one followed the path of technology and modernity, one's better nature would be revealed. Marie was trying to tell her something about the two of them. But whatever it was, Sadie did not answer it. What would be the point? They were so far away from each other. To send a postcard would be to feel the distance, and that would be unbearable.

When she looked carefully at the robot's face over the years, she found some days it didn't look male at all. All its features seemed feminine. It was an androgynous robot. In the future there would be no male or female, simply people.

All the Marys in Montreal

Although he did not know this, Louis was incapable of having male children. Every time one of his illegitimate children was pushed out of their wailing and hysterical mother's womb, the midwife announced the arrival of a girl. The mother found herself weeping even more profusely, knowing the baby didn't stand a chance in the world and would probably end up seduced and miserable like her.

They grew up all over the city. Since Mary was the most common name in Montreal, many of Louis's daughters were named Mary. Unlike Marie, who lived in the Golden Mile, all the other Marys worked for a living.

There was a Mary who worked with her mother as a leech collector. She waded out into the water with her arms spread as though she were involved in a religious rite. Her little plump body was covered in black leeches, as though she had just grown mustaches in the strangest of places. Her mother yelled for her to stand still. She trembled as her mother pulled them off one by one, dropping them into a jar to sell to the doctor.

There was a Mary who worked as a matchstick maker. She cut matches out of wood, dipped them in phosphorescent, and held them up to dry. There was a rumor that after you did this for a while something quite ghastly would befall you due to the phosphorescence. She imagined one day beginning to glow in the dark and being able to read by her own light. She imagined one day her hair going up in flames like a match. And everyone who had ever slighted her standing before her in fear.

There was a Mary who worked as a chimney sweep. Her mother had cut her blond hair short, so she could pass as a boy. She climbed out of the chimney and was completely covered in soot. Except for her brilliant blue eyes, which shone brighter than those of a boy. She held up her skinny black broom like it was the staff of a general and she coughed out a little black cloud of soot.

There was a Mary who worked with a man who passed as her real father, catching rats. They sold them to dog fighters. They would throw them into rings to fight with dogs. Her father wore leather gloves and picked up rats by the tails. She couldn't look at their faces. They were filled with so much rage at their predicaments. She had a dream that a rat walked up to her and said, "I hate you." And she screamed.

There was a Mary who lived with her uncles, who were grave robbers. Her job was to stand at one side of the cemetery and keep watch for any intruders. She had a bell in her pocket. She was supposed to ring it if she saw anyone coming. When they opened a coffin, there was a thin girl with blond hair holding flowers with white petals. The corpse was so fresh the flowers hadn't even wilted. They were all very careful with the girl's body because they didn't want to wake her. They whispered around the corpse. The last thing in the world they wanted was for the girl to wake up and realize she was dead.

One day this Mary would take the bell out of her pocket and ring it. And all the other Marys would rise up from their graves.

PART TWO

CHAPTER 16

Marie Antoine Is Apparently a Lady

The ballroom was swarming with marvelously dressed couples dancing to the twenty-piece ensemble playing fanciful tunes at the Midsummer Ball. But no one attracted more attention than Marie Antoine swirling in the arms of the handsome Philip Arnett, brother of the long-lost Sadie.

Marie Antoine was twenty-one years old and the undisputed queen of the Golden Mile. Everything she did was heralded as an event everyone had to attend. All the other ladies wanted to be friends with her and all the young men wanted to marry her.

The crinoline under Marie's dress had been designed to swing back and forth. It was a crafty design she had thought of herself and had suggested to the dressmaker. Given the price Marie was paying, the dressmaker said anything was possible. But when Marie took a twirl, the crinoline decided it was not done spinning and destabilized her.

There were often accidents whose cause lay in a crinoline. There was a man on hand with a bucket of water for girls who went up in flames. And five especially soft carpets had been placed at the bottom of the stairs for toppling girls.

Marie fell over, and her dress and crinoline went up over her head, making her do a backward somersault, which knocked over the woman next to her, creating a domino effect that caused all the young women to topple over. They all lay on the ground with their legs and arms in the air, flailing like a group of beetles that were stuck on their backs.

Sadie's brother helped her to her feet. Everyone in the room applauded. Marie held Philip Arnett's hand and took a little bow. Even falling over seemed enchanting when it was done by Marie Antoine.

ONLY A FEW HOURS EARLIER, Marie had been undressed and waiting for the dressmaker to deliver the stupendous outfit she would wear. The only thing she had on was a small oval locket she wore around her neck and never removed. While waiting, Marie was roaming around the house naked. The servants were used to seeing her that way and were no longer shocked. They would walk into the kitchen in the middle of the night to see Marie standing in a tiny undershirt and no drawers eating a bowl of strawberries and cream. The servants didn't really exist for Marie. She could not consider herself indecent in front of them.

She stopped in the kitchen. She had a sweet tooth. It was surprising that she wasn't fat since she ate nothing other than sweets. She found all other food boring. She picked up a cupcake on the counter and shoved it into her mouth, trying to eat it all at once. There was pink frosting all over her chin and black cake in her mouth. It was as though she had been buried alive in the ground, screaming with her mouth open. She stood up from the wooden chair, leaving behind two little misty moons that slowly disappeared as she walked away.

She walked down the hallway with an apple stuck in her mouth as though she were a pig. Her father said that she looked perverted. And to go to her room and put something on.

She put on as little clothing as possible. She had a little lace step-in chemise with silk shoulder straps—and a tiny silk pink rose as a top button. You could see the shadows of her nipples and her belly button and pubic hair beneath the white material. She put on a boudoir cap made out of lace with a silk yellow ribbon around it. It was supposed to hold her curls up, but she had so many, and she stomped around so much, they were bound to come toppling down. She put on a little pair of pink slippers that turned up at the toes with golden bells on them. Her father sighed when he saw her again in the parlor half-naked, but he couldn't help but delight in her utter unselfconsciousness.

She stuck a croissant in her mouth and then leaned over and let her pet pig bite into it. His name was Pitou. She called him Pitou and Tutu and Pipi and Petunia. He would crawl into bed with her. Whenever her father walked into the room, it seemed as though the pig and Marie had just been talking to each other. He had just interrupted a conversation that they were in the middle of having. The pig was wearing one of his bow ties.

This was what happened when a child didn't have a mother, he thought. They grew up wild. They grew up strange. He hoped marriage didn't change that. All the maids also wondered how Marie would change once she was engaged.

MARIE HAD HAD HER COMING-OUT ball the year before. She was introduced to all the eligible men, or boys as she had thought of them, in her neighborhood as potential suitors. She had known them all before of course. But they hadn't been presented to her in just this way. She was expected to begin a courtship with one of them. And then after a certain amount of time, she would elect to have him as her spouse. She would start a whole new life with him. But she did not want to start a new life with anybody. She was content the way she was.

But nobody, including herself, could imagine a future in which a young girl didn't marry. And if she didn't act as though it was something she was looking forward to, she would be socially shamed. But she wasn't indifferent to men. Marie went to dances regularly. She looked at the ear of a young man standing next to her at a ball and wanted to lean over and bite it. The idea that she might be allowed to lean over and bite his ear filled her up with warmth. She didn't know if it was attraction. It didn't seem to be love. All she knew was she had a desire to say that ear belonged not to the man whose head it was on, but to her.

A few months before, at the Spring Dance, she found herself enjoying one of the young men in the neighborhood's company more than others. He was short and had spectacles and curly hair. He made his curly hair stand up straight over his head in order to gain four inches. None of the other suitors worried about him. They couldn't imagine he was a threat until they heard the way Marie laughed at his jokes.

It was completely inappropriate. A woman was not supposed to laugh hysterically, especially when she was at a social gathering. There was something about it that was so overtly sexual. It made her chest move up and down and her forehead sweat. But Marie had never spent time with members of the opposite sex. She could never have had any idea of how delightfully idiotic men could be. And she was completely unprepared for the lovely elixir of physical attraction and bad jokes.

"Did you know the surface of the moon is reflective?" Marie said. "That's why it glows."

"You don't have to look for a mirror to brush your teeth," the young man answered. "You just look down at the ground beneath your feet."

"Do you think there's any point in traveling to the moon?" Marie asked.

"It's better to say you've gone than to actually go," he answered.

"When you travel all the way to the moon, you would certainly work up an appetite. You would need a spot of something to eat and some tea."

"I would certainly pack some cucumber sandwiches to eat on the way."

"The moon is farther than you imagine. You'll be in that balloon longer than you think."

"Right. Right. So bring a whole ham."

PHILIP ARNETT WALKED INTO THE ROOM while Marie was laughing. The hope of the Arnett family was now on Philip, who had also entered politics. Not having to compare himself to his younger sister had done wonders for his personality. There was really only room for one sibling to shine in every family. And that role was for the eldest brother. Every family is a cruel, intransigent monarchy.

Philip had grown up to be handsome. He knew what to do with his face now. He knew how to look at people in a way that made them feel slightly insecure. The Arnetts all had faces that gave them the impression of being intelligent. This impression allowed them to move ahead in politics. Although Philip wasn't especially smart, his lack of intelligence made him bitter, and that bitterness could come across as a superior sort of cleverness.

Philip had a chip on his shoulder the way the rest of the family did about their middle-class roots. He didn't believe he felt inferior because he was inferior. He thought he was inferior because others made him feel that way. He took his feelings of inferiority as an act of aggression against him. The Arnetts believed that if you wanted something badly enough, it should be yours. Like the rest of his family, Philip was covetous of status.

Philip was quite popular with young women. He seemed to look at others with a hint of disdain, and they found that intriguing. He was careful of every association he made, considering how it would affect his political career. When he saw Marie, his family's old obsession with her swelled up in his heart. He remembered Marie from when she was twelve years old. He remembered how excited the family had been by her presence. That infuriated him. He remembered seeing her from his window. She had piles of blond hair. The sun was shining on her head, setting her head on fire.

It was at that moment, when he saw Marie again still looking radiant, his heart swelling with an old contempt, that he decided he wanted to marry her.

He did not speak to her that night. He was irritated that she was speaking to another man.

MARIE WAS AT AN OUTDOOR tea party when Philip did approach her. There was a group of daffodils around Marie's chair. They were wearing baby bonnets to protect themselves from the sun. He handed her a love letter he had carefully composed. He leaned his arm over the table and, while doing so, upset the teapot, spilling the contents all over the table. Marie shrieked, as she was wearing a white dress. She took the paper from Philip's hands, thanking him profusely, and used it quickly to wipe up all the tea.

At the next social gathering, Philip asked Marie if he might sit with her. Marie told him a dream she had where she accidentally cut off her friend's finger with a cake knife. She had no idea what to do with it. She didn't want her friend to feel upset about her missing finger. So Marie stuck the finger in her pocket. But then she felt the finger slowly begin to wiggle in her pocket. Philip did not say anything. He did not know what to say to this foolish girl. He walked away upset.

〰

Marie's dress finally arrived with great ceremony. There were three assistants at the door. Two held the dress between them, as though they were carrying a fainting lady to a couch. The third assistant, a young boy, was carrying the crinoline hoops that went under the dress over his head, as though he were a bird in a cage. Marie had her maids hurry to her room to help her put on the elaborate dress. She spun around, making the hooped skirt spin, knocking a maid over. Marie knew she was going to cause a stir with this dress. She looked in the mirror and was pleased. She knew all the young men were going to want to dance with her. She sighed, thinking she would have to dance with Philip. And she was very uncertain how she felt about him.

When they were little, Sadie had confided many times to Marie that her brother was an idiot. Marie thought maybe he had changed. He must have something of Sadie inside him. She wondered if he would invite her to visit his home. And she could then look through Sadie's old room and her things. Surely they had left the room as it was. She pictured throwing herself down on the bed and inhaling the pillow deeply. If she inhaled strongly enough, all of Sadie would come back to her.

She thought Philip must be receiving news from Sadie. He must have letters. She was very curious what Sadie was up to. She wanted to talk about Sadie with somebody. That she'd be able to talk to him about Sadie was an enormous attraction. She felt the physical sensation of doing something she wasn't supposed to creep through her body.

Philip arrived at the Midsummer Ball feeling nervous, knowing Marie would be there. He was wearing a black tailcoat over a pair of white-and-blue-striped pants, and a white shirt with a starched collar and a bow tie. He had a top hat that looked as though it might topple off at any moment. He had read over his *Guidebook for Manners*. If you were polite and guided the conversation, you would be fine. A woman expected a man to have a strong sense of purpose and a career. He had examined the ink drawing of the man with a bow tie and a mustache on the cover.

He approached Marie and asked her to dance. Marie naturally accepted. As she was dancing with him, she began to notice a resemblance to Sadie in his face. It had never occurred to Marie that Sadie and Philip looked alike. But the more she looked at his face, the more she thought she could see similarities between Philip and Sadie. The more they moved about the room, the more she began to imagine she was in the arms of Sadie, and she adored that feeling.

THE MORNING AFTER THE MIDSUMMER BALL with Philip, Marie realized she got everything she wanted in life except for Sadie. When she was a young girl and first saw Sadie, she worried the other girl was unobtainable. She had been more surprised by Sadie's friendship than any gift she had ever received. But the impermanence of friendship frightened her then. It was as though she intuited it could not last.

Marie had felt a nagging sense of guilt ever since her postcard had gone unanswered. Whenever the name Arnett came up around Louis, as it occasionally did since the father was in politics, Marie's father got a disconcerted look about him, as though he were still wary of the Arnetts turning on them. So Marie never brought them up and therefore had no news of Sadie and no way of knowing what she was thinking or doing. This caused her to feel so ashamed about having blamed Sadie for the shooting of the maid.

Now that she had seen Sadie in Philip's face, she could not stop thinking about her. For the rest of the week, Marie felt as though her life was meaningless. Although she was busy all day, she felt strangely unoccupied. Although she excelled at everything, she felt she had accomplished nothing, and really couldn't do anything at all.

At the Sunday picnic, Marie walked over to Philip herself. A group of children with large hoops ran in front of her. She passed a table of elaborately decorated square cakes that seemed to resemble a miniature maquette of Versailles. She looked at him and announced, "You may court me, but only if you try to get Sadie back. I would like her to return to Montreal. I would like her as a sister-in-law."

"I will try my best," Philip said.

A FEW DAYS LATER, Philip was standing in the office of Louis Antoine, seeking permission to ask for his daughter's hand. Louis knew he should consider this younger man's proposition with sensitivity and poise. But looking at Philip, he was filled with so much contempt. He knew the Arnetts were social climbers. And as a social climber himself, he would never marry his daughter to one.

Louis was blue blooded himself even though his family had lost all their money. He had always had the ease and confidence of someone from an upper-class family. This boy was crude. He was rough around the edges. It was Philip's desperation that bothered Louis the most. The boy was so aware of all the advantages Marie could bring him, it would make it impossible for him to ever actually love her. There were so many things to love about Marie that had nothing to do with her wealth. She was intelligent. She was lazy, but when she put her mind to something, it was slightly perturbing how quickly she was able to master it. Philip would want to destroy all that.

"I can tell by your expression you already know my answer to that question," Louis Antoine said. "Because you know as well as I do you are no match for my daughter. She needs someone with a sense of humor. We are a family that likes to laugh. And you are dour. And maybe that's all right for some young women. But not for Marie. You'll bore her. She likes to be entertained. She dragged me all over the continent when she was still a girl, just to see new things. You want a wife who will stay at home and make you look good. That's not Marie. She will outshine you everywhere you go. And you will have to find ways to make her not glow so brightly. I love my daughter. Why on earth would I want her to marry you?"

"You are wrong about me, sir," Philip answered, staring hard at Louis.

"I can read a man like you. You think you are complicated, but you are an open book to me. I know what happens on the next page better than you."

Louis had held himself back from saying what he really wanted to add. Which was that the idea of the Antoines and the Arnetts united as a family was grotesque to him. He had paid Philip's sister's school fees for years and made financial contributions to his idiotic father's campaign. He hated how they were still always somewhere in his life, lurking. They would occasionally stand in his way, making their presence felt, as though they were temporarily blocking the sun, and then move away.

He knew when Philip walked out of the room this affair was not over. He might be done with the Arnetts, but the Arnetts were not done with him. The Arnetts would never be done with him.

LOUIS SPOKE TO MARIE ABOUT it at dinnertime. She and her father sat at opposite ends of a ridiculously long dining table. They would summon the waiter to them, whisper a message in his ear, and have him walk over to the other person to deliver it. They had found this great fun. Tonight, Louis was not in the mood for play.

"The Arnetts are going to bring up that ugly mess again. They are going to have me by the tail. They are going to pull every trick they have out of their hat. Honestly, it's going to be a travesty. I don't even know if I can eat tonight. The whole business is making me nauseous."

"Tell them I will let Philip court me, but I want them to bring Sadie back."

Louis was taken aback. "Why in the world do you want anything to do with that Arnett character?"

"I want Sadie back."

He had not expected this response from Marie. He understood men and their machinations. He could see their motives and their actions coming from miles away. He found them boring for just this reason. And even though Louis found women to be absurd, conniving, opaque, neurotic, and unpredictable, he had never met one he had found boring. Louis was reminded once again that all women are unknowable. They all have at least one secret that they are keeping from everybody else. A secret that changes everything you thought about them.

But he still hadn't expected Marie to have a secret. He had spent so much time with Marie. Her whole life, in fact. They had never been separated a single night. He had told her so many years before not to bring up or think about Sadie. And she hadn't. She had never mentioned Sadie after that moment. So he assumed she had forgotten her. He assumed the reason she had never brought Sadie up was because she was no longer thinking about her. But she had been pining for that girl all along.

What did he know about female friendship? He didn't know women could be so attached to each other. He assumed that they only spent time together when there were no men around. He was shocked.

It was the revelation that he did not understand Marie or any woman that swayed his decision. He was almost glad when Mrs. Arnett did arrive at his office, so he could get it over with. He consented to the engagement.

Marie was so bubbly and delightful. She would be destroyed by marriage. Louis couldn't bear for a man to look at her with contempt and disgust and to sneak off behind her back to enjoy himself with other women. He didn't think it was possible for a man and woman to be happily married. They had been trying it throughout human history and it never worked. It was the one thing about the world he was certain of. He was now consigning his daughter to a fate that would almost certainly be unpleasant. But what choice did he have?

A lily in the windowsill nodded off abruptly. The head of the flower dropped to the floor at Philip's feet, as though a woman had dropped her handkerchief in hopes that someone would pick it up.

CHAPTER 17

The Return of Sadie Arnett

Twenty-one-year-old Sadie Arnett was sitting in the communal room of her boarding school in England, reading a book. Sadie was wearing an abominable striped dress and black boots that had been polished to hide the scuff marks. She had grown up to be beautiful, of course. Her dark eyes were intimidating and her lips strangely red. She had been living in England for nine years. Many of the other girls had left much earlier, having being sent for by their families. She was the eldest girl there, and worked as a tutor to other students rather than going to class.

Sadie was ready to never be called for and to be cast out. She was aware this was a fate common to artists. And destitution was an asset to a writer's biography.

Sadie was abruptly summoned to the headmistress's office. The headmistress's collar was so tight, it looked as though the brooch had been pinned into her throat. She informed Sadie she would be returning to Montreal.

"And why is that?" Sadie asked.

"You should be delighted," the headmistress answered.

⤧

As THE SHIP SET SAIL from London to Montreal at the beginning of September, Sadie had a sense of how different she was from the last time she had sailed. She wasn't afraid of the ship. The ship was taking her to a place she knew very well. And she had read and thought so much about the world that nothing could really be considered the unknown anymore.

While she was sitting on the deck, she did not think of the family she would soon be reunited with. Her thoughts often returned, despite herself, to Marie. She would see Marie again. What would she think of her? She always imagined Marie was up to the most marvelous things. She would be embarrassed when they met again. All she had was a sketchbook filled with perverted observations to show for all the days and years she had been away. She could sense her characters in the sketchbook falling all over the place as the ship rocked, rolling around in their bloomers with their breasts hanging out. Her longing to see Marie and her resentment that her friend had seen so much more of the world than her was all mixed up in Sadie's mind. The convoluted thoughts of Marie caused her to puke on her boots. Or perhaps it was simply seasickness.

SHE STEPPED OFF THE SHIP. A porter carried a stack of trunks behind her. The porter was surprised by the weight of most of the packages because they were filled with books. Not at all the usual weightless frivolities that were in a woman's trunk. Her mother and father were waiting there. Sadie's father wore a bowler hat. He had a very thick mustache he wore turned down. He believed it made him look serious.

But Sadie believed it made him look sad and dour. She knew he was an established politician now and his continued success was the quest of the whole family.

She no longer thought of them as her family. Why should she? They clearly didn't love her. And by not loving her, they had given her permission to close her heart to them, to forget they existed. She had contempt for them as they had contempt for her. Whether the contempt had originated with her or with them, she couldn't say. It was in a part of her childhood memories she no longer had access to. She had assumed they would never send for her. She stopped in front of her mother and stood stiffly, refusing any display of affection. She shook her parents' hands.

OF COURSE MRS. ARNETT SHOULD have known this moment was coming. But some part of her had believed she would never have to see Sadie again. She was so used to her being gone that she couldn't imagine her here. The ocean had kept them safely apart. She was very alarmed by the notion of Sadie returning, even with the coup of marrying into the Antoine family. Naturally she could defend the exile to Sadie, but how could she explain never visiting her or sending her a gift or pocket money or anything at all?

The institution Sadie had been sent to was supposed to be one that ironed out the wrinkles in girls' personalities. But she was under no illusion this had been the case with Sadie. Sadie's will wouldn't have been broken. She knew Sadie had outwitted the school and was still a bitch.

Sadie had been so hateful before she left, when Mrs. Arnett hadn't done anything to merit it. Wouldn't it now be explosive? It might give her cancer. There was something powerful and dangerous about Sadie's hatred. She had known it when her daughter was a girl. And now Sadie was a grown woman.

But perhaps her intuition was wrong. Perhaps Sadie is different now, she thought. And she'll forgive me.

Mrs. Arnett had convinced herself she was a good person. She had acted in a way that would make everybody think of her as a good person. But Sadie thought differently of her. Sadie was the only person in the world who would look at her and say, *J'accuse.* She had a horrible feeling she was waiting for her final judgment. She saw Sadie in her cloak before anyone else did, looking very much like the Grim Reaper himself.

Mrs. Arnett was quite shocked when she realized her daughter was wearing the same cloak she had left in nine years before. When she had left, the cloak surrounded her completely, like a large blanket she disappeared under. Now it fit her perfectly. If it were not so hideous, she would have said the cloak had been made for her. But how shoddy and unladylike it was! Yet how could she complain about it when it was she who had given Sadie this cloak? And she had been wearing it every day for the past nine years?

She did not want to feel that she had visited this kind of shame on her daughter. She needed to remain the victim in this situation. She needed to remind herself that Sadie had visited shame on *her* and not the other way around.

Mrs. Arnett pulled herself up and looked her daughter in the face. Sadie appeared so different, and yet her expression was the same as it had been since she was three years old: one of condescension.

"How was your trip?"

"Awful, naturally."

Mrs. Arnett was a bit startled at Sadie's new accent. It was a mild one. It had the effect of not so much making her sound British as making her sound pompous and disdainful. Mrs. Arnett hated that she was intimidated by her.

WHEN THEY ARRIVED BACK at the house, Sadie went up to her old room. She was wondering if she would remember where her bedroom was, but she had no trouble finding it. Her mother followed in after her.

"Do you need some help with your clothes?" Mrs. Arnett asked.

"What clothes?" Sadie asked.

She took off her cloak and tossed it on the chair. Underneath she was wearing a genteel but shabby brown-and-gold-striped dress. It had been worn too many times. It hadn't occurred to Mrs. Arnett that Sadie had gone without so many things. Sadie could have written and asked for clothes. Either she or the Antoines would have sent her some. Or at least she believed she would have sent her some.

"Do you not like my attire? It seems to be making you uncomfortable. I was given castoffs from the other girls. There were some girls there from wealthy families, actual wealthy families, I mean, who enjoyed doing charitable deeds."

"You could have written for some clothes."

"Could I have? I thought it was made quite clear you wanted nothing to do with me when we parted. And should I have written for Christmas presents or a card on my birthday or on Valentine's Day? How silly! All I had to do was ask!"

"Well, that is behind us now. I think we must get you fitted for something quite elegant."

"Must we? But why? I'm not fit for society, being a murderess and all."

"That was a long time ago. I think everyone will be able to move past that. You're a grown woman. You were at a prestigious school all these years. I'm sure many of the girls here would appreciate having a peek at what a European education can do." Mrs. Arnett was trying to convince herself.

Sadie sat on an armchair next to a small table on which tea had been laid. She leaned back and crossed her legs in a pose she had to know was distractingly unladylike. She reached into the sugar bowl with her fingers instead of the tongs. She plopped no fewer than five sugar cubes into her tea. And then placed one on her tongue.

"Do what you must," Sadie said. "I could actually use a new dress simply for practical purposes. This one is too small. It was given to me two years ago and my chest has grown since then." She began to bend her arms every which way, stretching from the trip.

"The family fortunes have risen," Mrs. Arnett said. "We have three maids now. You'll have to look the part. Philip is doing extraordinarily well. Because of his background, your father still had an uphill battle that prevented him from reaching the goals he was capable of. But Philip will be able to have financial support and connections to make him a certain choice for premier and then prime minister. This house did wonders for your father. But Philip is going to have an even bigger one."

"Why is that? Where is Philip getting his sudden fortune from?"

"He is to marry Marie Antoine. We would like your help in that department."

Sadie burst into laughter. Mrs. Arnett looked infuriated and frustrated with her daughter. She abruptly left the room.

How ridiculous it was, Sadie thought, that they were trying to give Marie away to her asinine brother, Philip. Having been abroad so long had made her an outsider. And she could see the social machinations of her return so clearly, it was as though she was watching a poorly written, amateurish play. Her pull over Marie was being exploited so that it could advance the careers of her brother and her father. That was why

148

she was here. They were using her as a pimp in a way. Once again. But this time, she would have none of it.

A FEW MINUTES AFTER Mrs. Arnett left the room, Sadie heard the sound of thunder in the house. What in the world could that be other than a man storming up the stairs? She knew he was coming to put her in her place. Philip threw open the door. An oval painting of a woman fell from the wall as though she had fainted.

She was surprised at their physical resemblance. It was not the sort of thing you noticed as a child. But his face was so alien to her now, she noticed the shared features immediately. They stood in front of each other, two people who had come out of the same womb. And they couldn't really stand this fact. They could see right through the other, and neither was at all impressed.

"You've made our mother cry."

"Your mother. And I don't care."

"Are you seriously going to mess this up for everyone again?"

"How could I possibly do that?"

"You are going to be nice to Marie."

"Never."

His hand was around her neck before she knew what was going on.

"If you don't make Marie feel like joining this family, I will make sure you end up in a nuthouse."

"I cannot make Marie like you."

"We've already walked around the whole neighborhood for everyone to see."

Sadie was appalled. She had had so high an opinion of Marie all these years, but for what? She had grown up to be a fool. She had imagined her thriving and seeing the world and knowing everything about business and science. But no! God, no! She was engaged to her idiotic brother.

When Philip left the room, Sadie vowed to herself to make every effort to avoid the contemptuous Marie, whom she now fully blamed for denouncing her as a child. To hell with her, Sadie thought. If Marie was going to wed her brother, and bring her here to witness it, she would hold a marvelous grudge.

SADIE WAS SO UPSET at the news of Marie's engagement to Philip, she found herself unable to sit in her room and do anything, not even write. She decided to leave the house and go for a walk. She threw her awful cloak over her shoulders and pulled her hat down over her hair and eyebrows. And she left the house through the back kitchen door to avoid having to speak to her mother or brother.

Sadie marched around the neighborhood with her long cloak dragging over mud and horse shit on the street, muttering under her breath how angry she was at Marie for disappointing her. She found herself, quite by accident, in Marie's gardens. She had forgotten the geography of the neighborhood, but she had somehow, instinctively, ended up here. She saw the labyrinth. She couldn't help herself and wandered into it. Like any murderer, she wanted to return to the scene of the crime.

The last person she expected to see at the center of the labyrinth was Marie herself. Her heart leaped like a frog out of a child's fist. Sadie recognized her even though so many years had passed.

She hadn't thought to ever see Marie in the flesh again. But there she was, looking very striking. She was wearing her blond hair up in an incredible style. She wondered how many maids had worked on it. Sadie had never seen a bouffant so high in her life, and she didn't think she would ever see one that high again. Marie was carrying a small piglet in her arms. The piglet looked as though it were in a state of ecstasy. Sadie had probably interrupted Marie in an intense session of compliments.

As soon as she laid eyes on Marie once again, she was delighted despite herself. She had thought she was inoculated against Marie and had become immune to feelings about her years before. She had been freshly betrayed by Marie's engagement. But she saw Marie and was shocked by her body's reaction.

Perhaps there is such a thing as true love. What had she been doing the past nine years? Lying to herself? Distracting herself from a very central part of her personality, which was that she was metaphysically bound to Marie.

The last time they had been in this garden together they had stood facing each other with guns in their hands. It suddenly seemed as though Marie hadn't moved in all this time. As though she had stood there waiting for her to return for nine years.

"It's you!" Marie cried. "I knew you had come back. I was waiting for you to come visit me."

Marie dropped the piglet to the ground when she saw Sadie. The piglet let out a squeal of indignation and hurried off, its pride hurt.

Suddenly the women were unable to keep their hands off each other. They were enthralled by the physical changes in each other, and how they found each other even more beautiful. They reached out and put their hands on each other's hair. They played with each other's curls as though they were silk. They grabbed onto each other's ears and grinned. They put their hands on each other's cheeks. They gently pulled their faces together and kissed. Then Sadie pushed on Marie's body in order to distance herself from her, recollecting herself. Marie was engaged to her brother. She was not the same Marie she had left.

"Come have some chocolate with me!" Marie begged. "Every other girl around here is inept, to say the least."

"It is very nice to see you," said Sadie calmly. "I trust you are well. I must be returning home now."

"But why?"

"I'm expected of course. Aren't we always expected?" Sadie asked, and a slight sneer appeared on the side of her smile, like it was pulled up by a string at the corner.

Marie gave a small smile.

"Should we be friends again?" she said.

"Were we ever friends?"

"Of course we were. How can you say that to me?"

"We were similar back then, I suppose. It was possible for us to be friends. We both thought we were artists of some kind. But I was punished. And I was made to suffer. We can't really be expected to be friends anymore."

"I have suffered too."

"No, you haven't. Not really."

"Then why are you here?"

"I came to take a look at who I used to be, I suppose. I wanted to see just how far I had traveled and how much I have become. And all the things I know. I wanted to make sure it was you who were punished and not me. Your punishment is that you have become mundane and ordinary, and you have agreed to marry Philip."

Sadie turned away, feeling as if she had won something. She almost stepped on a squirrel as she stormed off. The animal's tail whipped all over the place, like the ostrich quill of a judge signing a death warrant.

DESPITE THE FAILURE OF THEIR CONVERSATION, Marie thought she would try again with Sadie. She paced back and forth in her room. She had to have more time with Sadie. She would have to create a situation wherein she could get Sadie to sit down and not budge. Marie invited Sadie to an embroidery circle at her home.

Marie sat at her desk in her undergarments and wrote with her favorite plume to Sadie an invitation for tea. She threw sawdust on the card. She held it up and shook it over her head, causing it to look momentarily like a startled bird that had been shot in the chest. She was in such haste to send the invitation she didn't want to wait for the ink to dry. She paused only because she was rather fond of her own handwriting.

Once a girl received an invitation to another girl's home, she could never refuse. It would be regarded as impolite. It would be regarded as her having a mind of her own. And while she was living under her mother's roof, she would never be allowed to do that.

She knew she was trapping Sadie, but she couldn't help it.

CHAPTER 18

The Heart Is an Ugly Thumper

Even though she found sitting in embroidery circles to be fraught with a certain level of anxiety, Marie was nonetheless very good at the craft. Her favorite subject was always roses. Roses seemed more alive than any other flower. So capturing their vitality was very difficult. She thought if she were able to capture a real rose, it would seem to move. There were pillows all over the house with her embroidered roses that refused to breathe.

The other girls had sat down and had begun embroidering by the time Sadie arrived late. Sadie sat down at the empty chair in the circle. She took off her hat, and her hair was unkempt and greasy, with pieces of it hanging in knots on her forehead. Everyone else's hair was immobile. Marie was flattered often for the immobility of her hair. Today, for instance, it was in a perfect mound of circular curls on her head. Their hair was like a group of hound dogs waiting for their meal to be dumped before them who would not budge a muscle before their master signaled for them to begin.

Sadie's physical appearance caused her to be immediately alienated. She sat sunken in the chair as though she were a male libertine. Her legs were kicked outward and crossed, displaying her filthy boots to everyone. The others knew she had been to a fancy boarding school. They figured she must be deliberately acting in a louche manner because she looked down on them. She was so used to fancier people. She viewed them as servants. They tried to make conversation. But their words were totally lost on Sadie, who continued to stare at Marie.

Sadie's presence caused Marie's heart rate to change and her lungs to inhale and exhale in a different way. It changed her inner temperature and her blood began to heat up. She felt circles of sweat begin to form under her armpits. The others observed the change in Marie's demeanor with displeasure. Sadie was stealing Marie's heart away, the same way she had when they were little girls.

Sadie took her embroidering out of her bag and began stitching.

"Would you like to see the rose I've been working on, Sadie?" Marie asked. "It's very realistic."

"A realistic rose. How original. By limiting what we can be realistic about, are we achieving realism at all? I didn't even know what my cunt looked like. And then one day I took a hand mirror and placed it there. Because I was so curious. I almost dropped the mirror, I was so in shock."

The girls had all stopped embroidering and were staring at Sadie, dumbfounded with shock themselves. But Sadie continued sewing away. After an hour of sewing, and not saying another word, Sadie handed Marie a kerchief. She had embroidered an anatomically correct heart on it.

"I went to see a surgeon's museum when I was in England," Sadie said. "This is what hearts are supposed to look like. When I laid eyes on what a heart actually looked like, much about affection and love made sense to me. Because love is quite grotesque when you think about it. We try to make it very neat and symbolic. But this is what it looks like."

It wasn't that Sadie wanted to destroy Marie. She wanted to destroy Marie's world. She saw that Marie had come to think of it as an acceptable world. She would show Marie how empty and inane it was. She couldn't help herself.

The other girls all thought Sadie had made something ugly, and they gave one another looks. But Marie felt like a fool. Her chin wobbled like the breast of a songbird.

TWO WEEKS LATER, MARIE INVITED Sadie to archery lessons. They stood on the lawn behind Marie's house, wondering whether the other still had excellent aim. Marie drew and hit the bull's-eye perfectly. The arrows in the black center of the target looked like a group of quills stuck into an inkpot.

"It's all very well to hit the center of a bull's-eye," Sadie said. "Especially when it is one you have been staring at for years. It is quite another to attempt to hit a target when you are under pressure."

"What do you propose? You can't possibly be murdering cats still. Do you want to go hunting? Shall I plunge my arrow into the beating heart of a moving deer?"

"No, nothing so extreme. I'm going to the theater later. So I don't have time to go hunting on my country estate the way you do."

Sadie reached into her pocket. She pulled out an apple and balanced it on her head. She stepped in front of the target.

"Shoot the apple off my head."

Marie raised her bow and arrow, but her whole body began to shake. She knew she could hit the apple were it nothing more than a red dot in the distance. But she could not take that kind of risk with someone's life, and certainly not with that of someone she adored! She remembered with an alarming clarity Sadie eating an apple after Agatha's murder. Sadie was trying to incriminate her for the murder she had gotten away with. She would have Marie murder again to prove her point, even if it involved she herself becoming a casualty.

Marie did not know how lowering the bow made her a coward, but it made her feel ashamed. Sadie pointed her finger at Marie's heart. Marie was too terrified to move, as if the finger had bullets in it. Sadie took the apple off her head and dropped it back into her pocket. As though she would need it again. As though this were something she went around doing regularly.

Sadie promised herself she would confront Marie until she realized it was better to be an outcast and returned to her former self. She walked off, having won the archery competition without having fired an arrow.

THE NEXT WEEK IN OCTOBER was the annual Thanksgiving Ball. It was made clear to Sadie there was no way she might get out of going. Sadie didn't try. She had known from her childhood everyone in the Golden Mile attended the Thanksgiving Ball. And besides, unlike every other event in the neighborhood, she quite missed going to a ball. She wanted to hear the orchestra and see the dancing. She had liked the excess of a ball and how it always brought peoples' emotions to a peak. There was always someone acting foolishly.

Sadie finally put on one of the dresses her mother had bought her. She placed her hair up on her head and jabbed it in place with pins. It was hardly much of an improvement on the way she had been wearing it lately. She didn't like the colors of the dress. It was beige with pink frills. It was made of so much chiffon she was worried the ash of her cigarette might set it on fire. But once she put her cloak on over it she felt more or less herself.

Sadie immediately ventured to the ballroom. Trees planted in large pots lined the dance floor, their branches decorated with candles, creating the effect of a magical forest. Through the makeshift trees, Sadie noticed Marie near the refreshment table. Marie was sweaty and animated and was lost in conversation with a group of men. She had clearly been there a while. Sadie watched as Marie knocked back her drink and then quickly had another, in a manner that was decidedly unladylike. She recalled how gluttonous Marie was. It was one of her absolute favorite things about her. The effects of the alcohol on Marie were immediate. Her cheeks became flushed and she stepped out onto the dance floor as though nothing could hold her back.

Since Marie couldn't feel Sadie's gaze, she was acting more naturally. Sadie's presence made her nervous, but clearly nobody else's seemed to. And men definitely did not intimidate her in the slightest. Marie toyed with the men, each one looking at her as though they were certain of her adoration. And then she would promptly drop from the man's arms as though he had never existed, and would pass into the arms of another. Sadie saw Marie could not be dominated by men. And yet she was remarkably attached to her brother. Sadie shrugged off a man who asked her to dance and gave him a contemptuous look so she could continue to focus on Marie.

Suddenly Mrs. Arnett was at her elbow. "You can't treat men that way," she whispered harshly.

"I can't be obsequious the way you are, Mother. Simply accept that."

"It wasn't solely because of the accident that you were sent away, Sadie. You were a difficult child. You refused to be loved. Can you imagine what that must feel like? To be rejected by your own daughter? You made me feel so bitter and unhappy. You looked at me with disgust. I was filled with self-loathing. I thought everything I did was unworthy and stupid. When I looked in the mirror I felt ugly. And I didn't feel like that until you came back."

Sadie was so habituated to this sentiment from her mother, she decided to strike back. "Fine!" Sadie yelled heading out onto the dance floor. "I will go and dance!" Sadie cut between a man and a swirling Marie. She caught Marie in her arms. Marie looked delighted as they spun around together, forcing everyone to move out of their way. Sadie caught a glimpse of her mother, who was fuming, and began to dance more ferociously. The heels of their boots hit the floor as though they were knocking on the doors of hell, asking to be let in.

"I wish I could always hold you like this," Marie said. "I wish a giant spider would come along and cast a web that wraps all around our bodies. We would be in a cocoon together. And when we finally came out, we would be different, more incredible creatures. We would look and realize we had the same bodies, but they would have colorful wings that spread out from them."

Sadie did not understand her own feelings; she did not know whether she wanted to kiss or strangle Marie. She didn't want to be put in the position of trying to trap Marie—to restrain her—to demand over and over again for the proof of her love. She did not want to spend her life waiting to be tossed away by Marie. Sadie suddenly felt like a man, and she found men ridiculous.

Sadie let go of Marie's arms and hurried off the dance floor. As Sadie stepped outside into the cold, there was a crow lifting its wing and spreading its feathers, like a man sticking his hand into a black leather glove. She inhaled deeply, thinking she had escaped. Did Marie expect her to fit into this world? It would be impossible. It was ridiculous. It didn't suit her personality at all.

Marie stood on the dance floor, confused, her arms stretched outward. She had felt the absolute pleasure of belonging to someone you actually wanted to belong to. She couldn't stand not knowing what was in Sadie's head. Sadie did not operate according to the rules of the

Golden Mile. Everyone else was predictable. Everyone else was under her and her father's thumb. She wanted to have her way. She wanted to know if Sadie loved her back. She wanted a commitment from Sadie. She felt like screaming in frustration.

She would accept playing this game where Sadie withheld her affection as long as she knew that, in the end, she would get her way. Sadie would spend the rest of her life in the Golden Mile and be her best friend.

Then she saw Mrs. Arnett. She knew Sadie abhorred her mother. But that didn't mean Marie couldn't use her to serve her purpose. Mrs. Arnett was underhanded. She was obsessed with the hierarchy of the Golden Mile. She would do Marie's bidding. She would do things for Marie that Marie had no right to ask her to do.

Marie was an intelligent, intuitive person, so she knew what she was doing was wrong. But she was also spoiled, so she went to do it anyway.

Mrs. Arnett was about to follow her daughter out of the hall in order to chastise her for leaving so abruptly when Marie stepped into her path.

"Have you seen Sadie's writing book?" Marie asked.

"I don't think she has one. I haven't observed her writing since she returned home."

"Yes, of course she does. Of course she must. She would never be able to stop writing. If you could just let me see the notebook. I know she's modest, so she hides it from others. So if you could let me see it without her knowing . . ."

"I haven't seen her with any notebook."

"She might hide it where she used to when we were little, underneath her mattress. If you bring it to me, I promise you I will honor my commitment to Philip. I want to be part of your family. I want you to be a part of mine. But Sadie is a dear friend of my youth and I want to make sure we are on good terms."

Marie was aware she was telling Mrs. Arnett where the secret door to Sadie's brain was and handing her the key. She did not care what else Mrs. Arnett found there—as long as she brought her back the fruit of knowledge she desired. Mrs. Arnett had no interest in what went on in Sadie's mind. She instead turned this meeting to her own advantage.

"Come over to dinner next Tuesday with your father, will you? We'll all be one family."

"Yes," Marie answered, and she grasped Mrs. Arnett's hands.

Mrs. Arnett's head was filled immediately with plans for the dinner. She went home and began preparations. She forgot all about the notebook. Sadie, meanwhile, was upstairs making her pen tear breathlessly across the page, the words like a black ribbon at the end of a dancing girl's braid as she recounted the tale of an orgy at a Thanksgiving Ball.

ON THE DAY OF THE DINNER, Sadie was standing out in front of her house. She had her old cloak on over a new pink dress her mother had bought for her. Her large, odd Napoleon hat was pulled over her hair.

She thought her parents were fools. It was idiotic to put her and Marie in the same room. Didn't they know? Their characters were both too strong. There was just no way they would ever be able to coexist peacefully. They could either resume their explosive love affair that would somehow bring down everyone around them or they ought to be on opposite sides of the Atlantic.

She thought, I will walk in and I will sit quietly for an hour. All I will have to do is perform being a well-mannered girl. It couldn't be that hard. She would do it just this once. There were girls at every dining-room table performing being good-mannered, so why couldn't she? There were girls in bedrooms performing desire and submission. There were girls in kitchens performing being hostesses. There were girls in parks performing being coy, delicate flowers or shrinking violets. Was there a girl anywhere in the city who wasn't performing?

A rat scampered across her boot. As if to remind her of the secret hidden life that existed in the walls and floorboards of the neighborhood. The repressed thoughts that were tucked away, chased into hiding. That was why girls were so afraid of rodents. If their repressed thoughts were to escape—and they were so potent—they would undo everything anyone thought of them.

Sadie caught the rat by its tail and held it up. The rat's black eyes looked like they were sewn on like round buttons. She wasn't at all squeamish. She spoke to the rat as though it were a person.

"Well, my friend, I would like to run away from here too. But like you, I'm feeding on their crumbs. What an absurd world, where genius is dependent on idiocy."

Animals quite liked Sadie. They listened to her. She had a facility with training them. For whatever reason, when she spoke to them, they cowered with adulation. Perhaps because, secretly, everything wants to be dominated. The rat, who had lived its entire life in exile and infamy, was suddenly domesticated.

She put the rat under her hat. And it snuggled in contentedly as though it were just another curl on a nineteenth-century girl's head.

SADIE WAS LATE FOR THE MEAL. Until she arrived, Marie appeared to be intrigued by nothing that went on during the dinner. The white taffeta of her skirt was in heaps around her, as though she had torn herself free from a butterfly net. She was oblivious to Philip and had asked several times after Sadie.

Marie suggested that if Sadie didn't come back on time, they could have another dinner. Sadie's mother nodded encouragingly at this proposal. But Louis yawned in lieu of confirming this idea. Louis was wearing a black tailcoat with velvet collars and gold buttons over a silver waistcoat. His blond hair was gelled into a wave that turned up at the side of his face as though he were standing in the wind. Clearly he was bored and had no intention of returning soon. He spent so much time in his mansion that his body had forgotten to follow the rules of social engagement. He really wanted to let out a huge fart. He wanted to take his pants off and fart.

He had a new magic lantern in the house. He wished he were at home, watching the animated slide show of a pretty French girl having her head cut off. That had to wait until the end of the meal, however.

Then at eight o'clock the front door burst open. Sadie entered in a way that drew attention to herself. She stomped into the dining room and paused, almost as though for effect. The way that a famous actor would when coming out from backstage. The maid rushed up to her to take her things. Sadie put her hand up to stop her.

Her mother insisted she come into the room and sit immediately.

"Take your hat off, Sadie."

Sadie just stared at her mother as she sat down, as though she had never seen her before in her life and couldn't imagine where her sense of authority came from.

"Sadie has a flare for eccentric costume, as you can see," Mrs. Arnett said harshly. "Despite what Sadie thinks, not all the habits she picked up in England are commendable. Take off that ridiculous hat, darling. We can barely see your charming face."

"I would really rather not. I haven't had time to fix my hair and it's an unsightly mess. Ungodly, you might say."

"Don't be absurd. Sadie has the most beautiful head of luxurious hair. Even when she was a baby. Other mothers couldn't believe it."

Sadie had slid into an empty place at the table. "Were you worried you had given birth to a tiny beast? I suppose it's an entirely hypothetical question, but if you gave birth to a goat, would you drown it or raise it?"

Philip used this pause in the conversation created by Sadie's absurdity to employ the tactics he had learned in his book of manners. He turned toward Marie.

"I find the new housing being built along the river to be a terrible eyesore," he said. "Having grown up in a beautiful home, I have no tolerance for hideous structures."

Marie half-turned to him in reply but didn't take her eyes from Sadie. "It's a necessary expenditure. There are boatloads of new citizens arriving every day at the port. There needs to be immediate and affordable housing for them. It's a necessary expenditure for our factory. And it is an excellent investment. The rent checks of the workers will pay it all back within a few years."

Philip was silenced, surprised by Marie's knowledge of the workings of factories. He was about to open his mouth to attempt to say something knowledgeable when his sister interrupted.

"The city is spreading like an infection," Sadie announced. "It's like a venereal disease.

"Everybody wants to live the lie that the city offers. Upward mobility. It allows you a new identity. You can change your past and your character. You can go from being a poor person to being a rich person. You can go from being a murderess to being a society girl."

The mention of murder went through the room like an electrical storm.

Sadie's father demanded the maid bring in another course, or summon someone to play music, something, anything, to shut his daughter up. Sadie rarely saw him this stimulated. He was standing up and waving his arms about like an emotional orchestra conductor.

"Don't you want to know the woman you are marrying?" Sadie

continued, unperturbed. "It's interesting. Women are either one thing or the other. I am indisputably wicked and terrifying, and she is sheltered and pure. And yet we are guilty of exactly the same crime. Can't we all just be a bit of both? I don't think I was the one who came off the worse in the bargain, to be honest. I rather prefer being accused of being rotten. I think it has really allowed me a greater scope of freedom. I thank the heavens every day that I'm unmarriageable. It saves me from this banal spectacle of courtship. Where two people try to hide as much of their personalities from one another as possible."

"Take off your hat, Sadie. Stop trying to be deliberately provocative," her mother insisted.

"May I be excused in order to take my hat off?"

"No. You'll take it off right this second. I've had enough of waiting for you."

Sadie stared at her mother, smiled politely, and returned her attention to Philip. "I think it's interesting that we never talk about the duel. I spoke about it so often in Europe. Think about it, Philip. No one will ever accuse you of being boring now. You'll be marrying a murderess."

In the middle of the uproar of voices, Sadie whipped off her hat. The rat came tumbling out onto the table.

MARIE'S FATHER SEEMED REMARKABLY UNFAZED while riding home in the carriage. The shadows of the trees stretched like stockings being pulled off feet. The cold air was as crisp as an apple that had just been bitten into.

"Don't worry about anything Sadie said, by the way. The minute a woman starts ranting or raving, no one listens to a word she says. I've never understood bitterness in women. Or women who can't get over a slight. So much shit happened in my life, but I don't go around bellyaching about it, do I? She acts as though she's been slighted. The fact was that girl was stark-raving mad as a child. I'm surprised nobody saw it. They were just as mad to bring her back, even if it's what you wanted. Once a woman has been off on an adventure, they are completely unknowable. They are unpredictable."

Marie didn't know what to think on the way home. She was quiet. Sadie was a more extreme, delicious version of herself. Marie was always into the newest things possible. She wanted the newest shoes, the newest dresses, the newest dance moves, the newest care, the newest inventions. And here was Sadie with the newest ideas.

Sadie walked into her bedroom. She was flushed and delighted from her spectacle and having quite effectively ruined the meal. Her mood changed quickly when she saw her mother in the center of the room, reading her notebook. The very book she had been so careful to keep out of the hands of authority figures. Why was she worried about them at all? The only authority figure a girl ever had to worry about was her mother.

Sadie knew everything was over. She should have turned and run out the door right then. But she had a perverse desire to hear what her mother had to say to her. Her mother hated her more than anybody else in the world did. There is something that holds us like a magnet to the person who hates us the most.

Sadie knew her mother had imagined horrible things about her personality and what she might be capable of. But this was beyond the scope of her imagination. And so her mother was the perfect audience for the book. If every writer has an ideal reader, that was what her mother was.

Sadie felt in many ways she had walked in on a partner having an affair. The book had had its way. That was what a book wanted most: to have the most corrupt and devastating effect. To change the world of those who read it. It was tired of just having young girls diddling themselves while reading it when it had a more grandiose desire to subvert order. The book wanted to change the world, and it was about to change Sadie's.

Mrs. Arnett looked up from the book at her. Her mother looked at her with such hatred but also with such superiority. Was hatred always informed by a sense of superiority? She could openly hate her daughter now that she had the upper hand.

"How in the world did you find my book?" Sadie inquired.

"Marie told me where it was."

"God! Marie!"

"You are reprehensible. You are grotesque. I see it now. You are sick. There is a sickness I could never see in you because you are my daughter. I denied what I knew. You shouldn't be walking around with people. You can't be here. I need to protect my family from you. You are wicked. How can you have even imagined these things, let alone write about them? You are poisonous."

"But did you think it was well written?"

When her mother leaped to the door, Sadie didn't move. Her mother closed the door behind her, quickly locking it. The lock made quite a clunking noise. The doors in these houses were monumental. They could turn any room into a prison.

Sadie stood there as though trapped in a cage. She would break all her limbs were she to jump from her window. She had never been locked up as a punishment before. At boarding school, the punishments were all public performances. But this was different.

She felt the rage come out of her like a destructive and uncontrollable natural force. Like a tornado whirling forward. She had no power to stop the propulsion. She flung her fists against the door over and over until they were bruised and bloody. She screamed obscenities until her throat was raw and hoarse. If they thought she was rude and inappropriate before, well, she'd let them know about what was really going on in her head. Finally, she flung a chair against the door. The chair broke into pieces.

She collapsed in an armchair. Having weathered her anger, she was exhausted. They had taken her freedom away. But perhaps she had never had any freedom. What choices had she ever been able to make? She had considered herself free in thought. But what did that freedom of thought really mean if you were living at the mercy of other people? If you had no freedom over your body. If someone could send you across the ocean and then bring you back at will, what did freedom mean?

She rose and then flopped onto the bed as though she had been forced to walk off the edge of a plank. Though her mind was roiling, as soon as her body hit the mattress she was swallowed by the sea. She fell deep into the deep, dark sea of sleep. She hadn't slept so well in ages.

When she woke up, she hazily put her dressing robe on in order to go down to the kitchen. They would probably have some new plan of exile for her, but what did she care? There wasn't anywhere that was more soul draining than here. They would send her back to England, perhaps.

She would be a teacher. It would be better than posturing like an eligible bride when she was clearly no such thing. She tried the door handle and found it still locked. Her anger rushed up inside her again.

She rang the maid's bell and then sat on the edge of the bed. She waited and no one came. She rang the bell again and then threw it across the room. Suddenly, there was the sound of a key turning in the lock. The click of it made her body flinch and jump as though she had heard someone cocking the safety on a gun.

The maid had a tray of coffee in one hand and with the other she put her index finger over her mouth and motioned for Sadie to be quiet. She closed the door behind her and set the coffee down next to the bed.

"You can't stay here, ma'am. It's dangerous. I see who they sent for. It's the madhouse."

Both their cheeks flushed red at once. It was the unmentionable term. The greatest fear of girls everywhere. They weren't going to make the mistake of exiling her this time. A person from exile might always return. Instead they would have her committed. The most socially approved way of ruining a girl. She would never be heard from again.

"Where do I go?" Sadie asked.

"Take your fancy dresses. No one will have seen anything the likes of them in the Squalid Mile. Someone will be your friend. You'll get yourself a male companion in no time. He'll show you about. It's not so hard. It's what I'd be doing if I looked like you."

"Where is the Squalid Mile?"

"Where is the Squalid Mile! I didn't think it possible not to know of the place! It's near where you got off the boat. Keep going east of there. It'll get noisier and noisier until you can't bear it. Then you'll be in the right spot."

"Is it nice there?"

"Of course not. Take your dresses! If you aren't going to wear them, you'll sell them for good money at the market."

Sadie began to quickly put on her old striped dress. The dress had been sleeping and was startled awake. The maid opened a large cloth bag and began to shove Sadie's other dresses into it.

Sadie hurried out through the maids' corridors. There were ways to escape through the servants' quarters, as they had been specifically designed for the master of the house to zip in and out of. Sadie left out the back of her house and hastened down the hill away from the Golden

Mile. She was very sorry to have to leave without the notebook. She had had such a wonderful relationship with it. And there were blank pages left in it. But perhaps it was books who determined when they were done and not their authors.

The wind blew under her cloak and flung it around her as though she were a matador. And wasn't she?

CHAPTER 19

The Squalid Mile

adie passed through a giant park on the side of the hill in search of a shortcut. She crossed over the grass field. The autumn ground was like a soft carpet under her shoes. The great big trees that had lost their leaves were stretching their arms as they always did. They let her pass by. They didn't reach down to grab her. They knew she had to go.

Sadie descended from the Golden Mile onto Sherbrooke Street, a large commercial street at the midpoint of the hill. The bright, large windows of the stores displayed beautifully crafted items. In the window of the millinery, one of the hats on display had cloth pink roses piled on top of it. Sadie paused to consider whether they were real.

Even in her frazzled state of mind, beauty could arrest her. As she stood for that brief moment in front of the display of hats behind the glass, she was aware of the life choice she was making. She was leaving behind this world and all its perfectly arraigned artifice. As she began to descend farther south toward the river, she was aware she was moving behind the scenes of beauty.

She was about to go to the neighborhood where all those cloth roses were crafted. There were apartments crowded with women who made the roses with slender fingers covered in tape from pinpricks. Drops of blood would spring up on their fingers like ladybugs. And their teeth were all ragged from biting threads. They slept in bunk beds, eight to a tiny room that no body heat could save from being cold. There were small clouds of breath that came out of their mouths as they slept and filled the city with fog the next morning.

Yes, she was going backstage. Before, she had had the opportunity to be one of the actors and perform onstage. Now, she was going into the darkness where the stagehands crafted their illusions.

As soon as she reached the Squalid Mile, the factories by the river were shooting up black clouds, which made everything dirty. The buildings and houses were ugly, made out of bricks in squat rows that covered each side of the street. The streets themselves had just been made and were dirt with planks of woods laid down row after row to create a sidewalk. And there were no trees. There were heaps of horse manure all over the road. She had to keep her wits about her.

There was filth everywhere. The stench of human excrement coming from the rows of outhouses in the alleys was unbearable. Sadie pulled a perfumed handkerchief out of her cloak pocket and held it up to her nose.

Sadie passed a young girl who was holding a basket of laundry in her arms and laughing uproariously. It was the exact type of laughter she had been punished for at boarding school. No one had ever told this girl she was supposed to control her laughter. Her laughter would have been interpreted as almost violent in the Golden Mile. What a way to live! How much more intense joy would be if you were allowed to express it. What came first: the feeling or the reaction to the feeling? Sadie wanted to write something that would be as joyous and uncontrollable and un-contained as this girl's laughter was.

She noticed the ways in which girls on the streets went out of their way to be pretty, even though they weren't given a penny to spend on their looks and were wearing tattered, out-of-fashion dresses. A girl, noticing young men were present, raised her skirt almost to her knee as she was stepping over a puddle. Her faded stockings, the color of pink roses, were visible for a brief second to anyone who was watching. Her legs and ankles were almost unacceptably pretty. She was suddenly, with her skirt raised, the most attractive girl Sadie had ever seen. Ah! to create beauty without a cent, that was remarkable!

There was a mother who could not have been more than fifteen, bent down in front of a perambulator. She began singing an absurd French ditty to the baby inside: "*If you stop crying, tonight I will give you a slice of the moon.*" These people had nothing material to promise and offer one another. So they offered one another descriptions of the moon and pirates at sea. They offered one another jokes and snippets of poetry.

In the Golden Mile everyone spoke English. Here the voices mixed in a loud tapestry of languages. Sadie could hear French and English. She also heard what she thought was Gaelic. She heard a group of men arguing in Yiddish and a woman speaking Creole. It made a marvelous, cacophonous symphony.

Suddenly the filth seemed to not matter and Sadie was taken in by everything she was seeing. Everything was a metaphor she wanted to write about. This was a landscape where people acted in an openly poetic manner. They wore their hearts on their sleeves. They were expressing their passions openly. They were expressing rage and longing out on the street. They weren't hiding anything from one another. They seemed fearless to her. How wonderful, Sadie thought, to have nothing to lose.

She passed a group of men lugging a large barrel up a narrow wooden staircase. The barrel slipped out of their hands and hurled itself back down the stairs. Sadie moved into the alley to get out of their way. She came immediately up against a couple fucking against a wall. The girl didn't even have her feet on the ground. Her ass was being held up by the man, and her legs in striped stockings were wrapped around him. His pants had been lowered and you could see his buttocks forcing themselves back and forth into the ruffles of her pink skirt and petticoats. Her legs rocked back and forth in her striped stockings. Her black boots might have once looked pretty enough, but the soles were almost worn through.

Sadie had read and thought and wrote and imagined so much about sex. And here it was. She couldn't believe her eyes. There was something almost supernatural about seeing an act you had previously experienced only in fiction. She could not believe this was how people in the Golden Mile made love. She had never seen anything as intimate as the looks on their faces. It was sex for pleasure. Neither expected anything but pleasure from the encounter. They were having sex for the sake of having sex. They didn't have expectations. They hoped to God there were no consequences, no babies, no diseases. They were risking their futures to have sex against a wall.

Up above her, strings of laundry were strung up from one building to another, blocking out the sky as though it were an enormous flock of birds. Sadie passed through the market. She saw a man moving some cups around a table while people tried to guess which one the ball was under. The cups moved around like horse hooves doing fancy footwork at a fair.

Sadie stopped in front of a puppet show. There were two characters. One was a rich fat man. The other puppet was a very petite lower-class girl in a simple dress. The fat man tried to convince her to raise her skirts and allow him to violate her. He flirted with her charmingly but emphatically. She refused all his advances in a witty, droll manner. Every now and again the fat man lost patience with this courtship and lunged for the young woman so he could pin her down and rape her. She ran screaming from him. There was a large group of children who had pressed themselves up to the front of the stage. Whenever the fat man lost control and tried to rape the girl, they would all burst out laughing and clap their hands.

Sadie was enthralled by the puppet show. She had been raised to think the arts were created by a group of refined individuals who were masters of their craft. They had learned and perfected it through the aid of great teachers. And the art they produced from the fulcrum was meant to amuse the very wealthy. It was created to reflect themes that would appeal to a wealthy man sitting in a reserved theater box with his wife. It was epic and noble. The wicked were punished. The usurpers realized the error of their ways and either committed suicide or subjected themselves to punishment by the morally pure.

This puppeteer seemed as interested in the tastes of a seven-year-old watching as he was with the grown-ups standing behind them. His play was remarkable and modern. He would never be able to perform this on a large stage. As a result, he had complete artistic freedom away from the morality police. He was unfettered by conservative ideas of theater.

As she watched the puppet who drank to excess and scratched its own ass, Sadie thought, How wonderful to say what you want to say!

Indeed, everyone was shouting their deepest secrets at one another. Their arguments were coming right out the windows. She closed her eyes and absorbed the violence that was spoken from one lover to another. She was delighted she was in a place where she was not the most shocking person. She would still seek to achieve that, but there was much to learn first. What fertile soil this was to plant oneself in as an artist, she thought.

This was now her world.

CHAPTER 20

Étude for Hands with Four Fingers

Mary Robespierre's salary from the factory went to her grandparents. She slept on a cot at the foot of their bed. She could hear them breathing and snoring. She could hear the dry skin between their toes as they moved them against each other. They sounded as though they were eating even when they were sleeping. They made the rooting, grunting noises of pigs. She watched them in their sleep. They were rolled in blankets like cocoons. They looked like well-fed maggots.

MAKING CAKES AT NIGHT was a way to escape everything. She had once asked her mother if she could come see the house where she worked, but her mother was emphatic it was out of the question. However, her mother would bring her books from the Antoine household to read. She brought her paints and paper that Marie had been encouraged to draw on but did not. Art was a revelation to Mary. Her world was drab and ugly. But she could create anything she wanted on the page. She might draw herself a white horse or small cottage covered with climbing vines.

Whatever it was, when she stared at it, it was perfectly alive. But the loveliest thing Agatha did was to smuggle baking ingredients from the Antoine household in her satchel.

Mary Robespierre found she was very much able to think her own thoughts when she baked. In fact, she was able to think more extravagant and complex thoughts while she was crafting elaborate cakes. She never would have become evil were it not for baking cakes. The cakes made her do it.

She sold the cakes at the street market, and they were always a success. Even in the cold air of the winter, people would stop to buy her cakes. Her grandparents insisted on taking the money she made. They rolled the bills up and tucked them into a tin can, and the roll made the temporary fluttering sounds of a bird being put in a cage. Mary thought this went too far. The cakes were part of her creative self. Her talent was the one thing she had ever felt belonged indisputably to her. Her talent was upset at her because everything it gave to her, she subsequently gave away to her grandparents. Her talent was giving her the tools she needed to survive in the world. Her talent told her she had to get away.

Sometimes being courageous and brave means getting rid of those who are dependent on you. Her grandparents were parasites. The more she obtained for herself, the more they would sponge off her.

Mary began to think about her future and how she might change her present circumstances. Mary had known since she was ten years old that Louis Antoine was her father. Her mother had told her before she died. Single mothers can never keep anything from their children. They have no one to talk to other than them at night. They sleep in the same bed as them and divulge everything, as though they were lovers. She knew ever since she had learned the truth to keep her mouth shut about it. She was a bastard, after all.

But lately Mary had carefully considered how she could use the information about her parentage to her advantage. She went to visit Jeanne-Pauline. The older woman screwed up her face in curiosity when Mary walked into the drugstore. Fine lines appeared all over her face, as though it were an intricate map of a city.

"Ah! You have come to cure yourself of your grandparents!"

"No, no. It's not for them at all."

"Ah, for yourself."

"Yes, I want something that will make me feel absolutely no pain."

Jeanne-Pauline looked at the girl, realizing she was stranger than the others. Whatever Mary was up to, it was probably wicked. She always liked girls with subversive and dangerous potential.

Mary was very careful about how she dressed the next morning. She scrubbed herself clean. She brushed her hair to get the grease out so the shimmeriness of the blond was noticeable. The blond hair was important because it would make her look young and pretty. She ran to the factory so she would appear flushed and out of breath and just the right amount of sweaty. Then she stopped outside the factory. She slapped her right cheek hard and suddenly with her right hand. Then, just as quickly, her left cheek with her left hand

Then she walked in with her shoulders back. It would happen in the morning. She went to her station and began to sew the sugar bags shut. She finished ten bags and then on the eleventh when she placed the cord to be snipped by the blade, she slipped her pinky finger under and she never knew what it was up to ever again.

Before the blood and the chaos that ensued, she picked up her finger, wrapped it in a kerchief and plopped it into her pocket. She had to be very careful about expressing her wants. If she didn't get them across quickly, she would end up with a pet turkey on a leash.

❧

THE FOREMAN DROVE WITH HER to the hospital. She made an unusual request from him on the way. She asked that she might be able to speak to Louis Antoine in person. She reached into her pocket with her un-bloodied hand and took out a square piece of paper. It was a calling card she had designed herself. Her name was beautifully written on it. You might easily mistake it for the card of a lady. It was odd to only have one calling card. But she hardly had a constant need for them. The foreman thought it odd indeed to be taking a calling card from a girl off the factory floor. He found it even stranger that a factory girl would summon the owner and expect her request to be delivered.

"Please tell him to come see me at the hospital, and I won't go to the papers."

The foreman supposed he did not have a choice and put the card into his pocket instead of tossing it out the window.

She sat on a chair at the end of the waiting room, with her hand bandaged up, waiting for Louis to arrive. For a moment she worried she had lost a finger for nothing. But then she saw him coming down the hallway, his dark ermine coat waving behind him. He looked at her and sat on a chair across from her.

This was the second time she had been in the same room as this man. The first time he had imprisoned her. This time he would free her. The trick was to ask this man for the right thing. If you asked for the wrong wish from this man, it would ruin you. You would go back to that moment for the rest of your life and wish you had kept your mouth shut. He looked at her with such a peculiar intensity, she felt she could make her request now.

"Do you remember me?" Mary asked.

"Yes, of course. We always meet under the most unfortunate circumstances."

"Do you think you are bringing me bad luck?"

"No, not at all. That did not cross my mind. It's your bad luck, wouldn't you say? I arrive afterward."

"You must think my family especially accident-prone."

"It was lucky you lost your little finger. You will still be able to use your hands and carry on most activities as though nothing happened."

"Was I lucky like my mother?"

He looked frightened. She could tell he was debating standing up and leaving. He clearly couldn't decide what he was feeling. And men did not like to be made to feel confused by women. He might call her bluff and not do anything at all for her. And truth be told there might not be any consequences for him. The factories were always on the brink of a revolt. But the revolt never happened. The rage of the masses has short-term memory loss.

Mary noticed his hesitation and then launched into action. "I would like to have my own bakery, and I would like you to give it to me. I have drafted all the proposals."

She moved very quickly. She snatched the rolls of paper from the inside pocket of her coat and spread them out on a nearby table. They were not there and then all of a sudden they were directly in front of him. Clearly her missing finger was in no way impeding her movements. There was a sketch of the outside of a small unused building next to the factory. In the drawing, it was no longer decrepit and had the name "Robespierre Bakery" painted in gold on the window. From that one drawing, he immediately saw she had talent. She had taken an eyesore of a building and had turned it into something darling and pretty.

There was a drawing of the interior. And then she unrolled a financial outline. It had the prices for all the appliances she would need. She had the amounts of ingredients she would need to start up, of course. She had every detail itemized, right down to the fee she would pay the sign painter to paint the words "Robespierre Bakery" on the glass in sparkly gold lettering. She spread her hands over the thin paper and it made the sound of a fire crackling.

She then cautiously handed him the financial details, which included the amount of money she would need from Louis for an investment. She wanted an extended lease on the building and property. She would have it for free for the first six months. After which she would be able to pay the rent herself.

"There are already plenty of bakeries in the neighborhood. What makes you so sure your cakes will sell?"

Her eyes lit up with anticipation when he said this. She was clearly delighted he had asked a question she had the exact answer to. She pulled out the rest of the drawings. She began unfolding them one by one. She kept glancing up. Even though Louis was her most cursed enemy, she still wanted to see his reaction to her drawings of cakes.

She knew there was something spectacular about her cakes. Although everything in her past would indicate that she should, Mary did not suffer from low self-esteem. She knew when she was good at something. She never doubted her potential. If anything, she was conceited. You needed that often-maligned quality to achieve greatness.

Louis had never described plans as beautiful before. But the drawings of cakes and cookies made him feel as though he were being presented with an astronomer's map of a perfect universe. He had no idea how she would execute these drawings and turn them into edible sculptures. But it was a noble enterprise. If he himself were to pass a window and see cakes that in any way resembled the ones she had drawn, he would have to buy them. They seemed too good to be true. And he had seen a lot of things in his day.

"They might seem improbable to you, but I have been making two dollars a week selling them at the street stalls. There's always more demand than I can meet."

Mary then went for her pièce de résistance. She pulled a small box out from the breast pocket of her coat. She laid it on top of all the plans and opened it. She saw Louis's eyes light up in amazement at the perfect chocolate ball with pink roses surrounding it. "It makes sense the factory should have a fine bakery," Mary said. "You want to be able to showcase what your sugar can do, don't you?"

Mary needed Louis to realize her dreams, but she also needed to see Louis to get her away from her grandparents. They would make sure they benefitted from her losing a finger and opening a bakery. Then it would all have been for nothing. "I want you to get my grandparents to leave me alone forever. I don't know how you would go about doing this. But I don't want to think about it. I'm poor; I don't know how to get people to do what I want them to do. You do."

AND SO, MARY ROBESPIERRE'S GRANDPARENTS were willingly paid off. And a little bakery was installed in a small shop in the shadows of the huge factory building. It would, of course, have difficulty distinguishing itself. How could any store in the presence of so much dinginess hope to emanate any sort of delight? She was unfazed. She had the opportunity to get out of the factory and she was going to.

❧

WHEN LOUIS WENT HOME AFTER speaking to Mary, he felt trapped. There was always a woman who was trying to get something from him. He began to think about his dead wife, Hortense.

He wished Hortense hadn't died. He wished he had treated her better. He thought if she were here right now, he would love her and he would have a life partner. And he was so alone in the world. Marie would be leaving. She would never adore him in the same way once she realized what he had allowed with her marriage. And at that moment he felt a wave of self-pity from which he would never recover.

Louis returned to his womanizing ways with a vengeance. No one was sure why.

CHAPTER 21

The Death of a Ladies' Man

Marie kept crying when she thought of Sadie and the exile she had caused. Perhaps her love was poisonous. Perhaps every time Marie tried to express her love, it would end up harming the object of her affection.

She had gone through so much effort to get Sadie back to Montreal. She would have preferred Sadie were still in Europe than be here but lost to her. When she heard that Sadie had run away to the poor parts of the city, she sent a man to find out whether this were in fact the case. He returned that evening with a report.

"I asked a group of streetwalkers whether they had seen anyone fancy strolling around. They knew someone who fit the description right away. They say she speaks with a British accent. Not because she's from England, but because she thinks she's better than everybody else."

"Yes, that's her."

"She had ink all over her fingertips. She always carries a large black book for writing in around with her."

"Yes, yes, that's her."

"I just missed her apparently. If I'd have been there five minutes before, I would have seen her choking on an oyster she slurped too quickly."

He was not sure where she was living as of yet, but would be able to tell her soon. Marie shook her head no and wept in frustration. She couldn't bear to hear Sadie's adventures for a spell. Because no matter what Sadie was doing, it was infinitely more fascinating than what she herself was engaged in. Sadie was wandering around in the realms of the new. She remembered the old poem that had caused so much strife between them. Sadie had gone off to Goblin Market.

Marie found Philip's resemblance to Sadie to be almost painful now. She hated that all the Arnetts had been privy to everything in Sadie's notebook but she hadn't. They thought it was all filth, but she was sure she wouldn't. She would have thought it was beautiful. She still wanted to ask whether Sadie had written about her. But she felt that even if Sadie had, it would be in a manner her mother and brother might not even recognize. Sadie might have written about a rose in a way Marie would recognize as herself.

Her attachment to Philip only served to alienate her from Sadie. Sadie saw her as one of them. She felt like ending the engagement. But she knew it would cause a scandal. She and her father never cared about scandal, given that they were the most powerful and richest family in the Golden Mile, but the Arnetts were a special case. It infuriated her that they had this power. She cursed the stupid maid Agatha, who was stupid enough to run in front of a bullet and tie her to Sadie's wretched family for life. She felt trapped and frightened by the Arnetts. If this was the way they had treated Sadie for acting out on her own and doing what she pleased, what would they do to her?

She sat dutifully and miserably with Philip on a park bench in front of a pond the ducks had all abandoned to fly south. The air was cold, and she pulled her fur wrap tightly around her neck. There was a red leaf that floated to the surface of the water like an image appearing in a developing photograph.

"Have you had any news from Sadie?" Marie asked.

"She's insane. She'll end up dead in the river. As you know, we all read her diaries, and quite frankly, she's the type of girl who ends up cavorting with men. She has no virtue. And when she allows herself to be murdered, it will honestly be a godsend for the family."

"It is strange to hear you talk that way about your sister."

"Perhaps. I am sorry she is to be your sister-in-law once we are married."

"I wish only one thing from you," Marie said.

"What is that?" Philip said, eyeing her suspiciously.

"You stop trying to put Sadie away in the madhouse. I just want you to let her be."

"If that makes you happy. As long as she doesn't interfere with the family, we are happy to pretend she is dead. It would be a scandal to have her put away. It is better for everybody if she simply disappears."

In that way Marie felt at least she had made some effort to protect Sadie. Even though Philip had expressed he was acting in his own interests, she liked to feel she was protecting Sadie by staying with him. She reflected on her own tragic nobility for a moment.

She wished she could marry Sadie instead of Philip. Sadie would be forced to stand next to her and be photographed. And that photograph would hang on the wall. Sadie would be forced to live with her and have breakfast with her every morning. Sadie would have to tell her where she was every moment of the day. She would be legally bound to her. Marie had never quite realized the potential for imprisonment marriage was. It startled her. She didn't know what to think.

THEN LOUIS DIED SUDDENLY OF a heart attack. The facts behind his death were not known to the general public. But he had died doing what he loved best.

He was on top of a maid from Dominica named Flore. She had a petite body and a large round head, which always gave the impression she was somehow defying physics by not toppling over. He was amazed at his own prowess. He loved to put the full weight of his body on a girl. He always found it made them come faster. He loved the intensity of it all. He loved pounding away at a girl. He was always thrilled by how much force a woman's body could take while being fucked. In any other circumstance when you showed them force, they were hurt and wounded.

He liked giving women orgasms. In that way he could never feel guilty about seducing the women. It could never be considered rape if the girls had an orgasm. He turned their orgasms against them. He considered their orgasm to be a form of consent.

He kept thrusting into Flore harder and harder. He kept banging harder and she kept moaning louder with more pleasure. And then she came. And he felt her come so hard. His whole body rocked and shook with it. He felt his body seize up. She was crying out in joy and didn't seem at all aware of what his body was going through. He was frightened by her orgasm. He looked into her eyes, trying to figure out if she knew what she was doing, but her eyes were squeezed shut. She had left him. She had forgotten all about him. She was imagining someone younger, someone more handsome, someone she would probably make love to next.

He couldn't breathe. His chest tightened violently, as though he were being crushed. He wanted to get off of her. Her orgasm seemed to have struck him like a bolt of lightning. He couldn't struggle against it anymore.

Louis had never properly grieved for his wife before. Everyone said he would. Everyone offered him advice about how it was going to feel and how he would be able to recover from it. They said it would take him about two years for the feelings of grief to lessen. And so he had waited for two years. He expected the emotions to come. But they never did. He felt no inkling of them. People said they could come out of nowhere, like a surprise. But they never did.

Suddenly now he thought back on his wife. Hortense had been the only woman who had been kind to him his whole life. Hortense, who had offered him the world. How could it be possible that grief was still there, after all these years, fully formed, waiting for him?

THREE OTHER MAIDS BURST INTO the locked room, responding to Flore's hysterical screams. When they opened the door, they found her pinned beneath Mr. Antoine's body. They ran in to shift the man. They pulled his body over onto his back.

They took a moment to stare at his naked body quietly, sharing a feeling of collective revulsion. It was strange to look at a body that had once been so vibrant and full of life but that was now a shell. A body without its personality always seemed too odd and unfamiliar. It was as though someone they had never met before was lying in the room. The features seemed like caricatures of Louis's. It was like looking at a wax figure of him at a museum.

And none of them had ever seen him with a penis that wasn't erect.

IN THE DAYS FOLLOWING HER father's death, Marie walked down the hallway in her nightgown, looked pressed upon, as though she had been summoned by girls playing with a Ouija board.

And Marie, who had already been struggling with loneliness, gave up on the struggle. It seemed unkind not to suffer at that moment if she could. Whereas before she would have done anything to stop her loneliness, now she welcomed it in the room like a rush of dark water. And she spread her arms and allowed herself to be submerged in it. She floated through the house in the water. She floated above her bed. Her whole body seemed drenched in tears. And she never wanted to stop crying.

How could this be? She had thought she and her father were inseparable. She woke up sobbing at the top of her lungs in the middle of the night, as though she had just been born: A strange creature with only two arms and two legs, and one stupid single broken heart.

Marie was shocked how empty the house was without him. She kept calling out to her father and realizing he could not answer. She would suddenly sit up and wonder, Where is Papa? I haven't seen him in so long. Then she would realize in a sudden gasp of recognition that he was not there. That he would never be there. And this sick, empty feeling inside her was something she would have to get used to for the rest of her life, and that seemed unbearable.

She realized how many of her daily rituals included Louis. She missed coming to the breakfast table, where the two of them sat half-dressed in their enormous robes, and giving him a big kiss on the lips. And they would eat piles of pastries smothered in warm jam and hot cream and be utterly content.

MARIE WAS NOW IN CHARGE of all the money. The factory money, her father's money, her mother's money. Her immediate reaction was to begin spending it in an extravagant manner. The idea of spending as much money as she possibly could was comforting. It gave her a physical pleasure. She realized that was what funerals were for. The only way to counter the ugliness and uncertainty of life was to tackle it in an aesthetic manner.

When the funeral was held, there were twenty-five blond children dressed in black suits walking ahead of the horses under the white wintery sky. She had wanted them to be blond so their hair contrasted against their dark clothing. There was one very slim boy in front. He had a beautiful face. The most beautiful of children's faces always looked sad.

Then came the row of black horses, each with black feathers on their heads. There was a white horse with black spots and a wreath of black roses in its mane being led by a girl in a black dress and an enormous black ribbon in her hair. The carriage that held Louis's body was completely covered in white roses. Marie thought white roses were appropriate because she thought of her father as the most sensitive man she had ever met. In her mind, he was innocent to the darkness of the world, and always insisted on living in a light-filled castle.

She was almost glad that in some ways her father's death coincided with Sadie's disappearance. It was a distraction. A parent's death was inevitable. The heart knew how to deal with it. Even if it was the most beloved parent in the world, the heart knew how to deal with it. But when someone you love abandons you, a sort of madness sets in. And to be honest, anything painful can be pleasurable if it distracts from the madness.

She appreciated being in a period of mourning.

IN THE DAYS FOLLOWING THE FUNERAL, Marie sat at her father's desk in his office at home. She held her back perfectly straight and crossed her hands in front of her. She made eye contact with whoever spoke to her.

There were lawyers around her who were talking all at once. In their dark suits they seemed like a forest surrounding her. Marie's blond hair made her look like a clearing in the woods the light still managed to shine into. They were speaking about things she couldn't quite understand and in a manner she couldn't follow. She had learned so much about factories on her travels, and she was certain she inherently understood her own, but the reality of actually running one was, of course, quite different. They all had papers and documents and scrolls and portfolios. They were waving pens at her. Although every fiber in her body felt intimidated, she was not going to sign anything she didn't understand. She knew that much. She knew not to give any of her power away.

Now that Louis was gone, the party was in many ways over. She could never get away with the things he had gotten away with. She could not act the way she had before. She was an unmarried woman. She was suddenly under a microscope. They were waiting for a single gesture to criticize and tear apart. If an itch sprung up somewhere on her body and she went out of her way to scratch it, she would be branded as loose. Everyone would be disgusted by her, no matter how much money she had.

She had always taken the estimation of people around her for granted. That something she considered so integral to herself could be taken away now was terrifying. She felt the loss of Louis's protection. She felt like a gazelle surrounded by lions. Of course they were going to come for her. How could they not?

"We shall decide all of this in the coming weeks," she said. "After I have had a chance to peruse these documents. I look forward very much to working with you gentlemen and hearing your concerns one by one."

✦

LATER THAT DAY, LOUIS'S SOLICITOR sat down with her. He had light-brown eyes, the color of a murky pond, and she waited for something to emerge from their depths. He explained to Marie she would never be able to run such a large house by herself. It was impossible. She didn't want to do such a thing anyway. She shouldn't be bothered with something so mundane. Since she was only twenty-two and a woman, he was prepared to assign a legal guardian to her who would continue to look after her. Marie was taken off guard by the comment, as it was something she had not considered.

"No. Why would I want that? Why would I give away all my agency to someone else? I'm not a child. I'm not anyone's daughter now. And I never intend to be again."

"I understand, miss. These are difficult times for you. We will not bother you with important decisions right now anyway. We will wait to speak to Mr. Arnett about it."

"Mr. Arnett?" Marie asked, genuinely taken aback that Philip would be expected to have a say in this matter.

"We will wait until you are married and everything is in its proper place. Everyone has assumed their proper roles. He is going to be re-sponsible for you."

"Don't be stupid," Marie answered, her body stiffening a little to deflect her injured pride.

"Are you prepared to speak to the factory workers? You have to an-nounce your father's death and that you are the new owner."

"Yes, of course," she said, although she most certainly was not.

❦

ON THE DAY SHE WAS to give her speech, Marie's hands were shaking all morning. She had known exactly how she was supposed to act at her father's funeral. She had seen that kind of performance so many times before. And it came organically to her. She had seen any number of young women looking tragic and bereft at funerals. But she had never seen a young woman addressing a crowd of workers.

Because of her new position in life, she knew she had changed. But she could not see herself from the outside. She did not know what this change would look like. But other people would. It wasn't the type of change you could see in the mirror. It was the type of change you had to see reflected back in other people's faces.

Marie stood above the workers on the steel bridge over the factory floor. They were waiting on her word to see whether they were going to be able to eat or not. This was what power looked like. It was people looking up at you and hanging on your every word.

"As you all have heard, my father, Louis Antoine, recently passed away. He was a wonderful man, full of life and love, and I will miss him every day for the rest of my life. But I want you to know that I possess and will uphold all of his best attributes. You might think it strange that a woman so young should now be the owner of this factory, your factory. I know I have much to learn, but I will learn it. And I would like to learn from you too. I have no family now, and I would like to think of you all as one. I want us to do great things together. And I want you to know I am here for all of you."

The factory workers applauded. Marie felt a huge surge of love rise up from below her. It brought tears to her eyes.

She would order the factory foreman to be kinder to the workers and to give the children lunch breaks. Owning the factory had meant something different to her than it had to her father. For him it meant having a massive house and being able to purchase any delightful thing that crossed his mind. But for her it was about power and responsibility. She was this factory. It was her face on the bags of sugar that were being shipped all over the province.

She could not have a husband. She felt it, the disastrous import of what it would be like to be married. For most women, the realization came afterward. After the ceremony. After the leftover cake had been poked at by the fingers of children and was lying on the ground. After the bottoms of their stockings were stained with blood from dancing. After the pearl necklace had broken and had fallen on the floor. After you didn't know whether what you experienced in the wedding bed had been pleasurable or painful. It happened when it was too late. Realizations enjoyed occurring when they were most effective and poignant and you could do nothing about them. It was the realization that you owned nothing. You were nothing. You had lost your rights to be a person.

It came upon her as she was standing above all her workers. Her whole body felt as though it were about to be robbed of something. If she had a husband, nobody would look at her the way they did now. They would instead divert all their questions to him. She would look at them looking at someone else. But they would never look her in the eye. She would start to become less and less visible. She would disappear layer by layer, like a painting being painted in reverse. She would become paler and paler. Then she would be nothing but a sketch on a paper. Then you would look and see nothing but the snow.

Philip would use this factory and her to become an important political figure, if not the most. He was going to take all this power from her. In the same way her father had from her mother. It belonged to the women in the family, not the men. She was not going to give this to Philip; she was not going to give it to anyone. She wanted it for herself.

Freedom and power were one and the same and were interchangeable. They came hand in hand.

ONCE A PARENT IS DEAD, you find yourself recalling the advice they gave you. You remember ways you disappointed them, with a full awareness that you will never be able to make things right. Marie felt she had disappointed Louis by getting engaged to Philip. She went to kneel on his grave. She wrapped her arms around the gravestone. She kissed it all over.

"What can I do for you, Papa? How can I make you happy now? Remember how you said I was the thing that made you the most happy in all the world? How can I make you happy now? I'm not going to marry Philip. I will renounce my love for Sadie. I understand now. You expected more of me."

Marie stood by the grave until the sun went down and it started to get colder and colder out. She knew it would be unacceptable behavior. She knew everyone in society would be appalled at her decision. She couldn't break off an engagement; they had been walking together in public! But she would do it nonetheless.

After she left the graveyard, a deer with large antlers tiptoed through the tombstones like a maid carrying a candelabra through a dark hallway.

CHAPTER 22

The Violation

It was overcast a few days later and everyone looking out their windows was forecasting snow. There was an expectancy in the sky, as though it were waiting for a church bell to break it. The leaves on the pond were like stamps that had been steamed off a letter.

Marie decided she would end the courtship with Philip that afternoon. She felt good about her decision. She knew it was one she would not have been able to make before her father died, and she was proud of her new independence. She imagined Philip wouldn't be terribly upset about it. He must know it had been a strange bit of luck that had caused them to be together in the first place. She was too good for him. And in fact, she was too good for any of the men in the neighborhood. Sadie was gone and had taken all the blame of the murder with her. It was unnecessary to worry about the effects the murder might have on her reputation anymore. It had always been her father's preoccupation anyhow.

She went to walk with Philip in order to break the news cordially. She considered doing it by letter, but she wanted to get his answer right away in order to get it over with.

They walked up together into the mountain behind Marie's mansion in their coats and boots. Marie knew it was something she ought to do in private, in order to spare Philip a public humiliation.

"I have to tell you something," Marie said, stopping when they reached the bank of the stream.

"What is it?" Philip asked.

"I cannot marry you."

Philip was very, very quiet. He stared at Marie in a way she found physically threatening. The features on his face began to twist in an expression she had never seen before. She wondered why she had ever imagined he looked like Sadie. She looked and looked in his face, but Sadie was not there. Marie felt alarmed. She had an urge to run back to her house. But she stood there, waiting for Philip's response. The cloud of white breath coming from his nose began to expand.

"You think you're sweet and virtuous, but you're none of those things. You are a little bitch, Marie Antoine. And there's no way you can argue otherwise. I've watched you be cruel to all the other girls for years and years. I watched it and I always thought, I'm going to be the one who breaks that bitch. I'm going to pay her back for everything she has ever done. You belong to me. You think you're going to break off our courtship and make a fool of me? You are only here because my family arranged for Sadie to be punished for your crime. You owe my family everything."

Marie was taken aback by the brutality of his words. She had never heard a man speak to her in this way. And since it was alien to her, she knew it was something she shouldn't be hearing and knew it was inappropriate. She realized the words were sexual. And that these words were a form of dark foreplay. One that made the girl freeze and lose her sense of reality. And wasn't that the same effect unwanted kissing and stroking had on a woman?

As she realized what was happening, Marie turned to get away. She began to run. Her chest was heaving as her lungs and heart squeezed against her corset. She ran over the rocks of the stream.

Her foot sank in the soil. Her dress was sloshing through the mud and bramble. She felt as though she were in a dream as she was running from a possibly imaginary threat. She thought it was most likely Philip wasn't chasing her. And why in the world would he be? What could he possibly do to her now?

She stopped for a moment at an incline of trees. She stopped and turned to see Philip was right behind her. He knocked her to the ground.

She felt herself being flipped over and her crinoline fly up. She couldn't half see what he was doing to her. She couldn't reach him with her hands. It was as though her dress were conspiring to rape her too. She kicked with her feet violently as he began to thrust his hips up to her. His breeches were down and he was inside her.

She stood up and the front of her dress was soaked in mud. Philip had already begun to walk away from her. It had started to rain. She stood in the rain and waited for the downpour to wash the mud off her. Then the rain turned to snow and she had no choice but to go home.

MARIE YELLED OUT THAT SHE needed a bath immediately. She sank into the bath in her petticoats. And her maids poured pitchers of warm water on her. "Just keep doing that for a while," she said.

She knew from the way the maids looked at her that they understood what had happened. And also that it was something that happened on a more or less regular basis. This was part of life.

She stopped eating. She had always been so plump and jolly, but now she was growing thinner. She stared at herself in the mirror every day. She was glad she was changing physically because she couldn't accept that anything about her could remain the same. She looked at her face as though it were that of a stranger. Her eyes seemed to have gotten wider and bluer. She stopped bothering to put her hair up in different ways. She let it fall down all around her in a tangled knot of thin golden strands. She began wearing the same simple beige shift dress every day. When she got stains on it she didn't care. There was a coffee stain on the lace pattern above her breast that looked rather like the shape of Brazil. There was a menstrual blood stain on the back of her dress. It was a menstruation she was rather happy to see arrive.

She learned from the maids that Philip destroyed her reputation. He had sullied her character while he was outraged. And now he could not marry her. If he had waited patiently, he would have been able to use her ruin to make her marry him. Now he couldn't even sue her for breach of contract. She was certain that Philip was outraged because he had missed out on this fortune. That he still saw Marie as rightfully his and, more important, he saw her money as his. He had ensured that if she wasn't marrying him, she would never be able to marry anybody else either.

He did not describe it as rape. He told all the other men she had wanted it. He couldn't resist. She had thrown herself at him. She was so filled with lust and expertise, she had clearly done it before. He had to hold his hand over her mouth because she was crying out so loud from pleasure.

When she heard the rumors Philip was spreading, she felt as though she were cringing in the corner like a beaten dog. Because everyone in the Golden Mile gossiped about what happened to her, she felt they were complicit. They were assaulting her over and over again. She tried to pull herself together one morning and put on a fashionable poufy white dress. She overheard two maids recounting how Philip had said she was insatiable. She leaned against the wall as though to become invisible. She slid down the wall onto the floor like a heap of snow and waited to melt into a puddle.

Marie watched the snow fall down through her window. It suffocated everything. It put all the plants and trees and gardens to sleep. It emptied the sky of birds and silenced the noises of people and animals. It was as though the snow were putting an end to all of civilization. And Marie wished it would.

She knew she herself was not allowed to talk about what had happened to her. Once again she was supposed to be quiet about something traumatic in her life. Everyone in the neighborhood knew and they would all talk about it behind her back. But she wouldn't be permitted to talk about it herself.

Her idea of what it was to be a woman was being built all over again. You could not be pretty. You could not be cordial. You could not put the feelings of other people above your own. These were all instructions to make a woman weak so that any man could take her down.

She was like Mary Shelley bringing Frankenstein's monster to life. Because being raped felt very much like being murdered. She was reanimating a dead body. She was animating each of her fingers. She held them over her face while she was in bed and began to wiggle them. She spent a day looking down at her toes. She raised one leg up in the air and then the other. She sat up and looked at her breasts as though they had presented themselves on her body for the first time.

Although she felt more alone than ever, there was something about the rape that made her cease to miss her father.

She reexamined all her memories of sex. She had seen maids coming out of her father's room in various stages of undress with their hair a mess and their cheeks flushed. She had heard laughter from her father's room. She had thought of sex as a lark. She didn't know there was within it the seeds of such darkness and humiliation. She had always seen it from her father's point of view. She had seen it from the man's point of view. The man was in control. What power men had over women! Before, she had considered all the women coming out of her father's room to have been engaged in consensual behavior. What shame they must have felt, returning to their rooms.

Now she had a dream of crowds of naked women trying to get out of her father's room. Their nudity was not at all charming. It was grotesque. It was like looking at the bodies of looted soldiers on a battlefield.

She had always believed she and her father were on the same side. They were both wealthy and the maids were poor. But now here she was in the same position he had put the maids in.

And somehow this cured her of her grief for her father. The girl who had loved her father and had been so close to him had also died. She grieved the girl more. But somehow she no longer mourned Louis. As a philosopher once noted, you feel the loss of something until it is completely lost.

CHAPTER 23

Sometimes There Is a

Pearl in an Oyster

After her initial euphoria about her freedom, the reality of Sadie's situation began to sink in. She was so filled with shock, she couldn't feel anything yet. She knew her emotions were going to come back. She was terrified of them. It was like expecting an abusive, drunk husband to come back from the tavern.

Her rage, almost to her surprise, wasn't directed at her parents. She had always known they were idiotic fools who despised her for no reason. How could she be upset with them? Instead, she felt enraged at Marie. She had expected so much of Marie, and her old friend had let her down. She couldn't help but feel Marie was responsible for her being in this tiny room, forced to figure out how to exist in the world on her own.

How could Marie have turned over her life's work to her mother? It had been right after a moment when Sadie had let her guard down. When Sadie had shown her affection. Marie pretended to love her, but then she would get her into these circumstances. Marie was always living in the same cozy home while Sadie suffered the consequences of their weird passion. As a noisy cart filled with bottles passed her, Sadie lifted her face to the sky and yelled, "To hell with you, Marie Antoine! Your stupid games are going to kill me."

Sadie starting weeping. Her tears were boiling hot, as if they had been heating up on a little pot in her brain and had been boiled by her rage.

She had to find a way to deal with her outrage toward Marie. She went to the general store and traded her silk gloves for a notebook and a fountain pen. To make up the difference, the store owner put several coins in her hands. She would be able to eat and find a hotel later, she thought. She went to a small church and went to sit on a back pew to write. She would spend time with Marie on the page. Writing was a form of exorcism. It made whatever was happening in your mind exist in another realm. Somewhere where it could be contained and you could make philosophical sense out of it.

It would be fiction. The only way to capture the strangeness of that relationship was through allegory and make-believe. She would describe what might happen were they actually to spend their lives together, acting out their desires. Perhaps it could never come to be in the real world, but it was the type of thing that could happen in fiction.

Her feelings for Marie were all tangled in a huge knot. As she put her pen down to the paper, a string came out. She was unraveling that great ball of twine into a story. She paused for a moment. She needed to come up with two fictional names for the characters. She settled on Justine and Juliette.

SHE HAD LOST TRACK OF TIME writing all day when she became aware of how ravenous she was. When she stepped out onto the street at eight o'clock one night, the darkness seemed as wet and tense as a deer's nose. Sadie knew the Squalid Mile was dangerous. She felt it for the first time now.

Sadie wasn't used to eating all her meals standing up outside at stalls, especially in the cold. But they lined the streets of the Squalid Mile and she was frightened to go into one of the noisy taverns or chop shops. The only thing she could afford at one of the stalls without selling another article of clothing was oysters and a pastry. She slurped them at the oyster shack on the corner ravenously. She quite enjoyed knocking back a bowl of soup in the cold wind. Everything tasted saltier outside. Table manners were entirely irrelevant, as there was no table to sit at. It was definitely cheap.

There was a group of women around her under the awning of the oyster shack. They were eating and seemed indifferent to the cold. The dust from the coal in the air made their skin sparkle in the evening. They began talking about work that evening, and it was clear they were prostitutes. For the purposes of her book, Sadie's curiosity was piqued by the women's profession. Sadie asked a slender, curly haired prostitute about it.

"How are the men supposed to know that you are for sale?"

"Walk past a man and then turn around and look back at him. He'll know. That's an invitation. Sometimes I lift up my skirt just a bit higher than anyone would think was appropriate."

The women started laughing at this. Clearly they felt she raised her dress far higher than that.

She demonstrated to Sadie. She took a theatrical step back from the other women. The prostitute raised the front of her skirts and Sadie could make out her petticoats that were soiled. She had striped white-and-red stockings, and there was something so childlike about them. Sadie realized, looking at the prostitute's stockinged legs, just how young she was. She realized she had been mistaken about the girl's age.

She had thought her to be much older, but now realized she was only about fifteen years old.

"What's a fancy woman like you want to know for?" another prostitute, whose dark, slicked curls looked as though they had been painted on her forehead, asked her.

"What makes you think I'm fancy."

"The way you talk," they all answered at once.

"You want to work on this corner and take our business, do you?"

The prostitutes started surrounding her. They all started cursing her. She tried to leave, but they began pulling at her cloak.

"Your dress is expensive under there. Why don't you hand it over?"

Sadie was suddenly pushed up against the wall as the prostitutes began to tear at her clothes. A slender man wearing a long black coat and a beaten-up top hat stepped between Sadie and the women and held up his hand. The women backed away. Sadie was stunned to see she had a protector. The man was very young and strangely thin. He put his hand under Sadie's arm and led her away down the street. The man moved with a peculiar lightness, almost as though he were dancing. He reached into his breast pocket and pulled out a cigarette. He exhaled the smoke through his nose and it curled to form a white mustache. He looked at Sadie with his large eyes that were framed with very long lashes and smiled sweetly. Sadie didn't feel at all alarmed by the presence of a man as she usually did, which surprised her.

She was even more confused when the voice that came out of the slender man's mouth was high-pitched and soft, and clearly that of a woman.

THE SLENDER MAN WITH THE voice of a woman introduced herself as George and asked her to wait. George went back to the group of prostitutes, who were still hanging around nearby, and pulled a handful of flyers from her breast pocket to give them. The women looked at them dismissively.

George returned and again took Sadie by the arm. "Don't worry about them," George said. "They have strange ideas about having a good time."

As they walked away, Sadie half expected the women to come after her. Instead, all she could make out was the sound of them all laughing. She imagined that no matter what circumstances they found themselves in over the course of a day, they would end up having a good laugh about it. Laughter was like tossing a bucket of water on any inflammatory situation.

Sadie turned her attention to her protector. She was very odd-looking, and unattractive by any classical standards of beauty. But the way she walked in her masculine getup was charming. And she nodded and winked at everyone who passed as though there wasn't a single person she considered a stranger.

"What were those pieces of paper you gave them?"

"They are some pamphlets about women's suffrage. They were mailed to me by the suffragette society in New York City, if you can believe it. I wrote to them one afternoon, and they wrote me back! And sent along those flyers to educate my own countrywomen. My full name is George Danton, by the way. Actually, my given name is Georgina Danton, but you know, George suits me better."

"I'm Sadie. Sadie Arnett. Of 54 McGregor Avenue. Except not anymore, of course."

"It's lovely to meet you, Sadie Arnett of uncertain address."

George's sense of humor was infectious, and Sadie felt herself become calmer.

"You have an intelligent face. It's not one I would forget. What brings you to this neighborhood?"

"I ran away from my home in the Golden Mile."

"Do they have British accents up there now?"

"I lived in England for nine years. I've been here since the morning."

"I'm surprised you didn't have any run-ins before you met those women."

"I hope I don't run into them again."

"Well, come over to my home for a cup of tea then." George took off her top hat, twirled it on her finger, tucked it under her arm, and looked at Sadie.

"All right," said Sadie.

"Wonderful!" George said with great enthusiasm. Sadie wondered if she was dead and this was an angel, because people were never so amenable.

Sadie was surprised when George led her to a large house on the corner of a street that was brightly illuminated by gaslights. It was one of the few stone houses in the neighborhood. It had gorgeous wooden moldings below the peaked roof that were covered in carvings of symmetrical flowers. It had clearly once been a fancy farmhouse before the ghetto had sprung up around it. From the music coming out the window, the sound of women's laughter, and the men walking up and down the front stairs, Sadie deduced at once it was a brothel.

"I know the last thing you're in the mood to see right now are whores. But don't worry about it. These girls aren't worried about competition. If anything, they would welcome the help. As soon as Madame began advertising the brothel as exclusive, business has been booming. Nobody has any idea what she means by exclusive, though. Is it the girls who are exclusive? I don't think so. They show up at the door without shoes. Not ever even having had a bath in their lives."

"Do you work here? Are you exclusive?"

"No." George laughed. "But I'm certain I would be considered exclusive!"

George put her hand on Sadie's back and led her away from the front of the building. Sadie reflected on how gentle George's touch was. There was something naturally considerate about her. They entered through the back of the building. Sadie couldn't make out much of what was going on in the brothel. They were in the servants' quarters of the house. All she could make out was laughter and hysterical piano playing from the next room. George hurried her up a flight of stairs to a room in an attic, taking Sadie's hand when she needed to step over a pile of porcelain washbasins that had been left on a landing.

It was evident that George had done her best to render her attic room cozy. There was an oval-shaped painting of a deer standing on its hind legs. There was a cigarette burn in the painting. Everything was slightly damaged. That was how it came to be moved up to the attic, out of sight. There was a red carpet that had a large black hole in the middle indicating it had survived some sort of fire. And there was a bed whose mattress seemed to have been slept in for a hundred years.

"Do you want a drink?" she asked Sadie.

"Yes, I would. Thank you."

George handed her a tumbler of whiskey. Sadie drank it. It was as though she had needed a drink for months and had finally got one. Her body felt stiff and frozen and she felt the alcohol unthaw everything. She felt the notes of the piano from the parlor below coming through the floorboards and tickling her feet. She plopped her behind down on the couch, and a cloud of dust rose up around her that was illuminated by the lamplight, as though she were surrounded by fairies.

She noticed the books that were spread all over the room like cats. They lay around, waiting to be picked up again and perused. They liked the feeling of fingers running through their pages. She couldn't help but go look at them immediately. She held up *Jane Eyre*. "What did you think of this?"

"Oh, I loved it of course," George answered. "It's all about being ugly, isn't it? A girl who everyone thinks is ugly. But that doesn't bother her. It's her ugliness that makes her know she's alive."

"What did you think about her falling in love?" Sadie was very curious to hear this uneducated girl's take on the complexities of this novel.

"Oh, I believe writers think they have to put a love affair in a book. They don't necessarily make sense. I ignore them." George laughed. "But I quite liked *Frankenstein*. I love when the monster rips out the heart of Frankenstein's wife. I thought that was hilarious and grotesque and much closer to anything I've read about love lately."

Sadie did not tell George, but after she had read that book, she had that fantasy often. She imagined walking up to Marie. She imagined ripping her heart out. Then she imagined holding it up in her hand for Marie to see. It would still be beating. And Marie would know what it was like to have your heart ripped out for no reason at all.

"*Frankenstein* is divine. I often wonder how Mary Shelley came to be so bold."

"Have you read her mother's book? She said raising girls to be silly playthings made for a morally bankrupt society. She said the way people were raising girls could only make them miserable. And they had to value what was on the inside of them, not the outside. It really affected me when I read it."

"I think all women are beautiful," Sadie answered. "I saw a woman lying on the sidewalk and she had no teeth and a broken nose. And she was singing a bawdy and melancholic song in the sweetest voice. And I thought this woman is beautiful in the most ferocious of ways. The world is terrified of a certain type of monstrous woman. That's why they invented these ideas of ugly and beautiful. They say we are beautiful now because we are young and stupid. But the more we accomplish and have to say, the uglier we are described as being."

"How interesting! Perhaps Mary Shelley is her mother's monster. Sprung from her ideas into something monstrous. She animated her dead mother's idea of a free woman and had it walk around in the world, not at all dainty, but grotesque and murderous."

"Yes! I do like that notion." Sadie also had to admit it was extremely sophisticated and now wanted to know how George was able to have such ideas. "How did you come to read so many books? Did your mother give them to you as a child?"

"Do I look like I had a mother? No, mothers are hard to come by these days. Half of them decide right after giving birth they aren't up for it. And they just leave this world. Not that that's what happened to me. My mother took a look at my ugly face and decided it was best not to let the world know she was responsible for me."

Sadie was struck by this brazen attitude toward mothers. "How does that make you feel?"

"I must've gotten used to it by the time I was one year old because I certainly haven't thought of it since. But I've always been lucky to have women on my side. I had women who were probably way better than my mother could ever be. Jeanne-Pauline at the pharmacy began loaning me books when I was ten or eleven. I never thought I'd get through the first ones, because they were filled with so many new words. You don't hear any such words growing up in a brothel. But those books changed me. If you read enough books, they are bound to make a peculiar thinker out of you."

"I always wanted to be a writer. Even when I was a very little girl. I used to write poems to dead animals."

"I've never met a writer before! See, I knew you were special! How do you go about writing?"

"I have a thought, then I put it down on paper. But the thought becomes something quite different on paper. It develops and unfolds. It becomes a wonderful creature of its own. I would feel entirely alone if it weren't for writing. It's kept me such marvelous company. But it's not only that."

"What are you working on now?"

"A novel."

"I love novels! The madam used to beat me when she caught me reading them. I don't blame her. I neglected everything when I had a book in my hand. I didn't care about the world. I let screaming babies scream. I'd let them walk right out into the road and get run over by a carriage. I went and let her favorite cat get pregnant. I let a whore almost beat a customer to death because I couldn't put my novel down. She would pull on my braids when she caught me not behaving. Then one day I cut them off. She went to pull them and they weren't there anymore. We laughed about that for years."

George picked up three balls and began juggling them over her head. Sadie was intrigued by this elegant, masculine girl who seemed so comfortable in her skin and the neighborhood. She wanted to know what she knew. She liked the way George moved around seamlessly in this violent world. She had a grace that came from having lived in pants her whole life. Both Sadie and Marie had been restrained by wearing corsets and tight-fitting dresses. They were like puppets who attempted to portray grace through limited movements. She felt a sadness about who she and Marie might be right now if they had not always been ordered to have such constrained movements as young ladies.

She had to be sure to free her physical body as well as her mind.

"And you said you are not a whore, but yet you live here?"

"What man would pay money to sleep with me? I'm a midwife."

Sadie's eyebrows rose in surprise at this astounding and gruesome profession. "How many babies have you delivered?"

"So many. I have no idea. Sometimes the girls don't even want to look at the babies. They just want to cry. In those cases, I'm the only one who speaks to the baby. I tell it that it's going to be okay. Although it really isn't going to be okay."

"Wouldn't it be the most marvelous thing if we didn't have to be born from women?"

"If we were found in ostrich eggs. You could put the egg on a pillow under a lamp. And when it cracks and the human came out, they wouldn't belong to anyone."

"Do you like living here?"

"I've never lived anywhere else. But this room is wonderful. Honestly, I used to sleep under the kitchen table. That's where the children go. I never had a room when I was little. I would build myself a nest like a little dog. We all did. We even slept with the dogs if we were lucky. They were warm. We usually slept in each other's arms. When our breath was the same we all fell asleep. When I got to my own room, it was the best day of my life."

"I won't stay any longer then."

"Oh, no. I didn't mean it that way. I would love for you to stay."

"Why is that?"

"You are the most intriguing person I have ever met wandering around the Squalid Mile. There is a character from a book just walking about, I thought as soon as I saw you. And then I discovered you are a writer! You must stay awhile."

There was the sound of shouting and screaming coming from below. It sounded as though a man was being forcefully ejected from the brothel. George didn't seem to notice at all. The screaming moved to the street. Sadie couldn't help but go see what it was. George got up to lean out and look with her.

There was a young prostitute with her breasts hanging out yelling at a man who was scurrying off. "That is not right. Come back and I'll kill you with my bare hands. And what are the rest of you looking at? Do you think looking at my bubbies is free, do you? Well, let's see how many of you pay to come to see them this week. The memory of them is going to cost you everything you have. I'll see you soon. I'll take your whole paycheck to see my pussy."

"She's going to be famous that one. When they are full of life and arrogant, they do very well for themselves."

CHAPTER 24

Marie Antoine Strikes

Back at the World

The foreman stopped outside Marie Antoine's house in the summertime. He hadn't been to visit in quite some time, not since Marie's father had died. He was quite used to wealthy women having nervous breakdowns. But nothing he had witnessed had prepared him for the state the maids were in. A girl wearing a white shift dress with a black butler's tailcoat over it opened the door.

"Right this way, sir," she said with a slight Caribbean accent. Then she walked away without taking his hat or his jacket. And he was entirely unsure whether he was supposed to follow her or not.

He stepped over a pile of dog shit. There was a Great Dane walking around. It disappeared behind the corner like a sinister creature.

There was a group of maids sitting at the table playing cards. One of the girls was in her undergarments. She screamed and jumped up and ran out, to the amusement of the other maids.

He inquired after Marie. They looked at him quizzically, as though they had no idea who in the world he might be looking for.

"She doesn't see guests anymore. Who let you in here anyhow?"

"I'm here to speak about the Antoine factory."

"Well, look around for her then."

"Ask Sarah to fetch her."

"Sarah!"

The girl who had answered the door came running back in. She stopped in front of the man and put her arms akimbo. "I did say right this way, sir!"

Marie was sitting on a completely destroyed couch in a large room. She was wearing a beige dress that looked as though it was desperately in need of a wash. Her hair was down and there was a white flower in it that looked as though it had been stuck in there a day before or so and had been forgotten. She put her hand out to see his proposed changes. She read through them carefully for twenty minutes. At no point did she tell him to sit, nor did Sarah, who was perched on the arm of the couch reading over Marie's shoulder with one leg swinging back and forth, offer him a chair.

He imagined it was some sort of production that Marie, for whatever reason, was pretending to read the documents.

The Great Dane walked in and curled into a ball at Marie's feet. It resembled a large piece of driftwood that had settled on the beach. Marie raised one of her feet and placed her boot on the back of the dog as though it were an ottoman. He saw her stockings that were white and, although expensive, covered in runs.

When she was done, she handed over the documents. And she stared at him with a look of intelligence he hadn't been expecting at all. It threw him off, making him immediately terrified about what he had done. He had never seen such a look, except on the face of a young girl at the factory who demanded to see Mr. Antoine after she lost a finger. And the two girls looked remarkably alike.

"I'm not going to sign these."

"No," he answered. "Of course not."

He opened his mouth as though to say something else, to try to make an excuse to camouflage what he had actually done. But then he immediately realized it was futile. And he bowed his head.

"I will leave now, then."

He waited for a brief second for Sarah to show him to the door but then realized that was not going to happen. He walked out of the house. As he rattled in the back of the carriage, the only thing he wanted was to go back to being the man he was when he had woken up that morning.

MARIE DIDN'T THINK ANYTHING OF her visit from the foreman until two weeks later. A cold glass of water was tossed on her melancholia, waking her up. There was an attempt at a hostile takeover by a competing sugar company. It was one in Toronto. The foreman had gone to them, saying Marie was weak and now was the time to make their move. Marie couldn't believe this had happened.

She was disappointed with herself for not seeing it coming. She knew no one would come to her aid. The world would use her depression to take advantage of her. They had come to finish her off. She regarded the factory and everyone in it as being against her. She considered the factory workers had hoodwinked her as much as the managers had.

SHE FIRED THE FOREMAN AND had the secretary from the office at the factory come to her house during the day instead. The secretary understood the workings of the factory perhaps better than anyone. Although nobody actually gave her any credit or due. She had been working in the office since before Marie had been born.

She had pens and pencils stuck in the bun of her hair on her head. She had a habit of sticking them in there when she was working and then forgetting altogether they were up there. By the end of the day she looked like a sculpture of a crowned Virgin Mary or a porcupine.

She sat with Marie at the same desk. They pored over all the dealings of the factory together. Marie was not afraid of the secretary knowing her ignorance. The secretary explained everything to Marie from scratch, but Marie was a very fast learner, and the lessons from the American factory owners all came back to her. She also had a passion for the subject. And she began to catch on and excel at the business in a manner that very much impressed the secretary. And, in fact, impressed everyone around her.

They ceased to treat her like a fool they could steal the factory from and began to defer to her decisions and work with her. Many had never believed they would find themselves following the instructions and orders of a woman, but it all happened so smoothly, they soon forgot to consider the unusualness of the situation.

Working from home would mean she didn't have to deal with the workers directly. They could not manipulate her sympathies to the detriment of the factory. The workers wouldn't understand why she was about to make a major tightening of the belt at the factory. But everyone had to make sacrifices now. Or they would be eating sugar from another province.

Marie worked on the business from the moment she woke up and was still in her pajamas and drinking her coffee. History was created by violent, narcissistic men who vaunted their dreams at the expense of the working-class masses. History regarded these men as complicated. But there could be no doubt whatsoever that they got things done. They were like the volcanoes and earthquakes that formed the continents. Marie came out of her depression with a callousness she and no one else could have expected.

And so the changes began.

CHAPTER 25

A Brief History of a
Girl Named George

The first day they met, Sadie and George talked all night in the brothel's attic. They sat cross-legged on George's bed, facing each other, as it felt as though they had known each other a much longer time. Every time they laughed, the mattress wheezed like an older woman. George adored Sadie's intellect. She'd always wondered if she would seem stupid if she were around upper-class women. Sadie had gotten a first-class education, as much as a woman could have a first-class education, and they got along marvelously.

George began her story at the very beginning. She was born in the brothel. George didn't know until quite an advanced age that you were supposed to wear all your clothes at once. One prostitute walked by with a crinoline like a cage around her and nothing else. Another woman was wearing a pair of bloomers. Her corset was untied and she was wearing it open like it was a jacket. Another was wearing striped stockings and a see-through chemise. They were mostly in bloomers and petticoats and undershirts. It was an ordeal to get their dresses back on.

George was no great beauty. She must have inherited her father's looks. All the women in the brothel denied that they were her mother. She accused them all one at a time of being such. She would do it as a way of establishing intimacy. She would know this later. She didn't quite know what she was doing at that point. She felt as though she were propositioning them somehow.

But it was considered impolite to point out which of the whores was your mother. You belonged to the whorehouse. You didn't want to lower the sexual allure of your mother, did you? You pretended to be your mother's sister if you looked too much like her.

But George was indispensable. She did ten times the chores other girls did.

She wasn't the type of girl men noticed. But growing up in the brothel taught her invisibility. She was able to dart in and out of rooms while people were having sex in order to retrieve items, or check on violent thumping. She would whisk into a room and would take instructions from a prostitute who was on all fours and being thrust into from behind.

"Go move that bowl of water from the table. I'm terrified it's going to fall over."

Once a prostitute had her continue to jerk a man off while she ran to the bathroom. She didn't want him to lose his hard-on. He lay there and closed his eyes, stroking her arm and imagining a more beautiful woman, no doubt.

One of George's gifts was she wasn't afraid of the human body. And she wasn't afraid of other people's pain. She helped out during all the births. The women found themselves wanting her to be next to them. She would look in their eyes and tell them not to worry, and that they were doing beautifully. And they found themselves hypnotized by her.

She made the same gestures with her face as they did. It made them feel as though they weren't alone in their pain. When they yelled, she yelled with them.

Once she was called in by a prostitute on a particularly busy night. The prostitute needed a little help getting the man to come, and all the other prostitutes were busy. In situations like this, she ran in and tickled their balls or put her finger in their bottoms. She didn't mind. It was usually an action that was quite mechanical and would have been a waste of time for another prostitute.

She also went in a room to show out a Chihuahua that was trying to rescue its mistress from a client. After that, it became one of the details of life she automatically attended to whenever she heard a dog barking.

She helped the prostitutes get dolled up again so they could go down and get another client quickly. She helped them douche. She helped reapply makeup and find their shoes. She replaced articles of clothing that had gotten torn. She took the clothes down to the kitchen to work on them right away.

She thanked the Lord for having made her ugly. She didn't have to work as a prostitute. She helped with every other job there and she learned so much. Also, she didn't have to worry about getting pregnant.

THERE WAS A SKINNY MAN who'd left his pinstriped jacket behind one day. George had begged and begged for it. She wore it with a pair of pants a young boy who had lived in the brothel had outgrown. When you saw her from behind, with her hair up, you could sometimes mistake her for a young man. She felt she was recognizable because of that jacket. It made her different.

She kept her hair in two braids at the side of her head but then cut them off to stop the madam from pulling them.

"Good lord. It's such a pity that you cut your hair," Madame exclaimed. "It was your one good feature. Now you'll be even uglier than you were before."

George was delighted at her short hair. It made her feel lighter. She liked the way she looked in the mirror. She liked that she looked like a very modern girl. She bought some pomade like the men wore in their hair. She used big gobs of it to style her hair in different ways. Her favorite was to make it into a wild pompadour over her head.

SINCE GEORGE WAS NEVER GOING to be a prostitute, or get married for that matter, or go to school, Madame sent her with a suitcase and some money so she could have a short apprenticeship with a woman in Sainte-Adèle who was an expert in the secrets of pregnancy and childbearing.

George returned knowing all there was to know about the secret life of fetuses. She knew how to use forceps. In fact, she bought a pair for the brothel. She had a portmanteau of gynecological instruments that looked like the skeletons of small dragons. Everyone was impressed by her savvy in that regard. That she would be able to think of their needs before they happened. She reached into a womb and turned a breech baby around. She didn't have any qualms about it. She understood the human body as well as any anatomy student might. One prostitute was having terrible cramps. It was clear the baby had died. But her body hadn't yet miscarried it. George had no problem with the task of fishing the baby out.

And when any of them needed to terminate a pregnancy, George could do that in a jiffy. In fact, because she had never killed a girl, others from all over the city came to see her at the brothel.

She was surprised at how long some of these daughters and maids waited before asking her for an abortion. Some of them would lie too.

They would tell her that they were only a month pregnant. And then when the baby came out, it would be so perfectly formed and tiny, obviously five or six months gestation. It looked like a perfect baby.

They would beg her to take it. She hated that. It was illegal. She would be thrown in jail. She had that bag filled with instruments she could never explain to authorities. She suggested they bury the babies in the garden. But they said the ladies of the house like to garden. And what would happen if they found the small skeletons in their hydrangea?

George might have carried on this way her whole life if one afternoon, when she was twenty-three years old, she had not come across a beautiful rich girl in a filthy cloak being accosted under the awning of an oyster shack.

CHAPTER 26

The Seven Lovely Sins

Sadie got a better look around the brothel in the morning. When the sunlight came up, you could see all the stains and destruction enacted on it. There were red wine stains on the wallpaper and floors. The carpets were black in the center where too many shoes had tread. You could make out what the carpets were intended to look like only along the edges near the walls. Then you could see they were green with yellow pineapples. The carpet had expected the delicate feet of Victorian girls walking soundlessly down the stairs. But instead it was the heavy footsteps of men with a girl flung over their shoulder with her ass in the air.

There really wasn't much use repairing the house. Because when the sun went down, all those stains and scratches vanished and the house looked fancy and illustrious all over again.

There were notches on the wall. They noted the height of some of the children who'd grown up in the brothel. George's name was there.

Sadie imagined George at four years old standing against the wall getting measured. And then turning around excitedly to see how tall she had gotten.

She knew she would become very good friends with George. It was very different from her friendship with Marie. George was so forthright and generous. It seemed she would share anything she owned and anything she knew. She trusted George, and she had never trusted anyone before. They had only just met and George was putting Sadie's feelings above her own.

Sadie was very interested in meeting the other women who worked at the brothel too. Madame was an older woman who wore a burgundy dress with an enormous skirt and a tight bonnet on her head. It was a mystery what might be found underneath her large skirt. One might imagine if she lifted it, there would be a small puppet theater underneath, where all the puppets were having delirious sex.

The women all came down for breakfast at one o'clock in the afternoon. Their stockinged feet hurrying across the landing were like a group of rabbits that had been flushed out of a bush.

Madame liked to hire exclusive prostitutes. And by exclusive, she meant women who were willing to engage in any theatrical and depraved requests without hesitation. Sadie was interested in the prostitutes working at the brothel. She thought she would one day write a book based on them. When she was finished with the book about herself and Marie, of course. She found the prostitutes were similar to the girls at boarding school. They had often been exiled for some peculiarity that made it impossible for them to live with their families. Sadie began to interview the girls, looking for the sin that had caused them to fall.

An Irish girl named Maureen's sin was Gluttony. She had been scorned by her family for being obese. This was a particular tragedy because she was rather pretty. So by gaining weight, she was ruining an opportunity that not all girls had. She had taken being beautiful entirely for granted. "When I eat, the whole world disappears. I feel like I'm a cloud in heaven."

It hadn't occurred to Sadie that being fat could be regarded as an offense that would cause you to be sent away like a murderess, like herself. The fat of Maureen's belly made it seem like she had the cutest baby pig on her lap.

A FRENCH GIRL NAMED MARTHE'S sin was Lust. "I was caught masturbating. I started touching myself. It was so wonderful. But I didn't know it was something other people knew about. So I thought I was doing it discreetly. I stuck a cucumber between my legs. I rocked gently back and forth. And I reached the point of ecstasy and I cried out. The reverend happened to be over for dinner that night."

LOUISA, AN ITALIAN GIRL WITH curly hair, was guilty of Sloth. "I was so lazy about my physical appearance." Sadie believed it immediately. The buttons of Louisa's vest were in the wrong holes. Her hair was lopsided on her head so that her hat was perpendicular to her ear. The madam was always sending her back to her room to straighten her attire up. She seemed incapable of looking immaculate like the other girls. The other day at dinner, she had a milk mustache over her mouth the entire evening.

A SLENDER, MIXED-RACE WOMAN NAMED Carol was guilty of Wrath. She had been bit by her mother's toy poodle. She had taken it by the throat with both hands and had strangled it.

ANNE, WHO WAS OF SCOTTISH descent and had come from a middle-class family, was accused of Envy. Before she got married, her sister shared everything with her. Her sister shared all her toys with her. If Anne admired a pair of stockings she was wearing, her sister let her try them on. If her sister discovered a pretty way of fastening her hair in a bun, she taught Anne the technique at once. But then she got married to a very handsome man and she had no part of it at all.

"How did you seduce him?" Sadie asked.

"I looked at him a few seconds more than was normal. I couldn't believe how easy it was."

Anne poured herself a glass of carbonated soda. Sadie stared at the bubbles rising from it. It was as though there were a tiny fairy drowning at the bottom of the glass.

RAMONA, WHOSE MOTHER WAS CHINESE, was so tall she seemed stretched like a shadow in the evening. She had been kicked out of her home for the sin of Greed. She had been gambling with her friends one night. She kept winning. Could she help it if she was lucky? She knew how to count cards. "What's the point of being good with numbers if you don't use it to make money? Gambling is what makes fortunes. They sent me here to teach me a lesson, but also because no one wanted to pay their debts to me."

"And did you learn your lesson?"

"You can't learn a lesson if it doesn't make any sense." She held out her two fists to Sadie. "Would you like to bet your hair ribbon on which hand a stone is in?"

SIOBHAN, WHO SWORE SHE WASN'T IRISH, was guilty of Pride. She rejected the advances of men too succinctly. She was honest and explained why she could not imagine herself married to them. I'm too intelligent to spend my days with you, she told one. I have to have someone I can converse with. Someone who is my intellectual equal.

"I went to a museum and I looked at the paintings of all the nudes. And all the statues. I realized none of them have breasts as beautiful as mine. Do you want to touch them?"

Siobhan held both breasts in her hands like she was offering two glasses of brandy.

"All right," said Sadie.

"Hold them," she whispered hoarsely.

CHAPTER 27

Mary Robespierre Has Balcony Seats

Mary Robespierre was not interested in making obscene amounts of money. She was content. She had so much more than she had ever dreamed of having. She got to do something she loved instead of going to the factory every day. She had come up with a harebrained scheme, and it had actually come to fruition. She had been insulted every day of her life. The freedom that came with not being emotionally abused was exhilarating. It made every day seem like the most perfect day on Earth. She supposed, because of human nature, she would begin to desire something more in life. But she had trouble imagining it. It was like trying to plan what you want to eat the next day after eating an enormous meal.

She worked happily in her bakery. There were piles of dough on the counter. They looked like older women sitting naked on the side of a public bath. Mary picked one up in her hands and threw it on the table. The flour lifted up all around her, and at that moment, a light snowfall descended all over the city.

WHEN THE BAKERY FIRST OPENED, because of its proximity to the factory, the factory manager had Mary bring cakes and pastries to their offices at lunchtime. She didn't have to make the cakes so pretty. They would have ordered from her anyway, since she was right next door. She made them beautiful for her own pleasure. She found it satisfying. She was obsessed with creating works of beauty. She sat with her pastry sleeves and knives, and nothing else in the whole wide world existed.

For many of the factory operators, the arrival of Mary's cakes was their favorite moment of their workday. They gathered around the cakes deciding which one caught their fancy. Looking at the cakes made odd, hidden parts of themselves come to light. One wondered why, at sixty-five, he was suddenly so drawn to a cake with pink icing and a cherry on top. Why did he feel like a shy little child at a birthday party?

Mary loved when the operators spent time perusing her cakes. When they had to take a very long moment before biting into one because they were about to destroy a work of art, Mary was delighted. It filled her with a pride no other feeling could compete with. Everybody has addictions to different feelings. They end up shaping the course of our lives. Those feelings become our north stars. Mary's north star was pride.

WHEN MARY HEARD LOUIS ANTOINE had died, she was taken aback. A cake she had been making lay on the kitchen table. It had fallen and resembled the belly of a woman who had recently given birth. Was she sad about Louis's death? No, how could she be? Louis had ignored her as a child and had spent no more than two hours of his life with her, both of which had made him squeamish and uncomfortable. She'd had to trade one of her fingers to see her father. She really couldn't afford to meet with him many more times. And yet he had given more to her than anybody else in the world ever had. She knew her protection was now gone. She wondered if Marie would come to the factory often. She knew Marie would notice their physical resemblance. She felt a perverse desire to show her face no matter how dangerous it turned out to be.

When Mary walked into the factory for the first time after Louis's death, she felt the current of anticipation running through the crowd. Everyone had stopped working and stood on the floor together beneath the balcony, waiting. And then Marie emerged above. Everywhere that Marie went, she glowed and attracted attention. But never nearly as much as she did when she was in the Squalid Mile. The sordid background threw the pink in her cheeks and the rich blond of her ringlets into relief. Her fingertips had a touch of pink at the ends of them. Her breasts were perfect globes that would never fall, as she would never be forced to breastfeed.

It was as though Marie were standing in a sketch for a painting but she was the only part that had been colored in.

They had never seen an outfit like the one she had on. She was in mourning and was dressed in black. But the black material of her dress was so expensive that it seemed to have different colors swarming around inside of it. They could never afford black like that. The black of their clothes was flat. It wasn't luminous. It wasn't a color. This black was a color. It was like looking at the river at night. There were beluga whales moving underneath the water. You couldn't see the sea creatures, but you could sense their shadows. You could feel their presence. There were mermaids twisting in the waves.

Marie was treating the balcony as though it were a stage. An observer might think she was unskilled and that she wasn't doing anything other than being herself. But Mary, having exactly the same body to work with, knew just how skilled Marie was. Mary was suddenly very envious. That was the thing she loved the most. Admiration. She could never get that kind of sycophantic love from baking. What must it be like to be admired and revered entirely for being yourself?

The nineteenth-century city was a squalid, infectious mess. Everyone was dropping dead all the time. There had been a great wave of people shitting themselves to death the year before. So you might think Louis having a heart attack and dropping dead was not the type of event that would raise any sort of sensation in this crowd. But when Marie described her father's passing, tears came to their eyes. They were devastated for Marie. They did not like to see her sad at all. At that moment, everyone in the factory felt Marie's life was more important than theirs. Her problems were grander and more epic. They were living her life vicariously. They gave up their entire identities at that moment to experience hers.

Mary could see it go to Marie's head almost immediately. Whatever Marie had been looking for in the crowd, she had gotten more than she expected.

Mary Robespierre could feel the electricity from the swell of emotions of the factory workers. It made her want to vomit from the intensity of it. If she were a doctor and placed a stethoscope against their chests, she would find their hearts were beating in rhythm. The power of a mob feeling the same emotion was hard to contain. It was like riding a temperamental stallion who had only recently been broken. You could lose control any minute. And he could crush you under his hooves. She wondered whether Marie understood that it could turn against her.

In any case, the feeling of affection would not turn that day. There was a feeling through the factory that now that Marie was their boss, all their problems were about to go away. They thought they might receive a slight increase in pay. Their minds couldn't help but wonder happily what that extra pay would allow them to buy. For a poor person, a penny is like a magic bean planted in their heads and from it springs the most incredible, almost preposterous, ideas.

NOTHING AT ALL CHANGED AT the factory for six months. And then in the summer and through the next winter, the changes began. Salaries were slashed, jobs made redundant, quotas pushed up. And most alarming, the machines were sped up. When she brought her cakes in, Mary began to notice the changes at the factory. She noticed the effects the extra workload was having on the women employed there. It was as though they were suffering from shock. There was a girl standing outside twitching. She kept raising her shoulders and allowing them to fall. There was a girl walking toward home from the factory who kept wiggling her fingers as though she were sewing.

There was a lot more yelling going on. Girls were getting into trouble because they weren't moving as fast as they could. Mary saw one of the overseers yelling at a girl. She couldn't hear the content of the argument because the noise of the machines drowned out their voices. But she could tell from their body language exactly what was transpiring, as though it were an excellent pantomime being performed onstage. The overseer was waving his arms and his lips were opening and closing, while the girl was cringing. His words were affecting her physically. They were like punches.

Mary thought about how language could crush a person. Particularly women. She recalled what it was like to be spoken down to. It hit you on the head like a hammer hitting a nail until you were nothing, only a piece of dirt on the ground. He wasn't even going to fire her, he was just getting her to be crushed and work in a state of humbled servility. The way women did at home.

It was usual for women to suffer abuse at home. There were no laws against it. It wasn't exactly socially acceptable, but everybody did it. But now here were girls who were being made to feel the way they did at home, at work. There was no difference between public and private worlds as far as girls were concerned. They were treated by everybody as though they were their daughters; you could say or do anything you wanted to them. They lived in a permanent state of humiliation.

Mary arrived at the factory very early one day to provide hot buns for a breakfast meeting. There were five girls all sitting outside the office of one of the foremen. They had been sent there to be reprimanded. They were hysterical about it. One got on her knees the moment the foreman walked out, begging his forgiveness for taking too long on a smoke break. She grabbed the foreman's ankles and he was visibly disconcerted. One took her boots off and hit herself on the head with them. It was rather extraordinary. Their mood was affecting everyone in the office. Mary considered perhaps on some level the girls knew what they were doing. They were performing their victimhood in a manner that upset the workings of the factory. If they didn't settle down, who knew what they were capable of?

Afterward, Mary felt the need to discuss the disturbing sights with someone. So she went off to see Jeanne-Pauline at the pharmacy. She found Jeanne-Pauline counting pills and putting them in containers.

"How are things?" Jeanne-Pauline asked without looking up.

"It's a mess over at the factory," Mary answered. "The women are in a particular fit. They are going mad. But they don't know they are going mad. They are acting in peculiar ways. They don't understand what they are doing. But I think this madness means that they are resisting." Mary warmed to her own idea. "Yes, they think they are getting sick. But they are resisting. They think all of their limbs are refusing to move. But that is their body resisting. They are throwing up their food. But that is their stomach resisting. They think they are suffocating their babies in their sleep. But they are just resisting. They are having sex in alleys, but they are just resisting. When they have nothing left, when they are all alone and broken down, then they might realize: Ah, I was resisting."

"Bravo, Mary. You have felt the revolutionary pulse in the skinny arms of women workers. And you will never be able to ignore it now."

After Mary left the store, Jeanne-Pauline reflected on how Mary had a wonderful way of thinking and a wonderful way of speaking. It was more revolutionary and violent than the girl herself was probably aware. She wondered what use she would make of it. She had the sort of violence needed for change. She had sacrificed a finger for her own personal cause. And it hadn't seemed to faze her whatsoever.

She made a note to herself that she would perhaps have reason to call on Mary's speaking skills sometime in the future.

CHAPTER 28

A Collaboration

Sadie settled in with George. She handed over a dress to the madam for rent, who promptly gave it to a beautiful fourteen-year-old prostitute.

The cold was so much more violent and temperamental in the Squalid Mile than it was in the Golden one. The inhabitants of the Squalid Mile brought out the worst of the winter's personality. It bullied the poor because it could. It cracked windows and blew open doors. It forced its way into homes and gave people chills and pneumonia. It twisted old people into pretzels, it aged young people by making them cranky and sore, and it murdered sweet children in their sleep. It pushed against residents as they tried to walk down the street. Drunks slipped on the ice and broke their necks. The frost bit and ruined many a nose. And factory girls coughed as though they smoked cigars. People were so covered in layers, they looked like they were books that had been soaked and bloated by the rain. When you saw the homeless sleeping on the church steps under all their coats and thin blankets, they looked like piles of newspapers.

But inside the brothel, the stove was pumped full of coal and the building was warm, as though you were naked and curled up in the belly of your mother, unaware that you would be shoved out one day. Sadie liked the feeling of hibernating, as she could concentrate on the dreamlike realm of her book undistracted. Sadie wrote for hours and hours. Her fingertips were always covered in ink. Sadie filled pages in a wonderful, unstoppable way. Watching her handwriting was like watching a cat playing with a string. She was a girl who had been born inspired.

George was fascinated with books. They were magical things. She had somehow never really considered the obvious fact that they had been written by actual human beings. And human beings who had all the same flaws and needs as any other. They sat at desks with their underwear on and their cats on windowsills and their pots of coffee getting cold. And they wrote down their ideas. They paused to eat soup, take a dump in the bathroom, look out the window, and masturbate, and then they sat down and continued to write.

"I notice you've been writing in a notebook. What are you writing about?" George asked.

"It's my novel that I mentioned. Would you like to read it?"

"Yes!"

George had believed from the instant she read the book that it was something of genius. She very much liked that the two main characters were passionate women. Neither were married to men. They seemed like pioneers in fiction to her. They were going off on an adventure. They were like Don Quixote and Sancho Panza. It was picaresque and funny. But George also knew that humorous books were often the most subversive ones. People became free in literature first. It was through books that new ideas entered the general population.

"The book is brilliant! Truly."

"I'm at a loss though," said Sadie. "I don't know how to finish it at all."

Sadie had looked up from her writing desk to discover she was in a deep forest. There was nowhere to grow. There was no pathway out. Every time she picked up the pen, new trees grew like beanstalks, wrapping around one another, growing so dense they would block out the sky. George sat down with her and they discussed the book.

It was as though George had a compass. She described the entire forest to Sadie. All its nooks and crannies. There were clearings with wildflowers growing in them. There were huge trees with roots that could reach out and trip you in order to get a look up your dress. She knew the way out of the forest. A path opened up before her feet.

Afterward, Sadie moved the tip of her pen like a sailboat over the waves on a most perfectly windy day. Her editing pen was making notes and slashes like a seabird dipping for fish.

GEORGE FELL QUITE NATURALLY INTO helping Sadie craft the novel. They sat at opposite sides of the desk they had pulled to the center of the room. Sadie scribbled away. When she was done with a page, George would read it and add comments. She gave her notes and crossed out paragraphs even though Sadie shouted in dismay.

WHEN THEY WERE DONE WORKING, George enjoyed pulling Sadie's boots off. The sound the shoelaces made as they were coming out was swift, like a pen writing on the page. She had one pair with buttons. She had a tiny tool for them. There was something so delicious about feeling the button pop out of the hole. Then George loved to hold

Sadie's feet and massage them. This was something all women loved. The heels and pointed toes of their boots always caused their feet to be in a perpetual state of agony.

She liked when Sadie was in various states of disrobe too.

Sadie liked wearing corsets. They held up her large breasts. She was wearing a dark-pink corset with a slip that was made out of several layers of lace, some of which had been torn at the bottom. George loved untying Sadie's corset. She loved the little gasp she let out when she was finished. And the great inhale she took before she pulled in the laces of the corset to tie it up. She had a white silk pair of underwear that she stepped into, pulled up over her shoulders and buttoned up. When she undid her corset, it was as though her breasts were free. She couldn't stand to have anything touching her breasts when she was ovulating because they were so sensitive.

Sadie had a pillow of sorts that protruded from the back of her crinoline. George would unbutton it. She would put it in Sadie's trousseau of clothes. But she longed to use it as a pillow. She wanted to inhale it and sit on it herself.

But she never saw anything more wonderful than when Sadie slept on top of the covers completely nude. She had a magnificent figure. She had large hips and a small waist and huge, full breasts. George had had her own bed for a while, but once Sadie moved in and she had gotten used to sleeping next to her, she felt she could never go back to sleeping in a bed alone again. She never woke up with a chill in the middle of the night. Sadie's body radiated so much wonderful, tender heat.

ON SATURDAY MORNINGS, ESPECIALLY ON cold days, all the girls liked to get together to smoke opium. They passed the pipe back and forth as though they were each trying to get a pretty tune out of a flute. The smoke from the pipes rose up in swirls around them, making them look like they were in an Impressionist painting.

Sadie loved smoking opium. It was as though your mind were a slate covered in complex mathematical equations. And then it was just wiped clean. It was as though a hunter had fired tranquilizer darts at the thoughts in her head and they fell to the bottom of her brain, comatose, and went to sleep.

It made her absurdly affectionate. She would lie next to George and stare at her with her eyes half-closed and say sweet things. One afternoon she was particularly extravagant: "You are a darling thing, George. How was it that you were born? You aren't supposed to have a brain filled with excellent thoughts. And yet you do. You are a wee little philosopher. And you were born and nobody wanted you. How in the world are you?" George started to laugh and agreed to smoke with her. The two women found themselves stoned and naked in each other's arms.

George tied a dildo around her hips with a large black ribbon. The black bow was tied above the crack of her ass. Sadie seemed to find this delightful. George climbed on top of Sadie's body and allowed the dildo to enter her ever so gently at first. When it was over, George lay on the bed with her arms propped behind her head and her chest stretched out so it looked flat. And her dildo was still pointing straight up in the air.

It was the first time Sadie had been penetrated so deeply by another person. She had felt her body anticipating the orgasm that was to come, like a rabbit in a magician's hat, waiting, waiting, waiting to leap out. She was surprised by the intensity of it when it finally occurred.

IN THE MORNING, SADIE LOOKED at George. There was something quite elegant about the way she looked wearing her dildo while she still slept. It was as though Sadie were looking at a unicorn, an enchanted creature standing in the room in her bare feet. What type of babies would the two of them have together? Would they be tiny wooden puppets?

She laughed at the ingenuity and absurdity of her own thoughts. But what she was most delighted about was that she had had sex and was free of commitment and consequence. Her sex life was off to an excellent start. She got out of bed and went to wash up in the bathroom.

George woke up and saw Sadie's boots on the floor. She couldn't believe Sadie's boots were on the floor where she had taken them off and left them. She picked up Sadie's cloak and wrapped herself in it and inhaled deeply. The smell of Sadie was all around her.

When she recollected the events from the night before, a frisson possessed her whole body. She could remember every detail about it as though it were happening right then and there. She kept replaying a moment where Sadie undid her corset and took off the chemise under it and her breasts were right there and they were so beautiful and full and perfect. And George had been staring at innumerable breasts her whole life, but she had never been so bedazzled by a pair. She had reached out for them and put one in her mouth and then the next one.

As she was going about her tasks for the day, she found herself daydreaming about Sadie. She looked out the frost-covered window as though she were looking through a wedding veil. She imagined she and Sadie going on adventures together. They were not adventures she had even been to on her own. They weren't the type of activity poor people engaged in. Everyone in the Squalid Mile was too busy, their lives too frenetic, for them to indulge in these leisure moments. If they managed to have a day off, they would drink themselves into a stupor and messily try to have sex before passing out.

She imagined them dressed in finery on the side of a ship waving to the masses as it pulled out to Europe. She pictured them on a rowboat in a pond. She was paddling the boat while Sadie sat under a parasol reading poetry out loud. She imagined the two of them on horses. George had never been on a horse before, but in the fantasy she rode perfectly. They were at a fast clip, bowing their heads to avoid branches. The wind was in Sadie's hair and it whipped everywhere, totally encircling her face at one point so it looked wrapped in a dark cocoon.

She imagined them having tea at a fancy restaurant where the walls were covered in pastoral murals of angels and naked children. And they selected macarons from a tiered tray and drank tea with flowers at the bottom that bloomed like tiny octopuses. And George knew all the correct manners.

George thought their lovemaking meant they were going to be together for the rest of their lives. Sadie was wondering who she would make love to next.

CHAPTER 29

The Price of Sugar

When the lawyer walked into her bakery one fall morning almost a year after Louis's death, Mary Robespierre considered it possible Louis had decided to help her. He might have left something for her in his will. He might have made some legal protection for her, for the day when Marie found out about their arrangement.

But Louis had not thought about her, and now Marie Antoine was making as many spending cuts as she could. The lawyer handed her his papers. He informed her the factory was rescinding the lease for the bakery. Her contract with Louis was being broken.

"I believe Marie Antoine will be willing to honor an arrangement her father made."

"She will be doing no such thing."

The bakery was now in the possession of the Antoine factory and the baker would have to report to the foreman. This was patently unfair. The reason the bakery was so successful was because of what she had done with it. She had built it from scratch.

❧

MARY PRESENTED HERSELF TO THE FOREMAN. She asked to be able to speak to Marie Antoine, but she was told that was not possible. Marie Antoine had given everyone explicit instructions—she did not want to see anyone who was disgruntled. And there were many of them. That was why she didn't make any exceptions. It didn't matter how many fingers Mary Robespierre cut off and tied ribbons around and sent her way, she would not get a meeting.

It always irked the foreman when he watched Mary Robespierre enter into the factory. This former factory worker arrived with her cakes and acted as though she were beholden to no one. She was so proud of her cakes and was only concerned what people thought of them. She didn't care whatsoever what people thought of her.

The foreman was quite pleased when he received the notice that Mary Robespierre was not to run the bakery independently. He wanted to punish Mary Robespierre. He wanted to punish her for being so dour and not smiling at him. He felt a surge of excitement at the prospect of destroying this girl. She was so ambitious. He could not wait to see her expression when she found she was at his mercy.

"Will the bakery still be under my direction?"

"I'm looking for a new baker."

Mary almost jumped at this news and was visibly flustered. "I put everything into this bakery. I built it from scratch. It has been successful. It will be more successful. I haven't done anything wrong. I did have an arrangement with Louis Antoine that I would not pay the rent for several months until the bakery got on its feet."

Mary reached into her inside pocket. She pulled out an envelope and placed it on the desk. The foreman put his fingertips on the envelope and pushed it back toward Mary.

"I'm sorry. I feel the bakery would do better under different leadership."

"Why? My cakes are regarded practically as works of art. Everyone likes them."

"There's no reason the bakery has to make the most ornate cakes in the world. They can really be made more efficiently. The point of the bakery should be that the overseers have something readily available to eat. There should be a man running the bakery. It will be more efficient."

Mary was silent for a moment. She stared at him without expression and asked, "What do I have to do to change your mind?"

He stood up and moved to the glass windows that made up the walls between his office and the factory. He closed the wooden Venetian blinds one by one. He had not put these blinds up. They had been put up before he moved into the office. These blinds served his purpose so well, he could not believe they were not invented directly for it.

Mary knew instantly what he was getting at. If she could cut off her finger, then she could very easily give up her virtue. She had no interest in her virtue. She didn't want to preserve her virginity for a husband, because she didn't want a husband. This did not seem like a very high price to pay. It would be over soon. She would have her bakery. The alternative wasn't something she wanted to consider. She did not want to go back to the factory line.

The foreman had Mary lean over his desk. She hiked her skirts up. He grabbed onto her blond hair and pulled it. He grunted as he entered her from behind, his large body curled against hers.

Mary was painfully in the present. She felt his sweat drip on her neck and his smell surrounded her. She stared out the window. The snow was falling, and she hated the snow. She saw some men loading bags of sugar onto a carriage. She hated them. And she hated the horse that was shaking its head as though furiously disagreeing with someone speaking next to him. She was so in the moment that everything happened at a terribly slow speed. The whole episode seemed interminable even though it wouldn't have lasted more than five minutes.

His body shuddered against hers. She knew there was a trick men could do that would not make her pregnant. But she didn't know what it was, so she could not ask for it. She hoped the hatred inside her would be enough to murder any fetus that tried to grow inside her.

He pulled himself off Mary as she leant across the table. When she stood back up, straightened her skirts, and turned toward him, her face was flushed, and for a moment he almost fell to the floor. Because he thought it was Marie Antoine standing before him. And she seemed quite prepared to kill him. He had accidentally fucked someone who had the power to crush him.

Then he realized it was Mary Robespierre. Of course. Of course. He had nothing to be afraid of. Of course she looked nothing like Marie. She was thinner. She was much more dour. Her teeth were yellow. Her hair was lanky. She looked at least eight years older. But he could never shake the vision out of his head. And he never touched Mary again.

MARY WAS FURIOUS, BUT HER anger wasn't directed toward the foreman. As soon as she walked into the bakery, she locked the door behind her and screamed. She smashed all the pans against the wall. Her face was covered in flour when she was done. Mary was enraged at Marie Antoine. This was her fault. She had debased her. How could Marie Antoine have entrusted Mary's fate to such a grotesque man? One might assume having a woman boss would put an end to this practice. But Marie was allowing this to happen to women at the factory and now to Mary herself.

Mary felt a new vitriol forming inside her. She had known herself to be bitter. She had not known if this was how she was naturally, or if it was a way she had become because of her grandparents. Whichever it was, that bitterness existed like a piece of coal inside her. And when her anger was lit, it burned long and hard. And there was no point in trying to blow it out; that only served to fan the flames. She had no choice but to let her anger burn slowly and steadily. She would be furious at Marie Antoine for a very long time.

She would have to quickly clean up if she wanted to make her orders for the morning. She would make Marie pay for this.

One day she would make Marie also feel small and easy to crush. She stepped outside the bakery to look up at the night sky and calm herself. There had been a general consternation that the stars were disappearing from the sky. But then it was discovered they were only becoming less visible because of the increased streetlamps in the city. So she was glad to spot a brilliant one that seemed particularly responsive to her requests. She wished that she would have revenge on Marie Antoine.

The bats were sleeping along the eaves of the bakery like rows of hanging umbrellas. They began to open their wings as though in preparation for a terrible storm.

CHAPTER 30

Backstage at the Music Hall

Sadie was sitting one early spring afternoon at the breakfast table with the other women of the brothel when the topic of her family came up. One of the prostitutes, Ramona, was reading the newspaper. She folded the top down and looked at the others.

"The morality police are trying to shut down the music hall again," Ramona said.

"They ruin everything! Which one is it?" Louisa asked. "Joseph Arnett or his son, Philip?"

"It's the son, Philip Arnett."

"That's Sadie's brother."

"Is it really?" Ramona asked, turning toward Sadie.

"Yes. I'm afraid so," Sadie answered. "What's he saying in the paper?"

"'The new lineup at the music hall is nothing more than a series of lewd theatrics, replete with sexual innuendos and indecent humor. The works serve no dramatic or edifying purpose. Rather, they serve to incite licentiousness in its audience. After viewing this performance, the audience members return home believing any indecent behavior is permissible.'"

"That sounds wonderful!" Sadie said. "We have to go see this spectacle. Will you take me, George?"

THE SPRING MADE EVERYONE IN Montreal, no matter what neighborhood, want to go out at night. Sadie and George crammed into the crowded music hall together. They sat at a table and ordered drinks. They shared a cigar together and laughed. They exhaled smoke as though the fires in their hearts had just been put out. George knew Sadie liked the attention they got when they were out together. Because Sadie was a natural provocateur. It gave her a thrill to be shocking and on the arm of another woman dressed like a man. And from the first moment Sadie Arnett had set foot in the music hall, she was in love with the spectacles presented there.

The crowd drank and yelled over one another through the musical acts, the magician, the lion tamer, and even the sword swallower. The music hall was different from the theater. The audience was rowdy. The theaters Sadie had visited as a child were places of culture and taste, where sophisticated people came. But the music hall let in those who were flamboyant and deviant. They used their cleverness for shocking observations and absurd conclusions. They carried on very public commentary on the acts taking place onstage.

Sadie listened to the snippets of conversation that reached her ears.

"Look at that magician. If that magician could really pull coins out of people's ears, why on earth would he be working at this ridiculous joint?"

"Why does that juggler have such a look of concentration on his face? I'd rather not see performers look as though they are about to take a crap. It's positively disconcerting."

"I think I saw a politician in the private booth. He lectures about morality and closing the theaters all the time. Give me a pervert who lives openly any day of the week."

"He's my ticket out of here. I'm not a virgin, but he doesn't have to know that. I've always been of the opinion the less your husband knows about you, the better."

A knife thrower came out onstage. He had long hair, a handlebar mustache, and a pointed beard. When his assistant came out, the crowd went wild, whistling and banging their glasses on the table. She was wearing an extraordinarily provocative white corset and a tiny skirt. She had on white boots that laced up to her knees and an enormous feather on her head. No woman would be allowed to wear such an outfit in real life. But in art and spectacle you were allowed so many more liberties. She walked assuredly, lifting up her knees as though she were a pony. The knife thrower sharpened his knives as she pranced about the stage.

Sadie looked at his expression. She could not, for the life of her, come up with any conclusive notion of how he felt about the woman he was about to throw knives at. Was he looking at her as though she were a piece of meat he was about to carve up? Or was he looking at her with affection? It seemed a combination of the two. She wondered whether they were lovers in real life. She concluded that they had to be.

How could two people go through this intense relationship that involved trust and humiliation and not become lovers? How could he allow any other man to make love to her when he had such ownership over her body in these moments?

The assistant twirled and trotted about to give the audience a look at her body. Sadie witnessed a flicker of irritation in the knife thrower's face, as the girl was stealing the show when it was his act. He was the one with talent. The girl was replaceable. He could have chosen any down-and-out pretty girl from the street who could hold still. But he was wrong. He didn't know it was her absolute subjugation that caused the act to be a success.

She disappeared backstage and returned with a large wooden wheel adorned with black-and-white stripes. She allowed the knife thrower to tie her to the wheel. He spun her, and her body blurred like the wings of a magical hummingbird for a moment before slowing slightly. The knives flew at her spinning body. Each time, the knife came so close to hitting her, it sliced a lock of hair off. Everyone in the audience was quiet so they could hear the sound of the knife through the air, the thud of it hitting the wood, and the ecstatic yelp that came from the mouth of the girl.

When the woman stepped off the wheel, with a giant smile on her face, Sadie felt so inspired. Here was a woman who was not afraid of the violence of men. A beautiful body was always in peril, but this woman openly enjoyed that threat. It made her feel alive. She was not afraid to face it.

As she was taking a bow, Sadie noticed a trickle of bright-red blood going down her stocking.

Sadie saw the woman behind the theater as she and George left to walk back to the brothel. She was wearing a large coat and was smoking a cigarette standing next to a portmanteau. Sadie abandoned George to go speak to her.

SADIE HAD A SEXUAL PENCHANT for performers. Once she had seen someone on the stage, they held an attraction no one else could.

On the days Sadie brought someone home from the music hall, George was barred from her bedroom, of course. Sometimes George knew who Sadie was in her room with, and other times it was a mystery.

It was always noisy, as performers are quite talented at projecting their voices.

George went to the bathroom one night and a clown she had seen onstage earlier in the evening was sitting on the toilet. He had white pancake makeup on his dark face and black diamonds around his eyes. Earlier he'd had a red circle for lips, but that had been kissed off.

There was a strongman she had seen at the variety hall in the kitchen one morning. He was wearing the same striped suit from the night before except it was untucked and had been put back on without any care. He was holding the three-year-old daughter of a prostitute on his hand up over his head. The little girl rocked like the top of a pine tree and looked frightened. But the women were all amused.

Although some of the performers clung to Sadie afterward looking for love, Sadie always tossed them aside in the morning. She didn't even seem to know them or recognize them. It was as though she were making love to the fictional character and not them.

George tried not to be upset with Sadie's affairs. She could ignore the men. But the worst was when she saw the tightrope walker slipping out the door in the early morning. She was wearing a large red velvet cloak, but you could see the silver of her shoes with large red stars painted on the sides.

SADIE SQUATTED OVER THE BASIN at the brothel. She was douching herself with a poisonous concoction George had made for her. A piano player had ejaculated inside her. She had asked him not to. But then his orgasm had detonated like a landmine he had touched with his toe.

Sadie found that when she wrote after a sexual adventure, she was so charged creatively. She sat down and wrote real and imaginary sexual escapades. She wasn't exactly sure why she included Marie in all the stories. When she picked up the pieces of her clothes and put them back on, she always found herself wondering what Marie would think of all this. The reason Marie would be the perfect audience for these stories was they came from the same place. She would understand the hilarity of all the moments. The lower classes were not aware of just how amusing they actually were.

CHAPTER 31

The Selfishness of Mermaids

There was a room filled exclusively with statues of nymphs in Marie's house. Her father had gone through a period where he was quite consumed with possessing them.

Marie walked by the room one spring evening and looked in the door. The nymphs were all in their various odd positions. The moonlight gave them the effect of looking very much alive. They were in states of ecstasy. They reminded her of being young. She was so wild at one age. Was that state of being unobtainable to her now? Was each nymph expressing a mood Marie would never experience again?

They were so unselfconscious. They reminded her of the ways she used to feel when she spent time with Sadie. The hysterical affection and admiration she had for her. But what made all those states glorious was they were unaware of the rest of the world. They existed in the state purely. The nymphs were all contorted in miraculous positions. It made them look as though they were flames that had escaped the fire for a moment. It was right before the moment where oxygen snuffed them out.

❦

MARIE RECOLLECTED HOW SHE ONCE loved when Sadie would read poetry to her. As she sat in the grass one afternoon while listening to a poem, a tiger strolled silently around her. All the air grew tense when a tiger was nearby. Marie had struggled against the urge to stand up and run.

Another time she found herself sitting on a rock in the middle of the ocean while listening to a Tennyson poem read by Sadie. The waves were coming up close to her. She held up her knees and feet and pulled up her dress so she wouldn't get her shoes and skirt wet. When she felt safe from the water, she turned her head around. She let out a cry. There was a mermaid with a huge tail sitting next to her. She was beautiful and her blond hair was in thick strands down her face like seaweed. But the tail was terrifying.

Then she learned that an actual mermaid had come to town. There were advertisements for its arrival in the dime museum pamphlets. Mermaids lived alone, unmarried and wild. Marie thought if she were to see someone else in her position, it would cure her of her profound solitude.

Marie paid admission to enter into the dime museum where the mermaid would perform. She moved through the rooms of the museum, taking in the other specimens on display. There was a bell jar with a small mummified demon. It looked like a baby monkey with bat wings. There was a stillborn baby who had apparently been found in an ostrich-egg shell. How in the world an ostrich had become impregnated with a human was a mystery of science. Miracles defied science and happened all the time.

She had to force her way through to get a seat at the front of the small theater at the rear of the museum. She heard the sound of the train of her dress tearing as someone stepped on it and she tried to move forward at the same time. But she didn't care. There was a slight degree of humility you had to sacrifice along with the ticket price in order to see something magical. You had to admit that human reason and progress were in some ways lacking. You had been a fool.

You believed in what you needed to believe in these places. She needed to believe in the mermaid. Mermaids had no role other than to be themselves. They were not mothers or sisters or daughters.

MARIE SAT WITH THE AUDIENCE in a dark theater around a stage on which a group of blue curtains hung around a square frame. The lights went on. The curtains were pulled apart. There was a tank of water in which a woman with an enormous blue fish tail was swimming.

Marie's heart fell. She wanted to fall to her knees and pray. It was as though you had pulled back a shower curtain to see the Virgin Mary standing there, a halo of light around her head as the sunlight reflects through the shower's downfall.

The mermaid swam in circles, as though her tail were a paintbrush an artist was trying to rinse the color from. She looked confined. She was in captivity. But that made her all the more appealing to the audience. They were looking at somebody who didn't want to be looked at.

She put the palms of her hands against the glass. They clung to it like starfish. She pushed her face up against the glass. She looked at the audience. It seemed as though it was so much harder for her to see the audience than it was for them to see her.

She pretended to be in need of mercy. But if she were in the ocean, she would be grabbing onto the feet of swimming children and pulling them to the bottom of the sea and would let them go as soon as they were dead. They would float back to the surface with their mouths open and their arms spread, as though they had just seen God.

The crowd was informed the mermaid's tongue had been removed. She was prevented from singing. If she sang, she would cause members of the audience to run onstage and crawl into her tank, where she would proceed to strangle them.

How many deaths was she responsible for? She would stick her head out of the water and sing to sailors and fishermen on boats. The fishermen would slit their own throats and toss their bodies in the water.

The mermaid swirled her body around, regaining her grace. She lifted her arms and body over the side of the tank. Her hair was limp on her face like seaweed. It looked so much better underwater. She ceased to seem like a watercolor painting being created right before your eyes.

The mermaid opened her mouth and a silence came out that was so lonely and powerless and sad, the curtains immediately dropped. And you did not want to see more or ask any questions about the mermaid for days.

MARIE RODE HOME IN HER carriage lost in deep reflection about what she had seen. The mermaid was stuck inside a tank. She had a tiny world in which to exist. But that wasn't only because she was in captivity but also because she was unique. She would not be able to breathe outside of it. She had nothing in common with those who lived outside the tank. And what was the point of conversation other than to find points of communality? The mermaid was on display for everyone to stare at in amazement. And wasn't that somehow the role Marie played in society as well?

Like Marie, because of her peculiar gifts and powers, the mermaid could not mingle with outsiders. So be it. Marie's social world was limited. It was a necessary result of being powerful. To be a woman in her position was as unusual and unheard-of as a mermaid. She wanted to exist in a world that allowed her to be herself uniquely. The mermaid, like her, too, had no mate. She was doomed to a life of celibacy. But that chaste fate was also a gift. It ensured she would never see herself in relationship to another person. In this way she would only ever be herself.

She didn't want to question whether the mermaid was real. She wanted to believe in it. She was looking for her reflection somewhere other than a mirror. And she had found it looking into the glass of the tank. It was all she needed to believe that she herself was possible.

Marie then thought about Sadie. Her friend was a weakness. She was fine with being alienated from everyone around her because she did not see them as her equal and found them frustrating and banal. But she had a longing for Sadie that had always caused her to act in rash ways that were her undoing. In order to be powerful and protected, she had to close that one door in her heart she kept wide open for Sadie but that others were able to sneak in through, the way her rapist had.

She needed Sadie to know. She wanted to tell her the door was shut. So she would stop wondering whether Sadie had forgiven her and might reach out to her. No, she wanted to quash any possibility that Sadie might want to be friends with her, even if it wasn't going to happen. Then she could get on with the business of being herself and be done with that emotional part of her. The part of her that missed Sadie was soft and sensitive and might prevent her from doing what she needed to do in life.

ONCE AGAIN, MARIE HAD NO trouble finding out where Sadie was. Marie had enough money to know whatever she wanted to in the city. There were already spies at the factory. Every factory had them. Their job was to figure out what was going on in the heads of the factory workers. Her spy gave her Sadie's address and, surprisingly, a phone number she could reach her by.

"Is this number in the Squalid Mile?"

"Of course it is, miss."

"I wasn't aware anyone had a telephone there."

"It's a high-class brothel, miss. They get what they want."

Marie's cheeks went red for a moment. She felt jealousy pounding like enemy soldiers at the gate. But she would not give in to it. Sadie was working as a prostitute. Men were enjoying her company for a paltry sum of money while Marie had tried everything to win her affection.

THE PHONE WAS RINGING. It sounded like a high-pitched scream of a woman who was being strangled. All the whores were staring at it. They were rather frightened by the idea of picking it up. They were superstitious about the new telephone. Sadie walked past them and picked it up herself. But the moment after she said hello, she wished she had done otherwise. Because she heard Marie's voice from the other line.

"Hello, Sadie."

Sadie didn't say anything back. She was so excited to hear Marie's voice, she felt her heart drop. It appalled her how she always had such a physical reaction to Marie's presence. And now she had a reaction to just her disembodied voice.

"I wanted to tell you I saw a mermaid. It made me think of you. It made me think of all the magical poems we used to recite to each other. Remember when you recited the poem about the mermaid to me? It made me think of that day."

Sadie didn't say anything, but Marie continued, unaffected by the silence. "And no one knows where this mermaid came from. There is only one they have discovered. And when you look at it, you're supposed to assume there are hundreds and hundreds more of it someplace. That it must come from a civilization of mermaids under the deep. But what if that is the only mermaid there is?"

"It wasn't real, Marie."

"I saw it so clearly I knew it was real. There was no way it couldn't be. It was more real than anything else around me. It was more real than the trees and the dogs. More real than the garden. More real than my house and my father. More real than us."

"That's not what you called to tell me, was it?"

"I've decided to no longer be your friend. I will no longer be in love with you. I am letting you go. I am going to be my own person now. I am going to get what I want out of this world. This is my good-bye. I don't want you to ever come look for me, and I will never, ever again seek you out. I wish you well, but I hope never to see or speak to you again."

MARIE PUT THE PHONE DOWN in her bedroom. Then she stood on her large balcony. The five-o'clock shadow began to appear on the chins of men all over the city. The sky was outrageously pink and blue. The night would soon arrive and a full moon was expected. How fantastic it would look! The moon shone because the sun looked at itself in the mirror. Would we even exist if we weren't vain?

Marie felt an incredible coldness. She had stopped pursuing, even on an imaginary level, the one person she loved in the world. Sadie was no more. Sadie was dead to her. But she was not mourning Sadie, she was mourning the part of her that had ever loved Sadie. She had put aside a love for a father and now she was setting aside the love of her youth. In the coming days she knew she would become a monster. She stood on the balcony letting the metamorphosis happen.

IN LESS THAN TWO MONTHS, the sun had beckoned all the flowers from the ground. It was making everything else more brightly colored too. It made Marie's dress redder, her jacket bluer. It made her hair a wild gold color.

There were two smaller sugar factories in Trois-Rivières and Quebec City. She went to visit each and bought them. Although one of the factories had asked whether it could maintain the family name, Marie was adamant it be changed to her own. When they explained the importance of the name, she looked at them coldly and said no. And they looked into her eyes and saw there was no emotion there. They signed the papers, shook hands, and departed from the room, hoping never to see her again. Marie signed quickly, her pen making the sound of a fencing sword slashing through the air.

When she took over a factory, she fired all their previous foremen. Why would she continue to employ people who had allowed the company to be run to the ground? She docked the salaries at one plant, saying they repeatedly missed the new quotas she had set. She made a point of hiring children, especially young girls. They were not strong, but she could get away with paying them half. She made sure her sugar was the only one being distributed in Quebec. She did this by cutting operating costs and temporarily lowering the price of her sugar. This forced competitors from other provinces out of business.

She turned on the lamp on her desk in the evening and the stars in the sky all turned on.

The moon was like a clown who hadn't completely wiped the makeup off his face.

CHAPTER 32

The Pensées of a Whore

After Marie had hung up the phone the day she had seen the mermaid, Sadie stood in the exact same position she had been in when she had picked up the receiver. The finality of what Marie had said was ruthless. She was usually enraged after engaging with Marie, but now she was numb. Marie was gone from her life and had left a great void. She was shocked by the sense of absence. She didn't know how she was supposed to do anything. It was as though she had lost both her arms and she was told she had to pick up something heavy.

Sadie was depressed for several weeks. She looked around herself and everything seemed drab. She was sitting on a chair that many, many cats had taken their frustrations out on. She was in a whorehouse. There was a Danish on a cracked plate covered in flowers and it was surrounded by flies.

She decided she had to finish her book. When she finished the book, she would be able to start a new chapter in her life. She would be able to stop thinking about Marie. She would be a published writer. She would be a renowned author. Or even if she wasn't a renowned author, she would be much closer to being a renowned author than she was before. She would have something in her life that completely usurped her feelings about Marie.

SADIE WAS SITTING AT THE kitchen table in the brothel several months later in the fall. There were three other prostitutes, dressed in their bloomers and undershirts, lounging in their chairs like a group of wilting white flowers that needed to be watered. They began speaking about the bag of sugar in the center of the table.

"Ugh. I can't stand that face," a prostitute said.

Sadie looked at the bag of sugar and did a double take. She had been used to Marie's face on the side of sugar bags growing up. She thought Marie would always be young and adorable and sweet-looking on the sides of sugar bags. She would appear there the way she had in Sadie's memory in the time before the murder of Agatha. But suddenly the image on the bag had grown up. The new silhouette was mature and stately. It was more beautiful than the previous one. Sadie wanted the silhouette to turn her head and explain herself.

She leaned forward and pulled the bag to her. It was as though she were holding Marie's head in her hands, but Marie refused to look her in the eye.

"My whole family works at that factory," a prostitute said. "Marie Antoine is a nightmare. She is a monster. She's so greedy. She's buying up all the sugar factories. She wants to be the most powerful woman in the country. I don't know what makes a person like that."

"She's in love with herself," another prostitute said. "She can't spend all the money she has in this lifetime. She spent more on a painting than my family earned in a year."

"I worked at her factory before coming here," the first prostitute said. "She almost doubled her profit by making us all work twice as hard. She only cares about herself. She's worse than any man really."

Sadie hadn't been following Marie's journey. As is often the case when we leave someone, we expect they have stayed in the same spot we left them, as though they are statues frozen in time. She imagined Marie still at the embroidery circle making rose after rose. She hadn't envisioned her taking over the factory and becoming a ruthless employer.

The more the women insulted Marie, the more Sadie felt proud of her old friend. This was the Marie she had been expecting when she returned to Montreal.

She allowed her brain to accept Marie's new social position. She laughed to herself. She decided she couldn't help but be pleased. It was quite incredible that a woman had acquired this status. Marie could have simply acted how her father had, accepting the wealth and being a socialite. But instead she had opted to expand her company, take the reins in her own hands, and become a business mogul. Marie was breaking barriers in the same way she was. Sadie felt that Marie had moved further ahead of her. She hadn't expected that. She left the table feeling an urge to work on her novel. She wanted it to be out in the world upsetting and provoking people the way Marie was.

Sadie felt distinctly like she had when she was waiting to go up for her recital of *Goblin Market* all those years before. Sadie knew back then she could not win by imitating Marie, but she had to be as extravagantly and fearlessly herself as Marie had been. It was as though she were standing on the edge of a pool of her own personality and Marie had pushed her in. Even then Marie had caused her to raise her game. Now she would too.

How could you not love someone who you secretly feared was better than you? And naturally their success terrified you because it meant they were going to move off to somewhere in the universe far, far above you. So, yes, occasionally you struck out against the love of your life.

Marie had moved up in the world. But Sadie would move down, so far down it would be spectacular.

A group of bats flew past the window of the brothel, as though they were shadow puppets who had escaped a child's wall.

SADIE ANNOUNCED TO GEORGE AND Madame that she was quite prepared to earn a living as a whore now. She didn't have any reservations about prostituting herself. She was ready to take her research to a whole other level. In any case, Sadie's money from selling her dresses had more or less evaporated.

"You don't have to work," George told Sadie. "You can stay in my room. I will support you."

"I don't want to be dependent on anyone. You know that, George; that last pamphlet you were handing out said as much. I'm not afraid of doing this for a living. I want to see what revelations lie in store for me. There are things you can only know through experimentation and not observation."

"You should have a specialization," Madame told her. "Then you can charge more money. And you don't have to turn as many tricks."

"Yes, I've been considering what exactly I want to do."

SADIE DRESSED IN A BLACK CORSET. She wore black boots that went up to her knees and had a black mask she tied over her eyes. And she had a series of whips and canes. She became a specialist in sexual torture. Men came to visit her from all over the city to be subjugated by her specifically.

When she entered the brothel, she did not enter as a blushing, ignorant bride to the bridal chamber. She had read up on erotica. She knew all the positions and obscene acts that were hidden in the minds of people of the time. She had so penetrated the lusts of the girls at the boarding school that nothing could surprise her. She had learned that within the mind of any single girl lay the greatest pornographic works. The fantasies of any girl could compete with the greatest pornographic works written by men.

She could tame a man the way she could tame a horse. And the man was much less of a monstrous beast. And so, in comparison, was frightfully easy to subdue. In fact, she had to hold herself back sometimes in order not to permanently damage or kill a man.

It was true that a woman was weaker than a man in physical strength. But a woman was filled with rage. And like any animal or prey, she had learned to be more manipulative and cunning in order to survive.

SADIE CONSIDERED THE ACTS SHE engaged in at the brothel to be a form of theatrical performance. She contemplated what each encounter had meant. Sex was, like theater, a way of enacting social structures. It was a satire on the relationship between man and woman.

Sadie reflected that both men and women were capable of orgasms. A man's orgasm was purely functional. It was to create babies. Without a man's orgasm, the human species would entirely discontinue. But a woman's orgasm had no purpose other than enjoyment. It existed outside of motherhood. The human race would continue whether or not women had orgasms. All the strict matrimonial laws were put in place because men didn't want to have to stake their future on female desire.

Each man she was with gave away the secrets of men's vulnerable relationship to a woman's sexuality. They came to Sadie because they were tired of battling it all day. They simply wanted to lay at its mercy.

The characters Justine and Juliette began to engage in more and more licentious behavior. Sadie had dabbled in sexual encounters in her first draft of the book, but now she put it front and center. She felt emboldened by Marie's life, her hours of honing her skill and her experiences in the brothel. There was no situation too perverse for her two young heroines to throw themselves into with glee, and in great detail. She knew her book had moved into the realm of the pornographic. In most pornography women were subjected to the desires of men. But Sadie would reverse that. In her book, women's desire would triumph. They would enter into this world of the bedroom and they would have their way. The fantasy would be constructed by their imagination and not that of a man. By understanding the landscape of perversion and pornographic desire, she was able to build a world wherein her female characters could act with ultimate freedom and uninhibited indulgence.

There were such new possibilities in writing from a perspective of female desire. That excited Sadie as an artist. Sadie wanted to put things in literature that had never been there before. In fact, putting experiences into books that hadn't been there before was the modus operandi of a writer. It was like being a butterfly collector. You didn't want the same common butterflies every collector had. You wanted the rare butterfly with black spots on its wings that only emerges at the witching hour and sheepishly tucks its antennae into the closing mouth of drowsy flowers.

SADIE WROTE IN THE EVENINGS after her theatrics. Her words squiggled onto the page like the laces of a girl running for her life with untied boots.

Sadie had no interest in making love to George anymore as she wrote through the fall and winter. When she was done with her peculiar shifts, she wanted to go straight to writing. They did not go out drinking at the music hall because the book called to her. Sadie always had a million questions for George. They were always quite technical and about the book. Sadie didn't think much about George in any respect outside of the book. George, on the other hand, felt bereft. She missed when Sadie would beg her to tell her a story about her childhood.

George decided she was being ridiculous. Writing this novel was the most important thing to Sadie, and George was an invaluable part of the process. The ladies' society meeting she attended always said women had to support one another's work, as they were all working on a common goal in the end. But when Sadie slammed her manuscript shut in the evening and stuck her quill in the inkpot, George felt as though she too had been put away for the night.

Sadie was always meticulous about putting her papers and writing instruments away. It seemed she enjoyed the ritual, which indicated that a hard day of writing was completed. George imagined Sadie taking her own skinny body apart as though it were a pen. She imagined Sadie unscrewing her legs and arms and putting them in the drawers of her desk. Sadie would put George's head in the large bottom drawer, turn the tiny lock, and then go about her business, taking her out again when the need arose.

George thought this bizarrely grotesque image was comforting. Because it would at least make her feel as though she belonged to Sadie. George never considered that it was the subject of the book, more than the act of writing itself, that was shutting her out.

George was perhaps the only reader who would look at Justine and Juliette and not realize Sadie was working on a love story, the aspect of novels she hated the most. George knew Sadie as a disgraced aristocrat who worked as a dominatrix at a brothel in the Squalid Mile. And she knew Marie as a coldhearted celibate business tycoon. But Justine and

Juliette were a version of Marie and Sadie who had never been separated. In this story, they had left the Golden Mile together and had gone on their adventures as one. Pornographic as their story was, Justine and Juliette existed in an Edenic land of childhood innocence. George did not recognize the two delightfully perverted aristocratic ladies as being at all psychologically accurate portraits of Marie and Sadie.

CHAPTER 33

The Unborn

George was delivering a baby one winter afternoon for a woman who refused to get undressed. She had on a white coat with blue flowers all over it. George had to beg her to take even that off. George knew this was going to be a difficult birth. Some women were more prepared for the ordeal of labor than others were.

"Please, I don't want to do this!" the pregnant woman yelled. "I've made a horrible mistake."

"Come back. Don't be silly," George cried. "I have something for the pain."

"This creature is trying to kill me. Let's wait for it to die inside me."

The moon was full. It looked like a breast engorged with milk because of all the babies crying in the night.

The women from the brothel came out of their rooms and surrounded the woman. They held her still. George held a little rag with chloroform over her face. She opened her mouth to curse and succeeded only in inhaling more deeply. Everyone was quick to catch her collapsing body. There is something strangely heavy about a pregnant woman. As they carried her, they could see the baby squirming in her belly like a child playing hide-and-seek behind a curtain. Perhaps she was right. Maybe the baby was a demon who was out to destroy her.

The woman begged for more chloroform. She had been in labor for so many hours. George was so tired, her body kept trying to escape her and drop to sleep somewhere. She began hallucinating. There was a moment when she was quite sure that she saw a goat sitting on a chair in the corner. It was a white goat. It had the body of a young girl and the head of a goat. It sat there knitting. She kept blinking, waiting for it to disappear. And when it did, she turned to the woman, and rather thoughtlessly, almost as though she were in a trance, administered more chloroform. The woman then fell unconscious and there was nothing George could do to rouse her.

George was panicking, thinking she had murdered the young woman. But she had to deliver the baby at least. George pulled the baby out with forceps. Its head looked like it was trying to fit through the neck of a sweater that was too small. The baby was small and dark blue and clearly never had any intention of having anything to do with this world. George looked at the umbilical cord. We are all born with the rope for our own hanging, George thought.

George was seated with the baby in her arms, feeling culpable. But then at last the mother began to rouse herself. George considered that this woman had so narrowly skirted death. But it had taken her baby instead.

While the mother was fastening her coat over her still-plump belly, she announced it had all turned out surprisingly for the best. It was natural. In the spring there were purple baby birds that had been tossed out of their nests by their mothers. Perhaps their wings didn't match. Or they sang out of tune. They were the color of the painted eyelids of young women who had been thrown out of their houses and had become prostitutes.

She stumbled over a chair on her way out because she was still groggy from the chloroform. George ran to help her, but she put her hand out to object. "Don't mind me. I'm simply still in a dream." She smiled sadly and walked out the front door.

GEORGE WENT INTO THE KITCHEN the next morning. She had had a rough night, but the girls always seemed to have rough nights. They were seated around the table that morning looking worse for wear. One girl's hair was in such a tangled nest above her head, it looked like it would be impossible to pull the knots out of it. The lower half of another girl's face was covered in smudged red lipstick. A girl had dark circles under her eyes. It was strange to see them under the eyes of a thirteen-year-old. It was as though she had been kept up from nightmares about monsters and witches living in the shadows, not from men making love to her.

One girl with no pants on had a visible handprint on one of her buttocks. A girl was holding up a hand mirror to look at the size of a hickey on her neck. Another girl came over with a chunk of ice and put it on the hickey. Their crotches were all sore from sex.

They were like soldiers after the night of a battle.

"I'm all out of chloroform," George announced. "Would anyone like me to pick something up for them at Marat's pharmacy?"

"I would never touch anything from that pharmacy," Ramona said. "The woman is a murderer. That's clear. She has so many poisons on her shelf, she's liable to give you the wrong one. And you'll wake up as a corpse."

"Don't be stupid," George said. "Jeanne-Pauline knows what she is doing. She's a genius."

"I didn't say she wasn't a genius. I said she was wicked. And she loves revenge. It gives her pleasure. So she's waiting for anyone to cross her path."

"She's a witch," said another girl. "She gives me the creeps every time I look at her."

GEORGE HAD A COMPLETELY DIFFERENT opinion of Jeanne-Pauline. She was an excellent pharmacist.

George would list the symptoms of a girl at the brothel, and Jeanne-Pauline would have the cure.

She also sold condoms. And suppositories and thermometers. All sorts of items the girls needed all the time.

Jeanne-Pauline had cures for ailments male doctors did not believe in. She had a tea made out of dandelions that would cure period cramps. There was a tea that treated the deep depression some women sunk into after they gave birth. She had a cream that treated the unbearable and inscrutable itch some women got on their private parts. There was a bottle that helped with hot flashes. There was an elixir that you rubbed on to cracked nipples to ease breastfeeding.

She had a series of miniature bottles that were meant to treat the spiritual condition of being a baby. Or, put more simply, to make the baby stop crying. They were filled with cocaine and gin and that type of thing.

Women came to the pharmacy because they felt much better talking to Jeanne-Pauline about their conditions than doctors. She never made them blush. She made them feel as though the most embarrassing condition was normal, because, of course, it was. There were other legitimate reasons to avoid male doctors. So many women's ailments were seen as being symptoms of hysteria. The doctor might, at any moment, determine the women should be locked up.

GEORGE HEADED TO THE MARAT pharmacy to pick up more chloroform. A dog passed by her. It looked troubled by its own hardships as it walked down the street. It had perhaps just read Darwin's essays and was wondering how its desire for love had led it out of the woods and to this. George still felt as though death were hanging around her. Hadn't it taken enough? George was especially superstitious that day, purchasing chloroform. She had almost killed a woman with it. So, like any child of the Squalid Mile, she looked about her for signs of impending doom.

As GEORGE WAS ABOUT TO enter the shop, another figure swished out of it, leaving the door open for her. George looked back to see who it was. For the very briefest of moments, George believed she got a glimpse of Death. It was wearing a black coat. She couldn't make out Death's face, as it was wearing a heavy fur hat and a scarf around the lower half of its head. But she saw the gloved hands hold up the ends of the coat as it neared a puddle, and then leap over it. Death was a girl. She could tell one thing from the shape of Death's feet, and the daintiness of the leap it took: Death was a girl.

George shuddered and considered turning back. But without the chloroform, the women in labor were always threatening to jump out the window. She didn't have the energy to pull them off the ledge.

THE BELLS ON THE DOOR jingled and Jeanne-Pauline's eyes perked up when she saw George.

"Ah! I was just thinking of you. Would you like to come in the back and have some tea? We have to finish our conversation about class warfare."

"I'm in a hurry. I need some chloroform. I'm all out. The Suffragist Society is having a salon next Tuesday. Everyone would be happy to see you."

"I don't know about that. Last time, I had the distinct impression everyone found my ideas too extreme."

"Of course not."

"What will be the topic of discussion?"

"We're campaigning to have Mrs. Parkhurst from the English society of suffragettes come give a speech in Montreal."

"I have no interest in the vote, my love."

"What? I can't believe you would think that."

"No. I have no interest in appealing to men rationally. We need to terrorize them. We should be in control first. And then they can ask us for the permission to vote. Men need to be held accountable for their crimes against humanity. There needs to be a reckoning."

George looked at Jeanne-Pauline, waiting for her to continue, to offer some sort of specifics. But Jeanne-Pauline didn't continue. She stared at George as though confident George could read her mind if she chose to. George chose not to. George was frightened of some of the ideas in Jeanne-Pauline's mind.

As George was leaving, Jeanne-Pauline took a magnifying glass out to read with. She held it up to her face. Her eye floated around it like a fish in a bowl.

As much as she found delivering babies difficult, George had come to hate performing abortions even more. She had stopped a year before, declaring it was too much for her to bear. When the girls came, they were so desperate and distraught, it would take her at least a day to be able to get rid of their moods. Their moods would cling to her like a smell.

But then a beautiful girl with strawberry-blond hair and wearing a green coat showed up, looking as though she might jump off a bridge if she were turned away.

Every girl who walked into the brothel looking for an abortion knew they were taking a risk and that their lives were endangered. But they didn't really expect to die. Unwed mothers always thought they were immortal and untouchable. They came to see George because they wanted their lives back. They wanted to have wonderful lives. When-ever something was ruining your life, you began to value the old life that had been taken away from you so much more. They came to her terrified. They considered having a baby a fate worse than death.

George was known for keeping girls alive. In many ways the abor-tion was a simpler procedure than delivering a baby. It was quiet and it was less messy.

George looked the woman up and down. Her green coat had been mended several times in an effort to keep it from looking tattered. The tips of her black boots had been carefully painted. Her fingernails had been clipped and her face was scrubbed clean. She had made herself immaculate. She even smelled like lilacs.

But the most magnificent thing about her was all her strawberry-blond hair. Despite all the obstacles that had been put in her path, she didn't think she could truly rail against fate because she had been blessed by a full head of perfect strawberry-blond curls. Not every girl had been given that. And her curls had always gotten her a little bit extra in life. When she was younger, her mother would send her to the butcher and not her other siblings, because the butcher always gave her a slice of meat that was a little bit bigger. People were always giving her a slice of life that was a tiny bit bigger. And that tiny bit was what she built her personality on.

She called George "sir" and held both her hands. The poor girl was idiotic enough to still believe the answer to one's problems were men. She was happy to see a male doctor because now her medical needs would be properly attended to. She told George her story. The owner of the shoe factory where she worked had gotten her pregnant. He had told her to come here. He had given her the address. He was the only one who knew. The whole affair had been a secret between them. He had made her keep it a secret. The girl thought secrets were special and made two people closer together than anybody else. She didn't know secrets were the enemy of women. Women should beware of the word "secret" at all costs.

George led her into a room where there was a bed in the middle. It was at the back of the house, away from everything else. It did have somewhat the feel of a cell. But that was so the sounds of screaming women in labor were not so loud in the rest of the brothel.

The girl took off her green coat. The white dress didn't have a single crease in it. George could see there was a slight stain at the bottom that had been scrubbed at. Despite the presence of faded stains all over the dress, it gave the impression of being clean. It looked as clean as the dress the Virgin Mary must have worn when she went door to door looking for a place that would give her an abortion. When she took off the dress, her petticoats were tattered at the bottom, like an envelope that had been messily opened with a finger and not a knife. Her poverty was revealed the more she became undressed.

It turned out the strawberry-blond girl had kept the baby inside her as a possibility much longer than she should have. And that possibility reacted very strongly to being negated. It no longer thought of itself as a possibility but as a hard truth. It saw its mother as a host. Like all children, it came to see its mother as a vessel to satisfy all its needs. When a mother neglects her child, the child reacts with an unprecedented fury.

The girl was sick for two days. Her face was covered in sweat; it made her look dewy. She looked as though fairies had placed a spell on her. She was enchanted. There was nothing George could do for her now. She was going to be led away into the woods. And on the morning of the third day, she was dead.

WHAT COULD THEY DO WITH the corpse? George made sure to put the green coat back on the girl. She had gone through so much trouble to keep it in good condition, it seemed only fair she should show up at the gates of heaven or hell wearing it. They folded her body into a large trunk. George looked at the girl once more. She was curled up as though she were a dreaming child. They hurried the body out of the brothel in the middle of the night. As they exited the brothel, snowflakes landed on their faces, melting into crocodile tears that steamed down their cheeks.

George reflected that the girl would not get a chance to say good-bye to anyone. She would not get to say good-bye to her siblings. She would not get to say good-bye to her parents. She would not get to say good-bye to her cat. She would not get to say good-bye to her neighbors. She would not get to say good-bye to the girls who worked on either side of her on the factory line. She would have to be replaced by another girl on the line. The girls on either side of her would have to slightly adjust themselves to the presence of a new body and then she would be gone.

What would people think happened to this girl? They would think she had been murdered. It was better for them to believe she had been abducted. Then they would believe that some sort of injustice had befallen her. Then she would at least evoke some sympathy. If they found her body in its actual state, everyone would think what had happened to her was her own fault. She had spoiled herself. She was a whore and perhaps it was better she was dead.

No one in the brothel thought it was George's fault. But she knew that no matter what anyone told her, she would blame herself. George had never killed a woman before. She felt like a murderer. She wanted to be prosecuted. She wanted to confess. She never wanted anyone to mistake her for an innocent. They should all know she was a murderer and treat her as such.

George was expecting the girl's ghost long before it finally showed up.

Since it was the age of invention, there would soon be no more ghosts. The houses were raised and fell apart so quickly, they were not at all appealing for ghosts. But the brothel was an older house. It had the types of nooks and crannies that ghosts enjoyed finding themselves in. Ghosts liked history. They also liked beautiful things. They had chairs they liked to continue to sit on. They had mirrors they liked to look in. Ghosts were truly in love with architecture. They got fixated on certain spots. And there was no one in the world who could convince them heaven might be a better place.

The ghost of the girl in the green coat would be in the strangest places. One morning George looked up and saw her lying on top of the kitchen cupboards. Another time, she was in the small backyard standing in the snow. She was sitting at the top of the stairwell and George was terrified to climb it.

George opened the bathroom door and the ghost was sitting on the toilet. She was on a chair in the parlor, holding a book in her hand, weeping: "I can't get past the first page, I keep reading it over and over again." She was sitting at the kitchen table with an egg in her hand. "Shhh," she whispered. "I'm waiting for it to hatch."

Each time George saw the ghost, she was utterly devastated. She had never been this upset. She found herself trembling in bed at night. It was as though she herself were lying at the bottom of an unmarked grave. Why did the girl seem to blame her? She didn't seem to blame her only for the abortion but also for getting pregnant in the first place. Did that make any sense? How was she responsible for this whole girl's life and any bad thing that had befallen her?

But reason would not let George off the hook. She decided the only way to have the ghost be at peace was to act as though she were responsible for all the young girls who were dying on tables and beds throughout the city.

It occurred to her that many of the girls who arrived at the brothel, either for work or for abortions, were in large part completely ignorant. They were so surprised by their own ruin, as though it had hit them like lightning and not through an inevitable path the world had set out for them. She thought they should at least know their story was a familiar one. Instead of helping girls once they were in this situation, wouldn't it be better to help them avoid it in the first place?

THERE WAS A TIME IN a young man's life when he paused and looked around at the world and determined how he wanted to be in it. And set forth on that adventure. George took off all her clothes and looked in the mirror. And all she saw there was a young man looking back at her. And the young man said, "You need to follow your path. You have to try to change the world and the way women live. That is who your true self is. That is where your talents lie."

CHAPTER 34

The Lady from the Mirror

Marie climbed into the back of her carriage after visiting the factory. It had been a full year since she had spoken to Sadie on the telephone and she had continued her ascension in the business world relentlessly. She had fired one of the overseers who had worked at the factory for fifteen years, and it had caused an emotional ruckus. But he was not implementing her decisions with enough efficiency and was second-guessing her choices. She felt as though she couldn't breathe because of the pollution. In the carriage she felt as though she were suffocating, and she opened the window as it was pulling away from the factory even though she knew this was quite a foolish idea. The streets down here stunk so badly, they always made her feel as though she were going to puke.

To her surprise, she smelled something quite splendid and lovely. It was coming from the bakery next to the factory. It smelled like cake. She was overcome by a deep craving to stuff her mouth full of cake.

She banged on the carriage to make it stop. She meant to send the driver in to commission some cakes. But when they pulled up in front, Marie was intrigued by the window display and decided to climb out and have a look herself. When she got up close, she saw, to her amazement, the roses on the cakes were actually icing.

Marie had heard about Robespierre Bakery. It had once been independent but was now affiliated with the factory. She could not recall whether this was her doing or not.

As Marie gazed closely into the window, she saw the reflection of her own face. Her hair was out of place, as a blond curl hung down on her forehead. She pushed the hair on her forehead to the side, but the curl didn't budge. She realized she wasn't looking at her reflection at all. She was looking at another woman. The woman looked so much like her it was quite startling. She stepped back from the window. The woman disappeared and the reflection of the street appeared immediately on the surface of the window where she had been.

Marie stepped inside the shop. The woman she had seen was standing there as though awaiting her. She was dressed in a white baker's dress with a large apron over top. Her hair was up in a messy bun and had a small white cap pinned to the back of it. Their clothes and social position were so different, no one else in the bakery was able to see the resemblance. But the women both saw it. Whereas it seemed to clearly amuse the baker, Marie was startled.

Her body knew information that her mind didn't. Her body sensed danger. Her nipples were erect. There was an electric current running through her body. She felt like she could touch an incandescent bulb and turn it on with her finger. She wasn't sure how her reflection had climbed out of her mirror and had escaped down here. Her reflection had always been so faithful.

"You are the baker?" Marie asked, hoping that speaking to the girl would break this spell.

"Why wouldn't I be?"

"Why would you be?"

"Am I the baker?"

"I am interested in looking at those roses."

"Those roses are of interest to you?"

"May I commission some of these and have them sent to my home?"

"You want to commission these and have them sent to your home?"

"Yes."

"Yes."

Marie couldn't make any sense of the conversation. The young woman took a small notepad out of a pocket in her apron.

"What is your name?"

"Marie."

"I am a Mary too. But you probably know that."

"How would I know that?"

"Isn't it obvious?"

Marie made a purchase, almost as if to have an excuse to leave the shop. She left with a box of cupcakes that were covered in blue waves. She opened the lid of the box. It was as though the waves were moving back and forth. She was like a giant holding the ocean in her arms. She had a peculiar feeling. It was the feeling of being lost at sea. The feeling was so big. She closed the lid of the box and hurried back to the carriage.

WHEN SHE ARRIVED HOME, MARIE handed the cupcakes over to the maids. They stuffed them into their mouths. She couldn't resist eating one herself. It was sublime. When she looked in the mirror later, her lips were still blue from the icing. As though she had just been murdered.

MARIE WAS INTRIGUED AND REPELLED by the other Mary. She could not get her out of her head. When she looked in the mirror, she didn't know whom she was looking at. She kept expecting her reflection to speak back to her. To tell her things she didn't know about herself.

She had always thought of herself as the prettiest and most cultured girl in the neighborhood. She had always believed she deserved special treatment because she was so splendid and unique. The idea of this kind of equality was horrifying. It was as if money didn't matter.

She had a dream she was in a hall of mirrors. There were a hundred reflections of herself. They were all reaching out to her as though they wanted her to come to them. But she held her hands tightly to her side, refusing to be beckoned. She was the original. She did not act in unison the way they did. But on the other hand, they were all acting in unison like an army.

She began to have recurring dreams of multiple Marys. There was a carriage of young women that stopped in front of her. She paused to allow the passengers inside to dismount. One by one they climbed out. There were six Marys who looked just like her. She wasn't even sure how all those Marys had managed to fit in the carriage. There was something terrifying about all the Marys. She knew there was no way to share everything she had with them. She would become one of them instead of the other way around. Why couldn't they allow her to be the exception?

She woke up in a cold sweat. Her blankets had crept to the end of the bed, as though they were an animal that was terrified of her. She realized from her dreams the Marys were coming for her.

MARIE DECIDED SHE WOULD GO and speak to Mary at the bakery again. She thought if she were to see Mary this time, she would realize they didn't look the same at all. And if anything, their similarities would prove to be superficial. She would get over this peculiar bewitchment.

She had just ended her obsessive attachment to Sadie, but this one was far more threatening to her sense of identity.

When Marie arrived in the bakery, she found herself pressed into the small space with a dozen other people, all of whom were jostling about, crying out in French to get the attention of the salesgirl. Marie wanted to get to the front so she could ask to see Mary. There was a sudden presence behind her back. She turned. There was Mary holding a box, standing in the doorframe.

Mary's shadow seemed to fall on Marie perfectly, causing only her to be in darkness while the rest of the shop was still bathed in light. It occurred to Marie she had never been able to lean in a doorway in public like that. Mary suddenly had so much power. She was in her element. She could do what she wanted in a way Marie could not. Mary made a gesture with her head that Marie should follow her. Marie hurried out.

"Would you like to come up to my room for some tea?" Mary asked. "I've finished work. I have to go to sleep in a couple hours. I work all night. I'm nocturnal now. I can hardly even stand to be in the sunlight. It makes me so sleepy."

Marie nodded slightly and followed her up the iron staircase that scaled the side of the building to the second floor. Marie was afraid to look down as she climbed. It seemed like an acrobatic feat, not something a person would do several times a day. She stood behind Mary on a small landing as she unlocked her door.

The apartment was incredibly dark. There was green paint on the walls that had chipped off in places. It was decorated in a very sparse manner. There were very few objects. There were two upholstered chairs. They had been sat on so many times the upholstering was almost black, although Marie could still make out the pattern of sparrows that had been embroidered into them. Marie was surprised the woman lived alone, even if it was a dingy apartment.

Marie realized how little she knew about anybody from this class. She didn't know anything about the pasts of her maids. It was as though they had appeared at her home fully formed.

Mary set her box on the counter and went to heat up some tea on the stove. The teapot was the first object in the apartment Marie had spotted that seemed to be of any worth. It was quite beautiful, crafted out of fine China with a green parrot painted on it. For some reason, she thought the girl must have stolen it. For a moment she was worried for her safety. Marie sat down at the small table.

"How old are you?" Marie asked suddenly.

"How old are you?"

"Twenty-four."

"Twenty-four."

"You are the same age as me?"

"You are the same age as me."

So it hadn't been the result of an awkward first encounter. This was very much the manner in which Mary acted whenever she was questioned. It had a strange rhetorical effect indeed. Mary intended to dominate this conversation and steer it wherever she wanted it to go.

Mary pulled on the ends of the gold bow on the cake box. The sides of the box all fell down, revealing a small round cake with white bows made out of frosting along the edges. She sliced a piece for Marie. She put it on a china dish that again looked too fancy for the apartment. She sat directly across from Marie.

Marie felt comforted when she held the saucer and the teacup in her hand. They were from her own world, of that she was sure. And the cup was probably so delighted to be held by her.

"Where are you from?" Marie asked.

"Where are you from?"

"Montreal, of course."

"Montreal, of course."

"Everybody in the city knows who I am."

"Everybody in the city knows who I am."

Marie looked closely into the other girl's eyes to see if she were deliberately provoking her, as though she were peeking into a keyhole trying to spy on the nocturnal, hidden activities behind it.

"My mother died when I was a baby," Marie said.

"My mother died when I was quite young."

"She killed herself."

"Mine was murdered."

"She was!"

"She was."

"And what of your father?"

"My father is your father."

"What do you mean?"

"What do you think I mean?"

"Do you have proof of this?"

"I have the bakery, don't I?"

"Because you lost your finger in one of his machines."

"Don't be stupid. You've seen what having a finger cut off gets you. It gets you a turkey. It doesn't get you your own business. Besides, it was only a pinky. Ask yourself what exactly a pinky is good for. And ask yourself, what could you trade a pinky for?"

Marie, naturally, had no idea how to answer this question. A white swirl of steam rose up off the tea like a naked girl climbing out of a bathtub.

"Let me tell you a story, since you seem to like stories," Mary said. "This is a story about us, two little girls who looked exactly the same. One of us was chosen. And one of us was buried. One of us was pampered. And one of us was crushed. One of us wore beautiful dresses and

297

one of us wore rags. One of us ate cakes and sweets. The other stayed up through the night making them more and more delicious. One demanded the cakes be more and more delicious. And the other complied. One wore beautiful rings on her hands. The other cut off her finger to be able to pay for a future. The whole time we thought the one who lived in the light was the one who was chosen. But this was not true. The one who was thrown in the dark was the one who had been chosen for a marvelous journey."

"No," Marie said assertively. "You saw me once. And you saw there was a resemblance between us. You are covetous by nature, and now you want what I have, but it isn't yours. It will never be yours. You think there's a way we could change places. That isn't true at all. We are nothing alike. I have worked for what I have. You don't have the character for it. You sneak around taking advantage of people. You tricked my father into giving you a bakery through your macabre antics. You might have convinced him you were his child. But I see you for what you are. A fake who wants to steal what isn't yours. You wouldn't even know what to do with it if you had it."

Marie stood up and left the apartment. She had no intention of listening to this nonsense anymore.

AFTER LEAVING, MARIE UNDERSTOOD WHY Mary Robespierre had upset her so much. She had suspected the truth from the moment she had laid eyes on her but hadn't wanted to admit it to herself.

Her father had been irresponsible. Her father had always had women in his bedroom. Of course he would have had other progeny. She hated that she was not his only child. There were so many people in the Squalid Mile who looked and acted like her and her father, and they fit right in. She had more in common with people of the Squalid Mile than with anyone in the Golden one. She could not stand that these people had an affinity with her. She blocked it out.

She had always looked down on that class. Her father had always shuddered and felt a great sense of unease whenever he was around factory workers. He would have a bad mood like a storm cloud follow him around the whole day after he had been with them. The cloud would then dissipate and he would be in a sunny mood again. What had affected him was seeing himself in those people and their sordid lots.

Marie had never experienced even an inkling of this. But now she knew exactly the feeling her father had fled from all those years before. She had seen her reflection in the Squalid Mile. She did not want to empathize with those people. She did not want to imagine what it felt like to be in a vermin-infested home. She did not want to know what it was like to have multiple children in her home. She didn't want to know what it was like to work in one of her factories.

These sensations were like cantankerous workers who tried to get her attention. But they were much more insidious. They snuck in underneath the doors. There was nothing that could be done to keep them out. They came through the walls. She felt as though she were being haunted. It took her a week to get the ghosts out of her head.

PART THREE

CHAPTER 35

Justine and Juliette

Sadie had written through the winter. George sat beside her with holes in the fingertips of her gloves crafting and editing the book. Sadie had little time to actually make love. She implied to George that once the book was done they would take some time off and engage in a real-life sexual escapade of their own. It put a joyous impetus in George's editing as she rewrote Sadie's madcap pages into a coherent narrative. It was as though they were a beast with two heads and four arms who together were creating something that surpassed the imaginations of any solitary, ordinary mortal. And in the spring of 1886, the book was done. The printer knew immediately he had a hit with the pornographic work Sadie handed to him.

OF COURSE, ONCE THE BOOKS were printed, there was still the question of selling them. Sadie's father had been campaigning so hard against immorality in Montreal, it was impossible to publish it with a legitimate publisher who would put it in bookshops. Madame was very willing to sell the books from the brothel. But George wanted to make them available to people who would not feel comfortable stepping foot in a brothel—namely, young girls.

George knew how everything worked in the underworld. Madame had her tentacles in all the different illegal enterprises of the city. They were all interconnected.

Having been sent everywhere on errands as a child, George had known everybody on the criminal side of the city since she was a little girl. She knew who was willing to sell contraband items. She went to the stores that were already involved in some sort of illegal activity. They were professionals in being clandestine.

She went to the bookie in his little shop with a slanted ceiling. He was a tall man with a gold tooth and a scar under his eye. When George was little, he let her sit on his knee and roll dice for him while he bit her ear. Because he considered her lucky. He had never imagined that he would ever have anything to do with the literary world.

She went to the saloon. The owner had a bulbous nose covered in veins. It looked like a broken teacup that had been glued back together. He had a cane with a swan head behind the counter that he would beat people with whenever they would get rowdy. The owner once gave her a shot of whiskey on her sixteenth birthday. She had fallen asleep almost immediately and had fallen off the barstool. He had had a soft spot for her since then. And said he would, of course, sell her books.

There was an apple merchant who was a regular at the brothel and well liked by all the whores. He always brought an apple along to give to the whore he was making love to. He liked the way girls' mouths tasted after they bit into apples. He showed George how to juggle apples when she was a girl and as she was tossing them in the air, one fell on her nose and broke it. He said he would sell them at his cart.

She still wasn't sure that young girls would feel comfortable buying books from any of these men. Then she thought of Jeanne-Pauline Marat's pharmacy. She went to see her.

"I've a book I'm going to publish. Will you sell it at your store?"

"That's an odd request. This isn't a bookstore."

"I'll leave you a copy, then, and you can decide."

Jeanne-Pauline picked up the book and stroked the cover with admiration.

"Oh my, George, you are meant for great and terrible things. You don't even realize it."

JEANNE-PAULINE CLOSED UP THE PHARMACY. She went into her apartment, which was at the back of the shop, carrying the book under her arm. She was always pleased to retreat to her apartment in the evening. She had never gotten over the thrill of it.

The truth was, she had always liked being alone. Women never got to be alone. That was too much of a luxury. Women always had someone to take care of. She had no one to take care of. She got to really do what she pleased. She left her clothes on the side of the bed. There was no one who would yell at her for leaving them there.

One of her most vivid memories of her wedding day was of being so cold. She was standing at the altar and she was trying so hard not to let her teeth chatter. She was wearing a lace dress. It had short sleeves. Her wedding veil was hanging down over her face and shoulders. It was the most inappropriate shawl. She was carrying a bouquet of white roses. They were trembling in her hands. She was afraid everyone would think she was terrified of being married. She wished she at least could wear gloves. The diamond on her wedding ring looked as though it were made out of ice.

She had pushed the bathtub so it was close to the fire. And that way the bathwater managed to heat up and stay warm as she was sitting in it. As though she were a giant dumpling sitting in a pot of stew. The warmth of the water made her forget the cold sensation of her wedding day. She was free. She settled into the bath to read the book.

WHEN GEORGE STOPPED BY TWO DAYS LATER, Jeanne-Pauline was very receptive to the idea of selling the books at her store.

"I'm very proud of you, George. I knew you would do something marvelous with your life since you were a very little girl. You were given a very powerful gift. You aren't attracted to men. And so no man has been able to curb any of your natural talents. The written word is a deadly thing.

"Of course you will be punished for it. But your punishment will be glorious. When a punishment is glorious, it is no longer a punishment, but a sacrifice."

"What do you think of the book?"

"It's completely preposterous and it's episodic. I've gone through my change in life, so I won't get as excited as many of the younger readers will. I do like that you've begun a press. You were too intelligent to spend the rest of your life working at the brothel and ending pregnancies. Not that that isn't a noble profession, but this is a new chapter in your life. I think this is just the beginning of your venture. When you begin publishing your own texts, that will be an extraordinary thing. You will have more interesting things to say than a spoiled aristocrat."

George bristled at this dismissal of Sadie. She had known for some time that Jeanne-Pauline didn't consider Sadie worthy of George's affections. She thought Sadie was using George and treating her as though she were disposable.

"And will you sell it at your store?"

"I've always been prepared to make a martyr of myself for a cause. Honestly, it's probably what has kept me going for so long. I've never been afraid of any death, including my own. I've lived so freely and fully, it would be an honor to be shot to death now. It isn't practical to live past a certain age, especially if you don't have any children. It's a wonderful thing. I've come to love being independent."

A criminal who disdains the law is a revolutionary.

JEANNE-PAULINE WAS ADEPT AT SELLING *Justine and Juliette*. Jeanne-Pauline made fake covers for the books sold at her store. She made an illustration of an orchid to go on it. She called it *A Quebec Book of Flora and Fauna*. She seemed to find this particularly funny, although no one else did.

Once George received a box from the printer, she would head straight to Jeanne-Pauline's, since there was always a demand for the books at her pharmacy. They sold more there than anywhere else.

Jeanne-Pauline began to sell packages of placebos. They were inexpensive, but the customers had to buy them in order to have the book. This way she could keep men from buying the book.

Men were the ones who would turn on you and report you to the police. She could look into women's faces and know they were reliable. Even if she were betrayed by a woman, she would accept that as a calculated risk. She could never tolerate being duped by a man.

She always kept the women in the store for several minutes before allowing them to leave with the book. If there was too much coming and going, it was bound to draw attention from the authorities. They didn't like to see women engaged in any furtive activity. They would by their nature be alarmed by women making money. "You really shouldn't be afraid of masturbating. It's a glorious thing. It's very soothing. It's a prescription for headaches," she would say to them.

EVERY PERSON WHO HAD AGREED to sell the book contacted George within two weeks of its publication, asking for more copies. George found herself going to and from the printer on a weekly basis. They could barely keep up with the demand. Word of the book spread through the city, and everyone seemed to want a copy. Sadie loved to spot copies of *Justine and Juliette* on the street. It was surprising to her that women from all different walks of life would read it. She saw a woman sitting next to a perambulator and reading it on a park bench. The twins inside the carriage were wrapped in each other's arms and her six-year-old was up in a tree.

She saw a girl in the back pew at a church. Her head was down and her lips were moving as she read. She wasn't reading the Bible, however. She had a copy of Sadie's book in her lap. She saw two girls on the trolley seated next to each other and sharing the book. One would try to turn the page, and the other would hold her hand up. They almost missed their stop.

She saw a young girl wink at a cat. She was holding Sadie's book under her arm. She saw a girl riding a bicycle and whistling. She saw the book in her basket. The girl was wearing a violet tailcoat that flew up behind her as she rode like a pair of racing sea otters.

Sadie thought she could tell when a woman had read her book. The woman seemed a little more bold. There was a skip in her step. Sadie wondered if it was a livelier type of girl who picked up the book to begin with, or if the book itself had the effect of making the reader livelier.

It wasn't just the fact that the book made a girl have an orgasm so intense that it made her more animated and bolder. It was the impression the characters in the book made on its female readers.

Justine and Juliette weren't at all interested in men. They were fascinated with each other and being free. This was a book that was telling readers they had a right to a different kind of drive.

They didn't have to become wives and mothers. Their desires might take them someplace else entirely.

One of the prostitutes had a sister who worked at the factory. She told Sadie there were girls at the factory who passed the book from one to the other. One girl began to hide a portion of her earnings in her boot. One girl refused to let her brother abuse her anymore. One girl ran away from home and no one knew where she went. It was said she had joined a traveling circus. Something inside her told her she would look good on the back of a horse after reading the book. One girl decided to go to college to be a doctor.

They often went back for second copies of the book to buy for friends so they, too, could experience this weird transformation. Others had seen the effects of the book on friends and came to get a copy of it for themselves, hoping it would also give them the courage to enact unique transgressions.

Other girls bought the book because they were simply horny and had no idea of the book's possibilities. It turned out that sexual awareness did not lead women to iniquity but toward empowerment.

SADIE WAS NOW TRULY A WRITER. Her original manuscript could not be taken away from her. It lived in the minds of others. The books would no doubt be decimated all over the city. But even if there was an attempt to burn them, there would always be one or two that survived.

Books were very much like rats. They went into the walls and hiding places. They proliferated in a secret way that was invisible. A single book could be passed around to twenty people. And when those people read the book, a copy existed in their head. And once a book is in someone's head, it has a way of spreading through ideas and conversation. And when someone who has read your book speaks to someone who hasn't, they transmit the world of the book without even knowing it.

As a runaway and then prostitute, Sadie had existed very much on the fringes, her name spoken in whispers in respectable company. But now she would be public again. Her name was all over the city. She felt a life change coming on, in the way a person feels an inevitable storm approaching.

Names often became common nouns instead of proper ones. The name Arnett was recognizable because of her father and brother's continuous involvement in city politics. She would change that. The name would belong to her. And when people heard the name, they would think of all her proclivities and inclinations and thoughts.

Although the name Arnett had connoted opposing decadence in art, now it would come to be that which it opposed. Thus the name would doubly be associated with naughtiness in art and the secret delight of perversion. Every family has a seed of its own destruction in it.

Anything Mr. Arnett proposed at public meetings would be met with snickers and derision. What in the world was weaker than not being able to control your own daughter? Fathers not being able to control their daughters was a much greater sign the moral fabric of society was slipping than the ribaldry of the theater. Her brother would be considered to be cut from the same cloth. And her mother, Sadie thought with delight, would no longer be able to pretend she didn't exist. In fact, her mother would be thinking about Sadie's existence every moment of her now wretched day.

DESPITE BEING PUBLISHED UNDER THE name Sadie Arnett, George felt very much ownership toward the book. She and Sadie began to make love more frequently. When they were spent, they liked to lie next to each other and spend hours describing what they had achieved. They were pleased with themselves. But the rush and pleasure of it was so great, it immediately made them terrified of it slipping through their fingers and them losing it. They needed more of this feeling. Suddenly all other epicurean delights paled in comparison to this one. Nothing tasted as sweet, music didn't move them in the same way. They were ready to start working on another novel.

Sadie stuck her quill into the inkpot. It drew up the ink like a feasting mosquito. She began scratching on her blank paper.

George liked that Sadie was writing books that shocked and provoked. But the tone was so aristocratic. The meanings were lost because of all the smut in the pages. She knew people read them to be titillated. And because they were filled with aspects of the taboo, they gave whoever owned them a thrill because they were carrying around a secret. Because they were filling their brains with things they shouldn't be filling them with.

But at the same time, George didn't believe they addressed the inequalities that women faced, and they didn't show them practical ways they could pursue the desire and joie de vivre the books had evoked in them. She wished there was a book everyone would read that delved into the way ordinary women lived. And how they were mistreated by everyone. How they were having their right to be happy exploited by the rich. A book about how women were exploited by their husbands. And their families. And society at large. How all girls were preyed upon, how a girl's talents were so unfulfilled and undermined in society.

CHAPTER 36

Read This Novel Naked

One afternoon, Marie looked out the window of her office into the backyard. It was the first day in spring that was warm enough for people to linger outside comfortably. She saw a maid sitting on an upside-down mop bucket. She was reading a book and was utterly transfixed. The wind kept trying to turn the page of her book, as though it were reading ahead of her and was eager to get to the next page. Another maid carried a mop bucket over to her, turned it upside down, and sat on it. And began to read over the other maid's shoulder.

Marie didn't read novels herself. Neither did she keep up to date on what was being published or causing a wave. She did, however, read the newspapers. She had every one of them delivered to her home in the morning. She read the pile with her coffee and her egg. She needed to keep abreast of everything happening in the city and country. She read with a large pair of scissors at her side. When she came across an article of interest to her or her business, she snipped it out.

But she was curious about the book the maids were reading. She kept watching them read. They were reading it with a fervid devotion, as though it were a romance novel. But at the same time there was a look of bemused intelligence to their expressions. They were engaging with the book in a way that was unusual in its intensity.

She called the first maid in later in the day. The maid stood in front of Marie's desk. She was a beautiful mixed-race girl.

"What was that book you were reading earlier?" Marie asked.

"What book is that, ma'am?" the maid asked, looking flustered.

"You were reading a book while sitting outside. I saw you from my window."

"I was on my break."

"Yes, I didn't say you weren't."

"I decided to read on my break. I did everything I was supposed to. I very much like working here. I like it so much better than the house where I worked when I was younger. If you don't want me to read, then I will not."

"We are having two different conversations. I don't care that you were reading. I want to know the title of the book."

The girl's cheeks turned a bright red. She looked down at her feet and then at Marie and then at the floor again.

"It's *Justine and Juliette*, ma'am," she answered with her eyes cast downward. "I was curious. I didn't know how many inappropriate things were in it until I read it. I had no idea."

"I've never heard of the book. Who is it by?"

"Sadie Arnett, ma'am."

Marie felt her eyes grow three sizes bigger. She always had that sensation when she was taken off guard. She never knew whether other people were able to notice. How could she not have known Sadie had written a book? How could she have missed the most important thing going on in Sadie's life? This was almost unbearably exciting news. She was feeling so many vulnerable and surprising feelings, she wanted to be alone. Even though she was quite good at keeping her emotions to herself, she might not be able to in this case.

And anyway, she wanted to feel these emotions to their fullest. She wanted to let her body shake and quake. She didn't want to make it hold back.

"Will you go to the bookstore at once and get me a copy?"

Marie reached into her pocket and took out a bill. It was enough to buy ten books. But naturally, it didn't matter to her. She would have given up her entire fortune, her house, to have a copy of that book in her hands.

"No, ma'am, you can't get it at a bookstore. It's a dirty book. It's illegal."

"Well, keep the money for yourself and give me your copy."

The maid had trouble suppressing her smile, knowing it was a tiny fortune she had just come by.

"I'll go get it from Lucy. She borrowed it from Rachel. I gave it to Sally to read and she was supposed to give it right back the instant she was done with it. But she gave it to Rachel. Never mind. You don't need to know this. I'm going to go find you the book!"

The maid turned and darted out of the room. Marie sat doing absolutely nothing, waiting for the maid to return. She could almost hear the girls scuffling about, as though she were listening to mice moving about in the walls. She tried to visualize where the maid might be. She was imagining her quite on the other side of the house. And she was startled when the maid appeared in the doorway with the book in hand.

The maid placed it gently on the table with an odd amount of ceremony.

Then as she was about to leave, she hesitated one more moment and said, "I don't think the character of Justine is much like you at all." She made a quick curtsy and rushed out the door.

Marie had no idea what to make of this statement. She opened the book and started reading. And suffice it to say, it was the rare afternoon during which Marie did not think of the factory at all.

MARIE'S FIRST IMPULSE UPON READING the book was to reach out to Sadie. For her, the book was a declaration of love. Sadie had been so disappointed in her when she had returned from England. How could she not be! Marie hadn't been bold enough then to forge a path on her own.

She wanted to rush down to the brothel and see Sadie. But she had made such a point on the phone about never speaking to her again, she felt she could not just show up. Perhaps Sadie would think she was starstruck and wanted to associate with her now that she was a famous author. And yes, of course this was true. But there was so, so, so much more to it!

They were both living out their dream now. And weren't both their dreams a shared one?

AFTER THE PUBLICATION OF *JUSTINE AND JULIETTE*, the Golden Mile began gossiping about Marie Antoine all over again. It was very clear to them who the Justine figure was meant to be. She was almost glad to give them something to talk about other than her being a megalomaniacal business tycoon. It made her feel something akin to pride. Marie felt she was meant to be the hero of a book. This was why she was lonely and couldn't relate to anybody. Her emotional life was meant to take place inside of a book. How could she ever have a true passionate love life in this stifling society? Instead, Sadie had created one for her in fiction.

Marie read the book three times. Funnily enough, even though everyone else thought of the book as pornographic, or at least transgressive, or at the very, very least adventurous, Marie found it to be a thing of great beauty. While Marie was busy rereading the book, there were so many people who began to object to its existence, declaring it obscene. The book was condemned by the morality police. This, of course, had the effect of making the book even more wildly popular. Marie kept abreast of the developments in the newspapers.

Naturally, the Arnetts had no intention of letting Sadie destroy their name without a fight. Sadie's father and brother began campaigning ruthlessly for the suppression of the book and the arrest of Sadie Arnett. They leveraged all the political power they had accumulated over the years into this cause. And Sadie Arnett found herself being dragged from the brothel while a huge crowd quickly converged to watch the arrest of this beautiful, notorious whore.

Per her request, Marie was notified immediately the morning Sadie was arrested for infringing on morality laws. Marie burst into action. Marie shifted an incredible amount of money around, and quickly.

The forces of corruption and anti-corruption were always at odds in the city. They were never won by any moral factor but instead by whoever could pay the most. Morality had been coopted by capitalism. Montreal was forever susceptible to bribery and corruption and fraud.

Marie bribed the official to drop the charges against Sadie. And also to make sure she was never held accountable for indecency again. Her books would be allowed to be published and sold in bookstores. Those who were shocked by the indecency in the book would be told they were ignorant, that the book was an allegory for struggle and strength. It was like a Roman statue of a nude. Its beauty transcended vulgarity.

No one would understand how Sadie Arnett had had her charges dropped and was released from jail without a trial. And people sometimes looked to the decision to allow *Justine and Juliette* to be sold in bookstores as the moment the city had turned completely mad: When a book about two amoral, promiscuous women would be deemed as having literary merit and people were too intimidated to criticize it.

Marie had paid everyone off before the Arnetts knew what was happening. Marie was also aware that freeing Sadie and allowing her words to be published freely would destroy the Arnetts. There were so many advantages to this move. She smiled when she thought of it. She had been waiting for the moment she would strike against them. She had waited until she had more power and she could take everything the Arnetts held dear away from them. What did they hold dear? It was their reputation. They wanted others to believe they were better, purer. They couldn't do it through money, so they were doing it through morality.

Marie went down to the police station herself to collect Sadie.

CHAPTER 37

Stockings

Sadie was sitting in a prison cell. There were pigeons on the cell's windowsill. They were rustling their wings, making the sound of someone tearing through books. One of the guards had given her a cigarette in exchange for her flashing her breasts at him. She inhaled and considered her situation. She had taken a risk. She would normally be outraged and terrified by her imprisonment. But, as she knew this arrest would be good for book sales, it was something an author had to endure. They couldn't keep her there very long. She knew Madame had strings she could pull to get her out.

Sadie began to pace in the cell. She would have felt better if they'd allowed her a notebook and pen to write with. Opening a notebook was like throwing open the shutters of a huge window and seeing crowds of people outside on the street. Being unable to write made the thoughts crowd in her head like a group of people trying to exit a theater on fire.

She waited. She waited.

It was the unknowing that was driving her crazy. She tried not to think about how she was always being punished for something she didn't consider a crime. Was it a crime to put into words how she felt about

Marie? Her relationship with Marie was the purest, most innocent part of her life. The period when she really had a connection with someone. She had liked Marie so much as a child, she would be chronically anxious about whether Marie liked her back. She couldn't imagine feeling like that again. It was the only time in her life she had made herself so vulnerable.

The book was about innocence. It was about delight. It was about connection. It was about true love. It was about how the rest of the world does not exist for true lovers. They would murder, rape, and kill for their love, but it was celebrated nonetheless. And is that not a beautiful thing?

Wasn't it beautiful? She was convinced she had written something of worth. So what if she used the female body and its sexuality as a metaphor for freedom and creation? She had liberated it from the shadows. She had used the language of female desire to create something great and unusual and beautiful. And even if she was in a jail cell, they could not convince her otherwise.

She had imagined Marie coming to see her after she wrote the book. She knew in many ways she had written the book all the while imagining Marie reading it. Marie had reached such heights, she felt the book had to be great to compete with them. She kept thinking, Is this good enough to compare to the wealth Marie has accumulated, to the social power Marie wields? She had found herself thinking as she had as a child, Are we really equals?

George had believed Sadie was writing the book with *her* as its principal reader. And that every time she made editorial choices it was with George in mind. But it was Marie. Nonetheless, it was George she was depending on now. She knew George was doing everything in her power to free her. George and Madame had always told her they had influence in the city. They had dirt on everyone who was in office. So many important men had come to the brothel and had let their guard down. They had enacted their most hidden and corrupt desires. Madame could blackmail so many men.

Sadie tried to have faith in George's machinations and tried not to worry. But at the same time she was aware there were men who would be above blackmail of that nature. They had never been to the brothel and they would laugh at, if not be outright disgusted by, a young woman who dressed like a man and attempted to sway their position.

Sadie was concerned about Madame's reach. If it were not for the fact that her father was in charge of the morality law, she would have been out by now. He was putting all his political leverage into having her locked up and punished. The only way he could protect his political career was to show he had defeated and silenced her.

George was up against men like her father and brother. They were cruel. And cruelty was not something George could negotiate with. There was nothing about their cruelty that made them vulnerable or that they could be called out on. They were men whose cruelty was domestic and was confined to women they possessed or were related to. This was largely socially acceptable and even encouraged. They were immune to the type of power Madame wielded.

When a guard came to the door and unlocked it, telling her she was free to go, she regretted immediately having ever doubted George. She felt such a flood of relief, it was akin to peeing in her clothes, releasing a bladder she had been brutally holding in. She rose from the bench, full of elation. It was such a relief, it was as though she were an air balloon. She felt the second she stepped out of the prison that the lightness might cause her to lift right off her feet and float into the air.

She was surprised to see an expensive carriage in front of the prison.

She did not assume the carriage was there for her. Perhaps another well-to-do prisoner was being released, although everyone she had seen while incarcerated was distinctly lower class.

This carriage had definitely descended from the Golden Mile. Sadie thought she had best get as far from that carriage as was possible. She felt a presence inside it. A presence so intense and aware of her, it could only be dangerous. She was about to distance herself from the carriage and head back to the brothel on foot when the door of the carriage opened. It stayed open, clearly waiting for her.

At this point there was nothing she could do other than approach it. A shining head of blond curls was framed in the doorway. It was Marie. Sadie had never been so surprised. Her heart started fluttering. As though she were a moth and Marie were a giant flame.

She had relegated Marie to fiction, where she could visit her. She had never expected to see Marie in the flesh again. But there she was. Marie had come for her.

Sadie climbed into the carriage. She sat across from Marie. The two were silent. They would both have liked to control and contain the smiles on their faces, but they could not.

"Do I owe you anything?" Sadie said finally.

"No, I don't even think I did this for you. I did it for myself. I did it for the future. What you are doing is so important. I have never responded to a book the way I did yours, and I am sure so many other readers felt the same way. No, Sadie Arnett. The world needs more books from you."

She took her hand in hers.

"Was the book about us?"

"It is absolutely fictitious."

"I found it so beautiful. It was so filled with pretty things. I very much like the way you write about sex. And the female body. When you want someone to touch you, when you allow someone to touch you, it is the most beautiful thing. Isn't it?"

"I don't know."

"You've completely destroyed my reputation, you realize. It was filled with conjecture before. But you've put an end to that."

"I can't edit myself when I write. It exists independently of me. I can't worry about what the consequences are. I have to write with an utter disregard for the idea that my work might destroy somebody else. In the same way I don't protect myself. I mean, I put us in the same boat, didn't I? In the book."

"That you did. You made us eternally conjoined. Do you know why I'm not that mad at you?"

"Because you're flattered?"

They both began to laugh.

"Will you take me back to the brothel? They'll be wanting to know I'm released."

"I'll have the driver deliver a note. I would just like to spend a little more time with you. In any case, we need to celebrate this most amazing day."

"Being released from prison?"

"I've made it so your books will never be challenged again. And they will be able to be sold in bookstores."

"Marie," Sadie said, and paused, visibly moved by this information. "You have given me the most extraordinary gift."

"It was my pleasure. I enjoy being able to do things for you more than anything else," Marie said. She looked at Sadie more closely, taking in how filthy spending a night in prison had made her clothes. "There's a store I want to take you to. I know you probably haven't been able to spend money the way you are supposed to. When I'm down, I spend money. There's an art to spending money. I have the most beautiful packages that arrive from Europe and all over the world. I had a pair of shoes arrive from China this morning. I think we should go buy stockings."

"I don't need new stockings."

"I think you do."

"And what do you base this on?"

"Raise your skirts for me. And show me the stockings you have on. If they are perfect and beautiful, I will leave you alone."

Sadie lifted her skirts. There were holes all over her stockings. Sadie laughed.

AND SO THEY WENT TO A STORE that specialized in stockings. Everything about stockings and the purchasing of them was erotic to Sadie. The way that the shop was so small. Because you didn't need that much room to display stockings. The way it was tucked away between two other stores. So that you walked by it without noticing if its contents didn't interest you but if you were looking for it, it was very easy to spot.

The salesgirl was reading a copy of *Justine and Juliette* behind the register when the women walked in. She put it down, not recognizing that the characters from the book were in her store. The erotic effects of the book were evident in her sleepy, sensual movement. All her gestures were so soft. She walked in her high-heeled boots without making any sound. She put everything in the shop in such perfect order. If she had control of the universe, everything would be pretty and perfect.

Even the way Sadie and Marie sat together on the bench awaiting the arrival of the box of stockings was erotic. The way they described what they wanted to the salesgirl was erotic. There were molds of disembodied feet standing one next to another wearing stockings. These were weirdly erotic too. It was as though Cinderella's foot had been cut off and was being preserved for posterity.

None of the stockings had any marks on them. There were no marks on the bottom. There weren't five round gray marks where your toes pressed down. There weren't any bloodstains on the heels. These were virgin stockings. They were as sweet and innocent as lambs.

Sadie and Marie both raised their skirts above their knees, admiring each other's stockings as they tried them on. They were infatuated by what they were looking at. The stockings Marie chose to put on had a pattern of climbing roses going up the calves. They were the most expensive pair of stockings in the store. She kept turning to see the roses. There were no guidebooks for women's pleasures. There were only guidebooks that instructed a woman on how to give other people pleasure.

"These are all so beautiful," Marie exclaimed. "We can't choose between them."

"It is cruel to make us choose," Sadie announced.

"We would like to have one of each."

Sadie held up a mannequin leg. "Do you think I could have this? There's something macabre about it that I quite like."

"Yes. Of course. You should also take that painting on the wall of a dog."

"You like that? I'm surprised."

"Not at all. I want to destroy it so no one else will ever have to lay eyes on it."

The women laughed. They left the store while the saleswoman quickly loaded the carriage with their purchases, including the mannequin leg and painting.

They had the carriage drive up to Sherbrooke Street. They spent the rest of the day on a mad shopping spree. They went to a large department store, buying whatever touched their fancy on each floor. They went to the dresses and bought at least twenty each. Their favorite part was standing in their underwear on risers facing each other while they were being fitted.

"Clothes feel magical the first time you wear them," Marie said. "When you wear them the second time, they never work. I can't wear the same dress twice."

"I paid for six months of rent with a single dress."

"Ridiculous. You must have been staying in a hovel. I think a month in a boardinghouse shouldn't cost more than a pair of my bloomers."

"Perhaps *your* bloomers. But I don't think anybody else's bloomers would do. Do you still have them imported from Paris?"

"My God. You remember that!"

"I've never been able to forget a single detail about you."

"How I've missed you, Sadie."

"We are so young. We have money and power. We don't have husbands. We can really do anything we want now."

They took each other's hands.

THEY WERE LITTLE GIRLS AGAIN. Their bodies no longer carried the baggage and scars of the lives they had both lived. Instead, they were luminescent. They were sharing an afternoon that had no past or future. They were back in Marie's garden. Flowers grew between their toes and fingers. There were butterflies around their foreheads. The smell of roses was everywhere.

"There is something so peculiar I wanted to share with you," Marie said. "I met a woman. She looks like me. She's completely mad, though. I don't know what to make of it."

"Why do you bother with her?"

"She looks exactly like me. Exactly."

"Let's go and meet her."

"I knew you would be curious about this phenomenon."

"We live in peculiar times. Anything is possible. If you don't have an open mind, you'll miss out on the whole adventure. What is reality anymore?"

"She says she is my sister."

"Well, your father was a notorious philanderer. I'm sure you do have siblings out there. What does it matter? The factory came to you from your mother anyhow. You'd have to worry if she was your mother's child too."

Marie was bolstered by Sadie's nonchalance. They climbed into Marie's carriage and instructed the driver to deliver them to the Robespierre Bakery. When they entered and the baker stepped out from the back, Sadie was dumbstruck. She wanted to immediately berate Marie for not telling her about the physical resemblance. But then she realized Marie had indeed told her. She kicked herself for interpreting anything as metaphorical. Particularly in this age of invention where metaphors were daily being converted into reality.

Sadie knew immediately the baker was using this uncanny resemblance to her advantage. She was doing it because she could. There was no way anyone of the lower classes could stop themselves from taking a stab at Marie—wanting to hurt Marie in some way. It is in the nature of the weak to torment the strong for no good reason, while the strong exploit the poor for the advancement of the world.

She was curious to see whether there was anything else, other than a general mean-spiritedness, behind this woman's relationship with Marie.

"Hello, I'm Marie's friend. Sadie Arnett."

"Yes, the famous pornographer. I know your work well."

"You look a lot like Marie. I will immediately concede that point. But although the resemblance is remarkable, I don't see that you have any other relationship to her."

"I know your story from the book. I suppose that's the joy of being a novelist, isn't it? You write your life. But you do it in a way where you take out all the negative qualities. You and Marie once committed a grave crime together. There's no mention of that in the book, is there?"

Sadie and Marie were quiet for a moment. They simply looked at Mary. Her baker hat was too large and was over her forehead, like a bag an executioner was about to pull down.

Sadie felt they ought to get the hell out of the shop. She took Marie's arm and pulled her onto the sidewalk. "We should not in any circumstance have anything to do with that woman again. She is obsessed with you. So what? So she looks like you. It's gone to her head. Don't even buy any cakes from her. They don't necessarily taste better than other cakes. I think she puts cocaine in the icing. They aren't necessarily good, they are addictive. She'll bloody well try to poison us."

"I was hoping you would tell me I had nothing to worry about."

"I believe it's worse than you think. What are you going to do about her?"

"I've made it my habit to ignore women of the Squalid Mile. They are always slightly hysterical."

"Not like that."

"I can't think properly when it comes to her. She shakes my sense of reality. I suppose I'll figure out what to do about her soon."

"Sooner is better than later. How does she know about what we did?"

"Who knows? She's obsessed with me. She knows everything."

"You have to deal with her, Marie."

Marie glanced at the bakery with an uncertain look. There was something about Mary that told her just to get away as fast as she could, and learn nothing else.

"She's from the Squalid Mile," Marie said definitively. "She has no power."

MARY ROBESPIERRE STOOD IN THE bakery watching the women through the window climb into Marie's extravagant carriage. She felt she had to pack all her anger inside herself so as not to explode. If she hurled herself at the women, she would be arrested and she would never have her revenge against them. She would have to bide her time until she found the opportunity to destroy the two of them.

The moment the two women were gone, Mary felt her anger explode like gunpowder. She threw a huge mound of dough on the table. She began to pound it as though it were a punching bag. She smashed it over and over again. Then she stuffed her face into it and screamed.

If Marie and Sadie had witnessed this scene, they might not have been laughing once again in the carriage as though all their problems in the world had been solved.

MARIE STEPPED OUT OF THE carriage and walked arm in arm with Sadie to the door of the brothel. "I used to be so jealous of you," Marie said. She put her head against her friend's shoulder. "I always thought you outdid me. No matter how much care I took getting dressed, I preferred whatever outfit you had on to my own. Whatever book you had in your hand seemed more interesting than whatever I was reading. If I was on my way to the zoo and I ran into you, I lost all interest in animals."

"Even the zebras?"

"Even the zebras."

Marie opened up the locket on her neck. She never opened it for anyone. And she wore it everywhere. Everyone felt a tinge of sadness and compassion for Marie when they saw that necklace. They supposed it contained a likeness of her mother and the only way she ever had any access to her mother's face was when she opened that tiny golden oval. When she was slightly out of her element or felt slighted in any way, she would put her hand around the locket. She let it warm up in the palm of her hand. She held it as though it were a gold coin and she was imagining what treat she could purchase with it.

Marie leaned forward so Sadie could see what it was. There were two small girls on either oval of the locket. On one was a blond girl with curly locks and unmistakable apple cheeks. And on the other side was a girl with black eyes and a mound of black hair. And when she closed the locket again, it made the sound of two people kissing.

CHAPTER 38

Drive a High Heel

Through My Heart

George could not bring herself to let Sadie languish in prison for even a few days. She knew Sadie didn't have a notebook, and she needed to write every day.

She had had a meeting with political men. It had been a humiliating experience for her. When men saw her for the first time, they were always upset. She knew they wanted to shake her and tell her even if she wasn't ugly, she should at the very least try to look feminine. She did not make any effort to appeal to their gaze. They had refused to listen to her.

Then George heard Sadie was miraculously out of jail, so she hurried home to the brothel to see her. On the way, George stopped at the carpenter's to pick up a dildo she had ordered. She wanted a dildo that was bigger than the penis of any of the men Sadie had been with. She carried it under her arm as though it were a magic wand. She thought of it as belonging to her. As being part of her body.

George loved when Sadie did things to her that a woman might traditionally do to a man. It thrilled her. Sadie came up to her and fastened the ascot around her neck. She felt such a sense of belonging. Another time Sadie leaned forward and used the hem of her sleeve to wipe a chocolate mustache off her top lip. George blushed with delight. Sadie was stepping down off a flight of stairs. She inadvertently put her arm out for George to hold her. And George never wanted to let go.

Whenever they made love, Sadie asked George to put the dildo on. She clearly liked to be penetrated. Once, Sadie requested she get a larger dildo. This was a request that would break the ego of many a man. But George merely had to go down to see the carpenter and have him fix this problem for her. The artisan told George the size she was asking for was far too big. But George told him to go ahead with it.

GEORGE BUMPED INTO MARIE AS she was leaving the building. Marie was confused by this young man. She usually felt her body tense up and become defensive whenever she was in the presence of a man, but she didn't feel that now. She was looking at a peculiar creature. She knew Sadie might be infatuated with this personality. Whoever they were, she wanted to get this peculiar being out of her way.

George stepped to the right as Marie simultaneously stepped to the left. George moved quickly to her left and Marie stepped to her right. George stepped to her right and Marie stepped to her left. This either went on for a few seconds or it went on for an eternity. And somewhere in an alternate reality, Marie and George were facing off against each other forever.

They both stopped finally and looked up at each other. George stepped to the side and lowered her head like a gentleman and allowed Marie to pass by.

Marie thought she should have reminded the person of how her name was on every sugar bag in the city. And everyone in the whole city was stirring a small scoop of her into their teacup. And they were drinking a little bit of her sweetness. Then she moved past as though George were a pesky, fleeting thought Marie was brushing out of her head.

But George immediately went from being irritated to being devastated. She was seized by loss and disbelief when she saw Sadie step out of the brothel wearing her cloak and carrying a portmanteau in her hand. It was partway open and she could see Sadie had all her writing materials inside. But why? She always knew Sadie came back home to her stacks of writing. Why was she taking her writing material with her? Was she planning to be gone for a day or two?

George couldn't bring herself to ask, in case the answer was yes. But she didn't have to because Marie's footman stepped out of the brothel carrying a trunk filled with Sadie's books, followed by a twelve-year-old prostitute carrying a box filled with Sadie's clothes and a stack of Sadie's hats on her head.

"George, darling. I'm going to go spend some time with Marie. We have so much catching up to do."

"You're taking all your things."

"Yes, of course. But I need a change of scenery. It's too difficult for me to be here. The police might barge in any day. I can't go through that again."

But she could tell by Sadie's demeanor she wasn't leaving because she was frightened. She was animated and excited. It was the first time she had seen Sadie giddy and enraptured by someone. She had assumed Sadie was incapable of these types of feelings. But now she knew better, and it broke her heart. She was capable of feeling these things. Just not for her.

"I thought you hated the Golden Mile," George said timidly.

"I do. I'm not going to the Golden Mile, really. I'm going to Marie's mansion. It's a world unto itself. I'll come see you again soon. I'll have a new draft of a book we can edit together."

George winced at this. She wished Sadie had said she would come back to visit or hold her. But she would come back for something self-serving and practical.

"Anyhow," Sadie said, "if I stay here, I'll wake up to an army of Marys trying to slit my throat."

George heard Marie's peal of laughter from inside the carriage. Obviously this statement had been made for Marie and not her, as George had no idea what it could mean. And then Sadie climbed into the carriage without even looking back at her.

The twelve-year-old was still on top of the carriage fastening the trunks as it began to drive off. Who knows how far it went before she was able to jump off.

George stood outside the brothel for a few moments after Sadie left. She realized it was Marie who had gotten Sadie out of prison, and this meant the two women were in each other's lives again. She would never be able to compete against Marie's power and charm. George's eyes were watery. As though the surface of a very still pool had been disturbed by a single stone.

GEORGE WENT TO HER ROOM. She sat on the bed next to the box. She opened the lid of the box and then closed it quickly. She found she couldn't look at it. Who was she to think she could ever have any use for a dildo that big? It had nothing to do with her. She was ashamed of it. She sat with her sexual organs in a little box. As though she were something you ordered from the store and you were meant to put together on your own.

She wondered whether Sadie preferred Marie because she was more typically a young woman. She loved the way Sadie described the female body in her books. But how did her body fit into this narrative? She did not see herself anywhere in fiction. And she did not see herself in Sadie's books either. They were a celebration of the female body, but they were not a celebration of hers.

There was a pile of new stockings lying on the floor like a group of condoms discarded after an orgy.

But Marie represented everything about the Golden Mile she hated, George thought with frustration to herself. George and Sadie were a team. Working and writing in the brothel had been what had inspired her novel. Why would she just drop it all? Hadn't her home been a home to Sadie? Had she, all this time, been regarding this place as a run-down dump? She was just staying here as some sort of lark and experimentation. Until she had an opportunity to go back to the Golden Mile.

George looked around her room. It had seemed so cozy before. She had always loved her attic room. Now it looked like a dump. The carpet was threadbare. The windowsill was covered in bird droppings. The only really expensive and beautiful thing in the room was a pair of boots Sadie had left behind underneath the desk as though a ghost, naked except for a pair of boots, was sitting there writing.

George picked up a pair of stockings. She took off her own clothes and put on the stockings. Then she went over and pulled on Sadie's shoes. She laced them up, then tottered over to the mirror. The high heels of the boots made her walk hesitantly, as though she were standing on thin ice that she might crash through at any minute. She looked in the full-length mirror to see if she looked feminine at all but found she rather looked as though she had been drawn by an artist with no skill and she was all awkward angles. She kicked off the boots.

What do you do when you are heartbroken? You feel terrified of your own emotions. George felt her emotions building above her like a storm cloud. The room was so filled with emotions it was as though it were filled with humidity. She had to get out of the room. She couldn't bear to lie on the bed where she and Sadie had made love. She had spent her whole life as a bachelor and hadn't minded it. But now the thought of having to spend the rest of her life alone was terrifying. It made her life seem so long and forlorn. She had been lucky enough to find someone she loved. But this person had chosen someone who didn't resemble her at all—and was, in fact, quite the opposite. She wanted to be with someone buxom and blond. Someone who smelled like roses and did everything prettily. If Sadie had left her for a man, things might have been easier. But she had left her for another woman.

George put her suit back on and left the brothel.

GEORGE WALKED TO A PART of the river where men gathered to sunbathe. It was probably the last day of the year they were able to do it before it turned cold. She wanted to lie down on the sand next to all the naked men. Their penises all sleeping to one side or the other.

She had been surrounded by women her whole life. At the brothel the women had always said she dressed like a boy and looked like a boy. They were the ones who had pointed that out to her. She was only dressing the way she felt comfortable and at ease.

But when they talked about romancing men, they never spoke about her. They left her out of these conversations entirely. If they were only attracted to men, they were not attracted to her. There had been a woman who had fooled around with George for a year. But the minute a man had come along, she had abandoned George abruptly. And how could she not, when being aligned with a real man brought a woman so much social standing in the world?

George wondered whether teetering between the genders made her impossible for people to take seriously. Perhaps it was because she did not really identify as a man or a woman that others could not see her as a proper person who had feelings and dignity and as much need for love as anyone else did.

But what could she do? The way she carried herself and dressed was the only way she could feel truly in her own skin. Were she to grow her hair and wear a dress and take on the mannerisms of a woman, she would feel as though she were awkward and unhappy, and as though she were pretending to be someone she was not.

George thought perhaps she should call herself a man. She avoided men in general, especially unfamiliar ones. They were the ones who would yell in her face she was ugly and needed to put a dress on. But she would go join them. She would take off her clothes and even though they would see she had female genitalia, they would understand that, on the inside, she was the same as them.

And if she were naked, she could not be accused of trying to be anyone but herself.

She took off her clothes. She lifted up a rock to put on top of them. The small bugs under the stone squiggled this way and that. They were like the leftover nuts and bolts and screws from the creation of the world.

She lay down naked near the men. It wasn't long before she found herself being dragged off by police for public indecency. The police officers put her in the back of their carriage. There was a beautiful man in the carriage as well. The man had rouge on his cheeks. He had a dress whose bodice was hanging too low on his body. His nipples were out. Anyone could see he had the nipples of a beautiful girl. She wondered whether they could switch body parts. If things could be that simple.

The next morning she was released with the young man she had been brought in with. George had spent the night in the women's ward. And she was exhausted from a night of long contemplation about her identity. The beautiful man had spent the night in the men's ward. His face was battered. His eyes were swollen shut like mussel shells that were impossible to open. His dress had been torn in several spots. He was no longer proud of it. He covered up the soiled dress with his cloak and hurried awkwardly down the street.

How tragic to be a man, George thought.

CHAPTER 39

Fifteen Minutes of Infamy

In the following days, George was filled with a rage she had never felt before. It sprouted thorny branches out of her heart. She had no idea rage was in the heart. She imagined it would be somewhere in the brain. She had felt many emotions in her stomach before. That was where sadness always seemed to be.

She had done everything she could to make Sadie's life better. She had dragged her off the street from where she was about to be murdered. She had given her a home. She had given her a community. Marie had more power in society than any other woman she knew. She owned the largest factory in the city, one that employed so many young and vulnerable girls. Marie had the ability to do right by them. But, instead, she exploited them all. George was shocked that Sadie did not factor all these mistreated girls into her evaluation of Marie's character.

Sadie had a grotesque and aristocratic taste.

George was reminded again that she didn't belong to anyone. Madame was the one constant in her life. She knew it was a source of joy to Madame that she was still alive. That it was proof in itself of a certain genius in George as a child. Madame had had other children left with her. They never lasted long. One darted out into the street. One managed to drown himself in a spaghetti pot of water. One never came home and remained a mystery to everyone. According to Madame, it was always a small mercy when they died.

She always believed it was George's ugliness that allowed her to survive. It's always a mistake to live off your looks. It was like eating nothing but sweets your whole life. Eventually it begins to rot your smile. George's ugliness made her clever. Madame believed that staying alive always involved a level of spitefulness. But Madame's joy and delight in her existence didn't exactly equate to love, did it?

George never longed for a mother so when she was little. In general, mothers were terrible people. She saw mothers allow their daughters to become prostitutes at eleven years old. They took their frustration out on their children. They beat them over the head with slippers. Generally, children put up with more abuse from their mothers than from anybody else in the world. Ordinarily if someone were to hit you with a shoe, you would either run away or try to defend yourself. But when a mother did it, the appropriate response was to cower. And ask her how she was feeling. And tell her not to feel bad for beating you.

Whenever George did something stupid as a child, she sat by herself and contemplated her actions. She berated herself for her stupidity. She made herself feel worse and worse as a form of punishment. Often in these moments, she isolated herself from all the other children. She sometimes took a chair to the corner and sat in it, facing the wall. She had no idea when she was supposed to get up from the wall since it was a mother who always determined whether you had stayed there long enough.

❧

GEORGE REALIZED THAT TO BE able to reject Sadie, she would have to become a writer herself. She had taken so much joy working on Sadie's projects. She was not prepared to give up on the literary arts even if she had been abandoned. It was now time to find her own subject matter.

George began to write about Marie. Her quill moved furiously, like the tail of a fox that was halfway down a rabbit hole murdering a family. George took the same subject as Sadie, ironically, but her approach was different. She wrote a pamphlet about the shocking expenditures Marie had made on a single afternoon. She thought the world had a right to know this young woman had purchased every variety of stocking in the shop. That she had purchased forty stockings at once. She said Marie's carriage was filled with similar purchases she had made throughout the day. That this was only one of her many stops, that the carriage was filled with fur coats. George naturally embellished the story a little. There was a rare white monkey she had purchased as a pet that was rummaging through a box of jewels.

Since the only establishment George had specified was the stocking shop, if anyone went there to check its veracity, the whole of her story would be certified true. She considered this to be fine journalism. It was certainly a cut above what any of her gentleman peers were doing. George left out Sadie from the spending spree. She wanted to destroy Marie and bring her down in the eyes of the world, and perhaps Sadie's as well.

Hyperbole was a necessary part of belles lettres. It wasn't really lying. Everything needed to be exaggerated in print to capture the emotions evoked in real life. That was why there were so many murders and high-stakes adventures with pirates in books. Otherwise, how else would you be able to convey the emotions that went on in a girl's head from the time she woke up in the morning until the time she went to bed?

When she was done, George looked at the letters on the page. They seemed to twitch like limbs that had recently been torn off insects.

GEORGE HAD NEVER ACTED IN a spiteful and malicious way before. But George had also never been heartbroken before. She knew there was a benefit for working-class people to learn how radically different the lifestyles of the upper class were from their own. That while the workers toiled and toiled away at the factories, achieving a bare level of sustenance, the owners were squandering the fortunes built on their backs in extremely lavish ways. Although she could justify her action by all these political reasons, she knew her motives were pettiness and jealousy. She knew she had to make a strike against Sadie or she would feel destroyed by her. She had to hurt Sadie so she could feel like a person again.

George set off down the street in her top hat. It joined the other top hats moving down the street, and they all looked like a group of chimneys on rooftops against the sky.

GEORGE BROUGHT HER WRITING TO the printers of broadsides on Saint Jacques Street. The man behind the desk looked her up and down dubiously, prepared to reject her efforts outright.

"This is very interesting. We've been publishing a series of broadsides attacking politicians and court hearings, but this is different. There's a heroine here. This is a beautiful woman behaving badly. Is it news? Is it something our readers need to know about? I'm not sure. But it might be a hit with female readers. And lord knows when they start reading something, they can't stop."

The broadside sold very well. Everyone wanted to heap scorn on Marie. She was a celebrity immediately. No one knew how to respond to her as a character in the broadside though. Whereas the publication of *Justine and Juliette* had caused the discussion around Marie to be smutty and glorious and exciting, the broadside made the city's sentiments to turn to hatred rather than awe. And this hatred was shared by a much wider audience than the young women who read the novel.

And truly the city became carried away in their gossip about Marie that fall. It was as though she had no feelings. She was allowed to be observed and speculated about. Everyone believed they had a right to judge her. And this was what, in part, made her so lovable. They loved that they were allowed to hate her.

MORE BROADSIDES AND CHAPBOOKS ABOUT Marie began to be published. Some George had written, but most she hadn't. The stories had escaped her and had become wildly inventive.

Everyone knew Marie from her profile on the sugar bags. It represented sweetness. It represented being able to eat cake instead of bread. So she was familiar enough to destroy. She was well known enough to want to topple. Because they had once loved her, they were more than delighted to tear her down.

One pamphlet described how Marie would have relations with five men a night. She was insatiable. She invited a duke from England over to make love to her. He was a very famous satyromaniac. She was always looking for new lovers. She sent a maid down to the lower quarters in order to find one for her. She sent her to the Squalid Mile because there was an unending supply of disposable bodies there. She slept with both women and men. Her preferred lovers were neither men nor women but virgins. She liked to instruct virgins in lovemaking. She had a twelve-year-old male lover. She made him call her Mama and she would pretend to breastfeed him. People imagined her toes twitching as she came like the feet of a girl hanging from the gallows.

THE POPULARITY OF HER BROADSIDE trashing Marie did not make George feel any better about herself. In fact, it was the contrary. She sat in a chair across from Jeanne-Pauline's register. The chair was squeezed in between two cabinets. One of which was filled with bottles of dried mushrooms. They looked like the appendages a witch had severed from children murdered in the woods. The other cabinet was filled with sprigs of plants that were still alive. There was an aloe plant that looked as though it was bent over and searching the ground for something.

George did not even know how a woman who had been devastated by another woman was supposed to act. She certainly didn't have literature on her side. No wonder she was not noticeable. She felt the most interesting thing about her was her relationship with Sadie. She did not know if she could go back to who she was before she knew Sadie. Being angry had distracted her from feeling sad. But now that the flurry of activity that anger sets off had subsided, she was even more sad. She was so lonely.

She was feeling very sorry for herself. She had never asked for anything from anybody. She had seen other children begging their mothers for affection and candy. There was no one she could ask anything from. That was what made her so happy, she thought. She didn't expect anything from other people. So she was never disappointed. She had expected so much from Sadie. It wasn't that she thought Sadie belonged to her but that she belonged to Sadie. And she thought Sadie would take care of that.

But this morning George had finally realized it was not a possibility. Sadie was not going to return. Because Sadie could not do anything she didn't want to do. Sadie couldn't do anything simply out of a sense of duty. She did not care for anything that did not give her a sense of personal pleasure. And George meant nothing to her.

Jeanne-Pauline seemed uninterested in Sadie. Although many of the girls in the neighborhood went to see Jeanne-Pauline for advice, it wasn't something that Sadie had ever done, or ever would do. Sadie never took advice from anyone. Jeanne-Pauline had always known Sadie considered herself above everyone in the neighborhood and only used them to amuse herself.

"Anger is a good thing," she told George. "So is pettiness. It sharpens your mind. It teaches you how to be wicked. Righteous anger can't teach you how to be wicked. It makes you demand justice. But petty grievances are like weeds that grow underneath sidewalks and find ways to undermine all that is rational and constructive in human civilization. You have learned to use words as weapons. You have learned to use words as a way to rally people's moods and desires and drives. They are now in a fit, enraged against Marie Antoine, with the mad fervor people reserve only for those who have crossed them in love. You are unhappy with this now and disappointed by the sordid results. But don't be. There is greatness here. Your darkness has planted the roots for greatness. I have known you since you were a very little girl, and you are the truest, most responsible person I have ever met. You have to fight against Marie Antoine and Sadie Arnett for the right reasons now, in order to achieve the collective good."

"Who am I to tell women what is right and wrong?"

"There are moments in time when the social hierarchy turns upside down. And those who were at the bottom are now suddenly at the top. We are at such a moment now. You should ask for what you really want. You should speak up now. There's a megaphone already up to your mouth. People will hear you."

CHAPTER 40

Wake Up the Servants

Marie had immediately set the maids to work the next day after Sadie had arrived. Some of them had descended into such a state of torpor over the past year they had difficulty even putting their shoes on. But within a few days they were back in vigorous motion again. Having grown up poor, and working since they were eleven and doing housework before, they had been conditioned to work. Marie went around switching them back on one by one, as though they were machines.

Now that Sadie was back, Marie felt a need to keep a proper home again. She wanted to make everything luxurious for Sadie.

Marie no longer ate in the kitchen. She had supper served in the enormous dining room in three courses. Sadie and Marie had their seats together at one end of the table. They consumed absinthe and stayed awake as long as they possibly could. Sadie laid her cheek on the surface of the table because she was so dizzy. Her head seemed to weigh a hundred pounds. Marie knocked her dishes out of the way and laid her head on the table to be at the same level as Sadie.

This happened every night. The maids would come and help them off to bed if they were in too peculiar a position. Once they passed out in the bathtub together. The maids came in every half hour to dump a pitcher of hot water into the basin so they didn't freeze.

When she was little, Sadie had felt the magic of this enormous house. But it had always made her jealous. Now that she lived here she was able to sink into it and admire it. The pillows on the bed swallowed her body and only her face was visible, as though it were being excavated by archaeologists.

THE TWO WOMEN LOVED TO sit together in Marie's enormous bathtub. Marie had felt too lonely and lost when sitting in this bathtub before. But now it became a favorite spot in the evening for the two women to immerse their bodies. The bath was big enough for them both to fit into easily. They filled the bath with bubbles, and it was as though the two of them were sitting in the clouds together.

That night a stack of broadsides Marie's assistant brought her were on a table next to the bath. Marie picked one up and read it out loud to Sadie.

"'Last week Marie Antoine summoned a fifteen-year-old citizen over to her carriage. Upon approaching the carriage, the boy was shocked to see Marie Antoine completely naked.'"

"Why is everyone so obsessed with your body? I feel as though somehow I might be the cause of this."

"In what way?"

"I made you into such a delicious fictional character, other people continue to make things up about you."

"Nonsense."

Of course, Sadie was in a sense responsible for the broadsides, although not for the reasons she believed. But she was oblivious to the level of rage and disappointment George was experiencing, and that it had provided the original impetus for these publications.

Sadie did not miss George at all. The rest of the world disappeared when she was with Marie. She enjoyed spending time with Marie so much, it made each day so full and seem to last a year. Each day was like a birthday party, a day at the beach, a visit to a world's fair. It sometimes crossed her mind that she ought to send a note to George, just to say hello and that the novel was coming along. But then there were always a hundred other more pressing and enjoyable things to do. In any case, she didn't see that George should have anything to complain about. She had spent the last years with her. She knew she was the most fanciful thing that had ever happened to George.

"They were never this way with my father, and he went around having sexual affairs with everyone," Marie said. "They can't stand having to listen to a woman. They imagine horrific sexual things happening to me. They think they can humiliate me with their wretched imaginations. Let them come. Let them get outraged. It's the price of doing business. If I didn't have any enemies, I could only consider my time on Earth an abject failure."

"Read me another one," Sadie said.

"'Marie Antoine imprisoned a young footman for a period of two weeks, during which time she fed him only cherries with her toes. He later went mad, wandering around demanding to be fed cherries.'"

Sadie laughed out loud. "My God, that's brilliant! I wonder who wrote that one."

Marie realized Sadie did not regard inhabitants of the Squalid Mile as threatening. Marie did wonder if Sadie's attitude would change because their friendship, as it became known, was bound to provoke the antagonism of the lower classes toward her. Then Sadie would realize what dangerous, libelous, violent monsters they were. But in any case, she had no intention of giving it too much thought that night.

"Let's go smoke some opium, shall we? Cleanse our brains of that nonsense."

They climbed out of the bath. When they were gone, the sheets of broadsides floated on top of the water. As they became soaked, the ink words turned into black goldfish, and swam off the page.

CHAPTER 41

When Martyrs Go for Tea

George decided to start her own press. George began to write pamphlets about the conditions of women in the factories. How they were underpaid, overworked, sexually vulnerable. George began publishing broadsides about contraception that she passed out at suffragist meetings and women's knitting circles and to women sitting together on stoops. This to her was the most important thing young women should know. To her surprise, George did not miss her collaboration with Sadie. The more time she spent away from Sadie, the more she felt the limitation of what they had worked on together. Her own passions rose to the surface.

She believed that the only way women could feel desires and allow them to be productive would be if they understood their bodies. She wanted them to know about withdrawal and contraception. If women could not control their reproductive organs, they could not be free. There was no use fighting for any other rights if these were not secured. They were prisoners to their own children. They simply could not take up any space in culture. They could not be scientists. They could not be politicians. They could not be artists.

She published a broadside about the need for safe and accessible abortions. It explained homemade recipes for abortions. She was terrified about the publication of this one, as she could be imprisoned for it, and she did not have a benefactor like Marie to get her out. Jeanne-Pauline offered to distribute it to women at her pharmacy. She rather liked the risk. In fact, she seemed to be most interested in doing whichever revolutionary actions took the most risks.

Jeanne-Pauline wrote a book herself, to be published by George's press. Because of the role Jeanne-Pauline had played in her life, George would have felt obliged to publish the book whether or not it was good. It turned out to be a very small book. It was a political pamphlet called *How to Kill Your Husband*. She described methods whereby women could murder their abusive husbands without drawing the attention of the authorities. One method included leaving a roller skate at the top of a flight of stairs.

Jeanne-Pauline situated spousal abuse as the most heinous of all crimes. If a woman was abused in her own home, then she must immediately consider the domestic sphere a war zone, wherein all domestic instruments were seen as weapons. A woman had a right to bludgeon her husband to death with a rolling pin. She had a right to slit his throat with a steak knife. Jeanne-Pauline did not see these actions as self-defense but as terrorist acts that created fear in men throughout the city. And caused other women to feel more free in their houses.

George considered whether it was ethical to release such a book in the city. She watched a woman at the drugstore counter open up the book with the small tips of her fingers. She seemed so physically delicate that anything might shock her. Instead she burst out laughing.

It turned out that most women came to regard Jeanne-Pauline's book as a work of satire. It became popular to read *How to Kill Your Husband* at dinner parties in upper-class circles.

Everyone laughed hysterically. It was the sort of morbid humor that was all the rage.

Jeanne-Pauline did not seem to care that her book was the object of ridicule. She had a satisfied look about her when she admired her published book. Her gray hair was in a twirled bun, like a brioche on top of her head. Perhaps she knew it came with the territory, that anytime a woman tried to be taken seriously, she would be met with derision. But she knew, nonetheless, she had planted a seed for murder in each of their minds.

GEORGE ARRIVED AT JEANNE-PAULINE'S APARTMENT one afternoon and was startled to say the least. Marie was sitting at the table in Jeanne-Pauline's living room. There was a plate full of macarons in front of her.

George thought Marie must have come to confront her about the broadsides.

"This is Mary Robespierre," Jeanne-Pauline said. "She is a very powerful speaker. She has an unusual, subversive manner of speaking. She's going to give a speech here next week. I thought you two might get along."

"It's fine to disseminate knowledge," Mary said, watching George. "But action is also necessary. We cannot have people understand that violence against the lower class is a crime until we witness someone being punished for it. Only then will people know the seriousness of their own crimes. Only then will they feel regret. Only then will they feel fear."

Even though George had accepted this wasn't Marie, her body continued to be alarmed as she stared at the girl.

"We'll prove we of the lower classes are violent animals. The way they always say we are."

Mary moved the macarons around on the table as though she were playing a game of backgammon. She stared at them as though she were contemplating her next move. She looked up at George.

"We don't have to prove our humanity to the upper classes. We need to terrorize them. Only then will they set us free. We need to be vicious."

"Things happen best when they happen slowly," said George. "You need to educate the woman worker and then she'll be respected by her employer."

"You have spent your whole life here. You see what you want to see. You don't want to realize how the upper classes see you. You are a means to their ends. Even your lover, Sadie, only used you for all your talents and skills. Then she tossed you into the garbage. We are always expendable. We create wonderful things, masterpieces, then they refuse to give us credit for anything. They say we did nothing at all. They say we have no knowledge or appreciation of beauty. Their names go in the history book. Not ours.

"Every great person has an underling they have crushed in order to step on and raise themselves up to be the greatest. Sadie is standing on your shoulders right now. I can see her black boots resting on them. It is a disturbing sight." George had the inclination to look at her shoulders while Mary continued. "What you are writing now has more relevance than anything she has written. And it is necessary for you to finish your political manifestos. Every piece of writing needs a climax. The climax of a political pamphlet has to occur outside in the real world. The climax of every political pamphlet is murder. That's what gives it its gravitas. You started this, but you don't know how to finish it."

"Together, you will finish it," said Jeanne-Pauline.

MARY'S FIRST SPEECH ON THE subject of unequal pay between men and women was in Jeanne-Pauline's living room. Many of the women were breastfeeding, as they wanted to make sure the children were silent while Mary was talking. Since Mary was perfectly bilingual, she delivered the speech in French or English, depending on what the majority of her crowd spoke, and sometimes she mixed the two. Despite George's hesitation, Mary's speeches were hugely popular with other women.

George handed out her pamphlets and tried to inform women about their bodies. She gave them a list of demands they could make at their workplace and how to go about organizing strikes. Mary, on the other hand, seemed content to drive them insane with her violent rhetoric.

George was nervous of the large crowd that had assembled in the marketplace the next week for her and Mary. She was more vulnerable than Mary was. Mary would be scorned for her ideas, but George would be reviled for existing in the body she did, whether she opened her mouth or not. Every time she left the brothel, she was putting herself in danger. George was adept at being invisible, at not drawing attention to herself, darting about so no one could get a good look at her. But when George stood in front of the crowd, in front of those women looking directly at her, waiting to hear what she had to say, she became unaware of her body. She felt something she had never felt before in public: she was comfortable in her own skin.

George and Mary's crowds grew larger. They began to have meetings in the park. It was a rare phenomenon to see young girls gathering for the purpose of establishing strength. There were so many of them. The more they had in their group, the more power they had to exert. They could not be fired by their employers or have their necks broken and be tossed into the river. They could not be disposed of, because there were simply too many of them.

Mary found that the size of the crowd did not really affect her enthusiasm for speaking. Whether there were four women in a kitchen or four hundred people at a park, she spoke as though she were warning them of an erupting volcano just outside their door. Once you have felt the public's gaze on you, it is almost impossible to go back. It is too exhilarating.

Mary began to wear a black ribbon around the stump of her cut-off finger. A young girl carrying a basket of laundry down the street had a black ribbon tied around her finger. It was nobody's business what the ribbon on their fingers was meant to remind them of. Perhaps it was to pick up a piece of lamb from the butcher shop. Or perhaps it was to go to a gathering of liberated women. One girl cut off a bit of the bright blue ribbon she wore in her hair. And she dyed it black and tied it around her finger. The ribbons were to remind them to be angry. The ribbons were a sign they had joined the revolution. They were ready to fight together.

The crowds were riveted by Mary and kept showing up despite the winter setting in. Their eyelashes stuck together with freezing tears and the tips of their noses were red. The cold made their lips bright red, as though they had been feasting on the carcass of a dead beast. They saw Mary Robespierre as one of their own. She had worked in factories, after all. She knew exactly what they had been through. She had also found a way to get out. She stood before them with her messy blond hair and her missing finger, and they would follow her anywhere. The ruffles down her skirt were like a series of waves about to break against the shore.

GEORGE AND MARY WERE AT a chop shop having lunch together one afternoon to plan their next gathering. George was very intuitive about people. Because she had grown up in a brothel, she had a whore's sense of intuition. She could ferret out ulterior motives. It was uncanny even to her. She did not know how she knew the information she did. It just popped into her head. She could tell a violent man before she even looked at him. There was a chill in the air. She felt the temperature drop slightly. She did not know whether the temperature had dropped in the room or in her body.

She thought there was something not quite right about Mary and her motivations.

George wanted to abolish the upper classes altogether. She thought the huge houses they lived in were too big for anybody. They ought to be turned into libraries and school and hospitals. They could easily be converted into apartment buildings that could each house a dozen factory families. Mary, on the other hand, openly coveted that lifestyle. Once she had Marie out of the way, she seemed to have every intention of walking into her house and taking her place.

"Imagine having Marie Antoine's wealth. Imagine what her bed is like. It must be enormous. You wouldn't even be able to fit such a thing into my room. It would be too heavy even. It would crash through the floor. I would sleep the sleep I was meant to sleep. I would dream my whole life all over again. I would always be dressed in the most beautiful clothes. I would drink my tea with sugar."

"How would you be any different than Marie?"

"I would have earned that place. I would slip into her petticoat. I would slip into her stockings. I would slip into her dress. I would slip into her shoes. We have to find whoever has stolen your place. And you have to take it back. For each of us living in the shadows, there is someone who has the same shape as them standing directly in their sunlight."

"You can't actually be talking about killing her. What's the point? We have to change the structures of factories. A new owner will take her place and do all the same things. There will always be another Marie."

"Then you must keep killing Marie until you are sure you have the real one and not the replica."

George could not be sure when Mary was speaking in metaphors. Then at one point she realized it didn't matter.

Mary took the last gulp of her soup. "Right now all Marie can do is think about me. I have invaded her thoughts. When she sits in front of an orchestra, it will be me hearing the music. When she watches a play, I am the one who follows the plot. When she eats ice cream, I am the one who tastes sweetness. All she tastes is ashes. Everything she touches will turn to death."

"When you talk like that, you sound bloody mad."

"What do you know about it?" Mary said to George. "You have all your fingers."

And she smiled. George had an irrational annoyance whenever Mary mentioned her missing finger. She didn't feel as if Mary had lost her finger in the same way other girls had. When Mary would mention her finger, George's sense of danger and suspicion would flare up. She wanted to grab Mary by her coat lapels and yell, "I am on to you, you sham!"

George was upset when Mary began to preach violence against women of the upper classes. This was unacceptable to her because she saw all women as being in the same boat. It was men who were oppressing them; they should not turn against one another.

"That's an interesting statement coming from you, as it was your diatribes against Marie Antoine that gained you your podium," said Mary.

"When I realize that was motivated by my petty ideas, I changed that around, right away."

Mary shrugged. "I deserve more. I deserve what they have."

Mary walked into her bakery. She turned on the lamp in the kitchen.

It made a stuttering, buzzing noise. It was as though there were a firefly inside it being exploited.

DESPITE THEIR DIFFERENCES, THE YOUNG women continued to give speeches together. George looked at all the eyes of the women in a crowd and she wanted the best for them. She felt so much empathy. Ever since the beautiful strawberry-blond girl had died, George had been looking for a way to help women, to actually change their lives. She had seen their vulnerability since she was so little. She had seen them when they first arrived at the brothel. They were skinny and angular. Their eyes popped out of their heads. They were terrified. They were beaten. They had lice. They hated themselves.

George wanted girls to have better lives. She wanted them to be paid more at the factories. Then it would be possible for them to marry who they wanted. They wouldn't have to marry at all. If they had terrible husbands, they would be able to leave them.

She wanted to go up to each one of them and tell them they were wonderful. And plant a dozen kisses on their faces. She wished she could give them each a portmanteau with an embroidered green rose on it filled with money and tell them all their dreams could come true. She wanted to babysit their children so they could go dancing all night. She wanted to put them on a train and tell them to see more than this mile of rotten houses they had been born into. She wanted to sit next to them on a beach while their hair dried, and feed them cake and tell them they were beautiful even if nobody else thought they were.

She had to make them believe they were valuable. What they wanted was worth fighting for. She wanted to tell them their desires were not little. They were monumental. That if they were squashed, it was a tragedy. If they wanted to have time to read a book in the evenings, that was as important as any of Napoleon's ambitions. Because what a triumph it was for any woman to have time for herself—and to be able to do something that benefitted her imagination alone.

How to do all this? she wondered. How to do all this?

When Mary looked at the crowd, she saw a group of identical faces. She blinked for a moment and it was as if every woman in the crowd had her face. There were a thousand of her, watching and waiting for what she was going to say. She knew she had their attention. She knew they were transfixed. She had put a spell on them.

They were looking at her, their heads as empty as Easter eggs, waiting for her to fill them with her thoughts. Their souls were as empty as pillowcases needing to be stuffed with goose feathers.

When she was happy, they would be happy. If she decided to be sad, so would they. If she was angry, they would be too.

She had so many fingers at her disposal now. She had been so right to give away one. Look how many she had in exchange. She could do anything with them. She could pick locks, she could slit throats, she could light fires. With enough fingers, she could pull a building to the ground.

They didn't know there was something wrong with their lives. They suspected it. But some of them weren't sure it could be better. One of them was probably worried she might lose the chocolat chaud she drank every Friday night. That the revolution was not worth jeopardizing that. They had to be rallied together in order to form a dragon of sorts, with Mary as the brain.

She would lead them into a revolution and a fight for equality even if they weren't ready for it. Because she was ready for it. And if you have a massive will, it is normal for you to build an army, for you to direct those with lesser wills to support your own. Some good would come of it for them. They would get the spoils of victory. If her goals were achieved, their rights would more or less inevitably be supported too.

She and Marie had the same father. They deserved the same life. Why had Marie been born with so much while she had been born with so little? That question, as it applied to her and Marie, could also be asked of the whole city. Why had the people in the Golden Mile been born with such wealth and privilege while those in the Squalid Mile had been born with nothing?

She made her personal situation into a universal one, and all the fingers in the crowd began wiggling, crawling off to do her bidding. And ironically, she didn't even have to make Marie the face of their collective rage because George had done it for her.

CHAPTER 42

The Revolution

Bodies of factory foremen began to turn up all over the place like scarecrows. One was the overseer at a plant who had whispered filthy words to young girls. He was awake for the briefest of seconds before he ascertained he was being accosted in his bed. There was a rag being forced down over his mouth. He grabbed at the arms of his assailant. They were skinny, so he knew they belonged to a woman. The chloroform on the rag put him straight back to sleep.

He woke up tied to a stake, dressed in undergarments from the factory he operated. He looked quite enticing. All the women who walked by whistled and made lewd comments. Did anyone who looked so provocative have a right to refuse being provoked? He had on a pair of exquisite leather shoes fashioned for a woman. He begged to be able to remove them because they were too small. They were tight around the toes and caused them to bend. His arched feet looked like those of a hanging bird.

Two very young girls wearing black masks over their heads climbed up on a stool behind him. He had no idea what they were going to do. He had not realized until that moment just how unpredictable little girls were. How had no one ever realized how violent they were? The young girls wore executioner's masks. They pulled the corset ribbons and his rib cage contracted. He couldn't breathe properly.

The foreman of the sardine factory, who handed over the paychecks of women to their husbands, also found himself tied to a stake all day. A plate of food from his icebox was placed at his feet just beyond his reach. A girl with a black mask held a dog on a rope. When the overseer begged that he was hungry, she let the dog go to eat his feast.

Another overseer, who was paying women half of what men were receiving, found himself tied to a stake wearing only his pants. There was a ladder standing up behind him. A small girl in a mask climbed up the ladder while lugging a bucket and slowly dumped it on his head. He shivered violently in the cold.

YOUNG GIRLS WORE THEIR MASKS even when they weren't going to a manifestation. They found them fun to wear in games of tag.

Everything was more fun with their masks on. They were able to be small monsters. With a mask on it was impossible to be evaluated as ugly or good-looking. They were freed from judgment and freed from authority. The masks were a small barrier that protected the girls from men. Men looked at them, but there was no way to read them. They were hidden behind their masks.

Men felt as though they were being stared at when they passed by the girls. They looked away and they still felt themselves being sized up and stared at behind their backs. They felt the eyes upon them all day. They didn't understand how this was permissible. Why didn't their mothers take the hoods off their heads, so they could go back to being little girls?

A man was walking home from work when he passed three girls

with masks on. One of the girls tossed a handful of jacks onto the sidewalk. They looked like a cluster of spiders, running over his shoes. He hurried on. He had the distinct impression the girls were following him. He thought that at any minute they would take their hairpins out and run after him with them. They would stab him. Or perhaps they would just insult him. He didn't know which was worse. He wished he hadn't taken such a dark side road home. He should have gone to Sherbrooke Street, which was well lit and populated. His feeling of unease did not abate until he was in his room and the door had locked. He felt like weeping with frustration. Because he wasn't sure whether he was afraid of the girls for no reason or if they had been genuinely threatening. That unknowing in itself was what made him feel so powerless. He didn't really have control over the situation.

He went to put a kettle on but then dropped it, startled. There was a thin girl with a beige mask on her head standing in the corner of the room. But after he blinked several times, he saw it was just the lamp of course. Every time he blinked, familiar objects turned into treacherous girls.

ONE MORNING, THE WOMEN WHO worked at the garment factory were all standing outside its door, blocking the entrance. There were so many women employed that the factory shut down without them. It was as though the machines were on the girls' side too. The quiet of the factory after the women left was peculiar. It was an uneasy silence.

The foreman at the garment factory read about what had happened to the three men at the other factories. There were some who told him that he should not bend to threats. He should never negotiate with terrorists. But there was something too unholy about the manner in which these indignities were happening. If he had men as his opponents, he would not be afraid in the same way. Men would fight with their fists. They would make their anger known. He could recognize the signs of an angry man. He could also understand what made them angry. But he didn't know what magic witchcraft women were capable of. Women were capable of anything.

Girls had as important a role in the garment factory as women did. They ran around on their little feet, darting in and out of the aisles. They scurried about like rats. Because they had started working at the factories so young, their bodies had become nimble and quick, adapting themselves to the frenetic pace of the machines.

He half expected these young girls to crawl out from underneath his bed. He was terrified of his maids. He thought they were all looking at him suspiciously. He felt all the women in the city were in cahoots. He had a dream all the girls in the factory descended upon him. They came after him with knives and forks. As though they meant to eat him alive.

A group of women passed him on the street. One of them whistled at him. He almost slipped on the ice and fell on his face because he was so threatened.

He conceded to all his workers' demands.

THERE WAS ALWAYS AN ELEMENT of creativity in the terrorist acts. That was because they were created by women, who had been raised in the decorative arts. They left chalk messages on the ground in the most perfect handwriting.

THEN ONE EVENING, A CROWD of girls from the sugar factory began a march up to the Golden Mile. Their black boots made the sound of a hailstorm. They could not keep quiet. Their murmuring and muttering grew and grew. Unlike the sound of a male crowd, their voices were high-pitched and sweet. And they made the most joyful cacophony. People rose from their sleep to poke their heads out the window to see this beautiful passage. There was a light fall of miniature snowflakes all around them.

They stuck their scrawny arms in the air. Although girls were supposed to be weak, these ones had been working in factories since they were twelve. And their arms were muscular and capable of anything. Their bellies always emitted a low rumbling. It sounded like the canons being dragged along with them.

They were on their way to Marie Antoine's house.

CHAPTER 43

A Group of Women Is
Called a Hailstorm

adie and Marie never discussed the revolution happening below, or the injustices of the women Sadie had lived with. Sadie had never really understood their plight. She had never been one of them. It wasn't the absinthe or the opium or the Champagne that was making the two women oblivious of the world around them. It was love, that great opiate. They became so entranced with each other that the rest of the world seemed irrelevant to them. It seemed like something that existed in the past before they had reunited and could never have any bearing on the present.

MARIE AWOKE ONE NIGHT TO the sound of a rock breaking a window at the front of the house. Although she never spoke of the revolution to Sadie, Marie knew exactly what was happening. It was the girls from the factories. She had been expecting them. Marie got out of bed. She quickly dressed herself in something simple. She didn't want help getting dressed. She was going to face these girls alone. She was going to meet them because she was one of them. Whether they wanted to admit it or not.

She left her hair down. She did not actually know how to look like one of them. She stopped for a moment to see her reflection in the mirror. Even though she was clothed, without her usual trappings she looked naked and too plain. It made her feel uncomfortable in her own skin. It was like she was looking at a stranger when she, of course, needed to feel like herself at the moment. She put a rose in her hair.

She opened the door of her balcony. It was a balcony that had been constructed to make whoever was standing on it appear stately. In fact, Marie had rarely gone out on this balcony during her whole life in the house.

If you were to take a peek at the balcony behind the house, you would find it littered with books and fans and a chess set, and a raccoon eating leftover cake on a tray. You would find a lounge chair covered in pillows that had the indentations of resting heads and etchings of strands of hair. But this front balcony was bare and unused.

Marie stood there quietly. The cold winter wind blew through her dress, but she didn't feel it. It was as though the window had been left open and a snow drift had blown in. The mob was already shouting demands at her. She could hardly make them out because everyone was screaming all at once. She did hear that they wanted her to come to her factory.

"Yes, I will go tomorrow," she said.

And they all went quiet. She was up on a balcony with a rose in her hair. But for a moment they all thought they were on the same level as her. They had spoken and she had listened. Marie turned and went back into her house. And the crowd decided to return home. They weren't quite sure what to do with one of their own.

If she were a man, they would have broken the windows and knocked down the doors. And dragged her outside onto the street to humiliate. When they humiliated men, they felt disgust and contempt for them. They then recognized this was how men regarded them all the time. And it made them even more enraged and merciless. But they didn't know what to make of Marie and her body. No one ever did.

They were also suddenly frightened of where they were. When they were in the Squalid Mile, they were able to escape easily into the walls and alleyways like fleeing insects. They had known how to dart in and out of sight since they were little girls. But here they were too exposed. The crowd dispersed.

When Marie looked back out the window, at the empty street, she noticed three young girls standing there still. They had black bags over their heads. They were small and seemingly weak. But they were all her executioners. The girls all held their hands up with their fingers spread. She shuddered. If you were to count the number of fingers on each girl's hand, none of them would add up to ten.

MARIE CLIMBED INTO BED WITH SADIE, who stirred in her sleep and asked, "Who were you talking to?"

"The revolutionary girls were at the window."

"Really?" Sadie said. "You should have woken me up." And she fell back to sleep.

The next day, as Marie climbed into her carriage, Sadie ran after her and hopped into the seat next to her friend and said, "I have an errand to run." Marie let her off a few blocks before the factory, and they agreed to meet later.

Marie stood in the office of her factory dressed in her business wear. She wore a dark-blue dress and a large navy-blue hat that tipped severely over one eyebrow.

She wanted to speak to the foremen about the state of the factory before addressing the workers. She felt the tension from all the workers on the factory floor below her. She felt the spell she once weaved was still able to hold them. But she felt it was less. She felt it begin to let up. There was a stillness. But it was the stillness before a storm. It was a pregnant silence. It was a vicious silence. It was the silence of someone biting their tongue.

The foreman explained there was great unrest in the factory. There was practically an uprising of sorts. The perhaps unusual aspect of this insurgence was that its most radical contingent were young women. She must know there were women all over the city who seemed to be engaged in a collective insanity.

"It might be better to hold off on the Philadelphia acquisition and use the money to meet some of their demands," he said.

Marie had been presented an opportunity to purchase a sugar factory in Philadelphia. It would be her first expansion into the United States. It required an enormous investment on her part. This money could have been spent to improve the conditions and pay at her Montreal factory.

Marie wondered about what she had implicitly promised the girls the other night. She wondered if she owed them anything. Then she thought about Mary Robespierre. No, she decided. Like Mary, what they wanted deep down was to take her place. They would be rotten to her if they had the chance. She had been given a unique opportunity to rise above the lot of the common girl. If they wanted to get ahead, they would have to find another way than spoiling her dreams. She and Sadie were different from these girls, and she would keep it that way.

"No," she said. "I'm moving forward with the Philadelphia acquisition."

"Are there any of their demands you could meet? Perhaps a shorter working day for the children?"

"Not now. If they worked harder, we would have money for it. I'm not giving up my plans for them."

Marie felt all the eyes on her as she stepped out of the foreman's office. Everyone was waiting. They wanted to get a look at her, especially the men in the crowd. She knew they had all been saying the most obscene things behind her back.

She stopped on the platform to look down at everyone. The faces of the men all looked up at her. They were all round and identical. She was giving them their moment to speak to her. If they had any idea how to speak to a woman in power, they might have said something to her that would have changed her stance.

There were wonderful things about her. She had been a beautiful girl. She had been full of life. There was a time when she thought she would have spent her whole life reciting poetry. There was a time in her life where she would have given them anything they asked for. In fact, the night before when it was only the girls at the window, she had been ready to give them what they wanted. But now that she saw all the men mixed in with them, she recoiled. She could not be kind to that class; they spoke of her as though she were an object. She felt the hatred and disgust in the room.

They looked at her as though she were a whore. She accepted their judgment of her. It curdled her blood. She walked along the bridge and down the stairs. The whole time she was thinking they might suddenly cry out at her. But they didn't say a word as she was walking down the stairs. They didn't say a word as she was walking out the door. She tilted her head ever so slightly, so her hat covered her face but so it didn't look as though she were avoiding them. She had effectively turned her back on the women who had come to her window the night before. But they were part of this group who would never love her. She could not separate the women from the rest of the mob of workers. They would be outraged when they found out they had been duped by her femininity. She had effectively declared war against them. And once she left the building, she didn't look back.

CHAPTER 44

Sadie Arnett's Head Rolls

up a Mountain

After she had been dropped off by Marie, Sadie intended to cut across the market square to go to the brothel. She wanted George to read something of hers and give her feedback. She knew George was writing hysterical diatribes against Marie, but she didn't assume it had anything to do with her. She wanted to try to win their friendship back. Moments after the carriage pulled away, Sadie saw a woman with white pancake makeup on her face balanced on an upside-down bucket. "They want to work me to the bone. I am a dead factory worker!" the woman yelled. Sadie quite appreciated the insanity of the rebellion. She felt lucky to be in this place at this time. There was a sort of theatricality to it.

She saw a thirteen-year-old girl who had stuffed her dress in a manner that made her look pregnant. "I am giving birth to a child who will go hungry its whole life," the girl shouted.

Sadie passed by drawings women had made all over the walls. There were drawings of rich men with nooses around their necks. There were drawings of hands with missing fingers with blood spurting out of them. They were using their talents not to seduce men but to demand recognition.

Sadie enjoyed every spectacle very much and considered herself, as a former resident of the Squalid Mile, a participant.

Hearing the noises of a rally, Sadie walked toward it, her cloak wrapped tight around her. It had snowed the night before and she was surprised these were still being held despite the cold. She moved through the crowd toward the podium that had been created by pushing a group of boxes together. Sadie stopped when she spotted George near the podium. She had never seen George look more beautiful. Her hat was off. Her short black hair was blowing up in the air over her head into a pompadour. Her tie was fluttering as though both ends were black birds attempting to mate. George looked stately and important. She had found a way to be famous in her own right.

Sadie was startled when she saw Marie climbing onto the podium wearing a long black wool coat that had a large hole in the elbow. But she quickly realized why she was up there when Mary Robespierre began speaking. That psychopath was hypnotic. But Sadie had recognized her peculiar talent for speaking when they had met.

"They eat sweets and our teeth rot," Mary proclaimed to the crowd. "We bathe and they are clean and we are still covered in grime. We give birth and we breastfeed their babies, while our children drink horrid water. Our children dance on the street corner and their pockets are filled with the coins they earn. We sew beautiful clothes but we end up in rags. We spend all day putting brand-new soles on brand-new shoes, but there are holes in our own. Our stockings are soaked. Our bodies are cold.

"They take away any meaning to our lives. There is no point to our days. We go through motions all day long. We don't know why. Only so we aren't cold, but we are freezing. Only so we aren't hungry, but we are still starving.

"The law doesn't allow us to be violent. The law won't let us get the fruits of our actions. We are puppets on strings. They say we are a tragedy. It makes them feel good about themselves when they see how foolish our theater is."

She held up her fist in front of her, as though she were staring at an imaginary knife. All the girls in the audience mimicked her gestures.

"I say we take a knife and we cut off those strings."

She turned her fist to the side and made a swift motion with it, as though she were slitting a throat. All the girls made the same motion.

"What gives them the authority to tell us what to do and what not to do? They are only human. They aren't gods. They have us believe that when we steal it is a crime. But when they steal, it is for the common good. You say, I don't not have permission to act this way. That is why I give you permission to do so. I, Mary Robespierre, a woman of the Squalid Mile, gives you permission to fight back.

"If they take away your childhood, take away their old age. If they take away what you have made, take away everything they own. If they take your food, poison it.

"I declare all criminal actions to no longer be such. All crime shall now be considered justice. Crime will be the great reckoning. You are now all bandits. You are lowlifes. You are thieves. You are villains. You are free.

"Let me speak to you now of a traitor in our midst. It is Marie Antoine's best friend, Sadie Arnett." Sadie turned red in shock as Mary continued. "She has already professed her love for Marie Antoine in her decadent book *Justine and Juliette*. They are one and the same. They were raised mere houses away from each other. They played the same make-believe games. All they both ever wanted was power. Sadie

Arnett has been infiltrating the revolution. She is a spy. She brings word of everything we do straight to Marie Antoine."

There was a general stirring among the crowd.

"What are the two of them capable of when they are together? They are capable of your worst nightmares. Do not put anything past them. If now you find yourself thinking, But they are just women, just like me, just like my sisters, just like my friends. They have hands and breasts and feet just like I do. They are capable of carrying children just like I am . . ." Mary paused and said, "I have personally been a victim of one of their sadistic crimes. In a game, for sport, for amusement, fourteen years ago, Sadie Arnett and Marie Antoine shot my mother in the heart and killed her."

Sadie was startled by the accusation. She looked toward George, and at that moment their eyes met. Sadie was certain George would somehow tone down the statement, or subtly indicate how she was to escape this situation. She waited while George continued to stare straight at her.

"There she is!" George cried, pointing to where Sadie was standing. Everybody in the front of the crowd turned to look. Sadie also turned. So she would look like one of the crowd, desperately eager to catch sight of Sadie Arnett and to bring her to their new tribunal of justice.

Sadie began to move through the crowd quickly. Her cloak was a perfect disguise. Everyone would be looking for some outlandish clothing. They would not expect Sadie Arnett to be wearing a tattered, nondescript cloak.

She realized she and George were no longer on the same side. George could not be her friend.

She had somehow thought of herself as classless because she was an artist. She was a member of the bohemian class, at least. But the crowd was right. When women were this angry, they were always right.

She hurried into the carriage parked on the corner, where Marie was sitting inside leafing through some documents, waiting for her.

"The revolution is after me," Sadie said, climbing in beside her friend.

"People have been pursuing you your whole life. They had always been trying to stop you from being yourself. You are a brand-new type of woman. More and more of you will be born in the next century. There will be an army of women created in your image. That is why everyone is making such an effort to destroy you. But you are back home with me now. I will protect you. I will make sure no one causes you to flee in the night ever again. You can spend the rest of your life writing. You can write all your wonderful novels."

"Thank you," Sadie said. And she meant it.

THAT EVENING, THE TWO WOMEN decided to get high to nullify the effects of the collective rage directed toward them earlier. It was now the two of them against the entire city. They were both despised by the lower and upper classes. Marie thought it was the first time she had been happy since she was a child. Marie stared at the smoke rising from the opium pipe. The smoke began forming into the illustrations of children's novels. She understood why sailors were attracted to smoking opium. The smoke told the story of a long voyage at sea all in the space of a brief minute. There was a ship on top of waves that was struggling not to capsize. A dragon reared its head out of the depths, a whale flipped upside down in the air, and mermaids reached from above the water for sailors. Enormous waves began to rear up and the ship tried to ride on top of them. But it could no longer manage and the waves rose up and swallowed the ship. Then Marie inhaled the small ocean and a sea of calm filled up her whole body. It drowned all her worries and left a great nothingness in its wake.

Marie was on the daybed. She raised her stockinged leg in the air like a cobra entranced by a flute. Sadie leaned on her stomach on the lounge chair like a caterpillar on a leaf looking at her pretty friend.

Marie never brought up men or marital prospects. Relationships with men seemed so common and mundane to Sadie, it hardly seemed worth inquiring into Marie's reasons. When she did think about it, she assumed Marie had avoided marriage for the obvious reasons: whoever would marry her was bound to try to manipulate her fortune. Nonetheless, she wondered whether Marie had ever experienced any horniness, and how it was she had never been curious enough to experiment.

"Why didn't you ever take a lover?" Sadie asked Marie.

"I thought it was too dangerous to be romantically involved with a man."

"I could never be terrified of men. They are too inept and insecure. But I understand your reservations."

Sadie had attributed Marie breaking off her engagement with her brother to her friend's coming to her senses. There was hardly any mystery to that. But she found herself curious as to the exact circumstances of his jilting. And thought it would be an interesting story to hear.

"How did you ever break it off with my brother?"

"The only thing I ever liked about him was he looked so much like you."

"How did he take it?"

Marie stared at Sadie. Marie was silent. A boiling tear dropped down Marie's cheek. Her tear fell onto the page of a manuscript lying on the small table next to her and it turned the word it landed on into a black sea creature swirling around in the saltwater.

Sadie sat up. "That asshole."

Sadie hadn't spent much of her royalties. She went to the bank the next day and bought up the mortgage and the debt on her childhood house. It was the one thing they had that allowed them to live in the Golden Mile. This would effectively exile them. She quite liked the poetic justice of that. Vengeance is an art form when in the hands of women. She laughed at the beautiful stupidity of it.

Sadie planned to sit outside the house on the day her family moved out. She would then inform them it was she who had bought the house. But she found herself in the clutches of a hangover that kept holding on to her and begging her to stay in bed. So Sadie decided her family was not at all worth the effort of getting up in the morning, something she loathed to do. She called the solicitor and told him to inform her family of the purchase. She then lay back down, falling into a cloud of fantasies, picturing her family's shocked faces in her head, and her laughter turned into giggling and then to murmuring and then she fell asleep.

SADIE DIDN'T HAVE A CENT LEFT, but she wasn't worried in the least. She sat down to write a new novel, one that would be wilder than *Justine and Juliette* and sell even more copies. She immediately felt the power of the new novel pulling her in. It was as thrilling as ever. The cursive on the page was like the yarn of a sweater unraveling. The more she wrote, the more naked she felt.

Sadie found she rather liked not working with George. She was not held back by George's insistence on universal themes. She was living in a decadent imaginary world. She reveled in depicting outrageous sexual antics. She was writing about extreme freedom.

Women were never supposed to put themselves first above all else. History was the foul record of men putting themselves first. Yes, it was replete with grotesque injustices. But it had enabled them to make their mark. It was the only way to know the self, Sadie believed. She was not after breaking down the boundaries between classes the way George was. But she was certainly attempting to blast through the walls that were put around the female imagination, saying it was not at all kind or proper. If women in society did not mirror the portraits she was describing, it meant society was itself a prison.

When she was done, she could not give her book to George's press. She had no difficulty finding another press, one much bigger than George's. The book was sold not only in Montreal but began to cause controversy all over North America and Europe. Sadie began to revile and intrigue readers all over the world, much to her delight. The name Sadie Arnett became synonymous with intellectual and sexual decadence. She was twenty-six and on her way to becoming a phenomenally successful and wealthy writer.

CHAPTER 45

The Etching on Your Fingertip

In a good mood after her Philadelphia acquisition, Marie went to visit a gallery owner. He brought her to the atelier of an artist who had been working on some dark illustrations. The gallerist knew Marie had a penchant for images of women in peculiar circumstances. They walked up three flights of stairs to a large, open attic apartment. The artist was wearing a pinstriped coat and was leaning against the wall, biting his ink-stained fingernails. Marie's delicate shoes stepped over the squalor on the floor in order to look at the etchings hanging on the walls. She immediately admired the fineness of the artist's lines. The etchings looked as though they had been created from single pieces of black thread. And if you picked up the string, it would all untangle and there would be nothing left on the page.

She stopped in front of one wall and her heart was like a teacup that had knocked over and spilled warm tea into her whole body. There was a series of etchings illustrating the poem *Goblin Market*. It was the poem she and Sadie had both performed and that had been the cause of their falling-out. Everything else around her disappeared. She heard the gallerist suggest she come look at something on the other side of the room, near where the artist was hovering, but Marie stood transfixed looking at the series of etchings.

The first one was an illustration of the two sisters who had set out together for a walk in the woods. One had dark hair and the other was fair. They reminded her so much of herself and Sadie. It was uncanny. She leaned forward to get a better look.

She looked at the drawing of the blond. She looked so naïve. Her vulnerability and ignorance were what made her beautiful. She was acting in a manner that made her seem genteel and lovely, but also asinine. She was endangering herself but also her sister. Her dark-haired sister was mercurial and wicked-looking. She viewed the world with suspicion. You could tell she had very often worn that expression, as her face now looked permanently suspicious.

The next etching was of the goblins in the woods who were setting up their fruit market. They were all male. She had no idea how they procreated. Perhaps they masturbated onto a tree trunk and then a bole formed on the side of it that grew and grew until it morphed into a goblin. The goblins all seemed to have melded with the woods.

One had tiny mushrooms sprouting from his neck. One looked so much like a frog he must get insulted when he was called one. There was a naked goblin whose skin was so loose he looked like a flaccid penis. Perhaps when he got excited, he grew three times the size and his skin became taut.

In the next illustration, the girls encountered the goblins. The blond sister seemed oblivious to how grotesque they were. She was only obsessed with the fruit, which did not look like real fruit but rather like jewels. There were apples that had not come from a tree but that must have been grown underneath the earth. A bear had been slaughtered and when it was cut open, there was a pomegranate in place of its heart. The goblins knew how to find fruit in places no one else knew to look.

In the next etching, the blond-haired sister was sick because she had eaten the fruit. She was lying in bed delirious with fever. Again, Marie was reminded of herself. She had always cast herself as a victim to get Sadie to do what she wanted. And, sure enough, in the next etching, the dark-haired sister went back to the woods to deliberately eat the fruit and find an antidote.

In order to save her sister, she had to endure the same fate as her. But she endured it while knowing it wasn't going to be easy. She tasted the fruit, knowing it was poisonous. Marie suddenly wondered whether she was dangerous for Sadie. She created traps for Sadie to walk into.

Although they both endured a horrific poisoning, the sisters knew what the fruit tasted like. And they were inextricably bonded. Sadie had known the true meaning of this poem. Sadie's interpretation had been much more astute than Marie's. In any case, it had played out in real life. Life had shown her darker interpretation to be more accurate.

Marie bought the series of etchings for Sadie.

WHEN MARIE GOT BACK TO her home in Montreal, it was very late and Sadie was asleep. She put the etchings away so she could give them to her on a special occasion. Marie looked at Sadie sleeping in her bed. Her breasts were like loaves of bread rising in the night. Sadie was back. Sadie was finally back. And Marie was going to make sure she protected that. She looked so splendid and beautiful and at rest. She would not let anyone touch or disturb her friend's repose. The outside world would be kept outside.

When word got out that the Philadelphia acquisition had gone through and Marie Antoine had not made good on her promises, a mob of women spent the night in a frenzy. They could not believe they had been betrayed by a woman. This seemed to be the most heinous of betrayals. Marie lacked any empathy for other women. She was worse than a man. No, she was a monster. They decided a more concerted, organized opposition was needed to take down Marie Antoine. They needed men on their side this time. And a general strike at the factory was called.

Marie had had more than enough of the revolting workers and revolutionaries. She declared that anyone who did not return to work in the morning would be fired immediately.

The next week Marie had a group of new workers sent into the factory to replace the ones who had been fired. There were police and guards to protect them when violence broke out. And there was no doubt in anyone's mind that violence would break out.

Later, all the papers would describe how it had been the female workers who had put up the most frightening and bizarre acts of rebellion. It was almost impossible to convey the level of mass mania if one hadn't been there. The whole scene was surreal and disturbing. One girl swung a cat by its tail and let it fall on the heads of the scab workers. There was a naked woman with a mask who launched a can of red paint in the face of a police officer.

A girl was throwing snowballs from the roof of the factory. How she had got up there, no one could say. But no one seemed quite ready to dispense with the possibility that she had flown.

The jeering, because it came from women, was high-pitched and shrill. The reporters were forced to resort to mythological analogies to describe it. They were harpies and banshees. Because they had never heard this sound before, they could not describe it as simply as a group of angry women who wanted their rights.

⁓

One evening Sadie took a break from her new manuscript and stood up to stretch her limbs. She walked over to the window to gaze out. Whereupon she discovered something very peculiar. She could not quite comprehend what she was seeing. Because she had been writing for hours, she felt she might be hallucinating. She opened the window and the cold rushed in, as though it had been waiting outside for hours to be let in. Sadie leaned her head out and yelled, "Marie! What in the world are you doing in that tree?"

"What do you mean?" Marie's voice said from behind her.

Sadie jumped and almost toppled over. She turned and Marie was coming up to the window next to her. Sadie pointed to the tree. They both looked at Mary Robespierre, who was standing on one of the bare branches.

"Murderers!" Mary yelled at the top of her lungs. "There must be justice for murderers!"

"Oh, for fuck's sake," Marie said. She closed the window and the blinds.

Marie and Sadie stood looking at the blinds for a good ten minutes. As though Mary might come through the curtains at any moment, as though they were in some terrible play. Finally, they both approached the window again and peeked around opposite sides of the curtain. The tree branches were empty, as though Mary had fallen off like the last autumn leaf.

"Thank God," Marie said.

"Has this happened before?" Sadie asked, still startled.

"She pops up once in a while. The last time she was in the labyrinth pretending to be shot. It used to trouble me so much. But now I'm rather used to it. She'll get bored eventually."

"Bored! We killed her mother. Were you aware of that?"

"She's mentioned it."

"Well, she's capable of anything. Clearly. She was sitting in a tree a minute ago."

"People get so hung up on their mother's death. I mean that's what mothers do, don't they? They die all the time."

Marie walked away from the window and out of the room, leaving Sadie utterly confused.

MARIE FELT SHE UNDERSTOOD Mary Robespierre in a manner Sadie didn't. She knew they were similar in many ways. For this reason, she felt there was a commercial solution to this problem. With enough money, this tiny entrepreneur would be silenced. She had no illusion the leader of a revolution might want a better world blessed by equality. Mary Robespierre was ambitious. She wanted the power and wealth that eluded her because of her lowly birth. Once she was at the top of the hierarchy, she would come to love inequality as much as the next wealthy person.

Marie decided she would draw up the paperwork to offer Mary ownership of the bakery. She would also offer to purchase whichever local bakeries she considered competition and would hand over the properties to her.

Marie went through her father's papers. She found the rescinded lease that had been transferred over to Mary with her father's signature on it. She could only conclude that her father had made this exchange in an attempt to placate the girl for her mother's death. This arrangement had temporarily been satisfactory, but now she had become greedy and wanted more. So what? thought Marie. She would give the psychopath what she wanted.

But then something else caught Marie's eye: a dark black envelope.

She opened it up and the first thing she pulled out was a death certificate for a girl. The parents were Mr. and Mrs. Louis Antoine. She had died when she was four months old.

Marie discovered another birth certificate. It was for twin daughters. The mother was Agatha Robespierre and the father was Louis Antoine. There was a legal adoption paper by which Louis Antoine had adopted one of the twins from Agatha.

Her heart was fluttering like a butterfly that had finally emerged from a cocoon. She felt all the blood drain out of her as though she had been shot in the chest. She fell onto the floor on her ass. A maid stuck her head in the door to see if she was all right. And Marie screamed to be left alone. The enormity of what she held in her hands was too much for her to bear. Mary had rights on everything she owned. Her house was not hers. Her factory was not hers. Marie's shadow could take everything away from her. Her reflection in the mirror had betrayed her.

She had shot her own mother. But it was too late for her to ever think that way. It was too late for her to consider Agatha her mother. Your mother is who you grow up thinking is your mother. She had grown up thinking her mother was a sadness. A sadness she had escaped.

She understood the revulsion she had always felt toward Agatha when she was young. Every time the woman had shown her any affection, she was overtaken by an urge to push the woman down the stairs. She had been entirely justified. Agatha could have ended her fortunate life at any moment. And now she understood the terrible feeling of ill ease Mary had given her—the feeling there was something more dangerous about Mary than anyone else.

She was thankful she and Sadie had shot Agatha. She did not have to worry about her speaking this abominable truth anymore. She was certain Mary did not even know this truth. She knew Louis was her father, but nothing else. But she would do away with Mary before she ever learned the truth. She needed to act immediately. She had learned the best way to deal with any situation was not to ruminate about it, but to act. She had also learned that people should not just be punished for the crimes they committed but for the ones they were going to commit.

CHAPTER 46

A Fable of Sadness

Louis's wife never blamed him for her sadness. How could she when it had always been there even when she was a girl? Hortense had always wanted people to leave her alone. But she wanted Louis's attention. She liked when he was physically close to her. Her body felt happier. Her thoughts stopped processing so quickly. She didn't feel as intelligent. And that was a good thing. He was so handsome. Everything about him seemed imbued with masculinity. She had never felt physically attracted to someone before him. When she looked down at the carriage floor and saw her feet next to his feet, the difference in size excited her. She felt as if she really belonged to him and it was the first time she ever felt she belonged to anyone.

After they married, they went to the country to live in her family's cottage while their new house was being built. She was happy there. It was where she retreated to in her childhood. She knew the names of all the flowers. She inscribed the birds she spotted in her great notebook. When she was all by herself chasing butterflies and collecting insects, she became distracted to such an extent she forgot her sadness. If she could somehow have devoted herself to that world, perhaps she could have found a way out of her depression. But everybody kept interrupting her.

Louis had never been in the country before. He was glad they were away from everyone in society. He felt his friends were mocking him for having married Hortense. They brought along one young, pretty red-haired maid with them. Louis made love to the maid a few times in the country, but it gave him no joy, and he stopped the affair immediately. To his own surprise, he preferred Hortense's company.

Hortense sensed his surprise affection. They were both comfortable around each other once they discovered how much they enjoyed having sex. And when she was pregnant, she was really truly beautiful. The doctor came and told them they should be gentle making love while she was pregnant. But Louis couldn't stop himself. He loved touching her belly.

Hortense told him all about her sadness. How it took over her life. How she didn't see any point to living. He hated when she described this sadness because she had been born with so much privilege. He was the one who had a precarious spot in society. He was the one who had had to struggle. She promised him her sadness was in her past. But he noticed a hesitation in her eyes. The house was ready when she was almost due to deliver. And he thought they would return to the city a happy family.

The red-haired maid was obviously pregnant herself. No one mentioned it. Louis was grateful the maid didn't seem interested in bringing it up.

Louis was terrified of what his baby with Hortense would look like. He began to see Hortense objectively again, from the eyes of others, who would undoubtedly think she was ugly. Hortense was not beautiful to him anymore. He hoped the baby would take after him and not Hortense. He never prayed for anything. He personally considered God a fool. And he thought of every scientific advancement as being a slap in God's face. He tried to get his hands on any technological gadget to prove what side he was on. But he went to a church and lit a candle and prayed his baby would be beautiful. He could not stand the idea that his child would have to go through life being ugly. It was a handicap, a disability, especially if you were a woman. He could understand how an ugly man might find meaning for himself in the world. But what was the point of an unattractive woman? He finally reconciled himself to trying to love the baby no matter what it looked like. It was a good thing, too, as the baby was uglier than he could have imagined. The baby looked exactly like Hortense.

He didn't like the character of this skinny baby either. He sensed she would have the same eccentricities as her mother. She would think too much. She would be an intellectual. She would also be consumed by words and books. And what point did literature serve other than to make women horribly depressed?

After the baby was born, Hortense became more melancholic. She didn't want to see Louis or the baby. She cried all day long. Once he came in the room and she was hitting her head with a pillow, screaming, Don't you understand? Why can't you understand what I feel like?

And he was angry at her for not being happy with him when she didn't even deserve him.

He took her moods personally. She wouldn't let him in her bedroom to touch her.

Hortense exacerbated his own sense of being unlovable. And so he punished her. He went to the city and began to have affairs again. He made her feel even more unlovable in order to feel superior himself. Her unattractive exterior mirrored the ugliness that was deep inside him. She retreated more to her room. Then after she didn't come out for two days, they broke through the door and found her hanging by the neck from a noose she had made out of the belt of a robe.

❧

LOUIS WENT TO THE CITY to deal with the sugar factory and his new role as owner. He was at his office when he received a telegram from his maid with the most terrible surprise. His and Hortense's baby had died.

When he arrived home, Agatha handed him the death certificate and a dried rose from the baby's funeral.

At dinner, of course, he noticed that Agatha was not with child anymore. When she saw Louis looking at her, Agatha asked him if he wanted to hold his babies. She hurried into the next room and came back with a perambulator. Louis looked in the carriage. The two infants were staring up at him. They looked exactly the same. They both had blond hair. They both had blue eyes. They both had sweaty curls that stuck to their foreheads. They both looked like him. He was taken aback to see children that resembled him. He might never have known this joy.

One of the children began to cry when he looked at her. She gave him a look of hatred. He was a grown man, but he took it personally. He thought a person was born with a look of hatred. She would have that look of hatred in her eyes her whole life. It was as impossible to change as eye color. The other baby girl opened her mouth in what could only be described as a grin. She looked at Louis with such love and recognition. Here was someone who would forgive him for whatever he did. She would make him feel good about himself. Finally, it was someone who loved him at first sight. Finally, it was someone who looked at him as though he were blameless.

"Take her," Agatha said. "No one needs to know she doesn't belong to Hortense."

Louis did not have a choice if he wanted to have the fortune. If Hortense's child was dead, the fortune would pass to her aunt and uncle and he would be out on the street again. But he never believed that was the reason he took Marie. He always thought it was love at first sight. And he needed a partner in crime, as he and Marie together perpetuated a grand fraud. He cared as little for the other twin as he did for all his other bastards lurking somewhere in the streets of the Squalid Mile.

And so it was that one of Agatha's children would have all the wonders money could buy. The other would learn to bake wonderful cakes.

CHAPTER 47

Your Shadow Is on Fire

Marie burned the birth certificate of the twin girls that night. She put her lit cigarette in the center of it. The singed circle spread out like a solar eclipse. She sat up into the late hours. She stared into the fire as though she were staring at the bakery she had ordered to be set on fire. She almost wanted to have a carriage bring her down to the factory so she could witness the destruction. It would be too peculiar that she was there. And that peculiarity would have turned into suspicion.

She had arranged the fire carefully so it would burn only the bakery and none of the surrounding buildings. And certainly not the factory. She was waiting and waiting for the phone call that would inform her the bakery was on fire. When the phone did ring, it startled her. She resented that the ring was able to upset her steely composure. It made her realize she was not nearly as collected as she believed.

"Was there anyone inside?" she asked.

"No, ma'am, thank the Lord. The woman who runs the bakery was inside, but she managed to get out."

"Thank you," Marie said.

She should have known she could not kill Mary.

She thought this threat might have done the trick anyhow. Now Mary would know exactly who Marie was and not to mess with her. It was time to put a boot on the heads of these grasping revolutionaries and push them back down the stairs they were trying to climb. Marie was a factory owner. She knew you had to strike terror into the workforce. You had to make an example of people. It was a great kindness, in a way, because it showed the others what would happen to them if they behaved badly.

There was still one log in the fire burning; its flames were like the red hair of Agatha flying behind her as she hurried down the corridor to reach the labyrinth.

MARY'S FACE LIT UP AS she stared at her bakery in flames. The snow all around the bakery had melted to wet puddles, as though it had mistaken the fire for the summer sun. Mary's shadow was monstrous. It kept lunging forward as though it were trying to get its hands around someone's neck to strangle them. The flames were in her eyes, making them appear red in color. Her dress was covered in soot. It was as though she had been stained by the nighttime. Part of her hair had been singed badly. The sleeve of her dress had been torn off, and her shoulder was bleeding from a gash. A blister on her palm rose, making it look like she was holding a jellyfish. She might have felt physical pain if she wasn't so consumed by anger. Anger was an analgesic. Anger set fire to all the other feelings and emotions and used them as combustibles. The fire made her face turn red and orange and look as though she had two black eyes. She had been awake making cakes when the building erupted in flames. Had she been sleeping, she would have been dead.

Staring at the fire made her feel like a wolf. The fire was pushing her back out into the wilderness. It wanted her to put her tail between her legs and disappear. She could not die if her reflection was alive and well.

She supposed she ought to be thankful to Marie. Marie Antoine was born to go to extremes. That was clearly what she was doing in this instance. Mary might have become complacent were it not for this. She might have accepted the status quo. She was earning enough money at her bakery that in about ten years she would be middle-class herself. She felt all the rough drafts of possible life plans set themselves on fire in her brain. There was the nasty cackling of fire both inside and outside her head.

Of course Marie must have discovered the truth. She had been waiting for Marie to put two and two together. For her to realize why they looked so much alike. Marie had acknowledged Mary's power with this attempted murder. Only your enemy can tell you how powerful you are. If they showed fear, it was like putting a knife in your hand. If they showed anger, it was handing you a gun. At that moment, stepping away from the fire, she knew just how dangerous she was. She was a walking stick of dynamite, and Marie had just lit her fuse.

Tears poured down her soot-covered cheeks, and the streaks revealed the colors underneath. Her face resembled a Renaissance painting being restored.

Mary smiled, knowing she had to take this story to its logical conclusion. She felt her missing finger twitching. As though it needed to be put into action. It needed to start in on a new project. There was nothing quite like trauma to stir the creative juices.

JEANNE-PAULINE WAS BEHIND THE COUNTER in her shop. Her hair was wrapped in a braid around her head. It was chilly, so she was wearing her fox stole over her black dress. The fox stole looked as though it were waiting for a moment to bite. Jeanne-Pauline lifted her head up from her book and looked out the window. Mary was standing outside. She was far enough from the door that she could be considered to be in the middle of the street.

With her face bathed and cleaned by tears, she looked more like Marie than ever before. It would have been obvious to anyone who saw them standing side by side that they were twins.

The wind was causing the light snowfall to form into different eddies. They resembled girls hurrying off after they'd been caught naked in the master's room.

Jeanne-Pauline knew that Mary was coming in to propose a plan to her. She knew exactly what the plan was going to be. She didn't believe it was appropriate to go to the door and invite or entice the girl in. This was the type of idea someone had to come to on their own without any pressure from anyone else. It had to be motivated by a perfect and clear-headed desire.

Jeanne-Pauline didn't have to consider whether she wanted to be involved. She didn't have any need to examine her own motives, or weigh pros against cons. She had been waiting several years for Mary to come to her with this plan. She knew from the first time Mary Robespierre had spoken to her, they had already begun planning this together.

Mary's curls were jumping up and down in the wind. They were ready to move forward. Her dress blew from behind her. It was also ready to launch into action. Jeanne-Pauline looked back down at her book and didn't raise her eyes again until she heard the bells on her door jingle loudly.

"I have a plan. I need your help."

"Of course," Jeanne-Pauline said. Her mouth formed into an expression. Ordinarily, it might be called a smile. But it was so calm and deathly that it seemed to need a new noun.

Mary left the shop with a paper bag under her arm. She took a small snuff box out of her pocket and opened it. She held it in her right hand and then tipped the contents onto her left fist. She took a deep snort and her eyes filled with power and glory.

CHAPTER 48

The Winter Ball

There was a snowstorm raging in Montreal in both the Golden and Squalid Miles. The ground was slippery. It made you slide backward as you walked forward, as though you had to keep going back to the beginning of a sentence in a book. The wind was being vicious. It was banging at the windows of the houses of the poor like a landlord who hadn't been paid. The slush made a sucking noise as boots stomped through it, like the sound of a noisy beast eating.

The women down below in the Squalid Mile were waging a war against Marie and Sadie. They had denounced them as oppressors. But the two young women sitting on their couches, their satin-embroidered slippers perched on ottomans, did not identify themselves as such. No oppressor actually sees themselves as one. They, like everyone else, are too busy identifying themselves as victims. Drops of water were falling off the icicles above the heated windows like the fangs of wolves salivating.

It was Sadie's idea to throw a ball.

They used to sit together in the park. They liked to sit on the roots that surrounded a giant tree as though they had been tossed into a den of snakes. All the other girls would observe them and be so jealous. They were like two little witches working on their magic spells. No one else had magical powers, so no one was invited to join them. Sadie wanted to reclaim that feeling.

It was as though this were their wedding. She wanted to pay honor to their friendship. She wanted everyone to know they were now a unit. They would not be separated again. It had been easy to always come for the two of them separately. But they were untouchable now.

Sadie wanted all of the Golden Mile to see how happy she and Marie were. She wanted them to see her family had been thrown out. They had had to leave the Golden Mile and live in the middle-class area below the hill. She was all that remained of the Arnetts now, and it was her morality that would reign over the party. They say the best revenge is living well, but does that mean living well in itself, or does it mean letting your enemy suffer by seeing how well you are living?

And Marie said, yes, why not, bring them all in. She was no longer afraid of the judgment of anyone in the Golden Mile. They seemed irrelevant to her. She wasn't ashamed of what Philip had done to her. He had enacted his violence on another incarnation of her. She wasn't a person who could be touched now. Men sometimes had trouble looking her in the eye because they felt intimidated. In her years of seclusion, she found that she hadn't become more sensitive or wary about people in her neighborhood. She had become indifferent to them. They seemed to hardly exist. Her parameters of experience now extended far past the Golden Mile. Women were expected to have such narrow circles of reference. They seemed very middle-class to her.

Marie realized her friendship with Sadie was the thing she was most proud of in the world. She would really do anything for it.

SADIE SAW THE BALL SHE was staging as revolutionary. From now on, they would determine the new morality of the neighborhood. Marie had the financial capital and Sadie had the cultural capital to be able to usher in a new era. They would no longer be afraid of the small, petty morals that made women into mindless centerpieces at a dinner table. They would show everyone that ambitious women ended up with the same rewards and power ambitious men did. They would not be filled with shame. They would be admired and envied, she was sure of it. If you had money, she figured, why wouldn't you be a decadent libertine? Money should be able to buy you moral virtue in this new age of capitalism.

Naturally, there was no one in the city who could resist accepting an invitation to this ball.

They were tempted by seeing the interior of the mansion that had been closed completely to the public for so many, many years. They were going to be meeting Justine and Juliette in person. How many times in their life would they have the opportunity to live in a novel?

MARIE HAD DECIDED TO DRESS as Marie Antoinette. She didn't want to wear a wig. She could create a confabulation with her real hair, she was certain. She was blessed with a wonderful head of hair. It would be like desecrating something, like ruining a public statue, to cover it up.

Everything was working out for her. It was as though the evening fit her like a glove. It was a myth that money couldn't buy you happiness. The snow was coming down like sugar sprinkled onto oatmeal so that it would be sweet just as she liked it. The whole world was going to be just as she liked it.

As she stepped out of her room into the hallway, she saw Sadie waiting for her, dressed as a young Marquis de Sade. She had on a white wig that swooped up into a pompadour, with a small ponytail at the back with an enormous black ribbon affixed to it, and a long black cloak that swooped out at the bottom and black leather boots that went to her knees. She looked dashing. They interlinked their arms and headed down the hallway and the stairs together. They would enter the ballroom as an inseparable, triumphant pair.

There was a sigh of admiration when Marie and Sadie stepped onto the ballroom floor dressed as the beautiful couple. Marie's gorgeous hair was entwined in braids and loops with small birds and cherries and a boat perched on top as though riding the waves. And her enormous dress had so many shades of pink, it was as though the world's most beautiful garden had been condensed into it. Sadie's long cloak spilled onto the floor around her as though she were leaking black ink. She looked so intimidating and superior to them all.

Perhaps what Marie had done that had most befuddled the denizens of the Golden Mile was that she had risen far up above them. She had created a class for herself. In the same manner that they didn't actually care about the working class because they didn't see them as people, Marie no longer really thought of the Golden Mile residents as people or cared whatsoever about their ideas or opinions.

She and Sadie had invited them over as a sort of audience. They were creating a new form of theater. It was one in which they played themselves. They invited and encouraged people to come and tell stories about them.

As the guests arrived, the snowflakes had begun falling outside, blinking on and off like fairy lights. They were happy to wear costumes, as it offered them permission to abandon their regular roles and abandon themselves to the world of Marie Antoine and Sadie Arnett.

There were too many Napoleons in the ballroom that night. Marie had considered putting a limit on how many Napoleons could come to her party. But then she decided to simply let it happen naturally.

Anne Boleyn was laughing. She was exhibiting her neck to everyone around her. There was what appeared to be a blood-soaked bandage tied around her neck. Queen Elizabeth was wearing a tall red wig that had tilted to the side. She had her legs on Sir Lancelot's lap as she was popping colorful macarons into her mouth. Robin Hood was peeing out a window in the hallway.

These characters from history gave the attendees at the ball license to act grandiose and wild. They were more licentious and more vain. They weren't worried about their reputations. If there was anything these figures proved, it was that degeneracy paid off.

There was a sort of sickness that set in after midnight. You couldn't feel that much joy without beginning to feel nauseous. Joy makes everyone ill. The ones who weren't used to feeling joy, who were solitary and melancholic most days, were the first to go. The lightweights were passed out. Cleopatra had fallen asleep on the toilet seat with her chin on her fist. Then the happy ones, who sought out ecstatic moments on a regular basis—they were still awake. They weren't going to be taken down by a small amount of joy. They were the true epicureans. They were ready.

And just like the old days when her father was still alive, this was when Marie began to shine as the true queen of the ball. She was like an athlete who waits for their opponent to tire before they make a display of their prowess.

At one in the morning, Marie was twirling with a ribbon around her waist. She was engaged in a ribbon dance. A wide ribbon was wrapped around a woman's waist. It was then pulled by a man, and the woman spun out to the side of the room. Marie unfurled like the petals of a flower. It was a pretty thing to watch. Sadie walked up to her on the dance floor. She held Marie's face in her hands and kissed it all over. Then they began dancing together without any intention of letting go this time. Everyone cleared the dance floor to observe this peculiar friendship.

They danced like they had no feet but were swinging around as though they were two swirling puppets in the hands of a careless puppeteer.

It was then that Marie clapped her hands and announced to Sadie, "I have a gift for you!" She hurried over to a structure that had been brought out while they were dancing and had been covered in a golden velvet cloth. Marie pulled off the cloth, unveiling the series of etchings of *Goblin Market* that were standing on easels.

Sadie stood next to her friend, looking into the etchings, moved in a way she never had been before. She was bewitched by the illustrations that had once been the setting for their discord but now seemed to represent everything that was intimate and passionate about their relationship. The women both knew nothing could ever separate them again.

A maid came out and handed Marie and Sadie a plate with two cupcakes. The frosting on the cakes was in the shape of pink roses. Delighted to see a rose in the middle of winter, Marie sunk her teeth into one and devoured it.

Sadie stuffed the cupcake in her mouth whole. She immediately felt nauseous because of all the Champagne she had been drinking. She stood up, walked behind her chair, and vomited up the cake before she was able to digest it. She then lay on the floor with her eyes closed. She had been drinking so much Champagne, she knew she would eventually be sick. But she didn't mind. She really quite liked the feeling of throwing up. It was as though she had exorcized all her demons. Her head was so much lighter. She thought she and Marie had been as festive as anyone possibly could. She had at least lived this night to its fullest. They had had one night of unearthly delight.

Sadie opened her eyes when she began to hear the screaming. She sat up and saw Marie was bent over and shaking. Marie was breathing too heavily, as though her chest were a locomotive engine. A train pulling out of the station and beginning to speed up. "It's the cake," she said. "It's poisoned." She was so pale. She looked as though she were made of porcelain and if she fell over, her fingers would break off. Marie sunk into her dress as though it were a luxurious bubble bath. Sadie, suddenly sober, rushed over to her.

Sadie leaned into Marie's body, calling to her. But there were arms holding her back. She looked at the hands grasping her from behind. They had long twiglike fingers. Sadie shuddered and cried out. She felt the arms of the goblins begin to reach out and twist themselves around her. She turned to look at them. There were a hundred goblins all around her.

They looked as though their skin had been shrunken to stick to their bones. They looked like they were roots of trees that had been pulled up. They had grown under the earth. You would pull them up by the tail. They longed for the darkness and the feeling of being stuck in the cold and the dark. They stank like death.

The goblins pulled her hair. Their fingers were slimy. They stuck to her skin. Each fingerprint had to be pulled off her as though from a murder scene. She knew they didn't have the antidote at all. Marie was poisoned and there was nothing she could do. She fell to her knees and buried her head in Marie's chest and wailed so loud, even the goblins were afraid. They climbed inside her brain to hide.

~~~

OUTSIDE, THE SNOW WAS FALLING down in Montreal in a way that it never did anywhere else in the world. It was coming down so thick. Its snowflakes were made out of fur. They were in a snow globe that had been shaken wildly and then put back on the shelf ever so gently and allowed to rest. The roses were dreaming underneath the ground.

CHAPTER 49

Requiem for a Beautiful Monster

Everyone knew Marie had a penchant for beautiful funerals. A fleet of white horses was pulling a white sleigh behind the carriage that contained Marie's coffin. It looked like a circus caravan. A young boy seated next to the driver climbed off the sleigh. He went around back and pulled on a chain that raised the roof of the carriage.

Such a huge flock of doves burst out of the sleigh. The flocks of birds flew up like the pages of a manuscript tossed into the air. In fact, many had expected doves to come out of there. But they hadn't expected quite so many. No one could even say how that many doves had been shoved in there. It must have involved a certain amount of cruelty. But what is the point of contemplating cruelty once the damage is done?

They burst out. They appeared almost like a dark cloud. They spread in all directions for a moment, hysterical and desperate only to be free. Then once they were far up above the crowd and were far enough away that they could safely assume they were beyond the grasp of any human hands, they rejoined together as a group to decide the best way to fly out of the circumstance.

For many years later, that area of Montreal was plagued by more doves than was normal in any part of the city. You could hear them quietly making weeping noises. They were an echo of mourning.

For once there was no one who could complain about Marie's wealth. It wasn't as though she would be able to enjoy this display herself. They were the ones who were benefitting. And they realized that moving into the modern age, there was a certain cruelty that would disappear. But there would also be a kind of beauty that would disappear. This outrageous display. They enjoyed it while it was there. There would be a time when it would be impossible.

Equality was a banal idea. A way of life was dying with her, they believed.

Marie's death was the most important thing about her life. Murdered women were immortalized. She had not lost her personality or any of her spark by being murdered. She had become larger than life when she was killed.

And who really mourned Marie's death? She didn't have any close relatives who were bereft at her departure. She didn't have any close friends. The only people she knew were those maids who were employed by her. And they were all more sorrowful for their loss of employment than anything else.

But of course Marie did have a chief mourner. And everyone knew who it was.

CHAPTER 50

The Trial

When the detective arrived, his carriage almost drove right by the mansion. The mansion was so completely covered by the wiry rosebush with dried frozen petals that he mistook it for nature and didn't think it was part of human habitation. Instead he thought it was part of the mountain that rose up behind it. It was only when he realized he had gone a house too far that he had the carriage move backward. He stared at the rosebush and allowed the shape of the house to emerge.

He felt for a moment as though he were hallucinating. Or that he was in a fairy tale. And whenever something like that happens, you brace yourself for other strange things to happen.

Anything a little bit magical is terrifying. God forbid you should encounter a miracle.

One of the rosebushes pulled his hat right off his head. It made the wind blow unexpectedly on his bald scalp. And a strong current of unease ran through his body.

This murder had so much to do with women. It was a house filled with women. He was already entering something creepy. The only place where women found themselves in such proximity was the madhouse. He thought when women spent too much time alone, they always went mad. And when he entered the house he felt the same way.

THE QUESTIONING OF THE MAIDS proved to be strange. The detective had been warned that the maids in this household were known to be peculiar. They had a tenuous grasp on reality. Whenever he assembled his list of witnesses, he always prayed there would not be a teenage girl on it. Young girls seemed to love to confuse him and tie his brain in knots. He did think it peculiar the cupcake had been delivered to Marie and Sadie in particular.

"Weren't you at all suspicious about where these two singular cupcakes came from? And why?"

"Well, no sir. I knew where it came from."

"And where was it from?"

"It was Miss Antoine herself who gave me the cupcakes and said to bring them out to her and Miss Arnett when they looked happy and everything was in the swing of things, as they say. So when I saw her dancing with Miss Arnett and they looked pretty together, I thought now would be a good time to bring them out."

"Why were you selected to serve the cupcakes to them?"

"Because I'm the prettiest, I suppose. I mean, all the girls here are pretty but I still get singled out sometimes for being pretty, especially by the mistress."

"Are you trying to tell me she wanted to commit suicide?"

"I don't know anything about that. I'm only telling you what I observed. She came in the kitchen with the cakes."

"And did you observe anything unusual about her demeanor?"

"I don't know what a demeanor is."

"Was there anything different about her?"

"Yes! She was dressed shabby. You know how beautiful her way of dressing can sometimes be. So I thought she was in a costume. Everyone had on such funny getups that night. And her voice was different."

"How so?"

"Marie usually sings her words. But this time she was so serious-sounding."

"Interesting."

"Do you think Miss Antoine will get any better?"

"I don't think so. She's dead."

Another maid spoke up at that moment. "The cakes were such pretty things. They weren't made by Martha. Her cakes are always delicious. But they don't look pretty. She could never make a rose like that. Nobody here can. If they could, I would know it because I've been working on being able to do it myself. They were made by a cake genius."

THE DETECTIVE WENT TO LOOK at different bakeries in search of a similar cupcake. When he went into a small bakery on Sherbrooke Street, he was shocked when he saw Marie Antoine working in the back. He tried to make sense of it. For a moment he thought it was a hoax.

"Marie," he said.

And she answered, "Yes."

She might have tricked somebody else, but he was a detective. And he was smart. And his brain was able to figure these types of things out. Naturally it did not help that she was holding a tray that had rows of cupcakes covered in roses, quite identical to the ones everyone at the party had described seeing.

She was hauled in for murder.

THE TRIAL LASTED THROUGH THE SPRING. George was not called on to testify, but she sat at the back of the court observing it all. She was quite used to the cast of characters, but for everyone else in the courtroom, this was an electrifying spectacle. The culprit was more wonderful than anyone could imagine. It was straight out of a penny dreadful novel. They knew the closest thing in real life to fiction was murder. Murder was fiction made incarnate.

There was a play based on the trial. In it, Mary was presented as a jealous insane person. Her similarity in appearance to Marie consumed her and caused her to have a delusion that they had been switched at birth. Mary insisted to the court they were sisters, but this was ruled a falsehood only she believed and that had caused her to spend all her time plotting Marie's macabre death.

Mary's lawyers petitioned the court to have the play stopped. How could any jury be impartial when everyone in the city was crowding into a theater to watch their client murder Marie in a cold and deranged, hateful manner?

But after the trial, the moment Mary was declared guilty, her crime became fodder for every form of theater in the city. Even the hurdy-gurdy monkey's tune seemed to be singing about Mary.

The courts brought in Jeanne-Pauline Marat to testify that she had sold Mary arsenic. Jeanne-Pauline was, as expected, a hostile witness. She claimed she couldn't remember having sold anything to Mary, or ever having seen her in her shop.

"It's entirely possible that I saw her in my shop. But I don't have a particular memory of it. Girls and young women are always coming into my shop. There are so many of them at all times. They all look the same, don't they? We are meant to see girls as being interchangeable.

We are meant to see them as being shells. They have no real futures and personalities they can choose. You saw Mary and Marie happen to look very much the same. But don't all young girls look exactly the same?"

In the end, the prosecution didn't really need Jeanne-Pauline's testimony, as they had receipts for poison from her pharmacy. It was almost as though they had brought her in for the sake of a spectacle. Here was yet another murderer for the price of one. The trial had so much going for it.

What was most peculiar about the trial was that all the witnesses were women. They were in a play that had no parts for men.

JUST WHEN EVERYONE THOUGHT THE trial could not get any more delicious, Sadie Arnett arrived.

As the trial progressed, Sadie felt jealousy flood through her brain. She hadn't thought she could still feel jealous of Marie. They had both achieved their goals and they had felt equal in every way. But now Marie was all everyone talked about. How could she compete against someone's death?

She knew that in death Marie was more alive than she had been while breathing. Wherever her name came up in the city, everyone was able to picture her. She could appear before anyone now. Sadie felt the level of fame Marie had achieved meant she belonged to the masses and not to her. Marie was no longer Justine.

Sadie had always wanted to be part of the revolution. And now she would be. She would show them all who was the most eloquent writer and orator in the whole city. She would now appeal to them as a woman who would undoubtedly be demonized on the stand. That would make her known to everyone around her. Mary had tried to poison her, too, after all.

The trial was the only thing that got her out of bed. She sent her novel to a publisher in Paris that was interested in her work. She wanted her novel to be released as close as possible to the court date. She saw it as a chance for unparalleled publicity.

SADIE DID NOT WEAR HER beaten-up clothes and cloak to court. Her cloak had been at her disposal to render her invisible. She wanted to be as visible as possible. She arrived at court wearing a splendid outfit. She wore a dress with thick black and white stripes with an enormous bustle. It had a beautifully cut jacket. Her hair had been combed and arranged perfectly. On top of her hairdo she had a black bowler hat. She had black velvet gloves that fit her so perfectly, it was as though she had dipped her arms in black paint.

Everyone went silent when she appeared at the courtroom door. She wanted to present as a full-fledged aristocrat. Sadie caught George's eye as she climbed into the witness stand. But she quickly looked away, as she no longer belonged to the Squalid Mile and her friendship with George was no longer meaningful to her.

There had been some debate over whether to consider her one of the revolutionaries. But Sadie was not actually a revolutionary. She had only ever been in search of her own freedom. She was fighting against her own constraints. She was not at all interested in increased wages or child care, or the actual changes needed for women of the working classes to be free. Everything she wrote was from a place of privilege. Hers was a different conversation from the one the revolutionaries were having.

She had made her inner voice be heard unfiltered. Instead of changing who she was as a little girl, she had grown into an outrageous, exaggerated version of herself. She represented the fully realized feminine soul. She had turned femininity on its head. She had shown it as something wild and ferocious and very powerful. And the courtroom waited for Sadie to speak, knowing they would hear something unbridled.

The lawyers made Sadie account for her actions the night of the murder.

"What do you recall of that night?"

"There were Napoleons all over the place. Or perhaps I was seeing double. At one point I was making love to a strongman."

"What was this man's name?"

"I'm not sure. I always think of him as the strongman. That's what his job is. I saw him for the first time onstage at the music hall. Flavio the Extraordinaire, I think. Although I doubt his mother named him that."

There was sudden laughter throughout the court.

"Please tell the court what you do for a living," the lawyer said.

"I am a novelist of renown."

"Were you employed at a brothel located on 67 Dandelion Alley for a period of no less than two years?"

"'Employed' is an interesting word for it."

There was laughter again. No one had expected Sadie to be so charming. No one had expected to be laughing during a murder trial.

"What did men pay you to do, exactly?"

"My work at the brothel was a theatrical undertaking of sorts. I went to boarding school in England for nine years. I was forced to act in a submissive way toward men. They struck me with a whip so I would comply. What does all that conditioning do to you in the end? I thought I would try the opposite. I would attempt to dominate men. When a scroll curls up one way, you roll it in another."

"Did you enjoy this?"

"I took a certain amount of pleasure in my work. I thought I was good at it."

"Are you a sapphist?"

"I'm not fussy. I take what I can get."

The lawyer's face went bright red whenever the court audience laughed at Sadie. He decided to get to the point.

"Did you feel you and Marie Antoine were in danger for your lives from Mary Robespierre?"

"Oh, most certainly."

"Then why did you throw a ball?"

"The thrill, I suppose. I always take it as a compliment when someone wants to kill me. I wanted to meet some of my fans."

"So you consider Mary Robespierre to be a fan?"

"Oh, definitely not. She had a perfectly good reason to go about murdering the two of us."

"And what would that be?"

Sadie was feeling the rush of self-destructive behavior. It reminded her of being young, when there aren't supposed to be consequences for your actions. She had faced such an enormous consequence as a child, she had never considered any action frivolous afterward. She had played a game of make-believe, and it had murdered someone. She had fired an imaginary gun and then realized how deadly imaginary bullets were. She stood there in the witness box smiling in her black-and-white-striped dress. It was as though she were already standing behind bars.

"Marie and I shot and killed her mother when we were twelve. It's difficult to get over that sort of thing. Quite honestly, I'm surprised it took her so long to come for us."

"THIS IS A BEASTLY WORLD, and she only wanted her piece of the beastly pie!" was what Sadie screamed as she was leaving, escorted out by two officers. No one was ever sure if she meant Marie Antoine or Mary Robespierre. As it could apply to them both.

Sadie thought she would be hanged next to Mary. She would imagine it was Marie Antoine hanging next to her. Wasn't that always her fantasy? She wanted to be punished with Marie. When they hung with two bags on their heads, all that would be left were two dresses dancing with each other in the air.

Sadie was absolutely right that the trial would sell books. She had vendors selling the books outside the courtroom. *Justine and Juliette* sold the most copies. Although it was a work of fiction, Sadie gave them permission to market it as nonfiction. She was bringing Marie alive to them all. What an extraordinary life the two of them must have had. Living in the large mansion, playing cards and saying witty things to each other. They were Justine and Juliette.

But she was wrong about being hanged. Instead she was put in a carriage and driven back up the hill to the psychiatric institution, in which she would come to write the greatest books of her career. And the fact that the books were written by a woman who had been committed lent them a fabulous allure.

CHAPTER 51

Come to My Hanging and

Kiss Me Good-Bye

Mary didn't protest or care when they came to get her in her prison cell the day of her hanging. It was fall, she had turned twenty-seven, and she felt immortality all around her. She knew she had done something with her life and talents that had made the whole city notice her. She had caused half the city to go mad and help act out her revenge toward Marie. But her personal vendetta had created something beautiful and immortal. Women everywhere had come to believe they deserved more, and they had demanded more. She would not have the Antoine factory, but in the end Marie wouldn't either. She was satisfied with all she had accomplished. She had expanded what it meant to be a woman. In the papers it said she couldn't fully be considered a woman. And she was in agreement with this. She wasn't a woman or a man. She was something greater than the two.

Young girls shouted her name as they brought her to the gallows.

MARY WAS SKATING ON THE LAKE once when she was very little when she fell through the ice. It was always said that if a person were to fall beneath the ice, they would never survive. But that was what made it so pleasurable to skate on top of it. It was beautiful, but it was also very dangerous.

You felt the fleetingness of life. Death was right beneath you. There was a thin line of ice between life and death.

Every child in Montreal was warned about ice. Which was a trickster. Which was out to get you. You could kiss it and your lips would be fastened to it forever. You could hold a doorknob and find your hand stuck. You thought the ice was beautiful. It allowed you to skate far, far out onto it. And then it cracked and swallowed you whole. It would bite off your ears or your nose. There was something almost medieval in its barbaric practices. It tried to pass itself off as being dignified and above everything else. But really it was savage. It liked to bury people alive. It would make the sound of young girls singing in the woods. You would go off to hear what it was. And then find yourself lost.

Mary was being very respectful of the winter the day she fell through the ice. She had on a heavy blue overcoat that had a hood sewn into the top. The coat was so heavy it always fell off the hook a few times after you tried to hang it up, like a drunkard having trouble standing up. She had three pairs of white tights on. She had a dingy white fur hat on her head. She didn't like any winter activity other than skating.

She liked the eeriness of skating above the river. She wondered about the life that was beneath her. She imagined whales and mermaids. The idea of it gave her such a fright, it sickened her to her stomach. Fright like that was delightful. It propelled you into action. There was a touch of the masochist in everyone.

She thought she had just fallen. But when her body hit the surface, she didn't stop falling but went right through it. She was stung by the cold. She saw all the people skating on top of her. They were all on their hands and knees trying to keep up with her journey. Did they want to save her, or was it all incredibly exciting to them? It was as though she were trapped in a mirror. Were they following her along as though she were a girl in a fairy tale who had met with a terrible fate?

Some men began to puncture and smash at the ice farther down the river. They opened a hole. They reached down and grabbed Mary. They pulled her out of the hole as though she were being born again.

She couldn't feel any of her body anymore. She couldn't feel her bones, although she wondered whether she had ever been able to feel her bones. She felt deep, deep in her body, all she was, was a pair of eyes staring at the world. She couldn't hear what anyone was saying. She was glad, because it was embarrassing to fall through the ice and be rescued like that, any way you looked at it.

Then she felt the noose snap her neck.

THE OLDER WOMEN OF THE CITY began a second uprising, much more radical and widespread than that of the young women. The second wave of the revolution had spread from the factories to the city at large. Women of all ages and walks of life began to revolt. They didn't even weigh whether Mary had the right to murder Marie. They were waiting for a catalyst to push them over the edge. The death of Mary Robespierre had made her into a martyr. All her views were validated. Suddenly Jeanne-Pauline's pamphlets were read in a different manner. Women took them at face value. They realized Jeanne-Pauline had been dead serious.

They realized that women's lives were in danger all over the city. And that women had a right to fight back any way they pleased.

They were tired of not being treated as though they were human beings who had a right to dreams and a right to a proper education and careers. There were fires at the university. Books were thrown into burning trash cans. Professors were chased out of their classrooms at knifepoint.

There were women who launched revolts in their own homes. They were tired of being raped and beaten by their husbands. They were so sick of their husbands drinking away their paychecks. They attacked their mates with frying pans and baking spoons and brooms.

There were maids who were fed up with being felt up in closets and having abortions and babies in infamy. They abhorred the thought of having no ownership over their bodies. They went after their masters with loaded chamber pots.

The girls in all the industries were disgusted at being paid less, of being insignificant, of not being included anywhere in the history of the Industrial Revolution, or anywhere in history at all.

There were corsets hanging all along the fence of the prison. There were girls who carried their bloomers on sticks. They all cried out for Mary's innocence and her right to revolt.

CHAPTER 52

A Room of One's Own

Oh, but wait. There is one more thing to tell that no one else knows. The only person who ever knew about it had died a long time before. You see, the death certificate for Louis and Hortense's child was a fake.

In truth, the ugly baby had not died. Agatha had swaddled up the baby and brought it on the train to Montreal. She walked deep into the heart of the Squalid Mile. In the Squalid Mile there were plenty of babies who had no history. They showed up unable to tell anyone where they had come from. It was impossible to keep track of which babies lived and which babies died. Agatha knocked on the brothel door at five in the morning. It was an hour when all the prostitutes had gone to bed finally. They would be so exhausted from fucking, nothing could wake them up. The rest of the city was still sleeping.

Madame had hurried Agatha into the brothel. She accepted an envelope of money from the woman and tucked it between her breasts. She then forged a death certificate herself. The baby had such clever black eyes. The madam had seen so many babies, she swore she could look into their eyes and see the character they would have for the rest of their lives. Madame liked the look of the baby immediately. She found its ugliness endearing. She knew it would give the baby a power. It would not fall into the traps pretty girls would. She was very eager to see what a girl this ugly would do with herself. She was determined the baby would survive.

Madame had advanced theories of the benefits of breastfeeding. Madame was a woman who made deductions. She noticed that children who breastfed longer had a tendency to stay alive. She insisted prostitutes who were breastfeeding let George suckle from their breasts. They didn't mind so much. They were less likely to get pregnant, and they weren't opposed to picking up a younger sobbing child and shutting it up for both their benefits.

George buried her head into the breasts of all the different women. There was a different size breast every night. Each one gave her a different sensation of comfort and pleasure. By being breastfed by different women, George grew up smart and alert and strong. And despite or because of her looks, she was brimming with an unassailable confidence for a child who had grown up orphaned and in a whorehouse.

GEORGE DID NOT HAVE ANY charges brought against her. She had avoided trying to implicate herself during the trial. She had been well aware that Mary would eventually get herself into this type of predicament. She had no inclination to argue for or against her. She did not think there was any good that was coming out of the trial. It was subverting the message of their movement. She was surprised the extent to which the others wanted to be part of it. She realized they were all engaged in far more risky behavior than she was. They would take any risk to make sure they were in the limelight. They had gone mad with a desire for self-importance. Especially her old love, Sadie Arnett, who had practically demanded to be dragged to the psychiatric facility. Although Sadie was proving prolific, George had no interest in any of that nonsense. She wanted to live a long, quiet, and productive life.

George had begun to make a modest living as a journalist. She moved into a small room on the third floor of a building. It was painted white and all the moldings were a pretty pale green color. It was small, but quite a lot of light came through the window. And it was a brand-new space for her.

George was pleased with the room. She was pleased with the size. She was pleased with the bed. She was pleased with the furniture. She was pleased with a round teapot. She put it on the heater to make tea. She set out her writing implements. George didn't know why people couldn't be satisfied by little things in this world.

George did not think of herself as a woman, and she didn't want to be a man either. She wanted to exist in a realm that was outside of gender. She thought there was a way to be a person. A person who wanted a better world outside of the structures that already existed and controlled people. She thought there was a way to exist as a person who cares.

She looked out the window. She saw a young woman walking briskly down the street with long red hair and dressed in a green coat. She took out a piece of blank paper and laid in on her table. She began to make footsteps in the snow of the white page.

CHAPTER 53

The Morning-After Pill

After the wave of insurgence in the city hit its high-water mark, it began to slowly sink. Everyone always thought they could maintain the fervor and zest of a revolution. But it was impossible. There was a moment when it was necessary to clean up the battlefield and bury the dead. There was a moment when it was necessary to wash the dishes and put the babies to bed. The revolution was seen as a great good. But now everyone had to nurse the wounds they had gained in the name of pursuing that which was right.

Many of the factories did indeed change. The factories could not operate again unless the women came back. And the women would not go back to work unless there were rules implemented to make children have an easier time at the factory. And so they were permitted to go to school and they were all given reduced working hours.

There were men who were union leaders who had not incited this insurgence. But they, nonetheless, took the credit for it. Their faces went in the history books and newspapers for being the architects and philosophers who had the presence of mind and intellect to find a way to protest industrialists using human beings as fodder to run their factories.

All the names of women who had participated and fought in the revolution were erased. They had been written in invisible ink. And then the history of men had been written over theirs in indelible ink. In order to see the history of the women you had to put the page up against the window and let a light shine through it. Then the history might dance like a shadow puppet against the wall.

In fact, in people's minds, it made sense that men would lead a workers' revolution, because they were the ones who worked in the factories. They were the ones who woke up in the morning and went to their jobs and earned a living. Women stayed home with the children. They took care of the housework. This was necessary business, but they couldn't understand what it was to wake up in the morning and earn money. Their husbands did that.

On a Monday a few months after the revolution in the Squalid Mile, an older woman walked down the street with a large staff. She banged on everyone's door telling them in was time to go off to their jobs. Remarkably soon afterward the people began to emerge from their doors. It was like the old woman was a child shoving a stick into an anthill.

The women woke up and splashed water on their faces. They pulled on their black stockings. When their big toes popped out of them, they sewed the hole closed with black thread.

Women who had their babies attached to their backs or were holding their little ones' hands hurried out their doors to head to the factories. Young girls, their coats missing buttons and fastened with diaper pins hurried out, their heads full of all sorts of romance, and ran down the streets to get to their stations on time. Older women with kerchiefs tied to their heads walked their arthritic limbs toward the factories.

There was a girl who was staring down a cat on the sidewalk. The cat had no intention of going anywhere. But neither did she. There was a girl who took a mouthful of water, tilted her face upward into the air and spit the water up as though she were a whale that had just emerged from the deep. There was a girl who was sewing at a sweatshop. She wrote the words "I HATE YOU" onto a piece of cloth and tucked it into the hem of a dress she was sewing.

There would be further uprisings in the city. To be alive is to be in a constant state of revolution. These girls would all grow up and come for the vote.

Acknowledgments

This book was edited by two very brilliant women, Jennifer Lambert and Alison Fairbrother.